KT-381-306

ISRAEL POTTER

HERMAN MELVILLE was born on August 1, 1819, in New York City, the son of a merchant. His father died when he was twelve, and Melville worked as a bank clerk and later an elementary school teacher before shipping off on a whaling vessel bound for the Pacific. Upon his return he published several books based on his experiences at sea, which won him immediate success. By 1850 he was married and had acquired a farm near Pittsfield, Massachusetts, where he wrote *Moby-Dick*. His later works, including *Moby-Dick*, became increasingly complex and alienated many of his readers. In 1863, during the Civil War, he moved back to New York City, where he died in 1891.

ROBERT S. LEVINE is Professor of English at the University of Maryland, College Park. He is the author of *Conspiracy and Romance*; *Martin Delany, Frederick Douglass, and the Politics of Representative Identity*; and *Dislocating Race and Nation*; and is the editor of a number of volumes, including *The Cambridge Companion to Herman Melville*; *The Norton Anthology of American Literature, 1820–1865*; and (with Samuel Otter) *Frederick Douglass and Herman Melville: Essays in Relation*.

Reading Borough Council

3412601018443 3

READING BOROUGH LIBRARIES	
Askews	
AF	£10.99

HERMAN MELVILLE

Israel Potter

HIS FIFTY YEARS OF EXILE

Introduction and Notes by ROBERT S. LEVINE

PENGUIN BOOKS

PENGUIN BOOKS

Published by the Penguin Group

Penguin Group (USA) Inc., 375 Hudson Street, New York, New York 10014, U.S.A.

Penguin Group (Canada), 90 Eglinton Avenue East, Suite 700, Toronto,
Ontario, Canada M4P 2Y3 (a division of Pearson Penguin Canada Inc.)

Penguin Books Ltd, 80 Strand, London WC2R 0RL, England

Penguin Ireland, 25 St Stephen's Green, Dublin 2, Ireland (a division of Penguin Books Ltd)

Penguin Group (Australia), 250 Camberwell Road, Camberwell,
Victoria 3124, Australia (a division of Pearson Australia Group Pty Ltd)

Penguin Books India Pvt Ltd, 11 Community Centre, Panchsheel Park, New Delhi - 110 017, India

Penguin Group (NZ), 67 Apollo Drive, Rosedale, North Shore 0632,
New Zealand (a division of Pearson New Zealand Ltd)

Penguin Books (South Africa) (Pty) Ltd, 24 Sturdee Avenue,
Rosebank, Johannesburg 2196, South Africa

Penguin Books Ltd, Registered Offices: 80 Strand, London WC2R 0RL, England

First published in the United States of America by G. P. Putnam & Co. 1855
This edition with an introduction and notes by Robert S. Levine published in Penguin Books 2008

1   3   5   7   9   10   8   6   4   2

Introduction and notes copyright © Robert S. Levine, 2008
All rights reserved

This text of *Israel Potter: His Fifty Years of Exile* was published in 1982 by Northwestern
University Press as part of Volume Eight of the Northwestern-Newberry Edition of *The Writings
of Herman Melville*, edited by Harrison Hayford, Hershel Parker, and G. Thomas Tanselle.
Reprinted by arrangement with Northwestern University Press.

CENTER FOR EDITIONS OF
AMERICAN AUTHORS
AN APPROVED TEXT
MODERN LANGUAGE
ASSOCIATION OF AMERICA

CIP data is available.
ISBN: 978-0-14-310523-7

Printed in the United States of America
Set in Sabon

Except in the United States of America, this book is sold subject to the condition that it shall not,
by way of trade or otherwise, be lent, resold, hired out, or otherwise circulated without the publisher's
prior consent in any form of binding or cover other than that in which it is published and without
a similar condition including this condition being imposed on the subsequent purchaser.

The scanning, uploading and distribution of this book via the Internet or via any other means
without the permission of the publisher is illegal and punishable by law. Please purchase only
authorized electronic editions, and do not participate in or encourage electronic piracy
of copyrighted materials. Your support of the author's rights is appreciated.

Contents

Introduction

Herman Melville's eighth novel, *Israel Potter: His Fifty Years of Exile*, was serialized in the July 1854 through March 1855 *Putnam's Monthly Magazine* and published as a book by G. P. Putnam & Company in March 1855. It garnered admiring reviews but low sales and then practically disappeared from the literary landscape, becoming almost as obscure as the self-proclaimed Revolutionary hero Israel Potter, whose 1824 auto-biographical narrative served as a crucial source for Melville's novel. In his dedication to *Israel Potter*, Melville imagines his eponymous hero one day emerging from the shadows to achieve "his popular advent." This introduction is informed by a similarly hopeful vision of a resurgence of interest in Melville's little-known Revolutionary novel. In *Israel Potter*, war is presented as an inchoate succession of violent and banal episodes in which participants have virtually no understanding of what is at stake or why they are doing what they are doing. Terroristic attacks on innocent civilians, brutal hand-to-hand combat, rampant explosions bringing about the instant deaths of scores of combatants, mass imprisonments and impressments, blurrings of national identities, and a lust for power constitute the Revolutionary War as depicted in Melville's novel. This is a novel for our times.

And yet the novel is much more than a cynical and despairing demythologizing of the American Revolution. It is also a comi-cally loopy work that mixes fictional with historical characters, skews historical chronologies, and depicts such celebrated his-torical figures as Benjamin Franklin, John Paul Jones, and Ethan Allen as tricksters, plotters, artful performers, and (especially in the case of Jones) killers. Among Melville's great achievements in *Israel Potter* are his bold characterizations of such distinctive figures, including the indomitable Israel Potter, even as he raises questions about their very distinctiveness, linking his main characters to the contingencies and confusions of their historical moment. Ultimately, Melville's tragicomic novel of the American Revolution works to unsettle fixed meanings of wars, individual lives, and nations, presenting the Revolution in antiexceptionalist terms as just another war that gives birth to just another self-regarding nation. Such a vision of the Revolutionary War may seem jaded, and it certainly went against the patriotic grain of Melville's times. But the novel is ultimately rejuvenating in the spirited way that it presses its readers to reflect on the value of wars that are made in the name of nations but not necessarily in the service of the ordinary people who inhabit them.

A trenchant comic novel of the American Revolution, *Israel Potter* can nonetheless prove to be a baffling and elusive read. Such are Melville's complex narrative strategies that it is sometimes difficult to discern the narrator's relation to his central character. Is he mocking Israel Potter or celebrating him? Additionally, there are jarring tonal shifts from comedy to tragedy; a looseness in the plotting typical of the picaresque; numerous references to arcane moments and figures in the Revolutionary War; and a rich, occasionally dense allusiveness to history, literature, philosophy, and the Bible that can send readers scrambling to encyclopedias, dictionaries, concordances, and endnotes. Though the novel received a number of glowing reviews when it was published in 1855, and went through three printings that same year, it never achieved the sales that its publisher was hoping for, selling well under ten thousand copies. A reviewer for the New York newspaper *Commercial Advertiser* declared in a March 1855 issue that *Israel Potter* is "an original and extremely graphic story of our revolutionary era, and is thoroughly saturated with American sentiment." But given the novel's relatively tepid sales, one suspects that Melville's contemporary readers didn't find the novel quite as "graphic" or exciting as this particular reviewer suggests, or even all that pleasing (or comprehensible) with respect to "American sentiment."

Still, ten years after its initial appearance in book form, the publisher T. B. Peterson took a chance with the novel, perhaps because of the potential appeal of its Revolutionary setting, and brought out two unauthorized printings of a slightly bowdlerized version in 1865. Thereafter, for the remainder of the nineteenth century (and for much of the twentieth century), *Israel Potter* lay hidden in the shadows, though in January 1888 there was at least one person interested enough in the novel to write Melville directly with his or her questions about how to make sense of it. Though the letter from this unknown correspondent has not survived, we can extrapolate from Melville's extant response that the letter writer had been frustrated by a recent reading of the novel and was reaching out to Melville for interpretive assistance. Melville offers the following guidance in a letter of January 31, 1888: "In what light the book entitled *I.P. or 50 Years of Exile* is to be regarded, may be clearly inferred from what is said in the Dedication."

So we turn to the dedication looking for clarity, and find that Melville archly dedicates his Revolutionary novel to "His Highness, the Bunker-hill Monument." The monument itself, completed in 1843, commemorated the first significant military conflict between the colonial army and British forces, the Battle of Bunker Hill, which took place on June 17, 1775, in Charlestown, Massachusetts, and came to be celebrated by Americans for its mythic status in inaugurating the Revolution that gave birth to the U.S. nation. In a speech of June 1825 on the laying of the cornerstone of the monument, the noted orator and politician Daniel Webster termed the American Revolution "the wonder and blessing of the world," and he made a special appeal to the approximately two hundred Revolutionary troops who had accompanied Lafayette to the dedication:

VETERANS OF HALF A CENTURY! When in your youthful days you put every thing at hazard in your country's cause, good as that cause was, and sanguine as youth is, still your fondest hopes did not stretch onward to an hour like this! At a period to which you could not reasonably have expected to arrive, at a moment of national prosperity such as you could never have foreseen, you are now met here to enjoy the fellowship of old soldiers, and to receive the overflowing of a universal gratitude.

One might read Melville's dedication to the Bunker Hill Monument as an effort to participate in the patriotic nationalism espoused by Webster and of great importance to his own family, for his grandfathers on both sides, Major Thomas Melvill and General Peter Gansevoort, were celebrated Revolutionary heroes. Or, given the demythologizing strategies of the overall novel, one might take the dedication as an ironic reminder of the nation's failure to live up to the Revolutionary ideals emblematized by the Monument, with the comically mock deference to a royalist-sounding "His Highness" suggesting a betrayal of republican principles. All of which is to say that Melville's supposedly clarifying letter may have left his inquiring reader at a loss.

Then again, perhaps the key to the dedication can be found in Webster's salute to the Revolutionary War veteran, for the novel that Melville dedicates "To His Highness the Bunker-hill Monument" tells the story of the Revolutionary War veteran Israel Potter, an actual historical person (1754?–1826?). Unlike the veterans celebrated by Webster, however, who are recognized for their services and "receive the overflowing of a universal gratitude," the "devoted patriot, Israel Potter," as Melville terms him in the novel's first chapter, never achieves such recognition. Instead, this little-known person, who supposedly fought heroically at the Battle of Bunker Hill, was denied a government pension by Congress after returning to the United States from a nearly fifty-year exile abroad, and died a pauper. In this respect, Melville can be seen as telling the story of a common man who does good work for his country but remains in the margins, unrecognized by his compatriots. By focusing on a patriot who was forced to struggle for his very survival, Melville may have been attempting to convey his own version of a key motif of his friend Nathaniel Hawthorne's *The House of the Seven Gables* (1851): "In this republican country, amid the fluctuating waves of our social life, somebody is always at the drowning-point." That Israel Potter spent most of his adult life in England would have simply added a transatlantic dimension to the darkly resonant vision that Melville had appropriated from Hawthorne's *House*, a novel that he admired.

And yet the fact is that Melville wrote *Israel Potter* around the time that he was despairing about his own lack of recognition as an author and wrestling with his own financial difficulties. Though he doesn't say as much to his unknown correspondent of 1888, one suspects that there was an autobiographical component to Melville's portrayal of the neglected Potter. After all, in a letter to Hawthorne of May 1851 written as *Moby-Dick* was going to press, the then thirty-one-year-old author accurately predicted that his great novel would be ignored by readers and reviewers, and that there would be grave economic consequences for the young man struggling to support his family: "Though I wrote the Gospels in this century, I should die in the gutter." Angered by the poor sales and mixed reviews of *Moby-Dick*, Melville wrote a caustic domestic novel, *Pierre; or, The Ambiguities* (1852), which featured a satirical attack on the genteel literary culture of his time. Unsurprisingly, *Pierre* sold fewer than two thousand copies, and during the late summer and early fall of 1852 received some of the harshest reviews ever accorded a work by a major American writer. The Boston *Post* termed the novel "utter trash"; the New York *Albion* called it "a dead failure," "objectionable," and an "incoherent hodge-podge"; and the New York *Evening Mirror* judged it "morbid and unhealthy." The New York *Day Book* went so far as to announce that "Melville was really supposed to be deranged, and that his friends were taking measures to place him under treatment," expressing the hope that as part of this treatment Melville would be "stringently secluded from pen and ink."

In the wake of these harsh reviews, Melville to some extent chose to give the appearance that he had adopted such seclusion, or indeed had that seclusion forced upon him by his friends. He went "underground," as some critics have termed this phase of his career, by writing short fiction and sketches for the popular magazines *Harper's New Monthly Magazine* and *Putnam's Monthly Magazine*, and publishing these works anonymously. During the period between 1853 and 1855, the regular publication of such fictions as "Bartleby the Scrivener" (*Harper's* 1853), "The Paradise of Bachelors and the Tartarus of Maids" (*Harper's* 1855), and "Benito Cereno" (*Putnam's* 1855) brought Melville a steady income (he was typically paid five dollars a page) and helped to restore his reputation, at least with the editors associated with *Harper's* and *Putnam's*.

With a resurgent confidence in his ability to find an audience, Melville continued his efforts to write longer fictional narratives. The evidence suggests that sometime in 1853 he finished a novel called *The Isle of the Cross*, but for reasons that remain murky, and perhaps forever lost to the historical record, was unable to find a publisher. The manuscript has not survived (or is waiting to be discovered). There is also evidence that in late 1853 he began a long narrative about tortoise hunting, for in May 1854 he wrote Harper and Brothers with the hope of publishing an extract in *Harper's* along with a serialization of a new work (*Israel Potter*). But *Harper's* had suffered a major fire at its offices in December 1853, which set back its publication schedule. So, unable to interest the editors at *Harper's* in the tortoise narrative or *Israel Potter*, Melville turned to the more politically liberal *Putnam's*, negotiating an advance payment of one hundred dollars (at the rate of five dollars per printed page) for *Israel Potter*, his one and only serialized novel. He would eventually earn $421.50 for the magazine serialization—a hefty sum for Melville at that time. The first installment of the novel, with the working title of *Israel Potter; or, Fifty Years of Exile: A Fourth of July Story*, appeared, appropriately enough, in the July 1854 *Putnam's*. Melville would eventually drop the subtitle and retitle the novel *Israel Potter: His Fifty Years of Exile* when it was published by G. P. Putnam & Company in the spring of 1855.

The novel did not come without controversy. In the pages of *Putnam's* itself, a reviewer in the May 1855 issue complained that Melville diverged significantly from his source text, the

1824 first-person *Life and Remarkable Adventures of Israel R. Potter*, and wondered what gave Melville the right to take such liberties in imagining Potter as linked, for example, with John Paul Jones. These remarks take us back to Melville's supposedly explanatory letter of 1888 about *Israel Potter*, for it is in the dedication to his novel that Melville addresses the Israel Potter source text. Melville's only other reference to the 1824 *Life and Adventures*, prior to the 1855 dedication, can be found in the journal he kept of his October 1849 through January 1851 visit to England and the Continent. In an entry of December 1849, Melville remarked on a typical day in London:

> Miserable rainy day. Treated myself to a sugar omelette, at the old place, for breakfast. Then went to the British Museum—closed. Then among the old book stores about Great Queen Street & Lincoln's Inn. Looked over a lot of ancient maps of London. Bought one (A.D. 1766) for 3 & 6 pence. I want to use it in case I serve up the Revolutionary narrative of the beggar.

There is no mention of when he obtained the Revolutionary narrative, which was no doubt Potter's, but it is clear from this entry that Melville had come to know London (which has an important place in *Israel Potter*) and wanted to know even more about the city and its environs for an anticipated future piece of writing about the Revolutionary "beggar." In the dedication to his 1855 novel, Melville states that "with a change in the grammatical person, it [*Israel Potter*] preserves, almost in a reprint, Israel Potter's autobiographical story," and that in his biographical novel about Potter, he aspires to present a common life that "should not have appeared in the volumes of [Jared] Sparks"—an editor and publisher known for bringing out biographies of great men in American history. In important ways, then, Melville implicitly suggests in his dedication that his historical novel will be raising questions about what constitutes a "great" life.

This Penguin Classics Edition of *Israel Potter* reprints approximately half of Potter's 1824 narrative, and readers will therefore be able to come to their own conclusions about Melville's accuracy in preserving Potter's story and about the possible significance of the many changes that Melville made to his source text when fictionalizing Potter's life. As can be quickly discerned from a comparative reading of the two texts, Melville follows the 1824 narrative rather closely for chapters two through six of his novel, and then for the most part leaves the narrative behind for his own fabulous inventions, such as the sequences of chapters featuring Benjamin Franklin, John Paul Jones, and Ethan Allen. (For these chapters, Melville drew on such diverse texts as Ethan Allen's *A Narrative of Colonel Ethan Allen's Captivity* [1799], Robert C. Sands's *Life and Correspondence of John Paul Jones* [1830], James Fenimore Cooper's *The History of the Navy of the United States* [1839], and the writings of Benjamin Franklin.) Even when closely adhering to Potter's 1824 narrative, however, Melville makes a number of changes, including moving from first- to third-person narrative, a change that allows him to present an ironically detached portrait of Israel Potter in an allusive and often elusive narrative that, unlike Potter's self-interested autobiography, attends to a range of interpretive perspectives.

To return one more time to the highly evocative dedication that Melville describes late in life as central to understanding the novel: It is crucial to note that Melville states in the dedication that the Potter narrative was "forlornly published on a sleazy gray paper," which is to say that the narrative was as marginal or beggarly as Potter himself, and that it was "written, probably, not by himself, but taken down from his lips by another." This point is worth emphasizing, for Melville is informing us that his own novel, which tells the story of a historical personage, draws on a first-person account that was itself a telling by another of the story of a historical personage. There is a slipperiness to the 1824 narrative, in other words, that Melville may have decided to develop as one of the main subjects of his novel. In this respect, both the 1824 narrative and Melville's 1854–55 novelistic retelling and reimagining can be taken as forerunners of Melville's 1857 novel *The Confidence-Man*, which focuses on the instability of character, the difficulties of interpretation, and the con games that inevitably accompany storytelling. The key to Melville's 1888 letter to his inquiring correspondent would appear to be that it offers no key at all. And perhaps that is the key to *Israel Potter*, which can be read as a reader-friendly version of the con games that will come to dominate the much more difficult and elusive *The Confidence-Man*. Viewed in this way, the 1824 *Life and Remarkable Adventures of Israel R. Potter* can be thought of as a source text that, rather than offering a clear foundation for interpretation, ultimately destabilizes interpretation, suggesting the radical instability of historical narrative—and indeed of history itself. There is no more powerful theme in *Israel Potter*; and the purported autobiography of the historical Potter (whoever that person may be) can be taken as an exemplary instance of such instability.

As the historians David Chacko and Alexander Kulcsar have demonstrated in their study of the historical Potter's 1824 *Life and Remarkable Adventures*, the book that claims to tell the history of an American Revolutionary veteran who fought heroically at Bunker Hill, and was subsequently exiled in England for nearly fifty years, is crammed with errors and inventions. Town records suggest that Potter was born in Cranston, Rhode Island, in 1754, not 1744; that he was a bastard child and not, as he claims at the outset, of "reputable parents"; that he probably did not participate in the battle of Bunker Hill; that he may have served as a British spy; that he probably did not meet with George III; and that there was no need for him to remain in England for nearly five decades, except by choice. There is evidence that Potter met with Benjamin Franklin in Paris, as Potter briefly mentions in his account (and as Melville then elaborates upon at length), but his meeting may have been for the purpose of embezzling funds for himself or as a function of his spying for England. Whatever the truth of these various matters, Melville would no doubt have known something of Henry Trumbull, the amanuensis and publisher of Potter's account, who was notorious for his production of wildly inaccurate histories, biographies, and autobiographies. (Melville probably did not know that the same year that Trumbull published Potter's narrative, one of his apprentices was arrested in Providence, Rhode Island, on a morals charge for selling pornographic materials published by Trumbull to minors.) Trumbull's stated reason for publishing the Potter narrative was to assist a Revolutionary veteran who had returned to the United States in 1823 in quest of a government pension, but Trumbull was also trying to cash in on the market for narratives by Revolutionary veterans. Potter's was one of the last of hundreds of such accounts in this very popular autobiographical genre.

Although Melville follows the basic details of the first half of Trumbull's narrative, his divergences from the 1824 source text were even more fanciful than Trumbull's own straying from whatever constituted the historical truth of Potter's life story. To highlight some of Melville's changes: Melville switches the opening setting of his narrative from Cranston, Rhode Island, to the Massachusetts Berkshires, thereby locating Potter in the region where Melville himself had been living since 1850 and thus in the larger context of the history of colonial Massachusetts. Melville's Potter is depicted as a disinterested patriot, whereas Trumbull's regularly speaks self-interestedly of his desire for a pension. Consistent with this change, Melville greatly expands upon Potter's possible meeting with King George III, making the king more appealing than in the source text and Potter himself into more of a feisty, patriotic democrat. Melville then goes off in new directions, inventing such scenes as Potter's near-death imprisonment in a secret recess of the mansion of a British squire; his plotting with the Paris-based Benjamin Franklin; his meetings with John Paul Jones and eventual participation in the famous 1778 naval battle between Jones's *Bonhomme Richard* and the British *Serapis*; and his witnessing of the imprisonment of the fiery Ethan Allen in the British coastal town of Falmouth. In Trumbull's first-person narrative of Potter, there is much concerning Potter's decades of poverty in England; Melville compresses that material and brings it to powerful focus in the Dantean chapter 24, entitled "The City of Dis." Trumbull's Potter returns to the United States in 1823, arriving first in New York City and then traveling to Boston, and at that time beginning the process of attempting to attain a pension; Melville's returns directly to Boston on July 4, 1826, and learns almost immediately that his pension request will fail. Trumbull tells yet another story of a Revolutionary veteran; Melville adds to Potter's story a panoply of Revolutionary heroes, a wealth of literary and historical allusions, and a shrewd narrative irony—all of which contribute to his efforts to address larger interpretive matters of history, biography, and nation.

Such complexities are addressed in relatively indirect fashion in the novel, for in a letter of June 1854 Melville insisted to his editor at *Putnam's* that *Israel Potter* will have "very little reflective writing in it; nothing weighty. It is adventure." In other words, Melville sought readers who liked a good story. A number of Melville's contemporary reviewers praised the book precisely for its storytelling, taking little note of its historical or political thematics, and early in the twentieth century the critic Yvor Winters declared that "*Israel Potter*, the life of an American patriot of the Revolutionary War, is one of the few great novels of pure adventure in English." Though the novel certainly has its share of rousing adventure, there is more going on in *Israel Potter* than might initially meet the eye, and even when Melville is telling a gripping, comical, and sometimes violent story, he is developing a rich symbolic history of his revolutionary (anti)hero.

The symbolic resonances of Potter's history are established in the novel's opening chapter, through Melville's brilliantly compact (and invented) account of "The Birthplace of Israel"—a chapter that links the Berkshires of Massachusetts to the English Puritans' conception of the New World as a New Canaan. Absolutely central to Melville's Revolutionary novel are the ironies built into Israel Potter's own name. The "Potter," with its associative linkages to Potter's Field (the traditional burial ground of the impoverished), serves as a predictor of the main character's eventual end in poverty. But what especially intrigued Melville were the millennial implications of his patriot's first name, which Melville emphasizes by using the pared-down "Israel" in chapter titles, thereby invoking the nexus of the biblical Israel, the United States as a New Israel, and the titular character. Ironies abound, for whereas the U.S. millennialist gives meaning to the world by apprehending typological scriptural parallels between the nation as New Canaan and the Israel of the Old Testament, Melville emphasizes disjunctions and chaos and, ultimately, the absence of meaning in the events, wars, and nations that he describes.

Using the opening chapter to establish the symbolic import (or lack of import) of Israel Potter's life history, Melville follows the basic outline of the 1824 Potter narrative in describing Potter's father's oppressive resistance to his marriage plans (thus conflating the tyrannical father with George III); Potter's subsequent three years at sea as a trader and adventurer; his return to New England and participation in the Battle of Bunker Hill; and his imprisonment by the British. The bulk of the novel is then made up of mostly invented escapades set during the period running from late 1775 to 1778. As described by the narrator, Potter while in England is regularly on the run, sometimes being imprisoned or impressed, and at other times operating as a free agent who nonetheless has little apprehension of the larger political or historical picture. Or, to put this in the vernacular, Israel Potter, as described in chapters seven through twenty-four, doesn't have a clue. He is enlisted as a spy for pro-American forces but has no idea what they are up to, nor does he have a clear understanding of what either Benjamin Franklin or John Paul Jones is doing in Paris. Though he fights in famous battles, he does not perceive their significance. The novel undermines the idea of a glorious patriotic march toward an eventual American victory in the Revolutionary War, and indeed never depicts the moment of victory. Instead, for nearly the entire novel Potter participates in the American Revolution as a confused, and for the most part baffled, historical actor.

In the concluding two chapters of the novel (which take us from the late 1770s to July 1826 and thus compact nearly fifty years into a small number of pages), Israel Potter, after working as a brickmaker outside of London, marries a shopgirl from Kent and has eleven children (ten of whom die). Like the Potter of Melville's 1824 source text, the Potter of Melville's novel eventually takes up the job of repairing chairs as a way of making a living. In the final chapter, when Potter journeys back to the United States, the Revolution returns to the forefront of the novel, but by this time the Revolution has become central to a self-aggrandizing national history, as in Daniel Webster's 1825 speech at Bunker Hill, from which Potter forever remains apart.

In *Israel Potter*, then, the American Revolution is presented as a random succession of events, some violent and some not, which do not necessarily yield anything worthy of celebration. There is little sense of progress or of a cohesive unfolding of a coherent national history; contingency and uncertainty are the order of the day. Melville's distinctive approach to representing the American Revolution becomes immediately apparent in the account of Potter's participation in the battle of Bunker Hill. Dismayed to find that his beloved had married while he was off at sea, Potter takes up farming, hears about the Battle of Lexington, enlists in the regiment of General Israel Putnam, and quickly finds himself within a chaotic scene of violence, the macabre highlight being Potter's effort to wrest a sword from what he fails to realize is the disembodied arm of a British soldier. The fighting comes to an anticlimactic finish with no sense that this is a pivotal conflict that has given new definition and momentum to the Revolutionary cause. Shortly thereafter, Potter is taken prisoner and put on the British frigate *Tartar*, and upon reaching England manages to escape dressed as an English sailor. Potter's first change of clothes initiates a succession of clothes changes that underscores just how easily identity can be altered and performed, and how easily individuals can end up on one or the other side of a battle. Readers familiar with Melville's *Redburn* (1849), *White-Jacket* (1850), and "Benito Cereno" (1855), among other works, know that clothes are central to Melville's presentation of the fungibility of personal and national identity.

The violence and seeming senselessness of the Battle of Bunker Hill, which Melville presents in a rushed present tense that conveys the immediacy of chaos and the absence of mythologized patriotic meaning, would seem to go against the grain of Melville's promise to his publisher George P. Putnam, affirmed in a letter of June 1854, "that the story shall contain nothing of any sort to shock the fastidious." There is actually much in *Israel Potter* that seems intended to shock the fastidious, such as the account in chapter 13 of Israel in tattered pants asking a British woman for a charitable handout, even as he notices that "a whitish fragment" of his genitals protrudes through "one loin of the rotten old breeches." In a subsequent scene in chapter 14, Israel, now forcibly serving on a British revenue ship, engages British officers in a wildly savage fight, during which one officer "caught Israel by the most terrible part in which mortality can be grappled," and Israel responds by grabbing another officer "round the loins, bedding his fingers like grisly claws into his flesh and hugging him to his heart." The barbarism of that battle, which Potter attributes to hearing the voice of John Paul Jones at sea, initiates a series of chapters in which Potter joins up with John Paul Jones to participate in some of the bloodiest scenes of the novel. As with the Battle of Bunker Hill, Melville for the most part presents bloody conflict in disrelation to Americans' retrospective celebration of the glories of the American Revolutionary War. Here, in chapters that are written in the past tense but, like the account of Bunker Hill, have the feel of a breathless present, Melville depicts what some historians have come to call the modern era's turn to total war. And he does so without offering pious judgments on the main participants.

The five key chapters on the martial John Paul Jones are chapters 15 through 19, which come after Potter has had a series of adventures in England and Paris, including meeting both Jones and Benjamin Franklin. As becomes apparent, Benjamin Franklin has shrewdly put Jones to the service of the American cause by granting him unchecked authority over sailors eager to fight the British. The narrator tells us that Jones "sailed without any instructions," and we are meant to realize that Franklin's omission of instructions is part of his genius. Franklin has unleashed a fighting machine who, when all is said and done, fights for the sake of fighting. Jones is unconcerned about national or revolutionary ideologies; there is never a moment when he seems to have reflected with any great insight on why he is fighting for the American cause. (For that matter, Franklin himself is presented as barely giving a thought to the issue.) And so, as with Bunker Hill, Melville depicts key naval battles of the Revolutionary War with a darkly comic violence that ultimately discloses the horrors that are covered up by the subsequent patriotic storytelling linking Jones to the glories of the American Revolution. Jones initiates his martial campaign by assaulting British civilian populations on the northern and western coasts of England. Thwarted in his initial plans to attack the inhabitants of Whitehaven and destroy the town, he nonetheless manages to burn all of their ships in harbor. Commanding Potter and a crew that enthusiastically supports his every move, Jones methodically continues his attacks on British coastal towns for approximately three months before "luck—that's the word" leads him to his great battle with the British naval ship *Serapis*.

The battle between Jones's ship, with the Ben Franklin–inspired name *Bonhomme Richard*, and the British *Serapis* is generally recognized as the first major sea battle between American and British forces. Jones became famous for supposedly saying, at a moment when it appeared that the battle was lost, "I have not yet begun to fight." Melville imports into the novel that apocryphal proclamation from nineteenth-century accounts, along with the outright fiction that Israel Potter was not only on board Jones's ship, but was also the person responsible for naming the ship in honor of Ben Franklin's Poor Richard—a name that Jones seconds because of his admiration for Poor Richard's famous proverb "God helps them that help themselves." Melville's description of the epochal battle in the much-admired chapter 19 for the most part follows his sources in Sands's *Life and Correspondence of John Paul Jones* and Cooper's *The History of the Navy of the United States*. On a summer night of 1778, under a full moon and off the coast of Yorkshire, hundreds of civilians on the cliffs look on as if war were a form of entertainment. But the promise of a traditional stately battle between two clearly defined sides quickly descends into utter pandemonium and atrocity, as approximately half of the men on both sides are killed (the dead number into the hundreds). Death breaks down national distinctions—"The belligerents were no longer, in the ordinary sense of things, an English ship, and an American ship"—and death trumps all in the cold waters off the northern British coast: "Into that Lethean canal," the narrator writes, "fell many a poor soul that night;—fell, for ever forgotten." Cannons burst apart, "killing the sailors who worked them." Cartridges ignite and explode, and more "than twenty men were instantly killed." The French ship *Alliance* arrives on the scene and inexplicably fires on Jones's ship, killing many others. By the end of this remarkable scene, Jones manages to gain control of the British vessel, even as his own ship sinks to the bottom of the sea. Melville's great reimagining of the unalloyed brutality of the encounter between the *Bonhomme Richard* and the *Serapis* concludes with the narrator posing a rhetorical question: "In view of this battle one may well ask—What separates the enlightened man from the savage? Is civilization a thing distinct, or is it an advanced stage of barbarism?"

In light of Melville's brutal account, the easy answer to such a question is that there are no great distinctions, which may be Melville's point. But it's equally likely that he is mocking such conventional pious posturing. Whatever his intentions, Melville follows the harrowing representation of battle with his most comical chapter, "The Shuttle," which depicts Potter stupidly allowing himself to be caught by the British enemy and then successfully feigning the identity of a British sailor by claiming to be one Peter Perkins. Melville's account in this comic chapter of how easily identities can be enacted and modified is consistent with the previous chapters' accounts of how national identities can collapse under the pain of death or the changing of clothes.

Throughout the novel, Melville works against fixed identities, narratives, and meanings. A recognition of the chameleonesque nature of identity may be the best way to approach the novel's key characters. True, Jones is a warrior, but he is also a feisty and amusing personage who seems rather modest about his abilities and is perhaps a version in extremis of all participants in war. The imprisoned patriot Ethan Allen, whom Israel Potter meets after successfully passing as English, may seem as wild and "savage" in his revolutionary energy as Jones, but one senses that he takes great pleasure in theatrically adopting such an identity while in an English prison, and one can only wonder what, if anything, would remain of Allen when the acting stops. Similar questions could be asked about Potter himself, who at times can seem like the scarecrow he encounters in a British farmer's field early in the novel. When all is said and done, Potter *is* as he is positioned and dressed.

Arguably the most problematic character in the novel is Benjamin Franklin, who has a significant role as the historical figure representing the heart and soul of the new nation. Most critics have regarded Melville's portrait of Franklin as highly condemnatory, and as part of a larger attack on the spiritless economic pragmatism and hypocrisy of the new nation itself. But in the context of the novel's destabilizing narrative strategies, it might make better sense to see Melville as comically piercing through the mythic Franklin in order to reveal a more interesting man. True, Franklin can appear to be a conniving hypocrite, arguing for temperance as he drinks his fine wines, counseling moral behavior as he pursues the ladies of Paris, urging economic prudence as he consorts as a Parisian dandy, and speaking in rational apothegms as he mystically dons a "conjuror's robe . . . with a skull-cap of black satin on his hive of a head." Melville's Franklin is ultimately wise and witty, a plotter and performer, who remains beyond the ken of Potter and the narrator. Melville concludes that there "was much benevolent irony, innocent mischievousness, in the old man," and he conveys his own Franklinian mischievous spirit in portraying him "in less exalted habitudes." Worldly and wise, and like Ethan Allen a brilliant performer, the ironically deconstructed Franklin of *Israel Potter*—a man who knows more than he lets on and never descends to deadly seriousness—is actually one of the more appealing accounts of Franklin in print.

In a Franklinian comic spirit, then, Melville offers much entertainment in *Israel Potter* and an almost relentless assault on high seriousness. That said, the novel in its final chapters becomes rather grim, and never more so than in the account of the impoverished Potter's relatively short period of time working near London as a brickmaker. Here Melville underscores the typological parallels between Israel Potter and the Israelites of the Old Testament, presenting England as similar to Egypt under Pharaoh, with the implication that an escape to the new Israel of the United States would possibly be redemptive. The narrator points to the ironies of Israel's situation as he toils in the brickyard thousands of miles away from the promised land: "He whom love of country made a hater of her foes—the foreigners among whom he now was thrown—he who, as soldier and sailor, had joined to kill, burn and destroy both them and theirs—here he was at last, serving that very people as a slave." But even as Israel Potter is being analogized to the Hebraic patriarchs of old, ironies remain, for this description underscores Potter's own savagery. Moreover, the narrator attributes to the beclouded Potter a guiding purpose for which there is little evidence in the novel.

Nevertheless, the depiction of Potter as a slave at the brickyard is worthy of note, for the slavery context of the American 1850s provides an important undercurrent to the novel. *Israel Potter* was published five years after Congress passed the Fugitive Slave Law of the Compromise of 1850, and it is surely no coincidence that Potter is presented as a fugitive. In chapter 1, after all, he is termed a "runaway rebel," and there are striking resemblances between Potter's continual efforts to escape from imprisonment and accounts in slave narratives of those runaway rebels' efforts to make their escapes. The scene in the English brickyards, which literally depicts Potter as a slave, helps to bring these parallels into focus. It is additionally worth noting that Melville began the serialization of *Israel Potter* the same year that saw the passage of the Kansas–Nebraska Act— the legislation that allowed settlers in the territories to choose whether they wanted to form free or slave states. That legislation sparked the bloody conflicts in Kansas and Nebraska presaging the Civil War. When Melville remarks on the battle between the *Bonhomme Richard* and the *Serapis* that "it was as if the Siamese Twins, oblivious of their fraternal bond, should rage in unnatural fight," it is difficult not to read into this imagery concerns about the fraternal violence that was on display in his own country during the mid-1850s. Shortly after the conclusion of the serialization of *Israel Potter* in *Putnam's*, Melville began a new three-part serialization of his great novella of slave revolt, "Benito Cereno," a work that, through its depiction of the hapless Captain Delano, portrayed the United States as a slave power on the brink of an apocalyptic racial war of extermination.

In the context of Melville's concerns about the persistence of slavery, which inform both "Benito Cereno" and *Israel Potter*, there is a heightened irony to Potter's eventual return to the United States in 1826 as an old man. The republican nation seems anything but the Promised Land he had dreamed of while laboring as an exile in England. Presented as a sort of Rip Van Winkle figure, Potter encounters a bustling, self-important post-Revolutionary world on the Fourth of July and is nearly killed by a carriage driver racing madly through the streets near Boston's Faneuil Hall. The masses are celebrating the heroes of Bunker Hill, but no one recognizes Potter. The prevailing mood of the final chapter is dismal and despairing, as Potter recalls the failed dreams of his youth and quietly fades from the novel (and from history). Though slavery is not explicitly mentioned in the final chapter, there are resemblances in mood and irony between Melville's 1854–55 novel of the American Revolution and Frederick Douglass's famous 1852 speech about the American Revolution. In "What to the Slave Is the Fourth of July?" Douglass points to the unfulfilled work of the American Revolution, proclaiming that the Fourth of July "is a sham; your boasted liberty, an unholy license; your national greatness, swelling vanity; your sounds of rejoicing are empty and heartless; your denunciations of tyrants, brass-fronted impudence; your shouts of liberty and equality, hollow mockery." Situating the reader with the exiled "slave" Israel Potter, who returns to the United States on the very Fourth of July that celebrates the fiftieth anniversary of the Declaration of Independence, Melville, through his "remote" historical fiction, conveys a similar sense of disillusionment, though without the clear political imperatives of Frederick Douglass.

Melville would appear to speak most clearly as a social critic earlier in the novel, when he analogizes the United States to John Paul Jones, and proclaims about the emerging new nation just before the battle between Jones's *Bonhomme Richard* and the British *Serapis*: "intrepid, reckless, predatory, with boundless ambition, civilized in externals but a savage at heart, America is, or may yet be, the Paul Jones of nations." The novel's bleak ending and this particular passage have encouraged recent critics to read *Israel Potter* as an attack on the nation not only for its failure to live up to its egalitarian ideals but also for its brutal policies of expansionism, its 1846–1848 war with Mexico, and its sustained support for slavery. But it is important to note that in the cataclysmic battle between the two ships, few distinctions are made between England and America, and in subsequent chapters Melville refers to the Napoleonic Wars and France's own implication in nationalistic violence. In his profoundly transatlantic and even global work, which is set mostly apart from the United States and in fact has only one chapter set in the new nation, Melville seems less intent on identifying the United States as particularly evil than on challenging all claims to national exceptionalism. The United States in this regard appears no better (or worse) than England, France, or the other nations that Melville alludes to over the course of the novel.

A historical novel that forcibly conveys how difficult it is to make sense of history, and that regularly reveals, as stated in chapter 18, "that . . . all human affairs are subject to organic disorder, since they are created in, and sustained by, a sort of half-disciplined chaos," may not be the best guide to social critique and reform. Instead, like Melville's other historical fictions, "Benito Cereno" and the posthumously published *Billy Budd*, the novel can be read as a guide to history, teaching us just how difficult it can be to discern clear patterns and meanings in that half-disciplined chaos, and by extension warning us of the risks of blindly following the lead of those who are overconfident in their ability to discern such patterns. This is a novel that can be humbling to all sides of the political spectrum. But it is also a novel that, by virtue of its comic energy, takes us on a romp through history even as it helps us to realize how little we know about its trajectories. Ironically, by the end of the novel, we come to know a little more by knowing a little less. Humbling and rejuvenating, *Israel Potter* is worthy of Melville's and our dedication.

—ROBERT S. LEVINE

Works Cited and Suggestions for Further Reading

SCHOLARLY EDITIONS OF *ISRAEL POTTER*

Israel Potter: His Fifty Years of Exile. Ed. Harrison Hayford, Hershel Parker, and G. Thomas Tanselle. Evanston and Chicago: Northwestern University Press and The Newberry Library, 1982.

Israel Potter: His Fifty Years of Exile. Ed. Hennig Cohen. New York: Fordham University Press, 1991.

SELECTED WRITINGS BY MELVILLE RELEVANT TO *ISRAEL POTTER*

Redburn: His First Voyage, Being the Sailor-boy Confessions and Reminiscences of the Son-of-a-Gentleman, in the Merchant Service. [1849.] Ed. Harrison Hayford, Hershel Parker, and G. Thomas Tanselle. Evanston and Chicago: Northwestern University Press and The Newberry Library, 1968.

White-Jacket; or, The World in a Man-of-War. [1850.] Ed. Harrison Hayford, Hershel Parker, and G. Thomas Tanselle. Evanston and Chicago: Northwestern University Press and The Newberry Library, 1970.

Moby-Dick; or, The Whale. [1851.] Ed. Harrison Hayford, Hershel Parker, and G. Thomas Tanselle. Evanston and Chicago: Northwestern University Press and The Newberry Library, 1988.

Pierre; or, The Ambiguities. [1852.] Ed. Harrison Hayford, Hershel Parker, and G. Thomas Tanselle. Evanston and Chicago: Northwestern University Press and The Newberry Library, 1971.

The Piazza Tales and Other Prose Pieces. [1839–1860.] Ed. Harrison Hayford, Alma A. MacDougall, and G. Thomas Tanselle. Evanston and Chicago: Northwestern University Press and The Newberry Library, 1987.

The Confidence-Man: His Masquerade. [1857.] Ed. Harrison Hayford, Hershel Parker, and G. Thomas Tanselle. Evanston and Chicago: Northwestern University Press and The Newberry Library, 1984.

Billy Budd, Sailor (An Inside Narrative). [Posthumous.] Ed. Harrison Hayford and Merton J. Sealts, Jr. Chicago: University of Chicago Press, 1962.

BIOGRAPHICAL STUDIES AND RESOURCES

Bercaw, Mary K. *Melville's Sources*. Evanston: Northwestern University Press, 1987.

Delbanco, Andrew. *Melville: His World and Work*. New York: Alfred A. Knopf, 2005.

Higgins, Brian, and Hershel Parker, Ed. *Herman Melville: The Contemporary Reviews*. Cambridge and New York: Cambridge University Press, 1995.

Leyda, Jay. Ed. *The Melville Log: A Documentary Life of Herman Melville, 1819–1891*. New York: Gordian Press, 1969.

Melville, Herman. *Correspondence*. Ed. Lynn C. Horth. Evanston and Chicago: Northwestern University Press and The Newberry Library, 1993.

Melville, Herman. *Journals*. Ed. Howard C. Horford and Lynn Horth. Evanston and Chicago: Northwestern University Press and The Newberry Library, 1989.

Parker, Hershel. *Herman Melville: A Biography*. 2 volumes. Baltimore: Johns Hopkins University Press, 1996, 2002.

Robertson-Lorant, Laurie. *Melville: A Biography*. New York: Clarkson Potter Publishers, 1996.

Rogin, Michael Paul. *Subversive Genealogy: The Politics and Art of Herman Melville*. New York: Alfred A. Knopf, 1983.

Sealts, Merton M., Jr. *Melville's Reading*. Columbia: University of South Carolina Press, 1988.

ESSAYS ON *ISRAEL POTTER*

Bellis, Peter. "*Israel Potter*: Autobiography as History as Fiction." *American Literary History*, 2 (1990): 607–26.

Blum, Hester. "Atlantic Trade." In *A Companion to Herman Melville*. Ed. Wyn Kelley. Oxford: Blackwell Publishing, 2006. 113–28.

Bryant, John. "*Israel Potter* Old and New." *Resources for American Literary Study*, 21 (1995): 261–73.

Chako, David, and Alexander Kulchsar. "Israel Potter: Genesis of a Legend." *William and Mary Quarterly*, 3rd series, 41 (1984): 365–89.

Christophersen, Bill. "Israel Potter: Melville's 'Citizen of the Universe.'" *Studies in American Fiction*, 21 (1993). 21–35.

Cohen, Hennig. "Israel Potter: Common Man as Hero." In *A Companion to Melville Studies*. Edited by John Bryant. New York: Greenwood Press, 1986. 279–313.

Cohen, Hennig. " 'Why talk of Jaffa?' ": Melville's *Israel Potter*, Baron Gros, Zummo, and the Plague." In *Savage Eye: Melville and the Visual Arts*. Ed. Christopher Sten. Kent, Ohio: Kent State University Press, 1991. 162–178

Davis, Clark. "The Body-Deferred: *Israel Potter* and the Search for the Hearth." *Studies in American Fiction*, 19 (1991): 175–87.

Ernest, John. "Revolutionary Fictions and Activist Labor: Looking for Douglass and Melville Together." In *Frederick Douglass and Herman Melville: Essays in Relation*. Ed. Robert S. Levine and Samuel Otter. Chapel Hill: University of North Carolina Press, 2008. 19–38.

Giles, Paul. " 'Bewildering Intertanglement': Melville's Engagement with British Culture." In *The Cambridge Companion to Herman Melville*. Edited by Robert S. Levine. New York and Cambridge: Cambridge University Press, 1998. 224–249.

Hiltner, Judith. "'A Parallel and a Prophecy': Arrest, Superimposition, and Metamorphosis in Melville's *Israel Potter*." *ATQ*, 2 (1988): 41–55.

Kelley, Wyn. "Melville and John Vanderlyn: Ruin and Historical Fate from 'Bartleby' to *Israel Potter*." In *Savage Eye: Melville and the Visual Arts*. Ed. Christopher Sten. Kent, Ohio: Kent State University Press, 1991. 117–126.

Lackey, Kris. "The Two Hands of *Israel Potter*." *College Literature*, 21 (1994): 32–45.

Post-Lauria, Sheila. "Magazine Practices and Melville's *Israel Potter*." *Periodical Literature in Nineteenth-Century America*, ed. Kenneth M. Price and Susan Belasco Smith. Charlottesville: University Press of Virginia, 1995. 115–32.

Reagan, Daniel. "Melville's *Israel Potter* and the Nature of Biography." *ATQ*, 3 (1989): 257–76.

Rosenberg, Brian. "*Israel Potter*: Melville's Anti-History." *Studies in American Fiction* 15 (1987): 175–86.

Temple, Gale. "Fluid Identity in *Israel Potter* and *The Confidence-Man*." In *A Companion to Herman Melville*. Ed. Wyn Kelley. Oxford: Blackwell Publishing, 2006. 451–466.

Zaller, Robert. "Melville and the Myth of Revolution." *Studies in Romanticism*, 15 (1976): 607–22.

BOOKS WITH SECTIONS OR CHAPTERS ON *ISRAEL POTTER*

Cagidemetrio, Alide. *Fictions of the Past: Hawthorne & Melville*. Amherst: University of Massachusetts Press, 1992.

Castronovo, Russ. *Fathering the Nation: American Genealogies of Slavery and Freedom*. Berkeley: University of California Press, 1995.

Colatrella, Carol. *Literature and Moral Reform: Melville and the Discipline of Reading*. Gainesville: University Press of Florida, 2002.

Dekker, George. *The American Historical Romance.* Cambridge and New York: Cambridge University Press, 1987.

Dillingham, William B. *Melville's Later Novels.* Athens: University of Georgia Press, 1986.

Dryden, Edgar A. *Monumental Melville: The Formation of a Literary Career.* Stanford: Stanford University Press, 2004.

Franklin, H. Bruce. *The Victim as Criminal and Artist: Literature from the American Prison.* New York: Oxford University Press, 1978.

Gilmore, Michael T. *The Middle Way: Puritanism and Ideology in American Romantic Fiction.* New Brunswick: Rutgers University Press, 1977.

Karcher, Carolyn L. *Shadow over the Promised Land: Slavery, Race, and Violence in Melville's America.* Baton Rouge: Louisiana State University Press, 1980.

Kelley, Wyn. *Melville's City: Literary and Urban Form in Nineteenth-Century New York.* New York and Cambridge: Cambridge University Press, 1996.

Keyssar, Alexander. *Melville's* Israel Potter: *Reflections on the American Dream.* Cambridge: Harvard University Press, 1969.

McWilliams, John P., Jr. *Hawthorne, Melville, and the American Character: A Looking-Glass Business.* New York and Cambridge: Cambridge University Press, 1984.

Rampersad, Arnold. *Melville's* Israel Potter: *A Pilgrimage and Progress.* Bowling Green, OH: Bowling Green Popular Press, 1969.

Reising, Russell T. *Loose Ends: Closure and Crisis in the American Social Text.* Durham: Duke University Press, 1996.

Samson, John. *White Lies: Melville's Narratives of Facts.* Ithaca: Cornell University Press, 1989.

Seelye, John. *Melville: The Ironic Diagram.* Evanston: Northwestern University Press, 1970.

Sten, Christopher. *The Weaver God, He Weaves: Melville and the Poetics of the Novel.* Kent, Ohio: Kent State University Press, 1996.

Winters, Yvor. *Maule's Curse: Seven Studies in the History of American Obscurantism.* Norfolk, Connecticut: New Directions, 1938.

CULTURAL AND HISTORICAL CONTEXTS

Allen, Ethan. *A Narrative of Colonel Ethan Allen's Captivity*. Ed. Stephen Carl Arch. Acton, Massachusetts: Copley Publishing, 2000.

Arch, Stephen Carl. *After Franklin: The Emergence of Autobiography in Post-Revolutionary America, 1780–1830*. Hanover, New Hampshire: University Press of New England, 2001.

Bailyn, Bernard. *Atlantic History: Concept And Contours*. Cambridge: Harvard University Press, 2005.

Cooper, J. Fenimore. *The History of the Navy of the United States*. 1839. Upper Saddle River, New Jersey: Gregg Press, 1970.

Dorson, Richard. *American Rebels: Narratives of the Patriots*. New York: Pantheon Books, 1953.

Kammen, Michael. *A Season of Youth: The American Revolution and the Historical Imagination*. New York: Alfred A. Knopf, 1978.

Linebaugh, Peter, and Marcus Buford Rediker. *The Many-Headed Hydra: The Hidden History of the Revolutionary Atlantic*. Boston: Beacon Press, 2000.

McWilliams, John. *New England's Crises and Cultural Memory: Literature, Politics, History, Religion, 1620–1860*. Cambridge and New York: Cambridge University Press, 2004.

Sands, Robert C. *Life and Correspondence of John Paul Jones*. New York: A. Chandler, 1830.

Thomas, Evan. *John Paul Jones: Sailor, Hero, Father of the American Navy*. New York: Simon and Schuster, 2003.

Williams, Daniel E., Ed. *Liberty's Captives: Narratives of Confinement in the Print Culture of the Early Republic*. Athens: University of Georgia Press, 2006.

Wood, Gordon S. *The Americanization of Benjamin Franklin*. New York: Penguin Books, 2004.

A Note on the Text

The text of this Penguin Classics edition of *Israel Potter: His Fifty Years of Exile* is taken from the Northwestern-Newberry volume edited by Harrison Hayford, Hershel Parker, and G. Thomas Tanselle (Evanston and Chicago: Northwestern University Press and The Newberry Library, 1982). The novel was initially serialized in the July 1854 through March 1855 *Putnam's Monthly Magazine of American Literature, Science, and Art*, and then was published as a book by G. P. Putnam & Company in March 1855. G. P. Putnam brought out two subsequent printings that same year. Because there were numerous errors in the 1855 volumes, including the dropping of the paragraph in chapter 24 beginning "On they passed," the Northwestern-Newberry editors conclude that Melville was not closely involved with the book's publication. They therefore take as their copy-text the *Putnam's* serialization (there is no surviving manuscript), and adopt only those variants from the periodical to book publication that they believe reflect Melville's authorial intentions, incorporating as well five of the eight editorial changes that Melville handwrote on his personal copy of the third printing of the novel. Although they correct obvious typographical errors, the Northwestern-Newberry editors preserve some of the spelling and usage inconsistencies that were standard fare of nineteenth-century periodical publishing.

ISRAEL POTTER:

His Fifty Years of Exile.

BY

HERMAN MELVILLE,

AUTHOR OF "TYPEE," "OMOO," ETC.

New York:

G. P. PUTNAM & CO., 10 PARK PLACE.

1855.

TO
His Highness
THE
𝔅unker-𝔥ill 𝔐onument

Biography, in its purer form, confined to the ended lives of the true and brave, may be held the fairest meed of human virtue— one given and received in entire disinterestedness—since neither can the biographer hope for acknowledgment from the subject, nor the subject at all avail himself of the biographical distinction conferred.

Israel Potter well merits the present tribute—a private of Bunker Hill,[1] who for his faithful services was years ago promoted to a still deeper privacy under the ground, with a posthumous pension, in default of any during life, annually paid him by the spring in ever-new mosses and sward.

I am the more encouraged to lay this performance at the feet of your Highness,[2] because, with a change in the grammatical person, it preserves, almost as in a reprint, Israel Potter's autobiographical story.[3] Shortly after his return in infirm old age to his native land, a little narrative of his adventures, forlornly published on sleazy gray paper, appeared among the peddlers, written, probably, not by himself, but taken down from his lips by another. But like the crutch-marks of the cripple by the Beautiful Gate,[4] this blurred record is now out of print. From a tattered copy, rescued by the merest chance from the rag-pickers, the present account has been drawn, which, with the exception of some expansions, and additions of historic and personal details, and one or two shiftings of scene, may, perhaps, be not unfitly regarded something in the light of a dilapidated old tombstone retouched.

Well aware that in your Highness' eyes the merit of the story must be in its general fidelity to the main drift of the original narrative, I forbore anywhere to mitigate the hard fortunes of my hero; and particularly towards the end, though sorely tempted, durst not substitute for the allotment of Providence any artistic recompense of poetical justice; so that no one can complain of the gloom of my closing chapters more profoundly than myself.

Such is the work, and such the man, that I have the honor to present to your Highness. That the name here noted should not have appeared in the volumes of Sparks,[5] may or may not be a matter for astonishment; but Israel Potter seems purposely to have waited to make his popular advent under the present exalted patronage, seeing that your Highness, according to the definition above, may, in the loftiest sense, be deemed the Great Biographer: the national commemorator of such of the anonymous privates of June 17, 1775, who may never have received other requital than the solid reward of your granite.

Your Highness will pardon me, if, with the warmest ascriptions on this auspicious occasion, I take the liberty to mingle my hearty congratulations on the recurrence of the anniversary day we celebrate, wishing your Highness (though indeed your Highness be somewhat prematurely gray) many returns of the same, and that each of its summer's suns may shine as brightly on your brow as each winter snow shall lightly rest on the grave of Israel Potter.

Your Highness'
Most devoted and obsequious,
THE EDITOR

JUNE 17TH, 1854.

CHAPTER I

The Birthplace of Israel

The traveller who at the present day is content to travel in the good old Asiatic style, neither rushed along by a locomotive, nor dragged by a stage-coach; who is willing to enjoy hospitalities at far-scattered farmhouses, instead of paying his bill at an inn; who is not to be frightened by any amount of loneliness, or to be deterred by the roughest roads or the highest hills; such a traveller in the eastern part of Berkshire, Mass.,[1] will find ample food for poetic reflection in the singular scenery of a country, which, owing to the ruggedness of the soil and its lying out of the track of all public conveyances, remains almost as unknown to the general tourist as the interior of Bohemia.

Travelling northward from the township of Otis, the road leads for twenty or thirty miles towards Windsor,[2] lengthwise upon that long broken spur of heights which the Green Mountains of Vermont send into Massachusetts. For nearly the whole of the distance, you have the continual sensation of being upon some terrace in the moon. The feeling of the plain or the valley is never yours; scarcely the feeling of the earth. Unless by a sudden precipitation of the road you find yourself plunging into some gorge; you pass on, and on, and on, upon the crests or slopes of pastoral mountains, while far below, mapped out in its beauty, the valley of the Housatonic[3] lies endlessly along at your feet. Often, as your horse gaining some lofty level tract, flat as a table, trots gayly over the almost deserted and sodded road, and your admiring eye sweeps the broad landscape beneath, you seem to be Boótes[4] driving in heaven. Save a potato field here and there, at long intervals, the whole country is either in wood or pasture. Horses, cattle and sheep are the principal inhabitants of these mountains. But all through the year lazy columns of smoke rising from the depths of the forest, proclaim the presence of that half-outlaw, the charcoal-burner; while in early spring added curls of vapor show that the maple sugar-boiler is also at work. But as for farming as a regular vocation, there is not much of it here. At any rate, no man by that means accumulates a fortune from this thin and rocky soil; all whose arable parts have long since been nearly exhausted.

Yet during the first settlement of the country, the region was not unproductive. Here it was that the original settlers came, acting upon the principle well-known to have regulated their choice of site, namely, the high land in preference to the low, as less subject to the unwholesome miasmas generated by breaking into the rich valleys and alluvial bottoms of primeval regions. By degrees, however, they quitted the safety of this sterile elevation, to brave the dangers of richer though lower fields. So that at the present day, some of those mountain townships present an aspect of singular abandonment. Though they have never known aught but peace and health, they, in one lesser aspect at least, look like countries depopulated by plague and war. Every mile or two a house is passed untenanted. The strength of the frame-work of these ancient buildings enables them long to resist the encroachments of decay. Spotted gray and green with the weather-stain, their timbers seem to have lapsed back into their woodland original, forming part now of the general picturesqueness of the natural scene. They are of extraordinary size, compared with modern farm-houses. One peculiar feature is the immense chimney, of light gray stone, perforating the middle of the roof like a tower.

On all sides are seen the tokens of ancient industry. As stone abounds throughout these mountains, that material was, for fences, as ready to the hand as wood, besides being much more durable. Consequently the landscape is intersected in all directions with walls of uncommon neatness and strength.

The number and length of these walls is not more surprising than the size of some of the blocks comprising them. The very Titans[5] seemed to have been at work. That so small an army as the first settlers must needs have been, should have taken such wonderful pains to inclose so ungrateful a soil; that they should have accomplished such herculean undertakings with so slight prospect of reward; this is a consideration which gives us a significant hint of the temper of the men of the Revolutionary era.

Nor could a fitter country be found for the birthplace of the devoted patriot, Israel Potter.

To this day the best stone-wall builders, as the best wood-choppers, come from those solitary mountain towns; a tall, athletic, and hardy race, unerring with the axe as the Indian with the tomahawk; at stone-rolling, patient as Sisyphus, powerful as Samson.[6]

In fine clear June days, the bloom of these mountains is beyond expression delightful. Last visiting these heights ere she vanishes, Spring, like the sunset, flings her sweetest charms upon them. Each tuft of upland grass is musked like a bouquet with perfume. The balmy breeze swings to and fro like a censer. On one side the eye follows for the space of an eagle's flight, the serpentine mountain chains, southwards from the great purple dome of Taconic—the St. Peter's of these hills—northwards to the twin summits of Saddleback,[7] which is the two-steepled natural cathedral of Berkshire; while low down to the west the Housatonic winds on in her watery labyrinth, through charming meadows basking in the reflected rays from the hill-sides. At this season the beauty of every thing around you populates the loneliness of your way. You would not have the country more settled if you could. Content to drink in such loveliness at all your senses, the heart desires no company but nature.

With what rapture you behold, hovering over some vast hollow of the hills, or slowly drifting at an immense height over the far sunken Housatonic valley, some lordly eagle, who in unshared exaltation looks down equally upon plain and mountain. Or you behold a hawk sallying from some crag, like a Rhenish[8] baron of old from his pinnacled castle, and darting down towards the river for his prey. Or perhaps, lazily gliding about in the zenith, this ruffian fowl is suddenly beset by a crow, who with stubborn audacity pecks at him, and spite of all his bravery, finally persecutes him back to his stronghold. The otherwise dauntless bandit, soaring at his topmost height, must needs succumb to this sable image of death. Nor are there wanting many smaller and less famous fowl, who without contributing to the grandeur, yet greatly add to the beauty of the scene. The yellow bird flits like a winged jonquil here and there; like knots of violets the blue birds sport in clusters upon the grass; while hurrying from the pasture to the grove, the red robin seems an incendiary putting torch to the trees. Meanwhile the air is vocal with their hymns, and your own soul joys in the general joy. Like a stranger in an orchestra, you cannot help singing yourself when all around you raise such hosannas.

But in autumn, those gay northerners, the birds, return to their southern plantations. The mountains are left bleak and sere. Solitude settles down upon them in drizzling mists. The traveller is beset, at perilous turns, by dense masses of fog. He emerges for a moment into more penetrable air; and passing some gray, abandoned house, sees the lofty vapors plainly eddy by its desolate door; just as from the plain, you may see it eddy by the pinnacles of distant and lonely heights. Or, dismounting from his frightened horse, he leads him down some scowling glen, where the road steeply dips among grim rocks, only to rise as abruptly again; and as he warily picks his way, uneasy at the menacing scene, he sees some ghost-like object looming through the mist at the roadside; and wending towards it, beholds a rude white stone, uncouthly inscribed, marking the spot where, some fifty or sixty years ago, some farmer was upset in his wood-sled, and perished beneath the load.

In winter this region is blocked up with snow. Inaccessible and impassable, those wild, unfrequented roads, which in August are overgrown with high grass, in December are drifted to the arm-pit with the white fleece from the sky. As if an ocean rolled between man and man, inter-communication is often suspended for weeks and weeks.

Such, at this day, is the country which gave birth to our hero: prophetically styled Israel by the good Puritans, his parents, since for more than forty years, poor Potter wandered in the wild wilderness of the world's extremest hardships and ills.[9]

How little he thought, when, as a boy, hunting after his father's stray cattle among these New England hills, he himself like a beast should be hunted through half of Old England, as a runaway rebel. Or, how could he ever have dreamed, when involved in the autumnal vapors of these mountains, that worse bewilderments awaited him three thousand miles across the sea, wandering forlorn in the coal-fogs of London. But so it was destined to be. This little boy of the hills, born in sight of the sparkling Housatonic, was to linger out the best part of his life a prisoner or a pauper upon the grimy banks of the Thames.[10]

CHAPTER 2

The Youthful Adventures of Israel

Imagination will easily picture the rural days of the youth of Israel. Let us pass on to a less immature period.

It appears that he began his wanderings very early; moreover, that ere, on just principles throwing off the yoke of his king, Israel, on equally excusable grounds, emancipated himself from his sire. He continued in the enjoyment of parental love till the age of eighteen, when, having formed an attachment for a neighbor's daughter—for some reason, not deemed a suitable match by his father—he was severely reprimanded, warned to discontinue his visits, and threatened with some disgraceful punishment in case he persisted. As the girl was not only beautiful, but amiable—though, as will be seen, rather weak—and her family respectable as any, though unfortunately but poor, Israel deemed his father's conduct unreasonable and oppressive; particularly as it turned out that he had taken secret means to thwart his son with the girl's connections, if not with the girl herself, so as to place almost insurmountable obstacles to an eventual marriage. For it had not been the purpose of Israel to marry at once, but at a future day, when prudence should approve the step. So, oppressed by his father, and bitterly disappointed in his love, the desperate boy formed the determination to quit them both, for another home and other friends.

It was on Sunday, while the family were gone to a farm-house church near by, that he packed up as much of his clothing as might be contained in a handkerchief, which, with a small quantity of provision, he hid in a piece of woods in the rear of the house. He then returned, and continued in the house till about nine in the evening, when, pretending to go to bed, he passed out of a back door, and hastened to the woods for his bundle.

It was a sultry night in July; and that he might travel with the more ease on the succeeding day, he lay down at the foot of a pine tree, reposing himself till an hour before dawn, when, upon awaking, he heard the soft, prophetic sighing of the pine, stirred by the first breath of the morning. Like the leaflets of that evergreen, all the fibres of his heart trembled within him; tears fell from his eyes. But he thought of the tyranny of his father, and what seemed to him the faithlessness of his love; and shouldering his bundle, arose, and marched on.

His intention was to reach the new countries to the northward and westward, lying between the Dutch settlements on the Hudson, and the Yankee settlements on the Housatonic. This was mainly to elude all search. For the same reason, for the first ten or twelve miles, shunning the public roads, he travelled through the woods; for he knew that he would soon be missed and pursued.

He reached his destination in safety; hired out to a farmer for a month through the harvest; then crossed from the Hudson to the Connecticut. Meeting here with an adventurer to the unknown regions lying about the head waters of the latter river, he ascended with this man in a canoe, paddling and poling for many miles. Here again he hired himself out for three months; at the end of that time to receive for his wages, two hundred acres of land lying in New Hampshire. The cheapness of the land was not alone owing to the newness of the country, but to the perils investing it. Not only was it a wilderness abounding with wild beasts, but the widely scattered inhabitants were in continual dread of being, at some unguarded moment, destroyed or made captive by the Canadian savages, who, ever since the French war,[1] had improved every opportunity to make forays across the defenceless frontier.

His employer proving false to his contract in the matter of the land, and there being no law in the country to force him to fulfil it, Israel,—who however brave-hearted, and even much of a dare-devil upon a pinch, seems, nevertheless, to have evinced, throughout many parts of his career, a singular patience and mildness,—was obliged to look round for other means of livelihood, than clearing out a farm for himself in the wilderness. A party of royal surveyors were at this period surveying the unsettled regions bordering the Connecticut River to its source. At fifteen shillings per month, he engaged himself to this party as assistant chain-bearer,[2] little thinking that the day was to come when he should clank the king's chains in a dungeon, even as now he trailed them a free ranger of the woods. It was midwinter; the land was surveyed upon snow-shoes. At the close of the day, fires were kindled with dry hemlock, a hut thrown up, and the party ate and slept.

Paid off at last, Israel bought a gun and ammunition, and turned hunter. Deer, beaver, &c., were plenty. In two or three months he had many skins to show. I suppose it never entered his mind, that he was thus qualifying himself for a marksman of men. But thus were tutored those wonderful shots who did such execution at Bunker's Hill; these, the hunter-soldiers, whom Putnam[3] bade wait till the white of the enemy's eye was seen.

With the result of his hunting he purchased a hundred acres of land, further down the river, toward the more settled parts; built himself a log hut, and in two summers, with his own hands, cleared thirty acres for sowing. In the winter seasons he hunted and trapped. At the end of the two years, he sold back his land—now much improved—to the original owner, at an advance of fifty pounds. He conveyed his skins and furs to Charlestown, on the Connecticut (sometimes called No. 4),[4] where he trafficked them away for Indian blankets, pigments, and other showy articles adapted to the business of a trader among savages. It was now winter again. Putting his goods on a hand-sled, he started towards Canada, a peddler in the wilderness, stopping at wigwams instead of cottages. One fancies that, had it been summer, Israel would have travelled with a wheelbarrow, and so trundled his wares through the primeval forests, with the same indifference as porters roll their barrows[5] over the flagging of streets. In this way was bred that fearless self-reliance and independence which conducted our forefathers to national freedom.

This Canadian trip proved highly successful. Selling his glittering goods at a great advance, he received in exchange valuable peltries and furs at a corresponding reduction. Returning to Charlestown, he disposed of his return cargo again at a very fine profit. And now, with a light heart and a heavy purse, he resolved to visit his sweetheart and parents, of whom, for three years, he had had no tidings.

They were not less astonished than delighted at his reappearance; he had been numbered with the dead. But his love still seemed strangely coy; willing, but yet somehow mysteriously withheld. The old intrigues were still on foot. Israel soon discovered, that though rejoiced to welcome the return of the prodigal son—so some called him—his father still remained inflexibly determined against the match, and still inexplicably countermined his wooing. With a dolorous heart he mildly yielded to what seemed his fatality; and more intrepid in facing peril for himself, than in endangering others by maintaining his rights (for he was now one-and-twenty), resolved once more to retreat, and quit his blue hills for the bluer billows.

A hermitage in the forest is the refuge of the narrow-minded misanthrope; a hammock on the ocean is the asylum for the generous distressed. The ocean brims with natural griefs and tragedies; and into that watery immensity of terror, man's private grief is lost like a drop.

Travelling on foot to Providence, Rhode Island, Israel shipped on board a sloop, bound with lime to the West Indies. On the tenth day out, the vessel caught fire, from water communicating with the lime. It was impossible to extinguish the flames. The boat was hoisted out, but owing to long exposure to the sun, it needed continual baling to keep it afloat. They had only time to put in a firkin of butter and a ten-gallon keg of water. Eight in number, the crew entrusted themselves to the waves, in a leaky tub, many leagues from land. As the boat swept under the burning bowsprit, Israel caught at a fragment of the flying-jib, which sail had fallen down the stay, owing to the charring, nigh the deck, of the rope which hoisted it. Tanned with the smoke, and its edge blackened with the fire, this bit of canvas helped them bravely on their way. Thanks to kind Providence, on the second day they were picked up by a Dutch ship, bound from Eustatia[6] to Holland. The castaways were humanely received, and supplied with every necessary. At the end of a week, while unsophisticated Israel was sitting in the main-top, thinking what should befall him in Holland, and wondering what sort of unsettled, wild, country it was, and whether there was any deer-shooting or beaver-trapping there; lo! an American brig, bound from Piscataqua to Antigua,[7] comes in sight. The American took them aboard and conveyed them safely to her port. There Israel shipped for Porto Rico; from thence, sailed to Eustatia.

Other rovings ensued; until at last, entering on board a Nantucket ship, he hunted the leviathan off the Western Islands and on the coast of Africa, for sixteen months; returning at length to Nantucket with a brimming hold. From that island he sailed again on another whaling voyage, extending, this time, into the great South Sea. There, promoted to be harpooner, Israel, whose eye and arm had been so improved by practice with his gun in the wilderness, now further intensified his aim, by darting the whale-lance; still, unwittingly, preparing himself for the Bunker Hill rifle.

In this last voyage, our adventurer experienced to the extreme, all the hardships and privations of the whaleman's life on a long voyage to distant and barbarous waters; hardships and privations unknown at the present day, when science has so greatly contributed, in manifold ways, to lessen the sufferings, and add to the comforts of sea-faring men. Heartily sick of the ocean, and longing once more for the bush, Israel, upon receiving his discharge at Nantucket at the end of the voyage, hied straight back for his mountain home.

But if hopes of his sweetheart winged his returning flight, such hopes were not destined to be crowned with fruition. The dear, false girl, was another's.

CHAPTER 3

*Israel Goes to the Wars; and Reaching Bunker Hill
in Time to Be of Service There, Soon After Is
Forced to Extend His Travels across the Sea
into the Enemy's Land*

Left to idle lamentations, Israel might now have planted deep
furrows in his brow. But stifling his pain, he chose rather to
plough, than be ploughed. Farming weans man from his sorrows. That tranquil pursuit tolerates nothing but tranquil meditations. There, too, in mother earth, you may plant and reap;
not, as in other things, plant and see the planting torn up by the
roots. But if wandering in the wilderness; and wandering upon
the waters; if felling trees; and hunting, and shipwreck; and
fighting with whales, and all his other strange adventures, had
not as yet cured poor Israel of his now hopeless passion; events
were at hand for ever to drown it.

It was the year 1774. The difficulties long pending between
the colonies and England, were arriving at their crisis. Hostilities were certain. The Americans were preparing themselves.
Companies were formed in most of the New England towns;
whose members, receiving the name of minutemen, stood
ready to march anywhere at a minute's warning. Israel, for the
last eight months, sojourning as a laborer on a farm in Windsor, enrolled himself in the regiment of Colonel John Patterson
of Lenox, afterwards General Patterson.[1]

The battle of Lexington[2] was fought on the 18th of April,
1775; news of it arrived in the county of Berkshire on the 20th,
about noon. The next morning at sunrise, Israel swung his
knapsack, shouldered his musket, and with Patterson's regiment, was on the march, quickstep, towards Boston.

Like Putnam, Israel received the stirring tidings at the plough.
But although not less willing than Putnam, to fly to battle at an

instant's notice; yet—only half an acre of the field remaining
to be finished—he whipped up his team and finished it. Before
hastening to one duty, he would not leave a prior one undone;
and ere helping to whip the British, for a little practice' sake, he
applied the gad[3] to his oxen. From the field of the farmer, he
rushed to that of the soldier, mingling his blood with his sweat.
While we revel in broadcloth, let us not forget what we owe to
linsey-woolsey.[4]

With other detachments from various quarters, Israel's regiment remained encamped for several days in the vicinity of
Charlestown. On the sixteenth of June, one thousand Americans, including the regiment of Patterson, were set about fortifying Bunker's Hill. Working all through the night, by dawn of
the following day, the redoubt was thrown up. But every one
knows all about the battle. Suffice it, that Israel was one of
those marksmen whom Putnam harangued as touching the enemy's eyes. Forbearing as he was with his oppressive father and
unfaithful love, and mild as he was on the farm; Israel was not
the same at Bunker Hill. Putnam had enjoined the men to aim
at the officers; so Israel aimed between the golden epaulettes,
as, in the wilderness, he had aimed between the branching
antlers. With dogged disdain of their foes, the English grenadiers
marched up the hill with sullen slowness; thus furnishing still
surer aims to the muskets which bristled on the redoubt. Modest Israel was used to aver, that considering his practice in the
woods, he could hardly be regarded as an inexperienced marksman; hinting, that every shot which the epauletted grenadiers
received from his rifle, would, upon a different occasion, have
procured him a deer-skin. And like stricken deers the English,
rashly brave as they were, fled from the opening fire. But the
marksmen's ammunition was expended; a hand-to-hand encounter ensued. Not one American musket in twenty had a bay-
onet to it. So, wielding the stock right and left, the terrible
farmers, with hats and coats off, fought their way among the
furred grenadiers;[5] knocking them right and left, as seal hunters
on the beach, knock down with their clubs the Shetland seal.[6]
In the dense crowd and confusion, while Israel's musket got in-

terlocked, he saw a blade horizontally menacing his feet from the ground. Thinking some fallen enemy sought to strike him at the last gasp, dropping his hold on his musket, he wrenched at the steel, but found that though a brave hand held it, that hand was powerless for ever. It was some British officer's laced sword-arm, cut from the trunk in the act of fighting; refusing to yield up its blade, to the last. At that moment another sword was aimed at Israel's head, by a living officer. In an instant the blow was parried by kindred steel, and the assailant fell by a brother's weapon, wielded by alien hands. But Israel did not come off unscathed. A cut on the right arm near the elbow, received in parrying the officer's blow; a long slit across the chest; a musket-ball buried in his hip, and another mangling him near the ankle of the same leg, were the tokens of intrepidity which our Sicinius Dentatus[7] carried from this memorable field. Nevertheless, with his comrades he succeeded in reaching Prospect Hill, and from thence was conveyed to the hospital at Cambridge. The bullet was extracted, his lesser wounds were dressed, and after much suffering from the fracture of the bone near the ankle, several pieces of which were extracted by the surgeon, ere long, thanks to the high health and pure blood of the farmer, Israel rejoined his regiment when they were throwing up intrenchments on Prospect Hill. Bunker Hill was now in possession of the foe, who in turn had fortified it.

On the third of July, Washington arrived from the South to take the command. Israel witnessed his joyful reception by the huzzaing companies.

The British now quartered in Boston suffered greatly from the scarcity of provisions. Washington took every precaution to prevent their receiving a supply. Inland, all aid could easily be cut off. To guard against their receiving any by water, from tories and other disaffected persons, the general equipped three armed vessels to intercept all traitorous cruisers. Among them was the brigantine Washington,[8] of ten guns, commanded by Captain Martindale. Seamen were hard to be had. The soldiers were called upon to volunteer for these vessels. Israel was one who so did; thinking that as an experienced sailor he should

not be backward in a juncture like this, little as he fancied the
new service assigned.

Three days out of Boston harbor, the brigantine was captured by the enemy's ship Foy, of twenty guns. Taken prisoner
with the rest of the crew, Israel was afterwards put on board
the frigate Tartar, with immediate sailing orders for England.
Seventy-two were captives in this vessel. Headed by Israel,
these men—half way across the sea—formed a scheme to take
the ship, but were betrayed by a renegade Englishman. As ring-
leader, Israel was put in irons, and so remained till the frigate
anchored at Portsmouth.[9] There he was brought on deck; and
would have met perhaps some terrible fate, had it not come out
during the examination, that the Englishman had been a deserter from the army of his native country, ere proving a traitor
to his adopted one. Relieved of his irons, Israel was placed
in the marine hospital on shore, where half of the prisoners
took the small-pox, which swept off a third of their number.
Why talk of Jaffa?[10]

From the hospital the survivors were conveyed to Spithead,[11]
and thrust on board a hulk. And here in the black bowels of the
ship, sunk low in the sunless sea, our poor Israel lay for a
month, like Jonah in the belly of the whale.[12]

But one bright morning, Israel is hailed from the deck. A
bargeman of the commander's boat is sick. Known for a sailor,
Israel for the nonce is appointed to pull the absent man's oar.

The officers being landed, some of the crew propose, like
merry Englishmen as they are, to hie to a neighboring ale-house,
and have a cosy pot or two together. Agreed. They start, and
Israel with them. As they enter the ale-house door, our prisoner
is suddenly reminded of still more imperative calls. Unsuspected
of any design, he is allowed to leave the party for a moment. No
sooner does Israel see his companions housed, than putting
speed into his feet, and letting grow all his wings, he starts like
a deer. He runs four miles (so he afterwards affirmed) without
halting. He sped towards London; wisely deeming that once in
that crowd detection would be impossible.

Ten miles, as he computed, from where he had left the bargemen, leisurely passing a public house of a little village on the

road-side, thinking himself now pretty safe—hark, what is this he hears?—

"Ahoy! what ship?"

"No ship," says Israel, hurrying on.

"Stop."

"If you will attend to your business, I will endeavor to attend to mine," replies Israel coolly. And next minute he lets grow his wings again; flying, one dare say, at the rate of something less than thirty miles an hour.

"Stop thief!" is now the cry. Numbers rushed from the road-side houses. After a mile's chase, the poor panting deer is caught.

Finding it was no use now to prevaricate, Israel boldly confesses himself a prisoner-of-war. The officer, a good fellow as it turned out, had him escorted back to the inn; where, observing to the landlord, that this must needs be a true-blooded Yankee, he calls for liquors to refresh Israel after his run. Two soldiers are then appointed to guard him for the present. This was towards evening; and up to a late hour at night, the inn was filled with strangers crowding to see the Yankee rebel, as they politely termed him. These honest rustics seemed to think that Yankees were a sort of wild creatures, a species of a 'possum or kangaroo. But Israel is very affable with them. That liquor he drank from the hand of his foe, has perhaps warmed his heart towards all the rest of his enemies. Yet this may not be wholly so. We shall see. At any rate, still he keeps his eye on the main chance—escape. Neither the jokes nor the insults of the mob does he suffer to molest him. He is cogitating a little plot to himself.

It seems that the good officer—not more true to the king his master than indulgent towards the prisoner which that same loyalty made—had left orders that Israel should be supplied with whatever liquor he wanted that night. So, calling for the can again and again, Israel invites the two soldiers to drink and be merry. At length, a wag of the company proposes that Israel should entertain the public with a jig; he (the wag) having heard, that the Yankees were extraordinary dancers. A fiddle is brought in, and poor Israel takes the floor. Not a little cut to think that these people should so unfeelingly seek to be diverted at the expense of an unfortunate prisoner, Israel, while jigging it up and down, still conspires away at his private plot, resolving ere long to give the enemy a touch of certain Yankee steps, as yet undreamed of in their simple philosophy. They would not permit any cessation of his dancing till he had danced himself into a perfect sweat, so that the drops fell from his lank and flaxen hair. But Israel, with much of the gentleness of the dove, is not wholly without the wisdom of the serpent.[13] Pleased to see the flowing bowl, he congratulates himself that his own state of perspiration prevents it from producing any intoxicating effect upon him.

Late at night the company break up. Furnished with a pair of handcuffs, the prisoner is laid on a blanket spread upon the floor at the side of the bed in which his two keepers are to repose. Expressing much gratitude for the blanket, with apparent unconcern, Israel stretches his legs. An hour or two passes. All is quiet without.

The important moment had now arrived. Certain it was, that if this chance were suffered to pass unimproved, a second would hardly present itself. For early, doubtless, on the following morning, if not some way prevented, the two soldiers would convey Israel back to his floating prison, where he would thenceforth remain confined until the close of the war; years and years, perhaps. When he thought of that horrible old hulk, his nerves were restrung for flight. But intrepid as he must be to compass it, wariness too was needed. His keepers had gone to bed pretty well under the influence of the liquor. This was favorable. But still, they were full-grown, strong men; and Israel was handcuffed. So Israel resolved upon strategy first; and if that failed, force afterwards. He eagerly listened. One of the drunken soldiers muttered in his sleep, at first lowly, then louder and louder,—"Catch 'em! Grapple 'em! Have at 'em! Ha—long cutlasses! Take that, runaway!"

"What's the matter with ye, Phil?" hiccoughed the other, who was not yet asleep. "Keep quiet, will ye? Ye ain't at Fontenoy[14] now."

"He's a runaway prisoner, I say. Catch him, catch him!"

"Oh, stush[15] with your drunken dreaming," again hiccoughed his comrade, violently nudging him. "This comes o' carousing."

Shortly after, the dreamer with loud snores fell back into dead sleep. But by something in the sound of the breathing of the other solider, Israel knew that this man remained uneasily awake. He deliberated a moment what was best to do. At length he determined upon trying his old plea. Calling upon the two soldiers, he informed them that urgent necessity required his immediate presence somewhere in the rear of the house.

"Come, wake up here, Phil," roared the soldier who was awake; "the fellow here says he must step out; cuss these Yankees; no better edication than to be gettin' up on naratal necessities at this time o'night. It ain't nateral; it's unnateral. D—n ye, Yankee, don't ye know no better?"

With many more denunciations, the two now staggered to their feet, and clutching hold of Israel, escorted him down stairs, and through a long, narrow, dark entry, rearward, till they came to a door. No sooner was this unbolted by the foremost guard, than, quick as a flash, manacled Israel, shaking off the grasp of the one behind him, butts him sprawling backwards into the entry; when, dashing in the opposite direction, he bounces the other head over heels into the garden, never using a hand; and then, leaping over the latter's head, darts blindly out into the midnight. Next moment he was at the garden wall. No outlet was discoverable in the gloom. But a fruit-tree grew close to the wall. Springing into it desperately, handcuffed as he was, Israel leaps atop of the barrier, and without pausing to see where he is, drops himself to the ground on the other side, and once more lets grow all his wings. Meantime, with loud outcries, the two baffled drunkards grope deliriously about in the garden.

After running two or three miles, and hearing no sound of pursuit, Israel reins up to rid himself of the handcuffs, which impede him. After much painful labor he succeeds in the attempt. Pressing on again with all speed, day broke, revealing a trim-looking, hedged, and beautiful country, soft, neat, and serene, all colored with the fresh early tints of the spring of 1776.

Bless me, thought Israel, all of a tremble, I shall certainly be caught now; I have broken into some nobleman's park.

But, hurrying forward again, he came to a turnpike road,
and then knew that, all comely and shaven as it was, this was
simply the open country of England; one bright, broad park,
paled in with white foam of the sea. A copse skirting the road
was just bursting out into bud. Each unrolling leaf was in very
act of escaping from its prison. Israel looked at the budding
leaves, and round on the budding sod, and up at the budding
dawn of the day. He was so sad, and these sights were so gay,
that Israel sobbed like a child, while thoughts of his mountain
home rushed like a wind on his heart. But conquering this fit,
he marched on, and presently passed nigh a field, where two
figures were working. They had rosy cheeks, short sturdy legs,
showing the blue stocking nearly to the knee, and were clad in
long, coarse, white frocks, and had on coarse, broad-brimmed
straw hats. Their faces were partly averted.

"Please, ladies," half roguishly says Israel, taking off his hat,
"does this road go to London?"

At this salutation, the two figures turned in a sort of stupid
amazement, causing an almost corresponding expression in
Israel, who now perceived that they were men, and not women.
He had mistaken them, owing to their frocks, and their wearing no pantaloons, only breeches hidden by their frocks.

"Beg pardon, lads, but I thought ye were something else,"
said Israel again.

Once more the two figures stared at the stranger, and with
added boorishness of surprise.

"Does this road go to London, gentlemen?"

"Gentlemen—egad!" cried one of the two.

"Egad!" echoed the second.

Putting their hoes before them, the two frocked boors now
took a good long look at Israel, meantime scratching their
heads under their plaited straw hats.

"Does it, gentlemen? Does it go to London? Be kind enough
to tell a poor fellow, do."

"Yees goin' to Lunnun, are yees? Weel—all right—go
along."

And without another word, having now satisfied their rustic
curiosity, the two human steers, with wonderful phlegm, applied

themselves to their hoes; supposing, no doubt, that they had given all requisite information.

Shortly after, Israel passed an old, dark, mossy-looking chapel, its roof all plastered with the damp yellow dead leaves of the previous autumn, showered there from a close cluster of venerable trees, with great trunks, and overstretching branches. Next moment he found himself entering a village. The silence of early morning rested upon it. But few figures were seen. Glancing through the window of a now noiseless public-house, Israel saw a table all in disorder, covered with empty flagons, and tobacco-ashes, and long pipes; some of the latter broken.

After pausing here a moment, he moved on, and observed a man over the way standing still and watching him. Instantly Israel was reminded that he had on the dress of an English sailor, and that it was this probably which had arrested the stranger's attention. Well knowing that his peculiar dress exposed him to peril, he hurried on faster to escape the village; resolving at the first opportunity to change his garments. Ere long, in a secluded place about a mile from the village, he saw an old ditcher tottering beneath the weight of a pick-axe, hoe and shovel, going to his work; the very picture of poverty, toil and distress. His clothes were tatters.

Making up to this old man, Israel, after a word or two of salutation, offered to change clothes with him. As his own clothes were prince-like compared to the ditcher's, Israel thought that however much his proposition might excite the suspicion of the ditcher, yet self-interest would prevent his communicating the suspicions. To be brief, the two went behind a hedge, and presently Israel emerged, presenting the most forlorn appearance conceivable; while the old ditcher hobbled off in an opposite direction, correspondingly improved in his aspect; though it was rather ludicrous than otherwise, owing to the immense bagginess of the sailor-trousers flapping about his lean shanks, to say nothing of the spare voluminousness of the pea-jacket. But Israel—how deplorable, how dismal his plight! Little did he ween that these wretched rags he now wore, were but suitable to that long career of destitution before him; one brief career of adventurous wanderings: and then, forty torpid years of pauperism. The coat was all patches. And no two patches were alike, and no one patch was the color of the original cloth. The stringless breeches gaped wide open at the knee; the long woollen stockings looked as if they had been set up at some time for a target. Israel looked suddenly metamorphosed from youth to old age; just like an old man of eighty he looked. But indeed, dull dreary adversity was now in store for him; and adversity, come it at eighteen or eighty, is the true old age of man. The dress befitted the fate.

From the friendly old ditcher, Israel learned the exact course he must steer for London; distant now between seventy and eighty miles. He was also apprised by his venerable friend, that the country was filled with soldiers, on the constant look-out for deserters whether from the navy or army, for the capture of whom a stipulated reward was given, just as in Massachusetts at that time for prowling bears.

Having solemnly enjoined his old friend not to give any information, should any one he meet inquire for such a person as Israel, our adventurer walked briskly on, less heavy of heart, now that he felt comparatively safe in disguise.

Thirty miles were travelled that day. At night Israel stole into a barn, in hopes of finding straw or hay for a bed. But it was spring; all the hay and straw were gone. So after groping about in the dark, he was fain to content himself with an undressed sheep-skin. Cold, hungry, foot-sore, weary, and impatient for the morning dawn, Israel drearily dozed out the night.

By the first peep of day coming through the chinks of the barn, he was up and abroad. Ere long finding himself in the suburbs of a considerable village, the better to guard against detection he supplied himself with a rude crutch, and feigning himself a cripple, hobbled straight through the town, followed by a perverse-minded cur, which kept up a continual, spiteful, suspicious bark. Israel longed to have one good rap at him with his crutch, but thought it would hardly look in character for a poor old cripple to be vindictive.

A few miles further, and he came to a second village. While hobbling through its main street, as through the former one, he was suddenly stopped by a genuine cripple, all in tatters too, who, with a sympathetic air, inquired after the cause of his lameness.

"White swelling,"[16] says Israel.

"That's just my ailing," wheezed the other; "but you're lamer than me," he added with a forlorn sort of self-satisfaction, critically eyeing Israel's limp as once more he stumped on his way, not liking to tarry too long.

"But halloo, what's your hurry, friend?" seeing Israel fairly departing—"where 're you going?"

"To London," answered Israel, turning round, heartily wishing the old fellow any where else than present.

"Going to limp to Lunnun, eh? Well, success to ye."

"As much to you, sir," answers Israel politely.

Nigh the opposite suburbs of this village, as good fortune would have it, an empty baggage-wagon bound for the metropolis turned into the main road from a side one. Immediately Israel limps most deplorably, and begs the driver to give a poor cripple a lift. So up he climbs; but after a time, finding the gait of the elephantine draught-horses intolerably slow, Israel craves permission to dismount, when, throwing away his crutch, he takes nimbly to his legs, much to the surprise of his honest friend, the driver.

The only advantage, if any, derived from his trip in the wagon, was, when passing through a third village—but a little distant from the previous one—Israel, by lying down in the wagon, had wholly avoided being seen.

The villages surprised him by their number and proximity. Nothing like this was to be seen at home. Well knowing that in these villages he ran much more risk of detection than in the open country, he henceforth did his best to avoid them, by taking a roundabout course whenever they came in sight from a distance. This mode of travelling not only lengthened his journey, but put unlooked-for obstacles in his path—walls, ditches and streams.

Not half an hour after throwing away his crutch, he leaped a great ditch nineteen feet wide, and of undiscoverable muddy depth. I wonder if the old cripple would think me the lamer one now, thought Israel to himself, arriving on the hither side.

CHAPTER 4

*Further Wanderings of the Refugee, with Some
Account of a Good Knight of Brentford Who
Befriended Him*

At nightfall on the third day, Israel had arrived within sixteen
miles of the capital. Once more he sought refuge in a barn. This
time he found some hay, and flinging himself down procured a
tolerable night's rest.

Bright and early he arose refreshed, with the pleasing prospect of reaching his destination ere noon. Encouraged to find
himself now so far from his original pursuers, Israel relaxed
in his vigilance; and about ten o'clock while passing through
the town of Staines[1] suddenly encountered three soldiers. Unfortunately in exchanging clothes with the ditcher, he could
not bring himself to include his shirt in the traffic; which shirt
was a British navy shirt; a bargeman's shirt; and though hitherto he had crumpled the blue collar out of sight, yet, as it
appeared in the present instance, it was not thoroughly concealed. At any rate, keenly on the look-out for deserters, and
made acute by hopes of reward for their apprehension, the soldiers spied the fatal collar, and in an instant laid violent hands
on the refugee.

"Hey lad!" said the foremost soldier, a corporal, "you are
one of his majesty's seamen! come along with ye."

So, unable to give any satisfactory account of himself, he was
made prisoner on the spot, and soon after found himself handcuffed and locked up in the Round House[2] of the place, a
prison so called, appropriated to runaways, and those convicted of minor offences. Day passed dinnerless and supperless
in this dismal durance, and night came on.

Israel had now been three days without food, except one
two-penny loaf. The cravings of hunger now became sharper;

his spirits, hitherto arming him with fortitude, began to forsake him. Taken captive once again upon the very brink of reaching his goal, poor Israel was on the eve of falling into helpless despair. But he rallied, and considering that grief would only add to his calamity, sought with stubborn patience to habituate himself to misery, but still hold aloof from despondency. He roused himself, and began to bethink him how to be extricated from this labyrinth.

Two hours sawing across the grating of the window, ridded him of his handcuffs. Next came the door, secured luckily with only a hasp and padlock. Thrusting the bolt of his handcuffs through a small window in the door, he succeeded in forcing the hasp and regaining his liberty about three o'clock in the morning.

Not long after sunrise, he passed nigh Brentford,[3] some six or seven miles from the capital. So great was his hunger that downright starvation seemed before him. He chewed grass, and swallowed it. Upon first escaping from the hulk, six English pennies was all the money he had. With two of these he had bought a small loaf the day after fleeing the inn. The other four still remained in his pocket, not having met with a good opportunity to dispose of them for food.

Having torn off the collar of his shirt, and flung it into a hedge, he ventured to accost a respectable carpenter at a pale fence, about a mile this side of Brentford, to whom his deplorable situation now induced him to apply for work. The man did not wish himself to hire, but said that if he (Israel), understood farming or gardening, he might perhaps procure work from Sir John Millet,[4] whose seat, he said, was not remote. He added that the knight was in the habit of employing many men at that season of the year; so he stood a fair chance.

Revived a little by this prospect of relief, Israel starts in quest of the gentleman's seat, agreeably to the directions received. But he mistook his way, and proceeding up a gravelled and beautifully decorated walk, was terrified at catching a glimpse of a number of soldiers thronging a garden. He made an instant retreat before being espied in turn. No wild creature of the American wilderness could have been more panic struck by a fire-brand, than at this period hunted Israel was by a red coat. It afterwards appeared that this garden was the Princess Amelia's.[5]

Taking another path, ere long he came to some laborers shovelling gravel. These proved to be men employed by Sir John. By them he was directed towards the house, when the knight was pointed out to him, walking bareheaded in the inclosure with several guests. Having heard the rich man of England charged with all sorts of domineering qualities, Israel felt no little misgiving in approaching to an audience with so imposing a stranger. But screwing up his courage, he advanced; while seeing him coming all rags and tatters, the group of gentlemen stood in some wonder awaiting what so singular a phantom might want.

"Mr. Millet," said Israel, bowing towards the bareheaded gentleman.

"Ha,—who are you, pray?"

"A poor fellow, sir, in want of work."

"A wardrobe too, I should say," smiled one of the guests, of a very youthful, prosperous, and dandified air.

"Where's your hoe?" said Sir John.

"I have none, sir."

"Any money to buy one?"

"Only four English pennies, sir."

"*English* pennies. What other sort would you have?"

"Why China pennies to be sure," laughed the youthful gentleman. "See his long, yellow hair behind; he looks like a Chinaman. Some broken-down Mandarin. Pity he's no crown to his old hat; if he had, he might pass it round, and make eight pennies of his four."

"Will you hire me, Mr. Millet?" said Israel.

"Ha! that's queer again," cried the knight.

"Hark ye fellow," said a brisk servant, approaching from the porch, "this is Sir John Millet."

Seeming to take pity on his seeming ignorance, as well as on his undisputable poverty, the good knight now told Israel that if he would come the next morning, he would see him supplied with a hoe, and moreover would hire him.

It would be hard to express the satisfaction of the wanderer, at receiving this encouraging reply. Emboldened by it, he now returns towards a baker's he had spied, and bravely marching in, flings down all four pennies, and demands bread. Thinking he would not have any more food till next morning, Israel resolved to eat only one of the pair of two-penny loaves. But having demolished one, it so sharpened his longing, that yielding to the irresistible temptation, he bolted down the second loaf to keep the other company.

After resting under a hedge, he saw the sun far descended, and so prepared himself for another hard night. Waiting till dark, he crawled into an old carriage-house, finding nothing there but a dismantled old phaeton.[6] Into this he climbed, and curling himself up like a carriage-dog, endeavored to sleep. But unable to endure the constraint of such a bed, got out, and stretched himself on the bare boards of the floor.

No sooner was light in the east, than he hastened to await the commands of one, who, his instinct told him, was destined to prove his benefactor. On his father's farm accustomed to rise with the lark, Israel was surprised to discover as he approached the house, that no soul was astir. It was four o'clock. For a considerable time he walked back and forth before the portal, ere any one appeared. The first riser was a man-servant of the household, who informed Israel that seven o'clock was the hour the people went to their work. Soon after, he met an hostler[7] of the place, who gave him permission to lie on some straw in an outhouse. There he enjoyed a sweet sleep till awakened at seven o'clock, by the sounds of activity around him.

Supplied by the overseer of the men with a large iron fork and a hoe, he followed the hands into the field. He was so weak, he could hardly support his tools. Unwilling to expose his debility, he yet could not succeed in concealing it. At last to avoid worse imputations, he confessed the cause. His companions regarded him with compassion, and exempted him from the severer toil.

About noon, the knight visited his workmen. Noticing that Israel made little progress, he said to him, that though he had long arms and broad shoulders, yet he was feigning himself to be a very weak man, or otherwise must in reality be so.

Hereupon one of the laborers standing by, informed the gentleman how it was with Israel; when immediately the knight put a shilling into his hands, and bade him go to a little road-side inn, which was nearer than the house, and buy him bread and a pot of beer. Thus refreshed he returned to the band, and toiled with them till four o'clock, when the day's work was over.

Arrived at the house, he there again saw his employer, who after attentively eyeing him without speaking, bade a meal be prepared for him; when the maid presenting a smaller supply than her kind master deemed necessary, she was ordered to re-turn and bring out the entire dish. But aware of the danger of sudden repletion of heavy food to one in his condition, Israel, previously recruited by the frugal meal at the inn, partook but sparingly. The repast was spread on the grass, and being over, the good knight again looking inquisitively at Israel, ordered a comfortable bed to be laid in the barn; and here Israel spent a capital night.

After breakfast, next morning, he was proceeding to go with the laborers to their work, when his employer approaching him with a benevolent air, bade him return to his couch, and there remain till he had slept his fill, and was in a better state to resume his labors.

Upon coming forth again a little after noon, he found Sir John walking alone in the grounds. Upon discovering him, Israel would have retreated, fearing that he might intrude; but beckoning him to advance, the knight, as Israel drew nigh, fixed on him such a penetrating glance, that our poor hero quaked to the core. Neither was his dread of detection relieved by the knight's now calling in a loud voice for one from the house. Israel was just on the point of fleeing, when overhearing the words of the master to the servant who now appeared, all dread departed:

"Bring hither some wine!"

It presently came; by order of the knight the salver was set down on a green bank near by, and the servant retired.

"My poor fellow," said Sir John, now pouring out a glass of wine, and handing it to Israel, "I perceive that you are an

American; and, if I am not mistaken, you are an escaped prisoner of war. But no fear—drink the wine."

"Mr. Millet," exclaimed Israel aghast, the untasted wine
trembling in his hand, "Mr. Millet, I——"

"*Mr.* Millet—there it is again. Why don't you say *Sir John*
like the rest?"

"Why, sir—pardon me—but somehow, I can't. I've tried; but
I can't. You won't betray me for that?"

"Betray—poor fellow! Hark ye, your history is doubtless a
secret which you would not wish to divulge to a stranger; but
whatever happens to you, I pledge you my honor I will never
betray you."

"God bless you for that, Mr. Millet."

"Come, come; call me by my right name. I am not Mr. Millet.
You have said *Sir* to me; and no doubt you have a thousand
times said *John* to other people. Now can't you couple the two?
Try once. Come. Only *Sir* and then *John*—*Sir John*—that's all."

"John—I can't—Sir, sir!—your pardon. I didn't mean that."

"My good fellow," said the knight looking sharply upon
Israel, "tell me, are all your countrymen like you? If so, it's no
use fighting them. To that effect, I must write to his Majesty
myself. Well, I excuse you from Sir Johnning me. But tell me
the truth, are you not a sea-faring man, and lately a prisoner
of war?"

Israel frankly confessed it, and told his whole story. The knight
listened with much interest; and at its conclusion, warned Israel
to beware of the soldiers; for owing to the seats of some of the
royal family being in the neighborhood, the red-coats abounded
hereabouts.

"I do not wish unnecessarily to speak against my own countrymen," he added, "I but plainly speak for your good. The
soldiers you meet prowling on the roads, are not fair specimens
of the army. They are a set of mean, dastardly banditti; who, to
obtain their fee, would betray their best friends. Once more, I
warn you against them. But enough; follow me now to the
house, and as you tell me you have exchanged clothes before
now, you can do it again. What say you? I will give you coat and
breeches for your rags."

Thus generously supplied with clothes, and other comforts by the good knight, and implicitly relying upon the honor of so kind-hearted a man, Israel cheered up, and in the course of two or three weeks had so fattened his flanks, that he was able completely to fill Sir John's old buckskin breeches, which at first had hung but loosely about him.

He was assigned to an occupation which removed him from the other workmen. The strawberry bed was put under his sole charge. And often, of mild, sunny afternoons, the knight, genial and gentle with dinner, would stroll bareheaded to the pleasant strawberry bed, and have nice little confidential chats with Israel; while Israel, charmed by the patriarchal demeanor of this true Abrahamic[8] gentleman, with a smile on his lip, and tears of gratitude in his eyes, offered him, from time to time, the plumpest berries of the bed.

When the strawberry season was over, other parts of the grounds were assigned him. And so six months elapsed, when, at the recommendation of Sir John, Israel procured a good berth in the garden of the Princess Amelia.

So completely now had recent events metamorphosed him in all outward things, that few suspected him of being any other than an Englishman. Not even the knight's domestics. But in the princess's garden, being obliged to work in company with many other laborers, the war was often a topic of discussion among them. And "the d—d Yankee rebels" were not seldom the object of scurrilous remark. Ill could the exile brook in silence such insults upon the country for which he had bled, and for whose honored sake he was that very instant a sufferer. More than once, his indignation came very nigh getting the better of his prudence. He longed for the war to end, that he might but speak a little bit of his mind.

Now the superintendent of the garden was a harsh, overbearing man. The workmen with tame servility endured his worst affronts. But Israel, bred among mountains, found it impossible to restrain himself when made the undeserved object of pitiless epithets. Ere two months went by, he quitted the service of the princess, and engaged himself to a farmer in a small village not far from Brentford. But hardly had he been here three weeks, when a rumor again got afloat, that he was a Yankee prisoner of war. Whence this report arose he could never discover. No sooner did it reach the ears of the soldiers, than they were on the alert. Luckily Israel was apprised of their intentions in time. But he was hard pushed. He was hunted after with a perseverance worthy a less ignoble cause. He had many hairbreadth escapes. Most assuredly he would have been captured, had it not been for the secret good offices of a few individuals, who, perhaps, were not unfriendly to the American side of the question, though they durst not avow it.

Tracked one night by the soldiers to the house of one of these friends, in whose garret he was concealed: he was obliged to force the skuttle,[9] and running along the roof, passed to those of adjoining houses to the number of ten or twelve, finally succeeding in making his escape.

CHAPTER 5

Israel in the Lion's Den

Harassed day and night, hunted from food and sleep, driven from hole to hole like a fox in the woods; with no chance to earn an hour's wages; he was at last advised by one whose sincerity he could not doubt, to apply, on the good word of Sir John Millet, for a berth as laborer in the King's Gardens at Kew.[1] There, it was said, he would be entirely safe, as no soldier durst approach those premises to molest any soul therein employed. It struck the poor exile as curious, that the very den of the British lion,[2] the private grounds of the British King, should be commended to a refugee as his securest asylum.

His nativity carefully concealed, and being personally introduced to the chief gardener by one who well knew him; armed too with a line from Sir John, and recommended by his introducer as uncommonly expert at horticulture; Israel was soon installed as keeper of certain less private plants and walks of the park.

It was here, to one of his near country retreats, that, coming from perplexities of state—leaving far behind him the dingy old bricks of St. James—George the Third was wont to walk up and down beneath the long arbors formed by the interlockings of lofty trees.

More than once, raking the gravel, Israel through intervening foliage would catch peeps in some private but parallel walk, of that lonely figure, not more shadowy with overhanging leaves than with the shade of royal meditations.

Unauthorized and abhorrent thoughts will sometimes invade the best human heart. Seeing the monarch unguarded before him; remembering that the war was imputed more to the self-will of the King than to the willingness of parliament or the nation;

and calling to mind all his own sufferings growing out of that war, with all the calamities of his country; dim impulses, such as those to which the regicide Ravaillac[3] yielded, would shoot balefully across the soul of the exile. But thrusting Satan behind him, Israel vanquished all such temptations. Nor did these ever more disturb him, after his one chance conversation with the monarch.

As he was one day gravelling a little bye-walk; wrapped in thought, the King turning a clump of bushes, suddenly brushed Israel's person.

Immediately Israel touched his hat—but did not remove it—bowed, and was retiring; when something in his air arrested the King's attention.

"You aint an Englishman,—no Englishman—no no."

Pale as death, Israel tried to answer something; but knowing not what to say, stood frozen to the ground.

"You are a Yankee—a Yankee," said the King again in his rapid and half-stammering way.

Again Israel assayed to reply, but could not. What could he say? Could he lie to a King?

"Yes, yes,—you are one of that stubborn race,—that very stubborn race. What brought you here?"

"The fate of war, sir."

"May it please your Majesty," said a low cringing voice, approaching, "this man is in the walk against orders. There is some mistake, may it please your majesty. Quit the walk, blockhead," he hissed at Israel.

It was one of the junior gardeners who thus spoke. It seems that Israel had mistaken his directions that morning.

"Slink, you dog," hissed the gardener again to Israel; then aloud to the king, "A mistake of the man, I assure your majesty."

"Go you away—away with ye, and leave him with me," said the king.

Waiting a moment, till the man was out of hearing, the king again turned upon Israel.

"Were you at Bunker Hill?—that bloody Bunker Hill—eh, eh?"

"Yes, sir."

"Fought like a devil—like a very devil, I suppose?"

"Yes, sir."

"Helped flog—helped flog my soldiers?"

"Yes, sir; but very sorry to do it."

"Eh?—eh?—how's that?"

"I took it to be my sad duty, sir."

"Very much mistaken—very much mistaken indeed. Why do ye sir me?—eh? I'm your king—your king."

"Sir," said Israel firmly, but with deep respect, "I have no king."

The king darted his eye incensedly for a moment; but without quailing, Israel, now that all was out, still stood with mute respect before him. The king, turning suddenly, walked rapidly away from Israel a moment, but presently returning with a less hasty pace, said, "You are rumored to be a spy—a spy, or something of that sort—aint you? But I know you are not—no, no. You are a runaway prisoner-of-war, eh? You have sought this place to be safe from pursuit, eh? eh? Is it not so?—eh? eh? eh?"

"Sir, it is."

"Well, ye're an honest rebel—rebel, yes, rebel. Hark ye, hark. Say nothing of this talk to any one. And hark again. So long as ye remain here at Kew, I shall see that you are safe—safe."

"God bless your majesty!"

"Eh?"

"God bless your noble majesty!"

"Come—come—come," smiled the king in delight, "I thought I could conquer ye—conquer ye."

"Not the king, but the king's kindness, your majesty."

"Join my army—army."

Sadly looking down, Israel silently shook his head.

"You won't? Well, gravel the walk then—gravel away. Very stubborn race—very stubborn race indeed—very—very—very."

And still growling, the magnanimous lion departed.

How the monarch came by his knowledge of so humble an exile, whether through that swift insight into individual character said to form one of the miraculous qualities transmitted with a crown, or whether some of the rumors prevailing outside of the garden had come to his ear, Israel could never determine. Very probably, though, the latter was the case, inasmuch as some vague shadowy report of Israel not being an Englishman, had a little previous to his interview with the king, been communicated to several of the inferior gardeners. Without any impeachment of Israel's fealty to his country, it must still be narrated, that from this his familiar audience with George the Third, he went away with very favorable views of that monarch. Israel now thought that it could not be the warm heart of the king, but the cold heads of his lords in council, that persuaded him so tyrannically to persecute America. Yet hitherto the precise contrary of this had been Israel's opinion, agreeably to the popular prejudice throughout New England.

Thus we see what strange and powerful magic resides in a crown, and how subtly that cheap and easy magnanimity, which in private belongs to most kings, may operate on good-natured and unfortunate souls. Indeed, had it not been for the peculiar disinterested fidelity of our adventurer's patriotism, he would have soon sported the red coat; and perhaps under the immediate patronage of his royal friend, been advanced in time to no mean rank in the army of Britain. Nor in that case would we have had to follow him, as at last we shall, through long, long years of obscure and penurious wandering.

Continuing in the service of the king's gardener at Kew, until a season came when the work of the garden required a less number of laborers; Israel, with several others, was discharged; and the day after, engaged himself for a few months to a farmer in the neighborhood where he had been last employed. But hardly a week had gone by, when the old story of his being a rebel, or a runaway prisoner, or a Yankee! or a spy, began to be revived with added malignity. Like bloodhounds, the soldiers were once more on the track. The houses where he harbored were many times searched; but thanks to the fidelity of a few earnest well-wishers, and to his own unsleeping vigilance and activity, the hunted fox still continued to elude apprehension. To such extremities of harassment, however, did this incessant pursuit subject him, that in a fit of despair he was about to surrender himself, and submit to his fate, when Providence seasonably interposed in his favor.

CHAPTER 6

*Israel Makes the Acquaintance of Certain
Secret Friends of America, One of Them Being
the Famous Author of the "Diversions of
Purley." These Despatch Him on a
Sly Errand across the Channel*

At this period, though made the victims indeed of British oppression, yet the colonies were not totally without friends in Britain. It was but natural that when Parliament itself held patriotic and gifted men, who not only recommended conciliatory measures, but likewise denounced the war as monstrous; it was but natural that throughout the nation at large there should be many private individuals cherishing similar sentiments; and some who made no scruple clandestinely to act upon them.

Late one night while hiding in a farmer's granary, Israel saw a man with a lantern approaching. He was about to flee, when the man hailed him in a well-known voice, bidding him have no fear. It was the farmer himself. He carried a message to Israel from a gentleman of Brentford, to the effect, that the refugee was earnestly requested to repair on the following evening to that gentleman's mansion.

At first Israel was disposed to surmise that either the farmer was playing him false, or else his honest credulity had been imposed upon by evilminded persons. At any rate, he regarded the message as a decoy, and for half an hour refused to credit its sincerity. But at length he was induced to think a little better of it. The gentleman giving the invitation was one Squire Woodcock,[1] of Brentford, whose loyalty to the king, had been under suspicion; so at least the farmer averred. This latter information was not without its effect.

At nightfall on the following day, being disguised in strange clothes by the farmer, Israel stole from his retreat, and after a few hours' walk, arrived before the ancient brick house of the Squire; who opening the door in person, and learning who it was that stood there, at once assured Israel in the most solemn manner, that no foul play was intended. So the wanderer suffered himself to enter, and be conducted to a private chamber in the rear of the mansion, where were seated two other gentlemen, attired, in the manner of that age, in long laced coats, with smallclothes, and shoes with silver buckles.

"I am John Woodcock," said the host, "and these gentlemen are Horne Tooke and James Bridges.² All three of us are friends to America. We have heard of you for some weeks past, and inferring from your conduct, that you must be a Yankee of the true blue stamp, we have resolved to employ you in a way which you cannot but gladly approve; for surely, though an exile, you are still willing to serve your country; if not as a sailor or soldier, yet as a traveller?"

"Tell me how I may do it?" demanded Israel, not completely at ease.

"At that in good time," smiled the Squire. "The point is now—do you repose confidence in my statements?"

Israel glanced inquiringly upon the Squire; then upon his companions; and meeting the expressive, enthusiastic, candid countenance of Horne Tooke—then in the first honest ardor of his political career—turned to the Squire, and said, "Sir, I believe what you have said. Tell me now what I am to do?"

"Oh, there is just nothing to be done to-night," said the Squire; "nor for some days to come perhaps, but we wanted to have you prepared."

And hereupon he hinted to his guest rather vaguely of his general intention; and that over, begged him to entertain them with some account of his adventures since he first took up arms for his country. To this Israel had no objections in the world, since all men love to tell the tale of hardships endured in a righteous cause. But ere beginning his story, the Squire refreshed him with some cold beef, laid in a snowy napkin, and a glass of

Perry,[3] and thrice during the narration of the adventures, pressed him with additional draughts.

But after his second glass, Israel declined to drink more, mild as the beverage was. For he noticed, that not only did the three gentlemen listen with the utmost interest to his story, but likewise interrupted him with questions and cross-questions in the most pertinacious manner. So this led him to be on his guard, not being absolutely certain yet, as to who they might really be, or what was their real design. But as it turned out, Squire Woodcock and his friends only sought to satisfy themselves thoroughly, before making their final disclosures, that the exile was one in whom implicit confidence might be placed.

And to this desirable conclusion they eventually came; for upon the ending of Israel's story, after expressing their sympathies for his hardships, and applauding his generous patriotism in so patiently enduring adversity, as well as singing the praises of his gallant fellow-soldiers of Bunker Hill; they openly revealed their scheme. They wished to know, whether Israel would undertake a trip to Paris, to carry an important message—shortly to be received for transmission through them—to Doctor Franklin, then in that capital.[4]

"All your expenses shall be paid, not to speak of a compensation besides," said the Squire; "will you go?"

"I must think of it," said Israel, not yet wholly confirmed in his mind. But once more he cast his glance on Horne Tooke, and his irresolution was gone.

The Squire now informed Israel that, to avoid suspicions, it would be necessary for him to remove to another place until the hour at which he should start for Paris. They enjoined upon him the profoundest secresy; gave him a guinea, with a letter for a gentleman in White Waltham,[5] a town some miles from Brentford, which point they begged him to reach as soon as possible, there to tarry for further instructions.

Having informed him of thus much, Squire Woodcock asked him to hold out his right foot.

"What for?" said Israel.

"Why, would you not like to have a pair of new boots against your return?" smiled Horne Tooke.

"Oh yes; no objections at all," said Israel.

"Well then, let the boot-maker measure you," smiled Horne Tooke.

"Do *you* do it, Mr. Tooke," said the Squire, "you measure men's parts better than I."

"Hold out your foot, my good friend," said Horne Tooke—"there—now let's measure your heart."

"For that, measure me round the chest," said Israel.

"Just the man we want," said Mr. Bridges, triumphantly.

"Give him another glass of wine, Squire," said Horne Tooke.

Exchanging the farmer's clothes for still another disguise, Israel now set out immediately, on foot, for his destination, having received minute directions as to his road; and arriving in White Waltham on the following morning, was very cordially received by the gentleman to whom he carried the letter. This person, another of the active English friends of America, possessed a particular knowledge of late events in that land. To him Israel was indebted for much entertaining information. After remaining some ten days at this place, word came from Squire Woodcock, requiring Israel's immediate return, stating the hour at which he must arrive at the house, namely, two o'clock on the following morning. So, after another night's solitary trudge across the country, the wanderer was welcomed by the same three gentlemen as before, seated in the same room.

"The time has now come," said Squire Woodcock. "You must start this morning for Paris. Take off your shoes."

"Am I to steal from here to Paris on my stocking-feet?" said Israel, whose late easy good living at White Waltham had not failed to bring out the good-natured and mirthful part of him, even as his prior experiences had produced, for the most part, something like a contrary result.

"Oh no," smiled Horne Tooke, who always lived well; "we have seven-league-boots for you. Don't you remember my measuring you?"

Hereupon going to the closet, the Squire brought out a pair of new boots. They were fitted with false heels. Unscrewing these, the Squire showed Israel the papers concealed beneath. They were of a fine tissuey fibre, and contained much writing in

a very small compass. The boots—it need hardly be said—had
been particularly made for the occasion.

"Walk across the room with them," said the Squire, when
Israel had pulled them on.

"He'll surely be discovered," smiled Horne Tooke. "Hark,
how he creaks."

"Come, come, it's too serious a matter for joking," said the
Squire. "Now my fine fellow, be cautious, be sober, be vigilant,
and above all things be speedy."

Being furnished now with all requisite directions, and a supply of money, Israel taking leave of Mr. Tooke and Mr. Bridges,
was secretly conducted down stairs by the Squire, and in five
minutes' time was on his way to Charing Cross in London;
where taking the post-coach for Dover, he thence went in a
packet to Calais,[6] and in fifteen minutes after landing, was
being wheeled over French soil towards Paris. He arrived there
in safety, and freely declaring himself an American, the peculiarly friendly relations of the two nations at that period,
procured him kindly attentions even from strangers.

CHAPTER 7

*After a Curious Adventure upon the Pont Neuf,
Israel Enters the Presence of the Renowned Sage,
Dr. Franklin, Whom He Finds Right Learnedly
and Multifariously Employed*

Following the directions given him at the place where the
diligence stopped, Israel was crossing the Pont Neuf,[1] to find
Doctor Franklin, when he was suddenly called to by a man
standing on one side of the bridge, just under the equestrian
statue of Henry IV.[2]

The man had a small, shabby-looking box before him on the
ground, with a box of blacking on one side of it, and several
shoe-brushes upon the other. Holding another brush in his
hand, he politely seconded his verbal invitation by gracefully
flourishing the brush in the air.

"What do you want of me, neighbor?" said Israel, pausing in
somewhat uneasy astonishment.

"Ah Monsieur," exclaimed the man, and with voluble politeness he ran on with a long string of French, which of course was
all Greek to poor Israel. But what his language failed to convey,
his gestures now made very plain. Pointing to the wet muddy
state of the bridge, splashed by a recent rain, and then to the feet
of the wayfarer, and lastly to the brush in his hand, he appeared
to be deeply regretting that a gentleman of Israel's otherwise imposing appearance, should be seen abroad with unpolished
boots, offering at the same time to remove their blemishes.

"Ah Monsieur, Monsieur," cried the man, at last running up
to Israel. And with tender violence he forced him towards the
box, and lifting this unwilling customer's right foot thereon,
was proceeding vigorously to work, when suddenly illuminated
by a dreadful suspicion, Israel, fetching the box a terrible kick,
took to his false heels and ran like mad over the bridge.

Incensed that his politeness should receive such an ungra-
cious return, the man pursued; which but confirming Israel in
his suspicions, he ran all the faster, and thanks to his fleetness,
soon succeeded in escaping his pursuer.

Arrived at last at the street and the house, to which he had
been directed; in reply to his summons, the gate, very strangely
of itself, swung open; and much astonished at this unlooked-
for sort of enchantment, Israel entered a wide vaulted passage
leading to an open court within. While he was wondering that
no soul appeared, suddenly he was hailed from a dark little
window, where sat an old man cobbling shoes, while an old
woman standing by his side, was thrusting her head into the
passage, intently eyeing the stranger. They proved to be the
porter and portress; the latter of whom, upon hearing his summons, had invisibly thrust open the gate to Israel, by means of
a spring communicating with the little apartment.

Upon hearing the name of Doctor Franklin mentioned, the
old woman, all alacrity, hurried out of her den, and with much
courtesy showed Israel across the court, up three flights of
stairs, to a door in the rear of the spacious building. There she
left him while Israel knocked.

"Come in," said a voice.

And immediately Israel stood in the presence of the venerable Doctor Franklin.

Wrapped in a rich dressing-gown—a fanciful present from
an admiring Marchesa—curiously embroidered with algebraic
figures like a conjuror's robe, and with a skull-cap of black
satin on his hive of a head, the man of gravity was seated at a
huge claw-footed old table, round as the zodiac. It was covered
with printed papers; files of documents; rolls of MSS.; stray bits
of strange models in wood and metal; odd-looking pamphlets
in various languages; and all sorts of books; including many
presentation-copies; embracing history, mechanics, diplomacy,
agriculture, political economy, metaphysics, meteorology, and
geometry. The walls had a necromantic look; hung round with
barometers of different kinds; drawings of surprising inventions;
wide maps of far countries in the New World, containing vast

empty spaces in the middle, with the word D E S E R T diffusely printed there, so as to span five-and-twenty degrees of longitude with only two syllables,—which printed word however bore a vigorous pen-mark, in the Doctor's hand, drawn straight through it, as if in summary repeal of it; crowded topographical and trigonometrical charts of various parts of Europe; with geometrical diagrams, and endless other surprising hangings and upholstery of science.

The chamber itself bore evident marks of antiquity. One part of the rough-finished wall was sadly cracked; and covered with dust, looked dim and dark. But the aged inmate, though wrinkled as well, looked neat and hale. Both wall and sage were compounded of like materials,—lime and dust; both, too, were old; but while the rude earth of the wall had no painted lustre to shed off all fadings and tarnish, and still keep fresh without, though with long eld its core decayed: the living lime and dust of the sage was frescoed with defensive bloom of his soul.

The weather was warm; like some old West India hogshead on the wharf, the whole chamber buzzed with flies. But the sapient inmate sat still and cool in the midst. Absorbed in some other world of his occupations and thoughts, these insects, like daily cark and care, did not seem one whit to annoy him. It was a goodly sight to see this serene, cool and ripe old philosopher, who by sharp inquisition of man in the street, and then long meditating upon him, surrounded by all these queer old implements, charts and books, had grown at last so wondrous wise. There he sat, quite motionless among those restless flies; and, with a sound like the low noon murmur of foliage in the woods, turning over the leaves of some ancient and tattered folio, with a binding dark and shaggy as the bark of any old oak. It seemed as if supernatural lore must needs pertain to this gravely ruddy personage; at least far foresight, pleasant wit, and working wisdom. Old age seemed in nowise to have dulled him, but to have sharpened; just as old dinner-knives—so they be of good steel—wax keen, spear-pointed, and elastic as whale-bone with long usage. Yet though he was thus lively and vigorous to behold, spite of his seventy-two years (his exact date at the time) somehow, the incredible seniority of an ante-diluvian seemed his. Not the years of the calendar wholly, but also the years of sapience. His white hairs and mild brow, spoke of the future as well as the past. He seemed to be seven score years old; that is, three-score and ten of prescience added to three score and ten of remembrance, makes just seven score years in all.

But when Israel stepped within the chamber, he lost the complete effect of all this; for the sage's back, not his face, was turned to him.

So, intent on his errand, hurried and heated with his recent run, our courier entered the room, inadequately impressed, for the time, by either it or its occupant.

"Bon jour,[3] bon jour, monsieur," said the man of wisdom, in a cheerful voice, but too busy to turn round just then.

"How do you do, Doctor Franklin," said Israel.

"Ah! I smell Indian corn," said the Doctor, turning round quickly on his chair. "A countryman; sit down, my good sir. Well, what news? Special?"

"Wait a minute, sir," said Israel, stepping across the room towards a chair.

Now there was no carpet on the floor, which was of dark-colored wood, set in lozenges, and slippery with wax, after the usual French style. As Israel walked this slippery floor, his unaccustomed feet slid about very strangely, as if walking on ice, so that he came very near falling.

" 'Pears to me you have rather high heels to your boots," said the grave man of utility, looking sharply down through his spectacles; "Don't you know that it's both wasting leather and endangering your limbs, to wear such high heels? I have thought at my first leisure, to write a little pamphlet against that very abuse. But pray, what are you doing now? Do your boots pinch you, my friend, that you lift one foot from the floor that way?"

At this moment, Israel having seated himself, was just putting his right foot across his left knee.

"How foolish," continued the wise man, "for a rational creature to wear tight boots. Had nature intended rational creatures should so do, she would have made the foot of solid bone, or perhaps of solid iron, instead of bone, muscle, and flesh.—But,—I see. Hold!"

And springing to his own slippered feet, the venerable sage hurried to the door and shot-to the bolt. Then drawing the curtain carefully across the window looking out across the court to various windows on the opposite side, bade Israel proceed with his operations.

"I was mistaken this time," added the Doctor, smiling, as Israel produced his documents from their curious recesses— "your high heels, instead of being idle vanities, seem to be full of meaning."

"Pretty full, Doctor," said Israel, now handing over the papers. "I had a narrow escape with them just now."

"How? How's that?" said the sage, fumbling the papers eagerly.

"Why, crossing the stone bridge there over the *Seen*"—

"*Seine*"[4]—interrupted the Doctor, giving the French pronunciation—"Always get a new word right in the first place, my friend, and you will never get it wrong afterwards."

"Well, I was crossing the bridge there, and who should hail me, but a suspicious looking man, who, under pretence of seeking to polish my boots, wanted slyly to unscrew their heels, and so steal all these precious papers I've brought you."

"My good friend," said the man of gravity, glancing scrutinizingly upon his guest, "have you not in your time, undergone what they call hard times? Been set upon, and persecuted, and very ill entreated by some of your fellow-creatures?"

"That I have, Doctor; yes indeed."

"I thought so. Sad usage has made you sadly suspicious, my honest friend. An indiscriminate distrust of human nature is the worst consequence of a miserable condition, whether brought about by innocence or guilt. And though want of suspicion more than want of sense, sometimes leads a man into harm: yet too much suspicion is as bad as too little sense. The man you met, my friend, most probably, had no artful intention; he knew just nothing about you or your heels; he simply wanted to earn two sous by brushing your boots. Those blacking-men regularly station themselves on the bridge."

"How sorry I am then that I knocked over his box, and then ran away. But he didn't catch me."

"How? surely, my honest friend, you,—appointed to the conveyance of important secret despatches—did not act so imprudently as to kick over an innocent man's box in the public streets of the capital, to which you had been especially sent?"

"Yes, I did, Doctor."

"Never act so unwisely again. If the police had got hold of you, think of what might have ensued."

"Well, it was not very wise of me, that's a fact, Doctor. But, you see, I thought he meant mischief."

"And because you only thought he *meant* mischief, *you* must straightway proceed to *do* mischief. That's poor logic. But think over what I have told you now, while I look over these papers."

In half an hour's time, the Doctor, laying down the documents, again turned towards Israel, and removing his spectacles very placidly, proceeded in the kindest and most familiar manner to read him a paternal detailed lesson upon the ill-advised act he had been guilty of, upon the Pont Neuf; concluding by taking out his purse, and putting three small silver coins into Israel's hands, charging him to seek out the man that very day, and make both apology and restitution for his unlucky mistake.

"All of us, my honest friend," continued the Doctor, "are subject to making mistakes; so that the chief art of life, is to learn how best to remedy mistakes. Now one remedy for mistakes is honesty. So pay the man for the damage done to his box. And now, who are you, my friend? My correspondents here mention your name—Israel Potter—and say you are an American, an escaped prisoner of war, but nothing further. I want to hear your story from your own lips."

Israel immediately began, and related to the Doctor all his adventures up to the present time.

"I suppose," said the Doctor, upon Israel's concluding, "that you desire to return to your friends across the sea?"

"That I do, Doctor," said Israel.

"Well, I think, I shall be able to procure you a passage."

Israel's eyes sparkled with delight. The mild sage noticed it, and added: "But events in these times are uncertain. At the prospect of pleasure never be elated; but, without depression, respect the omens of ill. So much my life has taught me, my honest friend."

Israel felt as though a plum-pudding had been thrust under his nostrils, and then as rapidly withdrawn.

"I think it is probable that in two or three days I shall want you to return with some papers to the persons who sent you to me. In that case you will have to come here once more, and then, my good friend, we will see what can be done towards getting you safely home again."

Israel was pouring out torrents of thanks when the Doctor interrupted him.

"Gratitude, my friend, cannot be too much towards God, but towards man, it should be limited. No man can possibly so serve his fellow, as to merit unbounded gratitude. Over gratitude in the helped person, is apt to breed vanity or arrogance in the helping one. Now in assisting you to get home—if indeed I shall prove able to do so—I shall be simply doing part of my official duty as agent of our common country. So you owe me just nothing at all, but the sum of these coins I put in your hand just now. But that, instead of repaying to me hereafter, you can, when you get home, give to the first soldier's widow you meet. Don't forget it, for it is a debt, a pecuniary liability, owing to me. It will be about a quarter of a dollar, in the Yankee currency. A quarter of a dollar, mind. My honest friend, in pecuniary matters always be exact as a second-hand; never mind with whom it is, father or stranger, peasant or king, be exact to a tick of your honor."

"Well, Doctor," said Israel, "since exactness in these matters is so necessary, let me pay back my debt in the very coins in which it was loaned. There will be no chance of mistake then. Thanks to my Brentford friends, I have enough to spare of my own, to settle damages with the boot-black of the bridge. I only took the money from you, because I thought it would not look well to push it back after being so kindly offered."

"My honest friend" said the Doctor, "I like your straightforward dealing. I will receive back the money."

"No interest, Doctor, I hope," said Israel.

The sage looked mildly over his spectacles upon Israel, and replied, "My good friend, never permit yourself to be jocose upon pecuniary matters. Never joke at funerals, or during business transactions. The affair between us two, you perhaps deem very trivial, but trifles may involve momentous principles. But no more at present. You had better go immediately and find the boot-black. Having settled with him, return hither, and you will find a room ready for you near this, where you will stay during your sojourn in Paris."

"But I thought I would like to have a little look round the town, before I go back to England," said Israel.

"Business before pleasure, my friend. You must absolutely remain in your room, just as if you were my prisoner, until you quit Paris for Calais. Not knowing now at what instant I shall want you to start, your keeping to your room is indispensable. But when you come back from Brentford again, then, if nothing happens, you will have a chance to survey this celebrated capital ere taking ship for America. Now go directly, and pay the boot-black. Stop, have you the exact change ready? Don't be taking out all your money in the open street."

"Doctor," said Israel, "I am not so simple."

"But you knocked over the box."

"That, Doctor, was bravery."

"Bravery in a poor cause, is the height of simplicity, my friend.—Count out your change. It must be French coin, not English, that you are to pay the man with.—Ah, that will do—those three coins will be enough. Put them in a pocket separate from your other cash. Now go, and hasten to the bridge."

"Shall I stop to take a meal any where, Doctor, as I return? I saw several cook-shops as I came hither."

"Cafés and restaurants, they are called here, my honest friend. Tell me, are you the possessor of a liberal fortune?"

"Not very liberal," said Israel.

"I thought as much. Where little wine is drunk, it is good to dine out occasionally at a friend's; but where a poor man dines out at his own charge, it is bad policy. Never dine out that way, when you can dine in. Do not stop on the way at all, my honest friend, but come directly back hither, and you shall dine at home, free of cost, with me."

"Thank you very kindly, Doctor."

And Israel departed for the Pont Neuf. Succeeding in his errand thither, he returned to Doctor Franklin, and found that worthy envoy waiting his attendance at a meal, which according to the Doctor's custom, had been sent from a neighboring restaurant. There were two covers; and without attendance the host and guest sat down. There was only one principal dish, lamb boiled with green peas. Bread and potatoes made up the rest. A decanter-like bottle of uncolored glass, filled with some uncolored beverage, stood at the venerable envoy's elbow.

"Let me fill your glass," said the sage.

"It's white wine, aint it?" said Israel.

"White wine of the very oldest brand; I drink your health in it, my honest friend."

"Why, it's plain water," said Israel, now tasting it.

"Plain water is a very good drink for plain men," replied the wise man.

"Yes," said Israel, "but Squire Woodcock gave me perry, and the other gentleman at White Waltham gave me port, and some other friends have given me brandy."

"Very good, my honest friend; if you like perry and port and brandy, wait till you get back to Squire Woodcock, and the gentleman at White Waltham, and the other friends, and you shall drink perry and port and brandy. But while you are with me, you will drink plain water."

"So it seems, Doctor."

"What do you suppose a glass of port costs?"

"About three pence English, Doctor."

"That must be poor port. But how much good bread will three pence English purchase?"

"Three penny rolls, Doctor."

"How many glasses of port do you suppose a man may drink at a meal?"

"The gentleman at White Waltham drank a bottle at a dinner."

"A bottle contains just thirteen glasses—that's thirty-nine pence, supposing it poor wine. If something of the best, which is the only sort any sane man should drink, as being the least poisonous, it would be quadruple that sum, which is one hundred and fifty-six pence, which is seventy-eight two-penny loaves.

Now, do you not think that for one man to swallow down seventy-eight two-penny rolls at one meal is rather extravagant business?"

"But he drank a bottle of wine; he did not eat seventy-eight two-penny rolls, Doctor."

"He drank the money worth of seventy-eight loaves, which is drinking the loaves themselves; for money is bread."

"But he has plenty of money to spare, Doctor."

"To have to spare, is to have to give away. Does the gentleman give much away?"

"Not that I know of, Doctor."

"Then he thinks he has nothing to spare; and thinking he has nothing to spare, and yet prodigally drinking down his money as he does every day, it seems to me that that gentleman stands self-contradicted, and therefore is no good example for plain sensible folks like you and me to follow. My honest friend, if you are poor, avoid wine as a costly luxury; if you are rich, shun it as a fatal indulgence. Stick to plain water. And now, my good friend, if you are through with your meal, we will rise. There is no pastry coming. Pastry is poisoned bread. Never eat pastry. Be a plain man, and stick to plain things. Now, my friend, I shall have to be private until nine o'clock in the evening, when I shall be again at your service. Meantime you may go to your room. I have ordered the one next to this to be prepared for you. But you must not be idle. Here is Poor Richard's Almanac,[5] which in view of our late conversation, I commend to your earnest perusal. And here, too, is a Guide to Paris, an English one, which you can read. Study it well, so that when you come back from England if you should then have an opportunity to travel about Paris, to see its wonders, you will have all the chief places made historically familiar to you. In this world, men must provide knowledge before it is wanted, just as our countrymen in New England get in their winter's fuel one season, to serve them the next."

So saying, this homely sage, and household Plato,[6] showed his humble guest to the door, and standing in the hall, pointed out to him the one which opened into his allotted apartment.

CHAPTER 8

*Which Has Something to Say
about Dr. Franklin and
the Latin Quarter*

The first, both in point of time and merit, of American envoys was famous not less for the pastoral simplicity of his manners than for the politic grace of his mind. Viewed from a certain point, there was a touch of primeval orientalness in Benjamin Franklin. Neither is there wanting something like his scriptural parallel. The history of the patriarch Jacob[1] is interesting not less from the unselfish devotion which we are bound to ascribe to him, than from the deep worldly wisdom and polished Italian tact, gleaming under an air of Arcadian[2] unaffectedness. The diplomatist and the shepherd are blended; a union not without warrant; the apostolic serpent and dove.[3] A tanned Machiavelli[4] in tents.

Doubtless, too, notwithstanding his eminence as lord of the moving manor, Jacob's raiment was of homespun; the economic envoy's plain coat and hose, who has not heard of?

Franklin all over is of a piece. He dressed his person as his periods; neat, trim, nothing superfluous, nothing deficient. In some of his works his style is only surpassed by the unimprovable sentences of Hobbes of Malmsbury,[5] the paragon of perspicuity. The mental habits of Hobbes and Franklin in several points, especially in one of some moment, assimilated. Indeed, making due allowance for soil and era, history presents few trios more akin, upon the whole, than Jacob, Hobbes, and Franklin; three labyrinth-minded, but plain-spoken Broadbrims,[6] at once politicians and philosophers; keen observers of the main chance; prudent courtiers; practical magians[7] in linsey woolsey.

In keeping with his general habitudes, Doctor Franklin while at the French Court did not reside in the aristocratical faubourgs.[8] He deemed his worsted hose and scientific tastes more adapted in a domestic way to the other side of the Seine, where the Latin Quarter,[9] at once the haunt of erudition and economy, seemed peculiarly to invite the philosophical Poor Richard to its venerable retreats. Here, of grey, chilly, drizzly November mornings, in the dark-stoned quadrangle of the time-honored Sorbonne,[10] walked the lean and slippered metaphysician,—oblivious for the moment that his sublime thoughts and tattered wardrobe were famous throughout Europe,—meditating on the theme of his next lecture; at the same time, in the well-worn chambers overhead, some clayey-visaged chemist in ragged robe-de-chambre, and with a soiled green flap over his left eye, was hard at work stooping over re-torts and crucibles, discovering new antipathies in acids, again risking strange explosions similar to that whereby he had al-ready lost the use of one optic; while in the lofty lodging-houses of the neighboring streets, indigent young students from all parts of France, were ironing their shabby cocked hats, or inking the whity seams of their small-clothes, prior to a prom-enade with their pink-ribboned little grizzets[11] in the Garden of the Luxembourg.[12]

Long ago the haunt of rank, the Latin Quarter still retains many old buildings whose imposing architecture singularly contrasts with the unassuming habits of their present occu-pants. In some parts its general air is dreary and dim; monas-tic and theurgic.[13] In those lonely narrow ways—long-drawn prospectives of desertion—lined with huge piles of silent, vaulted, old iron-grated buildings of dark grey stone, one al-most expects to encounter Paracelsus or Friar Bacon[14] turning the next corner, with some awful vial of Black-Art elixir in his hand.

But all the lodging-houses are not so grim. Not to speak of many of comparatively modern erection, the others of the bet-ter class, however stern in exterior, evince a feminine gayety of taste, more or less, in their furnishings within. The embellish-ing, or softening, or screening hand of woman is to be seen all over the interiors of this metropolis. Like Augustus Cæsar[15] with respect to Rome, the Frenchwoman leaves her obvious mark on Paris. Like the hand of nature, you know it can be none else but hers. Yet sometimes she overdoes it, as nature in the peony; or underdoes it, as nature in the bramble; or—what is still more frequent—is a little slatternly about it, as nature in the pig-weed.

In this congenial vicinity of the Latin Quarter, and in an ancient building something like those last alluded to, at a point midway between the Palais des Beaux Arts[16] and the College of the Sorbonne, the venerable American Envoy pitched his tent when not passing his time at his country retreat at Passy.[17] The frugality of his manner of life did not lose him the good opinion even of the voluptuaries of the showiest of capitals, whose very iron railings are not free from gilt. Franklin was not less a lady's man, than a man's man, a wise man, and an old man. Not only did he enjoy the homage of the choicest Parisian literati, but at the age of seventy-two he was the caressed favorite of the highest born beauties of the Court; who through blind fashion having been originally attracted to him as a famous *savan*,[18] were permanently retained as his admirers by his Plato-like graciousness of good-humor. Having carefully weighed the world, Franklin could act any part in it. By nature turned to knowledge, his mind was often grave, but never serious. At times he had seriousness—extreme seriousness—for others, but never for himself. Tranquillity was to him instead of it. This philosophical levity of tranquillity, so to speak, is shown in his easy variety of pursuits. Printer, postmaster, almanac maker, essayist, chemist, orator, tinker, statesman, humorist, philosopher, parlor-man, political economist, professor of housewifery, ambassador, projector, maxim-monger, herb-doctor, wit:—Jack of all trades, master of each and mastered by none—the type and genius of his land. Franklin was everything but a poet. But since a soul with many qualities, forming of itself a sort of handy index and pocket congress of all humanity,[19] needs the contact of just as many different men, or subjects, in order to the exhibition of its totality; hence very little indeed of the sage's multifariousness will be portrayed in

a simple narrative like the present. This casual private intercourse with Israel, but served to manifest him in his far lesser
lights; thrifty, domestic, dietarian, and, it may be, didactically
waggish. There was much benevolent irony, innocent mischievousness, in the wise man. Seeking here to depict him in his less
exalted habitudes, the narrator feels more as if he were playing
with one of the sage's worsted hose, than reverentially handling
the honored hat which once oracularly sat upon his brow.

So, then, in the Latin Quarter lived Doctor Franklin.
And accordingly in the Latin Quarter tarried Israel for the
time. And it was into a room of a house in this same Latin
Quarter that Israel had been directed when the sage had
requested privacy for a while.

CHAPTER 9

Israel Is Initiated into the Mysteries of Lodging-houses in the Latin Quarter

Closing the door upon himself, Israel advanced to the middle of the chamber, and looked curiously round him.

A dark tessellated floor, but without a rug; two mahogany chairs, with embroidered seats, rather the worse for wear; one mahogany bed, with a gay but tarnished counterpane; a marble wash-stand, cracked, with a china vessel of water, minus the handle. The apartment was very large; this part of the house, which was a very extensive one, embracing the four sides of a quadrangle, having, in a former age, been the hotel of a noble-man. The magnitude of the chamber made its stinted furniture look meagre enough.

But in Israel's eyes, the marble mantel (a comparatively recent addition) and its appurtenances, not only redeemed the rest, but looked quite magnificent and hospitable in the extreme. Because, in the first place, the mantel was graced with an enormous old-fashioned square mirror, of heavy plate glass, set fast, like a tablet, into the wall. And in this mirror was genially reflected the following delicate articles:—First, two bouquets of flowers in-serted in pretty vases of porcelain; second, one cake of white soap; third, one cake of rose-colored soap (both cakes very fra-grant); fourth, one wax candle; fifth, one china tinder-box; sixth, one bottle of Eau de Cologne; seventh, one paper of loaf sugar, nicely broken into sugar-bowl size; eighth, one silver teaspoon; ninth, one glass tumbler; tenth, one glass decanter of cool pure water; eleventh, one sealed bottle containing a richly hued liquid, and marked "Otard."[1]

"I wonder now what O-t-a-r-d is?" soliloquised Israel, slowly spelling the word. "I have a good mind to step in and ask

Dr. Franklin. He knows everything. Let me smell it. No, it's sealed; smell is locked in. Those are pretty flowers. Let's smell them: no smell again. Ah, I see—sort of flowers in women's bonnets—sort of calico flowers. Beautiful soap. This smells anyhow—regular soap-roses—a white rose and a red one. That long-necked bottle there looks like a crane. I wonder what's in that? Hallo! E-a-u—d-e—C-o-l-o-g-n-e. I wonder if Dr. Franklin understands that? It looks like his white wine. This is nice sugar. Let's taste. Yes, this is very nice sugar, sweet as—yes, it's sweet as sugar; better than maple sugar, such as they make at home. But I'm crunching it too loud, the Doctor will hear me. But here's a teaspoon. What's this for? There's no tea, nor tea-cup; but here's a tumbler, and here's drinking water. Let me see. Seems to me, putting this and that and the other thing together, it's a sort of alphabet that spells something. Spoon, tumbler, water, sugar,——brandy—that's it. O-t-a-r-d is brandy. Who put these things here? What does it all mean? Don't put sugar here for show, don't put a spoon here for ornament, nor a jug of water. There is only one meaning to it, and that is a very polite invitation from some invisible person to help myself, if I like, to a glass of brandy and sugar, and if I don't like, let it alone. That's my reading. I have a good mind to ask Doctor Franklin about it, though, for there's just a chance I may be mistaken, and these things here be some other person's private property, not at all meant for me to help myself from. Co-logne, what's that?—never mind. Soap: soap's to wash with. I want to use soap, anyway. Let me see—no, there's no soap on the wash-stand. I see, soap is not given gratis here in Paris, to boarders. But if you want it, take it from the marble, and it will be charged in the bill. If you don't want it let it alone, and no charge. Well, that's fair, anyway. But then to a man who could not afford to use soap, such beautiful cakes as these lying before his eyes all the time, would be a strong temptation. And now that I think of it, the O-t-a-r-d looks rather tempting too. But if I don't like it now, I can let it alone. I've a good mind to try it. But it's sealed. I wonder now if I am right in my understanding of this alphabet? Who knows? I'll venture one little sip, anyhow. Come cork. Hark!"

There was a rapid knock at the door.

Clapping down the bottle, Israel said, "Come in."

It was the man of wisdom.

"My honest friend," said the Doctor, stepping with venerable briskness into the room, "I was so busy during your visit to the Pont Neuf, that I did not have time to see that your room was all right. I merely gave the order, and heard that it had been fulfilled. But it just occurred to me, that as the landladies of Paris have some curious customs which might puzzle an entire stranger, my presence here for a moment might explain any little obscurity. Yes, it is as I thought," glancing towards the mantel.

"Oh, Doctor, that reminds me; what is O-t-a-r-d, pray?"

"Otard is posion."

"Shocking."

"Yes, and I think I had best remove it from the room forthwith," replied the sage, in a business-like manner putting the bottle under his arm; "I hope you never use Cologne, do you?"

"What—what is that, Doctor?"

"I see. You never heard of the senseless luxury—a wise ignorance. You smelt flowers upon your mountains. You won't want this, either;" and the Cologne bottle was put under the other arm. "Candle—you'll want that. Soap—you want soap. Use the white cake."

"Is that cheaper, Doctor?"

"Yes, but just as good as the other. You don't ever munch sugar, do you? It's bad for the teeth. I'll take the sugar." So the paper of sugar was likewise dropped into one of the capacious coat pockets.

"Oh, you better take the whole furniture, Doctor Franklin. Here, I'll help you drag out the bedstead."

"My honest friend," said the wise man, pausing solemnly, with the two bottles, like swimmer's bladders under his armpits; "my honest friend, the bedstead you will want; what I propose to remove, you will not want."

"Oh, I was only joking, Doctor."

"I knew that. It's a bad habit, except at the proper time, and with the proper person. The things left on the mantel were

there placed by the landlady to be used if wanted; if not, to be
left untouched. To-morrow morning, upon the chambermaid's
coming in to make your bed, all such articles as remained obviously untouched, would have been removed; the rest would
have been charged in the bill, whether you used them up completely or not."

"Just as I thought. Then why not let the bottles stay, Doctor,
and save yourself all this trouble?"

"Ah! why indeed. My honest friend, are you not my guest? It
were unhandsome in me to permit a third person superfluously
to entertain you under what, for the time being, is my own roof."

These words came from the wise man in the most graciously
bland and flowing tones. As he ended, he made a sort of conciliatory half bow towards Israel.

Charmed with his condescending affability, Israel, without
another word, suffered him to march from the room, bottles
and all. Not till the first impression of the venerable envoy's
suavity had left him, did Israel begin to surmise the mild superiority of successful strategy which lurked beneath this highly
ingratiating air.

"Ah," pondered Israel, sitting gloomily before the rifled
mantel, with the empty tumbler and tea-spoon in his hand, "it's
sad business to have a Doctor Franklin lodging in the next
room. I wonder if he sees to all the boarders this way. How the
O-t-a-r-d merchants must hate him, and the pastry-cooks too. I
wish I had a good pie to pass the time. I wonder if they ever
make pumpkin pies in Paris? So, I've got to stay in this room all
the time. Somehow I'm bound to be a prisoner, one way or another. Never mind, I'm an ambassador. That's satisfaction.
Hark! The Doctor again.—Come in."

No venerable doctor; but in tripped a young French lass,
bloom on her cheek, pink ribbons in her cap, liveliness in all
her air, grace in the very tips of her elbows. The most bewitching little chambermaid in Paris. All art, but the picture of art-
lessness.

"Monsieur! pardon!"

"Oh, I pardong ye freely," said Israel. "Come to call on the
Ambassador?"

"Monsieur, is de—de—" but, breaking down at the very threshold in her English, she poured out a long ribbon of sparkling French, the purpose of which was to convey a profusion of fine compliments to the stranger, with many tender inquiries as to whether he was comfortably roomed, and whether there might not be something, however trifling, wanting to his complete accommodation. But Israel understood nothing, at the time, but the exceeding grace, and trim, bewitching figure of the girl.

She stood eyeing him for a few moments more, with a look of pretty theatrical despair; and, after vaguely lingering a while, with another shower of incomprehensible compliments and apologies, tripped like a fairy from the chamber. Directly she was gone, Israel pondered upon a singular glance of the girl. It seemed to him that he had, by his reception, in some way, unaccountably disappointed his beautiful visitor. It struck him very strangely that she had entered all sweetness and friendliness, but had retired as if slighted, with a sort of disdainful and sarcastic levity, all the more stinging from its apparent politeness.

Not long had she disappeared, when a noise in the passage apprised him that, in her hurried retreat, the girl must have stumbled against something. The next moment, he heard a chair scraping in the adjacent apartment, and there was another knock at the door.

It was the man of wisdom this time.

"My honest friend, did you not have a visitor, just now?"

"Yes, Doctor, a very pretty girl called upon me."

"Well, I just stopped in to tell you of another strange custom of Paris. That girl is the chambermaid; but she does not confine herself altogether to one vocation. You must beware of the chambermaids of Paris, my honest friend. Shall I tell the girl, from you, that, unwilling to give her the fatigue of going up and down so many flights of stairs, you will, for the future waive her visits of ceremony?"

"Why, Doctor Franklin, she is a very sweet little girl."

"I know it, my honest friend; the sweeter, the more dangerous. Arsenic is sweeter than sugar. I know you are a very sensible young man; not to be taken in by an artful Ammonite;[2] and so, I think I had better convey your message to the girl forthwith."

So saying, the sage withdrew, leaving Israel once more gloomily seated before the rifled mantel, whose mirror was not again to reflect the form of the charming chambermaid.

"Every time he comes in he robs me," soliloquised Israel, dolefully; "with an air all the time, too, as if he were making me presents. If he thinks me such a very sensible young man, why not let me take care of myself?"

It was growing dusk, and Israel lighting the wax candle, proceeded to read in his Guide-book.

"This is poor sight-seeing," muttered he, at last, "sitting here all by myself, with no company but an empty tumbler, reading about the fine things in Paris, and I, myself, a prisoner in Paris. I wish something extraordinary would turn up now; for instance, a man come in and give me ten thousand pounds. But here's 'Poor Richard;' I am a poor fellow myself; so let's see what comfort he has for a comrade."

Opening the little pamphlet, at random, Israel's eyes fell on the following passages: he read them aloud—

"'So *what signifies wishing and hoping for better times? We may make these times better, if we bestir ourselves. Industry need not wish, and he that lives upon hopes will die fasting, as Poor Richard says. There are no gains, without pains. Then help, hands, for I have no lands, as Poor Richard says.*' Oh confound all this wisdom! It's a sort of insulting to talk wisdom to a man like me. It's wisdom that's cheap, and it's fortune that's dear. That ain't in Poor Richard; but it ought to be," concluded Israel, suddenly slamming down the pamphlet.

He walked across the room, looked at the artificial flowers, and the rose-colored soap, and again went to the table and took up the two books.

"So here is the 'Way to Wealth,'[3] and here is the 'Guide to Paris.' Wonder now whether Paris lies on the Way to Wealth? if so, I am on the road. More likely though, it's a parting-of-the-ways. I shouldn't be surprised if the Doctor meant something sly by putting these two books in my hand. Somehow, the old gentleman has an amazing sly look—a sort of mild slyness—

about him, seems to me. His wisdom seems a sort of sly, too. But all in honor, though. I rather think he's one of those old gentlemen who say a vast deal of sense, but hint a world more. Depend upon it, he's sly, sly, sly. Ah, what's this Poor Richard says: 'God helps them that help themselves.' Let's consider that. Poor Richard ain't a Dunker,[4] that's certain, though he has lived in Pennsylvania. 'God helps them that help themselves.' I'll just mark that saw, and leave the pamphlet open to refer to again.—Ah!"

At this point, the Doctor knocked, summoning Israel to his own apartment. Here, after a cup of weak tea, and a little toast, the two had a long, familiar talk together; during which, Israel was delighted with the unpretending talkativeness, serene insight, and benign amiability of the sage. But, for all this, he could hardly forgive him for the Cologne and Otard depredations.

Discovering that, in early life, Israel had been employed on a farm, the man of wisdom at length turned the conversation in that direction; among other things, mentioning to his guest a plan of his (the Doctor's) for yoking oxen, with a yoke to go by a spring instead of a bolt; thus greatly facilitating the operation of hitching on the team to the cart. Israel was very much struck with the improvement; and thought that, if he were home, upon his mountains, he would immediately introduce it among the farmers.

CHAPTER 10

Another Adventurer Appears
upon the Scene

About half-past ten o'clock, as they were thus conversing, Israel's acquaintance, the pretty chambermaid, rapped at the door, saying, with a titter, that a very rude gentleman in the passage of the court, desired to see Doctor Franklin.

"A very rude gentleman?" repeated the wise man in French, narrowly looking at the girl, "that means, a very fine gentleman who has just paid you some energetic compliment. But let him come up, my girl," he added patriarchically.

In a few moments, a swift coquettish step was heard, followed, as if in chase, by a sharp and manly one. The door opened. Israel was sitting so that, accidentally his eye pierced the crevice made by the opening of the door, which, like a theatrical screen, stood for a moment, between Doctor Franklin, and the just entering visitor. And behind that screen, through the crack, Israel caught one momentary glimpse of a little bit of by-play between the pretty chambermaid and the stranger. The vivacious nymph appeared to have affectedly run from him on the stairs—doubtless in freakish return for some liberal advances—but had suffered herself to be overtaken at last ere too late; and on the instant Israel caught sight of her, was with an insincere air of rosy resentment, receiving a roguish pinch on the arm, and a still more roguish salute on the cheek.

The next instant both disappeared from the range of the crevice; the girl departing whence she had come; the stranger—transiently invisible as he advanced behind the door,—entering the room. When Israel now perceived him again, he seemed, while momentarily hidden, to have undergone a complete transformation.

He was a rather small, elastic, swarthy man, with an aspect as of a disinherited Indian Chief in European clothes. An unvanquishable enthusiasm, intensified to perfect sobriety, couched in his savage, self-possessed eye. He was elegantly and somewhat extravagantly dressed as a civilian; he carried himself with a rustic, barbaric jauntiness, strangely dashed with a superinduced touch of the Parisian *salon*. His tawny cheek, like a date, spoke of the tropic. A wonderful atmosphere of proud friendlessness and scornful isolation invested him. Yet was there a bit of the poet as well as the outlaw in him, too. A cool solemnity of intrepidity sat on his lip. He looked like one who of purpose sought out harm's way. He looked like one who never had been, and never would be, a subordinate.

Israel thought to himself that seldom before had he seen such a being. Though dressed à-la-mode,[1] he did not seem to be altogether civilized.

So absorbed was our adventurer by the person of the stranger, that a few moments passed ere he began to be aware of the circumstance, that Dr. Franklin and this new visitor having saluted as old acquaintances, were now sitting in earnest conversation together.

"Do as you please; but I will not bide a suitor much longer," said the stranger in bitterness. "Congress gave me to understand that, upon my arrival here, I should be given immediate command of the *Indien*; and now, for no earthly reason that I can see, you Commissioners have presented her, fresh from the stocks at Amsterdam, to the King of France, and not to me. What does the King of France with such a frigate? And what can I *not* do with her? Give me back the 'Indien,' and in less than one month, you shall hear glorious or fatal news of Paul Jones."[2]

"Come, come, Captain," said Doctor Franklin, soothingly, "tell me now, what would you do with her, if you had her?"

"I would teach the British that Paul Jones, though born in Britain, is no subject to the British King, but an untrammelled citizen and sailor of the universe; and I would teach them, too, that if they ruthlessly ravage the American coasts their own coasts are vulnerable as New Holland's. Give me the *Indien*, and I will rain down on wicked England like fire on Sodom."[3]

These words of bravado were not spoken in the tone of a
bravo, but a prophet. Erect upon his chair, like an Iroquois, the
speaker's look was like that of an unflickering torch.

His air seemed slightly to disturb the old sage's philosophic
repose, who, while not seeking to disguise his admiration of the
unmistakable spirit of the man, seemed but ill to relish his apparent measureless boasting.

As if both to change the subject a little, as well as put his visitor in better mood—though indeed it might have been but
covertly to play with his enthusiasm—the man of wisdom now
drew his chair confidentially nearer to the stranger's, and putting one hand in a very friendly, conciliatory way upon his visitor's knee, and rubbing it gently to and fro there, much as a
lion-tamer might soothingly manipulate the aggravated king of
beasts, said in a winning manner:—"Never mind at present,
Captain, about the 'Indien' affair. Let that sleep a moment. See
now, the Jersey privateers⁴ do us a great deal of mischief by
intercepting our supplies. It has been mentioned to me, that
if you had a small vessel—say, even your present ship, the
'Ranger,'—then, by your singular bravery, you might render
great service, by following those privateers where larger ships
durst not venture their bottoms; or, if but supported by some
frigates from Brest⁵ at a proper distance, might draw them out,
so that the larger vessels could capture them."

"Decoy-duck to French frigates!—Very dignified office, truly!"
hissed Paul in a fiery rage. "Doctor Franklin, whatever Paul
Jones does for the cause of America, it must be done through
unlimited orders: a separate, supreme command; no leader and
no counsellor but himself. Have I not already by my services on
the American coast shown that I am well worthy all this? Why
then do you seek to degrade me below my previous level? I will
mount, not sink. I live but for honor and glory. Give me then
something honorable and glorious to do, and something famous to do it with. Give me the *Indien*."

The man of wisdom slowly shook his head.

"Everything is lost through this shillyshallying, timidity called
prudence," cried Paul Jones, starting to his feet; "to be effectual,
war should be carried on like a monsoon; one changeless deter-

mination of every particle towards the one unalterable aim. But in vacillating councils, statesmen idle about like the cats' paws[6] in calms. My God, why was I not born a Czar!"

"A Nor-wester rather. Come, come, Captain," added the sage, "sit down; we have a third person present, you see,"—pointing towards Israel, who sat rapt at the volcanic spirit of the stranger.

Paul slightly started, and turned inquiringly upon Israel, who, equally owing to Paul's own earnestness of discourse, and Israel's motionless bearing—had thus far remained undiscovered.

"Never fear, Captain," said the sage, "this man is true blue; a secret courier, and an American born. He is an escaped prisoner of war."

"Ah, captured in a ship?" asked Paul eagerly;—"what ship? None of mine! Paul Jones never was captured."

"No, sir, in the brigantine Washington, out of Boston," replied Israel; "We were cruising to cut off supplies to the English."

"Did your shipmates talk much of me?" demanded Paul, with a look as of a parading Sioux demanding homage to his gew-gaws; "what did they say of Paul Jones?"

"I never heard the name before this evening," said Israel.

"What? Ah—brigantine Washington—let me see; that was before I had outwitted the Solebay frigate, fought the Milford, and captured the Mellish and the rest off Louisbergh.[7] You were long before the news, my lad," he added with a sort of compassionate air.

"Our friend here gave you a rather blunt answer," said the wise man, sagely mischievous, and addressing Paul.

"Yes. And I like him for it. My man, will you go a cruise with Paul Jones? You fellows, so blunt with the tongue, are apt to be sharp with the steel. Come, my lad, return with me to Brest. I go in a few days."

Fired by the contagious spirit of Paul, Israel, forgetting all about his previous desire to reach home, sparkled with response to the summons. But Doctor Franklin interrupted him.

"Our friend here," said he to the Captain, "is at present engaged for very different duty."

Much other conversation followed, during which Paul Jones again and again expressed his impatience at being unemployed, and his resolution to accept of no employ unless it gave him supreme authority; while in answer to all this, Dr. Franklin, not uninfluenced by the uncompromising spirit of his guest, and well knowing that however unpleasant a trait in conversation, or in the transaction of civil affairs, yet in war, this very quality was invaluable, as projectiles and combustibles, finally assured Paul, after many complimentary remarks, that he would immediately exert himself to the utmost to procure for him some enterprise which should come up to his merits.

"Thank you for your frankness," said Paul; "frank myself, I love to deal with a frank man. You, Doctor Franklin, are true, and deep; and so you are frank."

The sage sedately smiled, a queer incredulity just lurking in the corner of his mouth.

"But how about our little scheme for new modelling ships-of-war?" said the Doctor, shifting the subject; "it will be a great thing for our infant navy, if we succeed. Since our last conversation on that subject, Captain, at odds and ends of time, I have thought over the matter, and have begun a little skeleton of the thing here, which I will show you. Whenever one has a new idea in anything mechanical, it is best to clothe it with a body as soon as possible. For you can't improve so well on ideas, as you can on bodies."

With that, going to a little drawer, he produced a small basket, filled with a curious looking unfinished frame-work of wood, and several bits of wood unattached. It looked like a nursery basket containing broken odds and ends of playthings.

"Now look here, Captain, though the thing is but begun at present, yet there is enough to show that *one* idea at least of yours is not feasible."

Paul was all attention, as if having unbounded confidence in whatever the sage might suggest; while Israel looked on, quite as interested as either; his heart swelling with the thought of being privy to the consultations of two such men; consultations, too, having ultimate reference to such momentous affairs as the freeing of nations.

"If," continued the Doctor, taking up some of the loose bits and piling them along on one side of the top of the frame; "if the better to shelter your crew in an engagement, you construct your rail in the manner proposed—as thus—then, by the excessive weight of the timber, you will too much interfere with the ship's centre of gravity. You will have that too high."

"Ballast in the hold in proportion," said Paul.

"Then you will sink the whole hull too low. But here, to have less smoke in time of battle, especially on the lower decks, you proposed a new sort of hatchway. But that won't do. See here now, I have invented certain ventilating pipes—they are to traverse the vessel thus"—laying some toilette pins along—"the current of air to enter here and be discharged there. What do you think of that? But now about the main things—fast sailing, driving little to leeward, and drawing little water. Look now at this keel.[8] I whittled it only night before last, just before going to bed. Do you see now how"—

At this crisis, a knock was heard at the door, and the chambermaid reappeared, announcing that two gentlemen were that moment crossing the court below to see Doctor Franklin.

"The Duke de Chartres, and Count D'Estaing,"[9] said the Doctor, "they appointed for last night but did not come. Captain, this has something indirectly to do with your affair. Through the Duke, Count D'Estaing has spoken to the King about the secret expedition, the design of which you first threw out. Call early to-morrow, and I will inform you of the result."

With his tawny hand Paul pulled out his watch, a small, richly jewelled lady's watch.

"It is so late, I will stay here to-night," he said; "Is there a convenient room?"

"Quick," said the Doctor, "it might be ill-advised of you to be seen with me just now. Our friend here will let you share his chamber. Quick, Israel, and show the Captain thither."

As the door closed upon them in Israel's apartment, Doctor Franklin's door closed upon the Duke and the Count. Leaving the latter to their discussion of profound plans for the timely befriending of the American cause, and the crippling of the power of England on the seas, let us pass the night with Paul Jones and Israel in the neighboring room.

CHAPTER 11

Paul Jones in a Reverie

"'God helps them that help themselves.' That's a clincher. That's been my experience. But I never saw it in words before. What pamphlet is this? 'Poor Richard,' hey!"

Upon entering Israel's room, Captain Paul, stepping towards the table and spying the open pamphlet there, had taken it up, his eye being immediately attracted to the passage previously marked by our adventurer.

"A rare old gentleman is 'Poor Richard,'" said Israel in response to Paul's observations.

"So he seems, so he seems;" answered Paul, his eye still running over the pamphlet again; "why, 'Poor Richard' reads very much as Doctor Franklin speaks."

"He wrote it," said Israel.

"Aye? Good. So it is, so it is; it's the wise man all over. I must get me a copy of this, and wear it around my neck for a charm. And now about our quarters for the night. I am not going to deprive you of your bed, my man. Do you go to bed and I will doze in the chair here. It's good as dozing in the crosstrees."

"Why not sleep together," said Israel, "see, it is a big bed. Or perhaps you don't fancy your bed-fellow, Captain?"

"When, before the mast, I first sailed out of Whitehaven[1] to Norway," said Paul, coolly, "I had for hammock-mate a full-blooded Congo. We had a white blanket spread in our hammock. Every time I turned in I found the Congo's black wool worked in with the white worsted. By the end of the voyage the blanket was of a pepper-and-salt look, like an old man's turning head. So it's not because I am notional at all, but because I don't care to, my lad. Turn in and go to sleep. Let the lamp burn. I'll see to it. There, go to sleep."

Complying with what seemed as much a command as a request, Israel, though in bed, could not fall into slumber, for thinking of the little circumstance that this strange swarthy man, flaming with wild enterprises, sat in full suit in the chair. He felt an uneasy misgiving sensation, as if he had retired, not only without covering up the fire, but leaving it fiercely burning with spitting faggots of hemlock.

But his natural complaisance induced him at least to feign himself asleep; whereupon Paul, laying down "Poor Richard," rose from his chair, and, withdrawing his boots, began walking rapidly but noiselessly to and fro, in his stockings, in the spacious room, wrapped in Indian meditations. Israel furtively eyed him from beneath the coverlid, and was anew struck by his aspect, now that Paul thought himself unwatched. Stern, relentless purposes, to be pursued to the points of adverse bayonets, and the muzzles of hostile cannon, were expressed in the now rigid lines of his brow. His ruffled right hand was clutched by his side, as if grasping a cutlass. He paced the room as if advancing upon a fortification. Meantime a confused buzz of discussion came from the neighboring chamber. All else was profound midnight tranquillity. Presently, passing the large mirror over the mantel, Paul caught a glimpse of his person. He paused, grimly regarding it, while a dash of pleased coxcombry seemed to mingle with the otherwise savage satisfaction expressed in his face. But the latter predominated. Soon, rolling up his sleeve, with a queer wild smile, Paul lifted his right arm, and stood thus for an interval, eyeing its image in the glass. From where he lay, Israel could not see that side of the arm presented to the mirror, but he saw its reflection, and started at perceiving there, framed in the carved and gilded wood, certain large intertwisted cyphers covering the whole inside of the arm, so far as exposed, with mysterious tatooings. The design was wholly unlike the fanciful figures of anchors, hearts, and cables, sometimes decorating small portions of seamen's bodies. It was a sort of tattooing such as is seen only on

thorough-bred savages—deep blue, elaborate, labyrinthine, caba-
listic. Israel remembered having beheld, on one of his early voyages, something similar on the arm of a New Zealand warrior,
once met, fresh from battle, in his native village. He concluded
that on some similar early voyage Paul must have undergone
the manipulations of some pagan artist.

Covering his arm again with his laced coat-sleeve, Paul
glanced ironically at the hand of the same arm, now again half
muffled in ruffles, and ornamented with several Parisian rings.
He then resumed his walking with a prowling air, like one
haunting an ambuscade; while a gleam of the consciousness of
possessing a character as yet unfathomed, and hidden power to
back unsuspected projects, irradiated his cold white brow,
which, owing to the shade of his hat in equatorial climates, had
been left surmounting his swarthy face, like the snow topping
the Andes.[2]

So at midnight, the heart of the metropolis of modern civilization was secretly trod by this jaunty barbarian in broadcloth; a sort of prophetical ghost, glimmering in anticipation
upon the advent of those tragic scenes of the French Revolution
which levelled the exquisite refinement of Paris with the blood-
thirsty ferocity of Borneo;[3] showing that broaches and finger-
rings, not less than nose-rings and tattooing, are tokens of the
primeval savageness which ever slumbers in human kind, civilised
or uncivilised.

Israel slept not a wink that night. The troubled spirit of Paul
paced the chamber till morning; when, copiously bathing himself at the wash-stand, Paul looked care-free and fresh as a day-
break hawk. After a closeted consultation with Doctor Franklin,
he left the place with a light and dandified air, switching his
gold-headed cane, and throwing a passing arm round all the
pretty chambermaids he encountered, kissing them resoundingly,
as if saluting a frigate. All barbarians are rakes.

CHAPTER 12

Recrossing the Channel, Israel Returns to the Squire's Abode—His Adventures There

On the third day, as Israel was walking to and fro in his room, having removed his courier's boots, for fear of disturbing the Doctor, a quick sharp rap at the door announced the American envoy. The man of wisdom entered, with two small wads of paper in one hand, and several crackers and a bit of cheese in the other. There was such an eloquent air of instantaneous dispatch about him, that Israel involuntarily sprang to his boots, and, with two vigorous jerks, hauled them on, and then seizing his hat, like any bird, stood poised for his flight across the channel.

"Well done, my honest friend," said the Doctor; "you have the papers in your heel, I suppose."

"Ah," exclaimed Israel, perceiving the mild irony; and in an instant his boots were off again; when, without another word, the Doctor took one boot, and Israel the other, and forthwith both parties proceeded to secrete the documents.

"I think I could improve the design," said the sage, as, notwithstanding his haste, he critically eyed the screwing apparatus of the boot. "The vacancy should have been in the standing part of the heel, not in the lid. It should go with a spring, too, for better dispatch. I'll draw up a paper on false-heels one of these days, and send it to a private reading, at the Institute. But no time for it now. My honest friend, it is now half-past ten o'clock. At half-past eleven, the diligence[1] starts from the Place-du-Carrousel for Calais. Make all haste till you arrive at Brentford. I have a little provender here for you to eat in the diligence, as you will not have time for a regular meal. A day-

and-night courier should never be without a cracker in his pocket. You will probably leave Brentford in a day or two after your arrival there. Be wary, now, my good friend; heed well, that, if you are caught with these papers on British ground, you will involve both yourself and our Brentford friends in fatal calamities. Kick no man's box, never mind whose, in the way. Mind your own box. You can't be too cautious, but don't be too suspicious. God bless you, my honest friend. Go!"

And, flinging the door open for his exit, the Doctor saw Israel dart into the entry, vigorously spring down the stairs, and disappear with all celerity, across the court into the vaulted way.

The man of wisdom stood mildly motionless, a moment, with a look of sagacious, humane meditation on his face, as if pondering upon the chances of the important enterprise: one which, perhaps, might in the sequel affect the weal or woe of nations yet to come. Then suddenly clapping his hand to his capacious coat-pocket, dragged out a bit of cork with some hens' feathers, and hurrying to his room, took out his knife, and proceeded to whittle away at a shuttle-cock of an original scientific construction, which, at some prior time he had promised to send to the young Dutchess D'Abrantes,[2] that very afternoon.

Safely reaching Calais, at night, Israel stepped almost from the diligence into the packet, and, in a few moments, was cutting the water. As on the diligence he took an outside and plebeian seat, so, with the same secret motive of preserving unsuspected the character assumed, he took a deck passage in the packet. It coming on to rain violently, he stole down into the forecastle, dimly lit by a solitary swinging lamp, where were two men industriously smoking, and filling the narrow hole with soporific vapors. These induced strange drowsiness in Israel, and he pondered how best he might indulge it, for a time, without imperilling the precious documents in his custody.

But this pondering in such soporific vapors had the effect of those mathematical devices, whereby restless people cipher themselves to sleep. His languid head fell to his breast. In another moment, he drooped half-lengthwise upon a chest, his legs outstretched before him.

Presently he was awakened by some intermeddlement with his feet. Starting to his elbow, he saw one of the two men in the act of slyly slipping off his right boot, while the left one, already removed, lay on the floor, all ready against the rascal's retreat. Had it not been for the lesson learned on the Pont Neuf, Israel would instantly have inferred that his secret mission was known, and the operator some designed diplomatic knave or other, hired by the British Cabinet, thus to lie in wait for him, fume him into slumber with tobacco, and then rifle him of his momentous despatches. But as it was, he recalled Doctor Franklin's prudent admonitions against the indulgence of premature suspicions.

"Sir," said Israel very civilly, "I will thank you for that boot which lies on the floor, and, if you please, you can let the other stay where it is."

"Excuse me," said the rascal, an accomplished, self-possessed practitioner in his thievish art; "I thought your boots might be pinching you, and only wished to ease you a little."

"Much obliged to ye for your kindness, sir," said Israel; "but they don't pinch me at all. I suppose, though, you think that they wouldn't pinch *you* either; your foot looks rather small. Were you going to try 'em on, just to see how they fitted?"

"No," said the fellow, with sanctimonious seriousness; "but with your permission I should like to try them on, when we get to Dover. I couldn't try them well walking on this tipsy craft's deck, you know."

"No," answered Israel, "and the beach at Dover ain't very smooth either. I guess, upon second thought, you had better not try 'em on at all. Besides, I am a simple sort of a soul,— eccentric they call me,—and don't like my boots to go out of my sight. Ha! ha!"

"What are you laughing at?" said the fellow testily.

"Odd idea! I was just looking at those sad old patched boots there on your feet, and thinking to myself what leaky fire-buckets they would be to pass up a ladder on a burning building. It would hardly be fair now to swop my new boots for those old fire-buckets, would it?"

"By plunko!" cried the fellow, willing now by a bold stroke to

change the subject, which was growing slightly annoying; "by
plunko, I believe we are getting nigh Dover. Let's see."

And so saying, he sprang up the ladder to the deck. Upon Israel following, he found the little craft half becalmed, rolling
on short swells almost in the exact middle of the channel. It
was just before the break of the morning; the air clear and fine;
the heavens spangled with moistly twinkling stars. The French
and English coasts lay distinctly visible in the strange starlight;
the white cliffs of Dover resembling a long gabled block of marble houses. Both shores showed a long straight row of lamps. Israel seemed standing in the middle of the crossing of some wide
stately street in London. Presently a breeze sprang up, and ere
long our adventurer disembarked at his destined port, and directly posted on for Brentford.

The following afternoon, having gained unobserved admit-
tance into the house, according to preconcerted signals, he was
sitting in Squire Woodcock's closet, pulling off his boots and
delivering his despatches.

Having looked over the compressed tissuey sheets, and read
a line particularly addressed to himself, the Squire turning
round upon Israel, congratulated him upon his successful mission; placed some refreshment before him, and apprised him
that, owing to certain suspicious symptoms in the neighborhood, he (Israel) must now remain concealed in the house for a
day or two, till an answer should be ready for Paris.

It was a venerable mansion, as was somewhere previously
stated, of a wide and rambling disorderly spaciousness, built,
for the most part, of weather-stained old bricks, in the goodly
style called Elizabethan. As without, it was all dark russet
bricks; so within, it was nothing but tawny oak panels.

"Now, my good fellow," said the Squire, "my wife has a
number of guests, who wander from room to room, having the
freedom of the house. So I shall have to put you very snugly
away, to guard against any chance of discovery."

So saying, first locking the door, he touched a spring nigh the
open fire-place, whereupon one of the black sooty stone jambs
of the chimney started ajar, just like the marble gate of a tomb.

Inserting one leg of the heavy tongs in the crack, the Squire pried this cavernous gate wide open.

"Why, Squire Woodcock, what is the matter with your chimney?" said Israel.

"Quick, go in."

"Am I to sweep the chimney?" demanded Israel; "I didn't engage for that."

"Pooh, pooh, this is your hiding-place. Come, move in."

"But where does it go to, Squire Woodcock? I don't like the looks of it."

"Follow me. I'll show you."

Pushing his florid corpulence into the mysterious aperture, the elderly Squire led the way up a steep stairs of stone, hardly two feet in width, till they reached a little closet, or rather cell, built into the massive main wall of the mansion, and ventilated and dimly lit by two little sloping slits, ingeniously concealed without, by their forming the sculptured mouths of two griffins cut in a great stone tablet decorating that external part of the dwelling. A mattress lay rolled up in one corner, with a jug of water, a flask of wine, and a wooden trencher containing cold roast beef and bread.

"And I am to be buried alive here?" said Israel, ruefully looking round.

"But your resurrection will soon be at hand," smiled the Squire; "two days at the furthest."

"Though to be sure I was a sort of prisoner in Paris, just as I seem about to be made here," said Israel, "yet Doctor Franklin put me in a better jug than this, Squire Woodcock. It was set out with bouquets and a mirror, and other fine things. Besides, I could step out into the entry whenever I wanted."

"Ah, but my hero, that was in France, and this is in England. There you were in a friendly country: here you are in the enemy's. If you should be discovered in my house, and your connection with me became known, do you know that it would go very hard with me; very hard indeed?"

"Then for your sake, I am willing to stay wherever you think best to put me," replied Israel.

"Well then, you say you want bouquets and a mirror. If those articles will at all help to solace your seclusion, I will bring them to you."

"They really would be company; the sight of my own face particularly."

"Stay here, then. I will be back in ten minutes."

In less than that time, the good old Squire returned, puffing and panting, with a great bunch of flowers, and a small shaving glass.

"There," said he, putting them down; "now keep perfectly quiet; avoid making any undue noise, and on no account descend the stairs, till I come for you again."

"But when will that be?" asked Israel.

"I will try to come twice each day while you are here. But there is no knowing what may happen. If I should not visit you till I come to liberate you—on the evening of the second day, or the morning of the third—you must not be at all surprised, my good fellow. There is plenty of food and water to last you. But mind, on no account descend the stone-stairs, till I come for you."

With that, bidding his guest adieu, he left him.

Israel stood glancing pensively around for a time. By-and-by, moving the rolled mattress under the two air-slits, he mounted, to try if aught were visible beyond. But nothing was to be seen but a very thin slice of blue sky peeping through the lofty foliage of a great tree planted near the side-portal of the mansion; an ancient tree, coeval with the ancient dwelling it guarded.

Sitting down on the mattress, Israel fell into a reverie.

Poverty and liberty, or plenty and a prison, seem to be the two horns of the constant dilemma of my life, thought he. Let's look at the prisoner.

And taking up the shaving glass, he surveyed his lineaments.

"What a pity I didn't think to ask for razors and soap. I want shaving very badly. I shaved last in France. How it would pass the time here. Had I a comb now and a razor, I might shave and curl my hair, and keep making a continual toilet all through the two days, and look spruce as a robin when I get out. I'll ask the squire for the things this very night when he drops in. Hark! ain't that a sort of rumbling in the wall? I hope there ain't any oven next door, if so, I shall be scorched out. Here I am, just like a rat in the wainscot. I wish there was a low window to look out of. I wonder what Doctor Franklin is doing now, and Paul Jones? Hark! there's a bird singing in the leaves. Bell for dinner, that."

And for pastime, he applied himself to the beef and bread, and took a draught of the wine and water.

At last night fell. He was left in utter darkness. No squire.

After an anxious, sleepless night, he saw two long flecks of pale grey light slanted into the cell from the slits, like two long spears. He rose, rolled up his mattress, got upon the roll, and put his mouth to one of the griffins' mouths. He gave a low, just audible whistle, directing it towards the foliage of the tree. Presently there was a slight rustling among the leaves, then one solitary chirrup, and in three minutes a whole chorus of melody burst upon his ear.

"I've waked the first bird" said he to himself, with a smile, "and he's waked all the rest. Now then for breakfast. That over, I dare say the squire will drop in."

But the breakfast was over, and the two flecks of pale light had changed to golden beams, and the golden beams grew less and less slanting, till they straightened themselves up out of sight altogether. It was noon and no squire.

He's gone a hunting before breakfast, and got belated, thought Israel.

The afternoon shadows lengthened. It was sunset; no squire.

He must be very busy trying some sheep-stealer in the hall, mused Israel. I hope he won't forget all about me till to-morrow.

He waited and listened; and listened and waited.

Another restless night; no sleep; morning came. The second day passed like the first, and the night. On the third morning the flowers lay shrunken by his side. Drops of wet oozing through the air-slits, fell dully on the stone floor. He heard the dreary beatings of the tree's leaves against the mouths of the

griffins, bedashing them with the spray of the rain-storm without. At intervals a burst of thunder rolled over his head, and
lightning flashing down through the slits, lit up the cell with a
greenish glare, followed by sharp splashings and rattlings of
the redoubled rain-storm.

This is the morning of the third day, murmured Israel to himself; he said he would at the furthest come to me on the morning of the third day. This is it. Patience, he will be here yet.
Morning lasts till noon.

But owing to the murkiness of the day, it was very hard to
tell when noon came. Israel refused to credit that noon had
come and gone, till dusk set plainly in. Dreading he knew not
what, he found himself buried in the darkness of still another
night. However patient and hopeful hitherto, fortitude now
presently left him. Suddenly, as if some contagious fever had
seized him, he was afflicted with strange enchantments of misery, undreamed of till now.

He had eaten all the beef, but there was bread and water sufficient to last by economy, for two or three days to come. It was
not the pang of hunger then, but a nightmare originating in his
mysterious incarceration, which appalled him. All through the
long hours of this particular night, the sense of being masoned
up in the wall, grew, and grew, and grew upon him, till again
and again he lifted himself convulsively from the floor; as if vast
blocks of stone had been laid on him; as if he had been digging
a deep well, and the stone work with all the excavated earth had
caved in upon him, where he burrowed ninety feet beneath the
clover. In the blind tomb of the midnight he stretched his two
arms sideways, and felt as if coffined at not being able to extend
them straight out, on opposite sides, for the narrowness of the
cell. He seated himself against one side of the wall, crosswise
with the cell, and pushed with his feet at the opposite wall. But
still mindful of his promise in this extremity, he uttered no cry.
He mutely raved in the darkness. The delirious sense of the absence of light was soon added to his other delirium as to the
contraction of space. The lids of his eyes burst with impotent
distension. Then he thought the air itself was getting unbear-
able. He stood up at the griffin slits, pressing his lips far into

them till he moulded his lips there, to suck the utmost of the open air possible.

And continually, to heighten his frenzy, there recurred to him again and again what the Squire had told him as to the origin of the cell. It seemed that this part of the old house, or rather this wall of it, was extremely ancient, dating far beyond the era of Elizabeth, having once formed portion of a religious retreat belonging to the Templars.[3] The domestic discipline of this order was rigid and merciless in the extreme. In a side wall of their second-story chapel, horizontal and on a level with the floor, they had an internal vacancy left, exactly of the shape and average size of a coffin. In this place, from time to time, inmates convicted of contumacy were confined; but, strange to say, not till they were penitent. A small hole, of the girth of one's wrist, sunk like a telescope three feet through the masonry into the cell, served at once for ventilation, and to push through food to the prisoner. This hole opening into the chapel also enabled the poor solitaire, as intended, to overhear the religious services at the altar; and, without being present, take part in the same. It was deemed a good sign of the state of the sufferer's soul, if from the gloomy recesses of the wall, was heard the agonized groan of his dismal response. This was regarded in the light of a penitent wail from the dead; because the customs of the order ordained, that when any inmate should be first incarcerated in the wall, he should be committed to it in the presence of all the brethren; the chief reading the burial service as the live body was sepulchred. Sometimes several weeks elapsed ere the disentombment. The penitent being then usually found numb and congealed in all his extremities, like one newly stricken with paralysis.

This coffin-cell of the Templars had been suffered to remain in the demolition of the general edifice, to make way for the erection of the new, in the reign of Queen Elizabeth.[4] It was enlarged somewhat, and altered, and additionally ventilated, to adapt it for a place of concealment in times of civil dissension.

With this history ringing in his solitary brain, it may readily be conceived what Israel's feelings must have been. Here, in this very darkness, centuries ago, hearts, human as his, had mildewed in despair; limbs, robust as his own, had stiffened in immovable torpor.

At length, after what seemed all the prophetic days and years of Daniel,[5] morning broke. The benevolent light entered the cell, soothing his frenzy, as if it had been some smiling human face—nay, the Squire himself, come at last to redeem him from thrall. Soon his dumb ravings entirely left him, and gradually, with a sane, calm mind, he revolved all the circumstances of his condition.

He could not be mistaken; something fatal must have befallen his friend. Israel remembered the Squire's hinting, that in case of the discovery of his clandestine proceedings, it would fare extremely hard with him. Israel was forced to conclude that this same unhappy discovery had been made; that owing to some untoward misadventure, his good friend had been carried off a State-prisoner to London. That prior to his going, the Squire had not apprised any member of his household that he was about to leave behind him a prisoner in the wall; this seemed evident from the circumstance that, thus far, no soul had visited that prisoner. It could not be otherwise. Doubtless, the Squire, having no opportunity to converse in private with his relatives or friends at the moment of his sudden arrest, had been forced to keep his secret, for the present, for fear of involving Israel in still worse calamities. But would he leave him to perish piece-meal in the wall? All surmise was baffled in the unconjecturable possibilities of the case. But some sort of action must speedily be determined upon. Israel would not additionally endanger the Squire, but he could not in such uncertainty consent to perish where he was. He resolved at all hazards to escape: by stealth and noiselessly, if possible; by violence and outcry, if indispensable.

Gliding out of the cell, he descended the stone stairs, and stood before the interior of the jamb. He felt an immovable iron knob; but no more. He groped about gently for some bolt or spring. When before he had passed through the passage with his guide, he had omitted to notice by what precise mechanism the jamb was to be opened from within, or whether, indeed, it could at all be opened except from without.

He was about giving up the search in despair, after sweeping with his two hands every spot of the wall-surface around him, when chancing to turn his whole body a little to one side, he heard a creak, and saw a thin lance of light. His foot had unconsciously pressed some spring laid in the floor. The jamb was ajar. Pushing it open, he stood at liberty in the Squire's closet.

CHAPTER 13

His Escape from the House, with Various Adventures Following

He started at the funereal aspect of the room, into which, since he last stood there, undertakers seemed to have stolen. The curtains of the window were festooned with long weepers of crape. The four corners of the red cloth on the round table were knotted with crape.

Knowing nothing of these mournful customs of the country, nevertheless, Israel's instinct whispered him, that Squire Woodcock lived no more on this earth. At once, the whole three days' mystery was made clear. But what was now to be done? His friend must have died very suddenly; most probably, struck down in a fit, from which he never more rose. With him had perished all knowledge of the fact that a stranger was immured in the mansion. If discovered then, prowling here in the inmost privacies of a gentleman's abode, what would befal the wanderer, already not unsuspected in the neighborhood of some underhand guilt as a fugitive? If he adhered to the strict truth, what could he offer in his own defence without convicting himself of acts, which, by English tribunals, would be accounted flagitious crimes? Unless, indeed, by involving the memory of the deceased Squire Woodcock in his own self-acknowledged proceedings, so ungenerous a charge should result in an abhorrent refusal to credit his extraordinary tale, whether as referring to himself or another; and so throw him open to still more grievous suspicions?

While wrapped in these dispiriting reveries, he heard a step not very far off in the passage. It seemed approaching. Instantly he flew to the jamb, which remained unclosed; and disappearing within, drew the stone after him by the iron knob. Owing to his hurried violence, the jamb closed with a dull, dismal and singular noise. A shriek followed from within the room. In a panic, Israel fled up the dark stairs; and near the top, in his eagerness, stumbled, and fell back to the last step with a rolling din, which reverberated by the arch overhead smote through and through the wall, dying away at last indistinctly, like low muffled thunder among the clefts of deep hills. When raising himself instantly, not seriously bruised by his fall, Israel intently listened;—the echoing sounds of his descent were mingled with added shrieks from within the room. They seemed some nervous female's, alarmed by what must have appeared to her supernatural or at least unaccountable noises in the wall. Directly he heard other voices of alarm undistinguishably commingled, and then, they retreated together, and all again was still.

Recovering from his first amazement, Israel revolved these occurrences. No creature now in the house knows of the cell, thought he. Some woman,—the housekeeper, perhaps,—first entered the room alone. Just as she entered, the jamb closed. The sudden report made her shriek; then, afterwards, the noise of my fall prolonging itself, added to her fright, while her repeated shrieks brought every soul in the house to her; who, aghast at seeing her lying in a pale faint, it may be, like a corpse, in a room hung with crape for a man just dead, they also shrieked out; and then with blended lamentations they bore the fainting person away. Now this will follow; no doubt it *has* followed ere now:—they believe that the woman saw or heard the spirit of Squire Woodcock. Since I seem then to understand how all these strange events have occurred; since I seem to know that they have plain common causes; I begin to feel cool and calm again. Let me see. Yes. I have it. By means of the idea of the ghost prevailing among the frightened household; by that means, I will this very night make good my escape. If I can but lay hands on some of the late Squire's clothing—if but a coat and hat of his—I shall be certain to succeed. It is not too early to begin now. They will hardly come back to the room in a hurry. I will return to it, and see what I can find to serve my purpose. It is the Squire's private closet; hence it is not unlikely that here some at least of his clothing will be found.

With these thoughts, he cautiously sprung the iron under foot, peeped in, and seeing all clear, boldly re-entered the apartment. He went straight to a high, narrow door in the opposite wall. The key was in the lock. Opening the door, there hung several coats, small clothes, pairs of silk stockings, and hats of the deceased. With little difficulty Israel selected from these the complete suit in which he had last seen his once jovial friend. Carefully closing the door, and carrying the suit with him, he was returning towards the chimney, when he saw the Squire's silver-headed cane leaning against a corner of the wainscot. Taking this also, he stole back to his cell.

Slipping off his own clothing, he deliberately arrayed himself in the borrowed raiment; silk small-clothes and all; then put on the cocked hat, grasped the silver-headed cane in his right hand, and moving his small shaving glass slowly up and down before him, so as by piece-meal to take in his whole figure, felt convinced that he would well pass for Squire Woodcock's genuine phantom. But after the first feeling of self-satisfaction with his anticipated success had left him, it was not without some superstitious embarrassment that Israel felt himself encased in a dead man's broadcloth; nay, in the very coat in which the deceased had no doubt fallen down in his fit. By degrees he began to feel almost as unreal and shadowy as the shade whose part he intended to enact.

Waiting long and anxiously till darkness came, and then till he thought it was fairly midnight, he stole back into the closet, and standing for a moment uneasily in the middle of the floor, thinking over all the risks he might run, he lingered till he felt himself resolute and calm. Then groping for the door, leading into the hall, put his hand on the knob and turned it. But the door refused to budge. Was it locked? The key was not in. Turning the knob once more, and holding it so, he pressed firmly against the door. It did not move. More firmly still, when suddenly it burst open with a loud crackling report. Being cramped, it had stuck in the sill. Less than three seconds passed, when, as Israel was groping his way down the long wide hall towards the large staircase at its opposite end, he heard confused hurrying noises from the neighboring rooms, and in another instant several persons, mostly in night-dresses, appeared at their chamber-doors, thrusting out alarmed faces, lit by a lamp held by one of the number, a rather elderly lady in widow's weeds, who, by her appearance, seemed to have just risen from a sleepless chair, instead of an oblivious couch. Israel's heart beat like a hammer; his face turned like a sheet. But bracing himself, pulling his hat lower down over his eyes, settling his head in the collar of his coat, he advanced along the defile of wildly staring faces. He advanced with a slow and stately step; looked neither to the right nor the left; but went solemnly forward on his now faintly illuminated way, sounding his cane on the floor as he passed. The faces in the doorways curdled his blood, by their rooted looks. Glued to the spot, they seemed incapable of motion. Each one was silent as he advanced towards him or her; but as he left each individual, one after another, behind, each in a frenzy shrieked out, "the Squire, the Squire!" As he passed the lady in the widow's weeds, she fell senseless and crosswise before him. But forced to be immutable in his purpose, Israel solemnly stepping over her prostrate form, marched deliberately on.

In a few minutes more he had reached the main door of the mansion, and withdrawing the chain and bolt, stood in the open air. It was a bright moonlight night. He struck slowly across the open grounds towards the sunken fields beyond. When midway across the grounds, he turned towards the mansion, and saw three of the front windows filled with white faces, gazing in terror at the wonderful spectre. Soon descending a slope, he disappeared from their view.

Presently he came to hilly land in meadow, whose grass having been lately cut, now lay dotting the slope in cocks;[1] a sinuous line of creamy vapor meandered through the lowlands at the base of the hill; while beyond was a dense grove of dwarfish trees, with here and there a tall tapering dead trunk, peeled of the bark, and overpeering the rest. The vapor wore the semblance of a deep stream of water, imperfectly descried; the grove looked like some closely-clustering town on its banks, lorded over by spires of churches.

The whole scene magically reproduced to our adventurer the aspect of Bunker Hill, Charles River, and Boston town, on the

well-remembered night of the 16th of June. The same season;
the same moon; the same new-mown hay on the shaven sward;
hay which was scraped together during the night to help pack
into the redoubt so hurriedly thrown up.

Acted on as if by enchantment, Israel sat down on one of the
cocks, and gave himself up to reverie. But, worn out by long loss
of sleep, his reveries would have soon merged into slumber's still
wilder dreams, had he not rallied himself, and departed on his
way, fearful of forgetting himself in an emergency like the present. It now occurred to him that, well as his disguise had served
him in escaping from the mansion of Squire Woodcock, that disguise might fatally endanger him if he should be discovered in it
abroad. He might pass for a ghost at night, and among the relations and immediate friends of the gentleman deceased; but by
day, and among indifferent persons, he ran no small risk of being apprehended for an entry-thief. He bitterly lamented his
omission in not pulling on the Squire's clothes over his own, so
that he might now have reappeared in his former guise.

As meditating over this difficulty, he was passing along, suddenly he saw a man in black standing right in his path, about
fifty yards distant, in a field of some growing barley or wheat.
The gloomy stranger was standing stock-still; one outstretched
arm, with weird intimation pointing towards the deceased
Squire's abode. To the brooding soul of the now desolate Israel,
so strange a sight roused a supernatural suspicion. His conscience morbidly reproaching him for the terrors he had bred in
making his escape from the house; he seemed to see in the fixed
gesture of the stranger something more than humanly significant. But somewhat of his intrepidity returned; he resolved to
test the apparition. Composing itself to the same deliberate
stateliness with which it had paced the hall, the phantom of
Squire Woodcock firmly advanced its cane, and marched
straight forward towards the mysterious stranger.

As he neared him, Israel shrunk. The dark coat-sleeve
flapped on the bony skeleton of the unknown arm. The face
was lost in a sort of ghastly blank. It was no living man.

But mechanically continuing his course, Israel drew still
nearer and saw—a scarecrow.

AN ENCOUNTER OF GHOSTS

Not a little relieved by the discovery, our adventurer paused, more particularly to survey so deceptive an object, which seemed to have been constructed on the most efficient principles; probably by some broken down wax-figure costumer. It comprised the complete wardrobe of a scare-crow, namely: a cocked hat, bunged; tattered coat; old velveteen breeches; and long worsted stockings, full of holes; all stuffed very nicely with straw, and skeletoned by a frame-work of poles. There was a great flapped pocket to the coat—which seemed to have been some laborer's—standing invitingly open. Putting his hands in, Israel drew out the lid of an old tobacco-box, the broken bowl of a pipe, two rusty nails, and a few kernels of wheat. This reminded him of the Squire's pockets. Trying them, he produced a handsome handkerchief, a spectacle-case, with a purse containing some silver and gold, amounting to a little more than five pounds. Such is the difference between the contents of the pockets of scare-crows and the pockets of well-to-do squires. Ere donning his present habiliments, Israel had not omitted to withdraw his own money from his own coat, and put it in the pocket of his own waistcoat, which he had not exchanged.

Looking upon the scare-crow more attentively, it struck him that, miserable as its wardrobe was, nevertheless here was a chance for getting rid of the unsuitable and perilous clothes of the Squire. No other available opportunity might present itself for a time. Before he encountered any living creature by daylight, another suit must somehow be had. His exchange with the old ditcher, after his escape from the inn near Portsmouth, had familiarized him with the most deplorable of wardrobes. Well, too, he knew, and had experienced it, that for a man desirous of avoiding notice, the more wretched the clothes the better. For who does not shun the scurvy wretch, Poverty, advancing in battered hat and lamentable coat?

Without more ado, slipping off the Squire's raiment, he donned the scarecrow's, after carefully shaking out the hay,

which, from many alternate soakings and bakings in rain and
sun, had become quite broken up, and would have been almost
dust, were it not for the mildew which damped it. But sufficient
of this wretched old hay remained adhesive to the inside of
the breeches and coat sleeves, to produce the most irritating
torment.

The grand moral question now came up, what to do with the
purse? Would it be dishonest under the circumstances to appro-
priate that purse? Considering the whole matter, and not forgetting that he had not received from the gentleman deceased
the promised reward for his services as courier, Israel concluded that he might justly use the money for his own. To
which opinion surely no charitable judge will demur. Besides,
what should he do with the purse, if not use it for his own? It
would have been insane to have returned it to the relations.
Such mysterious honesty would have but resulted in his arrest
as a rebel, or rascal. As for the Squire's clothes, handkerchief,
and spectacle-case, they must be put out of sight with all
despatch. So, going to a morass not remote, Israel sunk them
deep down, and heaped tufts of the rank sod upon them. Then
returning to the field of corn, sat down under the lee of a rock,
about a hundred yards from where the scarecrow had stood,
thinking which way he now had best direct his steps. But his
late ramble coming after so long a deprivation of rest, soon
produced effects not so easy to be shaken off, as when reposing
upon the haycock. He felt less anxious too, since changing his
apparel. So before he was aware, he fell into deep sleep.

When he awoke, the sun was well up in the sky. Looking
around he saw a farm-laborer with a pitch-fork coming at a
distance into view, whose steps seemed bent in a direction not
far from the spot where he lay. Immediately it struck our adventurer that this man must be familiar with the scarecrow;
perhaps had himself fashioned it. Should he miss it then, he
might make immediate search, and so discover the thief so
imprudently loitering upon the very field of his operations.

Waiting until the man momentarily disappeared in a little hollow, Israel ran briskly to the identical spot where the scarecrow
had stood; where, standing stiffly erect, pulling the hat well over

his face, and thrusting out his arm, pointed steadfastly towards the Squire's abode, he awaited the event. Soon the man reappeared in sight, and marching right on, paused not far from Israel, and gave him an one earnest look, as if it were his daily wont to satisfy that all was right with the scarecrow. No sooner was the man departed to a reasonable distance, than, quitting his post, Israel struck across the fields towards London. But he had not yet quite quitted the field, when it occurred to him to turn round, and see if the man was completely out of sight; when, to his consternation, he saw the man returning towards him, evidently by his pace and gesture in unmixed amazement. The man must have turned round to look, before Israel had done so. Frozen to the ground, Israel knew not what to do. But, next moment it struck him, that this very motionlessness was the least hazardous plan in such a strait. Thrusting out his arm again towards the house, once more he stood stock-still, and again awaited the event.

It so happened that this time in pointing towards the house, Israel unavoidably pointed towards the advancing man. Hoping that the strangeness of this coincidence might, by operating on the man's superstition, incline him to beat an immediate retreat, Israel kept cool as he might. But the man proved to be of a braver metal than anticipated. In passing the spot where the scarecrow had stood, and perceiving, beyond the possibility of mistake, that by some unaccountable agency it had suddenly removed itself to a distance; instead of being terrified at this verification of his worst apprehensions, the man pushed on for Israel, apparently resolved to sift this mystery to the bottom.

Seeing him now determinately coming, with pitchfork valiantly presented, Israel, as a last means of practising on the fellow's fears of the supernatural, suddenly doubled up both fists, presenting them savagely towards him at a distance of about twenty paces; at the same time showing his teeth like a skull's, and demoniacally rolling his eyes. The man paused bewildered; looked all round him; looked at the springing grain; then across at some trees; then up at the sky; and satisfied at last by those observations, that the world at large had not undergone a miracle in the last fifteen minutes, resolutely resumed his advance; the pitchfork like a boarding-pike now aimed full at the breast of the object. Seeing all his stratagems vain, Israel now threw himself into the original attitude of the scarecrow, and once again stood immovable. Abating his pace by degrees almost to a mere creep, the man at last came within three feet of him, and pausing, gazed amazed into Israel's eyes. With a stern and terrible expression Israel resolutely returned the glance, but otherwise remained like a statue; hoping thus to stare his pursuer out of countenance. At last the man slowly presented one prong of his fork towards Israel's left eye. Nearer and nearer the sharp point came; till no longer capable of enduring such a test, Israel took to his heels with all speed, his tattered coat-tails streaming behind him. With inveterate purpose the man pursued. Darting blindly on, Israel leaping a gate, suddenly found himself in a field where some dozen laborers were at work; who recognizing the scarecrow—an old acquaintance of theirs, as it would seem—lifted all their hands as the astounding apparition swept by, followed by the man with the pitchfork. Soon all joined in the chase; but Israel proved to have better wind and bottom than any. Outstripping the whole pack, he finally shot out of their sight in an extensive park, heavily timbered in one quarter. He never saw more of these people.

Loitering in the wood till nightfall, he then stole out and made the best of his way towards the house of that good-natured farmer in whose corn-loft he had received his first message from Squire Woodcock. Rousing this man up a little before midnight, he informed him somewhat of his recent adventures, but carefully concealed his having been employed as a secret courier, together with his escape from Squire Woodcock's. All he craved at present was a meal. The meal being over, Israel offered to buy from the farmer his best suit of clothes, and displayed the money on the spot.

"Where did you get so much money?" said his entertainer in a tone of surprise; "your clothes here don't look as if you had seen prosperous times since you left me. Why, you look like a scarecrow."

"That may well be," replied Israel very soberly. "But what do you say? will you sell me your suit?—here's the cash."

"I don't know about it," said the farmer, in doubt; "let me look at the money. Ha!—a silk purse come out of a beggar's pocket!—Quit the house, rascal, you've turned thief."

Thinking that he could not swear to his having come by his money with absolute honesty—since indeed the case was one for the most subtle casuist—Israel knew not what to reply. This honest confusion confirmed the farmer; who with many abusive epithets drove him into the road; telling him that he might thank himself that he did not arrest him on the spot.

In great dolor at this unhappy repulse, Israel trudged on in the moonlight some three miles to the house of another friend, who also had once succored him in extremity. This man proved a very sound sleeper. Instead of succeeding in rousing him by his knocking, Israel but succeeded in rousing his wife, a person not of the greatest amiability. Raising the sash, and seeing so shocking a pauper before her, the woman upbraided him with shameless impropriety in asking charity at dead of night, in a dress so improper too. Looking down at his deplorable velveteens, Israel discovered that his extensive travels had produced a great rent in one loin of the rotten old breeches, through which a whitish fragment protruded.

Remedying this oversight as well as he might, he again implored the woman to wake her husband.

"That I shan't!" said the woman morosely. "Quit the premises, or I'll throw something on ye."

With that, she brought some earthenware to the window, and would have fulfilled her threat, had not Israel prudently retreated some paces. Here he entreated the woman to take mercy on his plight, and since she would not waken her husband, at least throw to him (Israel) her husband's breeches, and he would leave the price of them, with his own breeches to boot, on the sill of the door.

"You behold how sadly I need them," said he; "for heaven's sake befriend me."

"Quit the premises!" reiterated the woman.

"The breeches, the breeches! here is the money," cried Israel, half furious with anxiety.

"Saucy cur," cried the woman, somehow misunderstanding him; "do you cunningly taunt me with *wearing* the breeches? begone!"

Once more, poor Israel decamped, and made for another friend. But here a monstrous bull-dog, indignant that the peace of a quiet family should be disturbed by so outrageous a tatter-demalion,[2] flew at Israel's unfortunate coat, whose rotten skirts the brute tore completely off; leaving the coat razeed to a spencer,[3] which barely came down to the wearer's waist. In attempting to drive the monster away, Israel's hat fell off, upon which the dog pounced with the utmost fierceness, and thrusting both paws into it, rammed out the crown, and went snuffling the wreck before him. Recovering the wretched hat, Israel again beat a retreat, his wardrobe sorely the worse for his visits. Not only was his coat a mere rag, but his breeches, clawed by the dog, were slashed into yawning gaps, while his yellow hair waved over the top of the crownless beaver, like a lonely tuft of heather on the Highlands.[4]

In this plight the morning discovered him dubiously skirmishing on the outskirts of a village.

"Ah! what a true patriot gets for serving his country!" murmured Israel. But soon thinking a little better of his case, and seeing yet another house which had once furnished him with an asylum, he made bold to advance to the door. Luckily he this time met the man himself, just emerging from bed. At first the farmer did not recognize the fugitive; but upon another look, seconded by Israel's plaintive appeal, beckoned him into the barn, where directly our adventurer told him all he thought prudent to disclose of his story; ending by once more offering to negotiate for breeches and coat. Having ere this, emptied and thrown away the purse which had played him so scurvy a trick with the first farmer; he now produced three crown-pieces.

"Three crown-pieces in your pocket, and no crown to your hat!" said the farmer.

"But I assure you, my friend," rejoined Israel, "that a finer hat was never worn, until that confounded bull-dog ruined it."

"True," said the farmer. "I forgot that part of your story. Well, I have a tolerable coat and breeches which I will sell you for your money."

In ten minutes more, Israel was equipped in a grey coat of coarse cloth, not much improved by wear, and breeches to match. For half-a-crown more, he procured a highly respectable-looking hat.

"Now, my kind friend," said Israel, "can you tell me where Horne Tooke, and John Bridges live?"

Our adventurer thought it his best plan to seek out one or other of those gentlemen, both to report proceedings, and learn confirmatory tidings concerning Squire Woodcock, touching whose fate he did not like to inquire of others.

"Horne Tooke? What do you want with Horne Tooke?" said the farmer: "He was Squire Woodcock's friend, wasn't he? The poor Squire! Who would have thought he'd have gone off so suddenly. But apoplexy comes like a bullet."

I was right, thought Israel to himself. "But where does Horne Tooke live?" he demanded again.

"He once lived in Brentford, and wore a cassock there. But I hear he's sold out his living, and gone in his surplice to study law in Lunnon."

This was all news to Israel, who, from various amiable remarks he had heard from Horne Tooke at the Squire's, little dreamed he was an ordained clergyman. Yet a good-natured English clergyman translated Lucian; another, equally good-natured, wrote Tristram Shandy; and a third, an ill-natured appreciator of good-natured Rabelais, died a dean;[5] not to speak of others. Thus ingenious and ingenuous are some of the English clergy.

"You can't tell me, then, where to find Horne Tooke?" said Israel, in perplexity.

"You'll find him, I suppose, in Lunnon."

"What street and number?"

"Don't know. Needle in a haystack."

"Where does Mr. Bridges live?"

"Never heard of any Bridges, except Lunnon bridges, and one Molly Bridges in Bridewell."

So Israel departed; better clothed, but no wiser than before.

What to do next? He reckoned up his money, and concluded he had plenty to carry him back to Doctor Franklin in Paris. Accordingly, taking a turn to avoid the two nearest villages, he directed his steps towards London, where, again taking the post coach for Dover, he arrived on the channel shore just in time to learn that the very coach in which he rode brought the news to the authorities there that all intercourse between the two nations was indefinitely suspended. The characteristic taciturnity and formal stolidity of his fellow-travellers—all Englishmen, mutually unacquainted with each other, and occupying different positions in life—having prevented his sooner hearing the tidings.

Here was another accumulation of misfortunes. All visions but those of eventual imprisonment or starvation vanished from before the present realities of poor Israel Potter. The Brentford gentleman had flattered him with the prospect of receiving something very handsome for his services as courier. That hope was no more. Doctor Franklin had promised him his good offices in procuring him a passage home to America. Quite out of the question now. The sage had likewise intimated that he might possibly see him some way remunerated for his sufferings in his country's cause. An idea no longer to be harbored. Then Israel recalled the mild man of wisdom's words— "At the prospect of pleasure never be elated; but without depression respect the omens of ill." But he found it as difficult now to comply, in all respects, with the last section of the maxim, as before he had with the first.

While standing wrapped in afflictive reflections on the shore, gazing towards the unattainable coast of France, a pleasant-looking cousinly stranger, in seaman's dress, accosted him, and, after some pleasant conversation, very civilly invited him up a lane into a house of rather secret entertainment. Pleased to be befriended in this his strait, Israel yet looked inquisitively upon the man, not completely satisfied with his good intentions. But the other, with good-humored violence, hurried him up the lane into the inn, when, calling for some spirits, he and Israel very affectionately drank to each other's better health and prosperity.

"Take another glass," said the stranger, affably.

Israel, to drown his heavy-heartedness, complied. The liquor began to take effect.

"Ever at sea?" said the stranger, lightly.

"Oh, yes; been a whaling."

"Ah!" said the other, "happy to hear that, I assure you. Jim! Bill!" And beckoning very quietly to two brawny fellows, in a trice Israel found himself kidnapped into the naval service[6] of the magnanimous old gentleman of Kew Gardens—his Royal Majesty, George III.

"Hands off!" said Israel, fiercely, as the two men pinioned him.

"Reglar game-cock," said the cousinly-looking man. "I must get three guineas for cribbing[7] him. Pleasant voyage to ye, my friend," and, leaving Israel a prisoner, the crimp,[8] buttoning his coat, sauntered leisurely out of the inn.

"I'm no Englishman," roared Israel, in a foam.

"Oh! that's the old story," grinned his gaolers.[9] "Come along. There's no Englishmen in the English fleet. All foreigners. You may take their own word for it."

To be short, in less than a week Israel found himself at Portsmouth, and, ere long, a fore-topman in his majesty's ship of the line, "Unprincipled," scudding before the wind down channel, in company with the "Undaunted," and the "Unconquerable;" all three haughty Dons bound to the East Indian waters as reinforcements to the fleet of Sir Edward Hughes.[10]

And now, we might shortly have to record our adventurer's part in the famous engagement off the coast of Coromandel, between Admiral Suffren's fleet and the English squadron,[11] were it not that fate snatched him on the threshold of events, and, turning him short round whither he had come, sent him back congenially to war against England, instead of on her behalf. Thus repeatedly and rapidly were the fortunes of our wanderer planted, torn up, transplanted, and dropped again, hither and thither, according as the Supreme Disposer of sailors and soldiers saw fit to appoint.

CHAPTER 14

In Which Israel Is Sailor under Two Flags, and in Three Ships, and All in One Night

As running down channel at evening, Israel walked the crowded main-deck of the seventy-four,[1] continually brushed by a thousand hurrying wayfarers, as if he were in some great street in London, jammed with artisans, just returning from their day's labor, novel and painful emotions were his. He found himself dropped into the naval mob without one friend; nay, among enemies, since his country's enemies were his own, and against the kith and kin of these very beings around him, he himself had once lifted a fatal hand. The martial bustle of a great man-of-war, on her first day out of port, was indescribably jarring to his present mood. Those sounds of the human multitude disturbing the solemn natural solitudes of the sea, mysteriously afflicted him. He murmured against that untowardness which, after condemning him to long sorrows on the land, now pursued him with added griefs on the deep. Why should a patriot, leaping for the chance again to attack the oppressor, as at Bunker Hill, now be kidnapped to fight that oppressor's battles on the endless drifts of the Bunker Hills of the billows? But like many other repiners, Israel was perhaps a little premature with upbraidings like these.

Plying on between Scilly and Cape Clear,[2] the Unprincipled—which vessel somewhat outsailed her consorts—fell in, just before dusk, with a large revenue cutter[3] close to, and showing signals of distress. At the moment, no other sail was in sight.

Cursing the necessity of pausing with a strong fair wind at a juncture like this, the officer-of-the-deck shortened sail, and hove to; hailing the cutter, to know what was the matter. As he hailed the small craft from the lofty poop of the bristling seventy-four, this lieutenant seemed standing on the top of Gibraltar,[4] talking to some lowland peasant in a hut. The reply was, that in a sudden flaw of wind, which came nigh capsizing them, not an hour since, the cutter had lost all four foremast men by the violent jibing of a boom.[5] She wanted help to get back to port.

"You shall have one man," said the officer-of-the-deck, morosely.

"Let him be a good one then, for heaven's sake," said he in the cutter; "I ought to have at least two."

During this talk, Israel's curiosity had prompted him to dart up the ladder from the main-deck, and stand right in the gangway above, looking out on the strange craft. Meantime the order had been given to drop a boat. Thinking this a favorable chance, he stationed himself so that he should be the foremost to spring into the boat; though crowds of English sailors, eager as himself for the same opportunity to escape from foreign service, clung to the chains of the as yet imperfectly disciplined man-of-war. As the two men who had been lowered in the boat hooked her, when afloat, along to the gangway, Israel dropped like a comet into the stern-sheets,[6] stumbled forward, and seized an oar. In a moment more, all the oarsmen were in their places, and with a few strokes, the boat lay alongside the cutter.

"Take which of them you please," said the lieutenant in command, addressing the officer in the revenue-cutter, and motioning with his hand to his boat's crew, as if they were a parcel of carcasses of mutton, of which the first pick was offered to some customer. "Quick and choose. Sit down, men"—to the sailors. "Oh, you are in a great hurry to get rid of the king's service, ain't you? Brave chaps indeed!—Have you chosen your man?"

All this while the ten faces of the anxious oarsmen looked with mute longings and appealings towards the officer of the cutter; every face turned at the same angle, as if managed by one machine. And so they were. One motive.

"I take the freckled chap with the yellow hair—him;" pointing to Israel.

Nine of the upturned faces fell in sullen despair, and ere
Israel could spring to his feet, he felt a violent thrust in his rear
from the toes of one of the disappointed behind him.

"Jump, dobbin!"[7] cried the officer of the boat.

But Israel was already on board. Another moment, and the
boat and cutter parted. Ere long night fell, and the man-of-war
and her consorts were out of sight.

The revenue vessel resumed her course towards the nighest
port, worked by but four men: the captain, Israel, and two officers. The cabinboy was kept at the helm. As the only foremast
man, Israel was put to it pretty hard. Where there is but one
man to three masters, woe betide that lonely slave. Besides, it
was of itself severe work enough to manage the vessel thus short
of hands. But to make matters still worse, the captain and his
officers were ugly-tempered fellows. The one kicked, and the
others cuffed Israel. Whereupon, not sugared with his recent experiences, and maddened by his present hap,[8] Israel seeing himself alone at sea, with only three men, instead of a thousand, to
contend against, plucked up a heart, knocked the captain into
the lee scuppers,[9] and in his fury was about tumbling the first-
officer, a small wash of a fellow, plump overboard, when the
captain, jumping to his feet, seized him by his long yellow hair,
vowing he would slaughter him. Meantime the cutter flew foaming through the channel, as if in demoniac glee at this uproar on
her imperilled deck. While the consternation was at its height, a
dark body suddenly loomed at a moderate distance into view,
shooting right athwart the stern of the cutter. The next moment
a shot struck the water within a boat's length.

"Heave to, and send a boat on board!" roared a voice almost
as loud as the cannon.

"That's a war-ship," cried the captain of the revenue vessel,
in alarm; "but she ain't a countryman."

Meantime the officers and Israel stopped the cutter's way.

"Send a boat on board, or I'll sink you," again came roaring
from the stranger, followed by another shot, striking the water
still nearer the cutter.

"For God's sake, don't cannonade us. I haven't got the crew to
man a boat," replied the captain of the cutter. "Who are you?"

"Wait till I send a boat to you for that," replied the stranger.

"She's an enemy of some sort, that's plain," said the Englishman now to his officers; "we ain't at open war with France; she's some blood-thirsty pirate or other. What d' ye say, men," turning to his officers; "let's outsail her, or be shot to chips. We can beat her at sailing, I know."

With that, nothing doubting that his counsel would be heartily responded to, he ran to the braces to get the cutter before the wind, followed by one officer, while the other, for a useless bravado, hoisted the colors at the stern.

But Israel stood indifferent, or rather all in a fever of conflicting emotions. He thought he recognized the voice from the strange vessel.

"Come, what do ye standing there, fool? Spring to the ropes here!" cried the furious captain.

But Israel did not stir.

Meantime, the confusion on board the stranger, owing to the hurried lowering of her boat, with the cloudiness of the sky darkening the misty sea, united to conceal the bold manœuvre of the cutter. She had almost gained full headway ere an oblique shot, directed by mere chance, struck her stern, tearing the upcurved head of the tiller in the hands of the cabin-boy, and killing him with the splinters. Running to the stump, the captain huzzaed, and steered the reeling ship on. Forced now to hoist back the boat ere giving chase, the stranger was dropped rapidly astern.

All this while storms of maledictions were hurled on Israel. But their exertions at the ropes prevented his shipmates for the time from using personal violence. While observing their efforts, Israel could not but say to himself, "These fellows are as brave as they are brutal."

Soon the stranger was seen dimly wallowing along astern, crowding all sail in chase, while now and then her bow-gun, showing its red tongue, bellowed after them like a mad bull. Two more shots struck the cutter, but without materially damaging her sails, or the ropes immediately upholding them. Several of her less important stays[10] were sundered, however; whose loose tarry ends lashed the air like scorpions. It seemed

not improbable that owing to her superior sailing, the keen cutter would yet get clear.

At this juncture, Israel, running towards the captain, who
still held the splintered stump of tiller, stood full before him,
saying, "I am an enemy, a Yankee; look to yourself."

"Help here, lads, help," roared the captain, "a traitor, a
traitor!"

The words were hardly out of his mouth when his voice was
silenced for ever. With one prodigious heave of his whole physical force, Israel smote him over the taffrail[11] into the sea, as if
the man had fallen backwards over a teetering chair. By this
time the two officers were hurrying aft. Ere meeting them midway, Israel, quick as lightning, cast off the two principal halyards[12], thus letting the large sails all in a tumble of canvas to
the deck. Next moment one of the officers was at the helm, to
prevent the cutter from capsizing by being without a steersman
in such an emergency. The other officer and Israel interlocked.
The battle was in the midst of the chaos of blowing canvas.
Caught in a rent of the sail, the officer slipped and fell near the
sharp iron edge of the hatchway. As he fell, he caught Israel by
the most terrible part in which mortality can be grappled.
Insane with pain, Israel dashed his adversary's skull against
the sharp iron. The officer's hold relaxed; but himself stiffened.
Israel made for the helmsman, who as yet knew not the issue of
the late tussel. He caught him round the loins, bedding his
fingers like grisly claws into his flesh, and hugging him to his
heart. The man's ghost, caught like a broken cork in a gurgling
bottle's neck, gasped with the embrace. Loosening him suddenly, Israel hurled him from him against the bulwarks. That
instant another report was heard, followed by the savage hail—
"You down sail at last, do ye? I'm a good mind to sink ye, for
your scurvy trick. Pull down that dirty rag there, astern!"

With a loud huzza, Israel hauled down the flag with one
hand, while with the other he helped the now slowly gliding
craft from falling off before the wind.

In a few moments a boat was alongside. As its commander
stepped to the deck, he stumbled against the body of the first-
officer, which, owing to the sudden slant of the cutter in coming

to the wind, had rolled against the side near the gangway. As he came aft, he heard the moan of the other officer, where he lay under the mizzen shrouds.

"What is all this?" demanded the stranger of Israel.

"It means that I am a Yankee impressed into the king's service; and for their pains I have taken the cutter."

Giving vent to his surprise, the officer looked narrowly at the body by the shrouds, and said, "this man is as good as dead; but we will take him to Captain Paul as a witness in your behalf."

"Captain Paul?—Paul Jones?" cried Israel.

"The same."

"I thought so. I thought that was his voice hailing. It was Captain Paul's voice that somehow put me up to this deed."

"Captain Paul is the devil for putting men up to be tigers. But where are the rest of the crew?"

"Overboard."

"What?" cried the officer; "come on board the Ranger.[13] Captain Paul will use you for a broadside."[14]

Taking the moaning man along with them, and leaving the cutter untenanted by any living soul, the boat now left her for the enemy's ship. But ere they reached it, the man had expired.

Standing foremost on the deck, crowded with three hundred men, as Israel climbed the side, he saw, by the light of battle-lanthorns,[15] a small, swart, brigandish-looking man, wearing a Scotch bonnet, with a gold band to it.

"You rascal," said this person, "why did your paltry smack give me this chase? Where's the rest of your gang?"

"Captain Paul," said Israel, "I believe I remember you. I believe I offered you my bed in Paris some months ago. How is Poor Richard?"

"God! Is this the courier? The Yankee courier? But how now; in an English revenue cutter?"

"Impressed, sir; that's the way."

"But where's the rest of them?" demanded Paul, turning to the officer.

Thereupon the officer very briefly told Paul what Israel had told him.

"Are we to sink the cutter, sir?" said the gunner, now advancing towards Captain Paul. "If it is to be done, now is the time. She is close under us, astern; a few guns pointed downwards, will settle her like a shotted corpse."

"No. Let her drift into Penzance,[16] an anonymous earnest of what the white-squall in Paul Jones intends for the future."

Then giving directions as to the course of the ship, with an order for himself to be called at the first glimpse of a sail, Paul took Israel down with him into his cabin.

"Tell me your story now, my yellow lion. How was it all? Don't stand; sit right down there on the transom. I'm a democratic sort of sea-king. Plump on the wool-sack, I say, and spin the yarn. But hold; you want some grog first."

As Paul handed the flagon, Israel's eye fell upon his hand.

"You don't wear any rings now, Captain, I see. Left them in Paris for safety."

"Aye, with a certain marchioness there," replied Paul, with a dandyish look of sentimental conceit, which sat strangely enough on his otherwise grim and Fejee[17] air.

"I should think rings would be somewhat inconvenient at sea," resumed Israel. "On my first voyage to the West Indies, I wore a girl's ring on my middle finger here, and it wasn't long before, what with hauling wet ropes, and what not, it got a kind of grown down into the flesh, and pained me very bad, let me tell you, it hugged the finger so."

"And did the girl grow as close to your heart, lad?"

"Ah, Captain, girls grow themselves off quicker than we grow them on."

"Some experience with the countesses as well as myself, eh? But the story; wave your yellow mane, my lion—the story."

So Israel went on, and told the story in all particulars.

At its conclusion, Captain Paul eyed him very earnestly. His wild, lonely heart, incapable of sympathizing with cuddled natures made hum-drum by long exemption from pain, was yet drawn towards a being, who in desperation of friendlessness, something like his own, had so fiercely waged battle against tyrannical odds.

"Did you go to sea young, lad?"

"Yes, pretty young."

"I went at twelve, from Whitehaven. Only so high," raising his hand some four feet from the deck. "I was so small, and looked so queer in my little blue jacket, that they called me the monkey. They'll call me something else before long. Did you ever sail out of Whitehaven?"

"No, Captain."

"If you had, you'd have heard sad stories about me. To this hour they say there that I,—blood-thirsty—coward dog that I am,—flogged a sailor, one Mungo Maxwell, to death.[18] It's a lie, by heaven! I flogged him, for he was a mutinous scamp. But he died naturally, some time afterwards, and on board another ship. But why talk? They didn't believe the affidavits of others taken before London courts, triumphantly acquitting me; how then will they credit *my* interested words? If slander, however much a lie, once gets hold of a man, it will stick closer than fair fame, as black pitch sticks closer than white cream. But let 'em slander. I will give the slanderers matter for curses. When last I left Whitehaven, I swore never again to set foot on her pier, except, like Cæsar, at Sandwich,[19] as a foreign invader. Spring under me, good ship; on you I bound to my vengeance!"

Men with poignant feelings, buried under an air of care-free self-command, are never proof to the sudden incitements of passion. Though in the main, they may control themselves, yet if they but once permit the smallest vent, then they may bid adieu to all self-restraint, at least for that time. Thus with Paul on the present occasion. His sympathy with Israel had prompted this momentary ebullition. When it was gone by, he seemed not a little to regret it. But he passed it over lightly, saying, "You see, my fine fellow, what sort of a bloody cannibal I am. Will you be a sailor of mine? A sailor of the captain who flogged poor Mungo Maxwell to death?"

"I will be very happy, Captain Paul, to be sailor under the man who will yet, I dare say, help flog the British nation to death."

"You hate 'em, do ye?"

"Like snakes. For months they've hunted me as a dog," half howled and half wailed Israel, at the memory of all he had suffered.

"Give me your hand, my lion; wave your wild flax again. By heaven, you hate so well, I love ye. You shall be my confidential man; stand sentry at my cabin door; sleep in the cabin; steer my boat; keep by my side whenever I land. What do you say?"

"I say I'm glad to hear you."

"You are a good, brave soul. You are the first among the millions of mankind that I ever naturally took to. Come, you are tired. There, go into that state-room for to-night—it's mine. You offered me your bed in Paris."

"But you begged off, Captain, and so must I. Where do you sleep?"

"Lad, I don't sleep half a night out of three. My clothes have not been off now for five days."

"Ah, Captain, you sleep so little and scheme so much, you will die young."

"I know it: I want to: I mean to. Who would live a doddered old stump? What do you think of my Scotch bonnet?"

"It looks well on you, Captain."

"Do you think so? A Scotch bonnet though, ought to look well on a Scotchman. I'm such by birth. Is the gold band too much?"

"I like the gold band, Captain. It looks something as I should think a crown might on a king."

"Aye."

"You would make a better looking king than George III."

"Did you ever see that old granny? Waddles about in farthingales,[20] and carries a peacock fan, don't he? Did you ever see him?"

"Was as close to him as I am to you now, captain. In Kew Gardens it was, where I worked gravelling the walks. I was all alone with him, talking for some ten minutes."

"By Jove, what a chance! Had I but been there! What an opportunity for kidnapping a British king, and carrying him off in a fast-sailing smack[21] to Boston, a hostage for American freedom. But what did you? Didn't you try to do something to him?"

"I had a wicked thought or two, captain; but I got the better of it. Besides, the king behaved handsomely towards me; yes, like a true man. God bless him for it. But it was before that, that I got the better of the wicked thought."

"Ah, meant to stick him, I suppose. Glad you didn't. It would have been very shabby. Never kill a king, but make him captive. He looks better as a led horse, than a dead carcass. I propose now, this trip, falling on the grounds of the Earl of Selkirk,[22] a privy counsellor, and particular private friend of George III. But I won't hurt a hair of his head. When I get him on board here, he shall lodge in my best state-room, which I mean to hang with damask for him. I shall drink wine with him, and be very friendly; take him to America, and introduce his lordship into the best circles there; only I shall have him accompanied on his calls by a sentry or two disguised as valets. For the earl's to be on sale, mind; so much ransom; that is, the nobleman, Lord Selkirk, shall have a bodily price pinned on his coat-tail, like any slave up at auction in Charleston. But, my lad with the yellow mane, you very strangely draw out my secrets. And yet you don't talk. Your honesty is a magnet which attracts my sincerity. But I rely on your fidelity."

"I shall be a vice to your plans, Captain Paul. I will receive, but I won't let go, unless you alone loose the screw."

"Well said. To bed now; you ought to. I go on deck. Good-night, ace-of-hearts."

"That is fitter for yourself, Captain Paul; lonely leader of the suit."

"Lonely? Aye, but number one cannot but be lonely, my trump."

"Again I give it back. Ace-of-trumps may it prove to you, Captain Paul; may it be impossible for you ever to be taken. But for me—poor deuce, a trey, that comes in your wake—any king or knave may take me, as before now the knaves have."

"Tut, tut, lad; never be more cheery for another than for yourself. But a fagged body fags the soul. To hammock, to hammock! while I go on deck to clap on more sail to your cradle."

And they separated for that night.

CHAPTER 15

*They Sail as Far as the
Crag of Ailsa*

Next morning Israel was appointed quarter-master; a subaltern selected from the common seamen, and whose duty mostly stations him in the stern of the ship, where the captain walks. His business is to carry the glass on the look-out for sails; hoist or lower the colors; and keep an eye on the helmsman. Picked out from the crew for their superior respectability and intelligence, as well as for their excellent seamanship, it is not unusual to find the quarter-masters of an armed ship on peculiarly easy terms with the commissioned officers and captain. This berth, therefore, placed Israel in official contiguity to Paul, and without subjecting either to animadversion, made their public intercourse on deck almost as familiar as their unrestrained converse in the cabin.

It was a fine cool day in the beginning of April. They were now off the coast of Wales,[1] whose lofty mountains, crested with snow, presented a Norwegian aspect. The wind was fair, and blew with a strange, bestirring power. The ship—running between Ireland and England, northwards, towards the Irish Sea, the inmost heart of the British waters—seemed, as she snortingly shook the spray from her bow, to be conscious of the dare-devil defiance of the soul which conducted her on this anomalous cruise. Sailing alone from out a naval port of France, crowded with ships-of-the-line, Paul Jones, in his small craft, went forth in single-armed championship against the English host. Armed with but the sling-stones in his one shot-locker, like young David of old, Paul bearded the British giant of Gath.[2] It is not easy, at the present day, to conceive the hardihood of this enterprise. It was a marching up to the muzzle.

The act of one who made no compromise with the cannonad-
ings of danger or death; such a scheme as only could have
inspired a heart which held at nothing all the prescribed prudence of war, and every obligation of peace; combining in one
breast the vengeful indignation and bitter ambition of an out-
raged hero, with the uncompunctuous desperation of a renegade. In one view, the Coriolanus[3] of the sea; in another, a cross
between the gentleman and the wolf.

As Paul stood on the elevated part of the quarter-deck, with
none but his confidential quarter-master near him, he yielded
to Israel's natural curiosity, to learn something concerning the
sailing of the expedition. Paul stood lightly, swaying his body
over the sea, by holding on to the mizzen-shrouds,[4] an attitude
not inexpressive of his easy audacity; while near by, pacing a
few steps to and fro, his long spy glass now under his arm, and
now presented at his eye, Israel, looking the very image of vigilant prudence, listened to the warrior's story. It appeared that
on the night of the visit of the Duke de Chartres and Count
D'Estaing to Doctor Franklin in Paris—the same night that
Captain Paul and Israel were joint occupants of the neighboring chamber—the final sanction of the French king to the sailing of an American armament against England, under the
direction of the Colonial Commissioner,[5] was made known to
the latter functionary. It was a very ticklish affair. Though
swaying on the brink of avowed hostilities with England, no
verbal declaration had as yet been made by France. Undoubtedly, this enigmatic position of things was highly advantageous
to such an enterprise as Paul's.

Without detailing all the steps taken through the united
efforts of Captain Paul and Doctor Franklin, suffice it that the
determined rover had now attained his wish; the unfettered
command of an armed ship in the British waters; a ship legiti-
mately authorized to hoist the American colors; her commander having in his cabin-locker a regular commission as an
officer of the American navy. He sailed without any instructions. With that rare insight into rare natures which so largely
distinguished the sagacious Franklin, the sage well knew that a
prowling *brave*, like Paul Jones, was, like the prowling lion, by

nature a solitary warrior. "Let him alone;" was the wise man's answer to some statesman who sought to hamper Paul with a letter of instructions.

Much subtle casuistry has been expended upon the point, whether Paul Jones was a knave or a hero, or a union of both. But war and warriors, like politics and politicians, like religion and religionists, admit of no metaphysics.

On the second day after Israel's arrival on board the Ranger, as he and Paul were conversing on the deck, Israel suddenly levelling his glass towards the Irish coast, announced a large sail bound in. The Ranger gave chase, and soon, almost within sight of her destination—the port of Dublin—the stranger was taken, manned, and turned round for Brest.

The Ranger then stood over, passed the Isle of Man towards the Cumberland shore,[6] arriving within remote sight of White-haven about sunset. At dark she was hovering off the harbor, with a party of volunteers all ready to descend. But the wind shifted and blew fresh, with a violent sea.

"I won't call on old friends in foul weather," said Captain Paul to Israel. "We'll saunter about a little, and leave our cards in a day or two."

Next morning, in Glentinebay, on the south shore of Scotland, they fell in with a revenue wherry.[7] It was the practice of such craft to board merchant vessels. The Ranger was disguised as a merchantman, presenting a broad drab-colored belt all round her hull; under the coat of a Quaker, concealing the intent of a Turk. It was expected that the chartered rover would come alongside the uncharetered one. But the former took to flight, her two lug sails staggering under a heavy wind, which the pursuing guns of the Ranger pelted with a hail-storm of shot. The wherry escaped, spite the severe cannonade.

Off the Mull of Galloway,[8] the day following, Paul found himself so nigh a large barley-freighted Scotch coaster, that, to prevent her carrying tidings of him to land, he dispatched her with the news, stern foremost, to Hades; sinking her, and sow-ing her barley in the sea, broadcast by a broadside. From her crew he learned that there was a fleet of twenty or thirty sail at anchor in Lochryan,[9] with an armed brigantine. He pointed his prow thither; but at the mouth of the loch, the wind turned against him again, in hard squalls. He abandoned the project. Shortly after, he encountered a sloop from Dublin. He sunk her to prevent intelligence.

Thus, seeming as much to bear the elemental commission of Nature, as the military warrant of Congress, swarthy Paul darted hither and thither; hovering like a thunder-cloud off the crowded harbors; then, beaten off by an adverse wind, discharging his lightnings on uncompanioned vessels, whose solitude made them a more conspicuous and easier mark, like lonely trees on the heath. Yet all this while the land was full of garrisons, the embayed waters full of fleets. With the impunity of a Levanter,[10] Paul skimmed his craft in the land-locked heart of the supreme naval power of earth; a torpedo-eel, unknowingly swallowed by Britain in a draught of old ocean, and making sad havoc with her vitals.

Seeing next a large vessel steering for the Clyde,[11] he gave chase, hoping to cut her off. The stranger proving a fast sailer, the pursuit was urged on with vehemence, Paul standing, plank-proud, on the quarter-deck, calling for pulls upon every rope, to stretch each already half-burst sail to the uttermost.

While thus engaged, suddenly a shadow, like that thrown by an eclipse, was seen rapidly gaining along the deck, with a sharp defined line, plain as a seam of the planks. It involved all before it. It was the domineering shadow of the Juan Fernandez-like Crag of Ailsa.[12] The Ranger was in the deep water which makes all round and close up to this great summit of the submarine Grampians.[13]

The crag, more than a mile in circuit, is over a thousand feet high, eight miles from the Ayrshire shore. There stands the cone, lonely as a foundling, proud as Cheops.[14] But, like the battered brains surmounting the Giant of Gath, its haughty summit is crowned by a desolate castle, in and out of whose arches the aerial mists eddy like purposeless phantoms, thronging the soul of some ruinous genius, who, even in overthrow, harbors none but lofty conceptions.

As the Ranger shot nigher under the crag, its height and bulk dwarfed both pursuer and pursued into nut-shells. The main-truck of the Ranger was nine hundred feet below the foundations of the ruin on the crag's top.

While the ship was yet under the shadow, and each seaman's face shared in the general eclipse, a sudden change came over Paul. He issued no more sultanical orders. He did not look so elate as before. At length he gave the command to discontinue the chase. Turning about, they sailed southward.

"Captain Paul," said Israel, shortly afterwards, "you changed your mind rather queerly about catching that craft. But you thought she was drawing us too far up into the land, I suppose."

"Sink the craft," cried Paul; "it was not any fear of her, nor of King George, which made me turn on my heel; it was yon cock of the walk."[15]

"Cock of the walk?"

"Aye; cock of the walk of the sea; look,—yon Crag of Ailsa."

CHAPTER 16

They Look in at Carrickfergus, and Descend on Whitehaven

Next day, off Carrickfergus, on the Irish coast, a fishing boat, allured by the Quaker-like look of the incognito craft, came off in full confidence. Her men were seized, their vessel sunk. From them Paul learned that the large ship at anchor in the road, was the ship-of-war Drake,[1] of twenty guns. Upon this he steered away, resolving to return secretly, and attack her that night.

"Surely, Captain Paul," said Israel to his commander, as about sunset they backed and stood in again for the land, "surely, sir, you are not going right in among them this way? Why not wait till she comes out?"

"Because, Yellow-hair, my boy, I am engaged to marry her to-night. The bride's friends won't like the match; and so, this very night, the bride must be carried away. She has a nice tapering waist, hasn't she, through the glass? Ah! I will clasp her to my heart."

He steered straight in like a friend; under easy sail, lounging towards the Drake, with anchor ready to drop, and grapnels[2] to hug. But the wind was high; the anchor was not dropped at the ordered time. The Ranger came to a stand three biscuits' toss off the unmisgiving enemy's quarter, like a peaceful merchantman from the Canadas, laden with harmless lumber.

"I shan't marry her just yet," whispered Paul, seeing his plans for the time frustrated. Gazing in audacious tranquillity upon the decks of the enemy; and amicably answering her hail, with complete self-possession, he commanded the cable to be slipped, and then, as if he had accidentally parted his anchor, turned his prow on the seaward tack, meaning to return again

immediately with the same prospect of advantage possessed at
first. His plan being to crash suddenly athwart the Drake's
bow, so as to have all her decks exposed point-blank to his
musketry. But once more the winds interposed. It came on with
a storm of snow; he was obliged to give up his project.

Thus, without any warlike appearance, and giving no alarm,
Paul, like an invisible ghost, glided by night close to land, actually came to anchor, for an instant, within speaking-distance of
an English ship-of-war; and yet came, anchored, answered hail,
reconnoitered, debated, decided, and retired, without exciting
the least suspicion. His purpose was chain-shot destruction.
So easily may the deadliest foe—so he be but dexterous—slide,
undreamed of, into human harbors or hearts. And not awakened
conscience, but mere prudence, restrain such, if they vanish
again without doing harm. At daybreak no soul in Carrickfergus
knew that the devil, in a Scotch bonnet, had passed close that
way over night.

Seldom has regicidal daring been more strangely coupled
with octogenarian prudence, than in many of the predatory enterprises of Paul. It is this combination of apparent incompati-
bilities which ranks him among extraordinary warriors.

Ere daylight, the storm of the night blew over. The sun saw
the Ranger lying midway over channel at the head of the Irish
Sea; England, Scotland, and Ireland, with all their lofty cliffs,
being simultaneously as plainly in sight beyond the grass-green
waters, as the City Hall, St. Paul's, and the Astor House, from
the triangular Park in New York.[3] The three kingdoms lay covered with snow, far as the eye could reach.

"Ah, Yellow-hair," said Paul, with a smile, "they show the
white flag, the cravens. And, while the white flag stays blanket-
ing yonder heights, we'll make for Whitehaven,[4] my boy. I
promised to drop in there a moment ere quitting the country
for good. Israel, lad, I mean to step ashore in person, and have
a personal hand in the thing. Did you ever drive spikes?"

"I've driven the spike-teeth into harrows[5] before now,"
replied Israel; "but that was before I was a sailor."

"Well then, driving spikes into harrows is a good introduction to driving spikes into cannon. You are just the man. Put

down your glass; go to the carpenter, get a hundred spikes, put them in a bucket with a hammer, and bring all to me."

As evening fell, the great promontory of St. Bees Head, with its lighthouse, not far from Whitehaven, was in distant sight. But the wind became so light, that Paul could not work his ship in close enough at an hour as early as intended. His purpose had been to make the descent and retire ere break of day. But though this intention was frustrated, he did not renounce his plan, for the present would be his last opportunity.

As the night wore on, and the ship with a very light wind glided nigher and nigher the mark, Paul called upon Israel to produce his bucket for final inspection. Thinking some of the spikes too large, he had them filed down a little. He saw to the lanterns and combustibles. Like Peter the Great,[6] he went into the smallest details, while still possessing a genius competent to plan the aggregate. But oversee as one may, it is impossible to guard against carelessness in subordinates. One's sharp eyes can't see behind one's back. It will yet be noted that an important omission was made in the preparations for Whitehaven.

The town contained, at that period, a population of some six or seven thousand inhabitants, defended by forts.

At midnight, Paul Jones, Israel Potter, and twenty-nine others, rowed in two boats to attack the six or seven thousand inhabitants of Whitehaven. There was a long way to pull. This was done in perfect silence. Not a sound was heard except the oars turning in the rowlocks. Nothing was seen except the two lighthouses of the harbor. Through the stilness and the darkness, the two deep-laden boats swam into the haven, like two mysterious whales from the Arctic Sea. As they reached the outer pier, the men saw each other's faces. The day was dawning. The riggers and other artisans of the shipping would before very long be astir. No matter.

The great staple exported from Whitehaven was then, and still is, coal. The town is surrounded by mines; the town is built on mines; its ships moor over mines. The mines honeycomb the land in all directions, and extend in galleries of grottoes for two miles under the sea. By the falling in of the more ancient collieries,[7] numerous houses have been swallowed, as if by an earthquake; and a consternation spread like that of Lisbon, in 1755.[8] So insecure and treacherous was the site of the place now about to be assailed by a desperado, nursed, like the coal, in its vitals.

Now, sailing on the Thames, nigh its mouth, of fair days, when the wind is favorable for inward bound craft, the stranger will sometimes see processions of vessels, all of similar size and rig, stretching for miles and miles, like a long string of horses tied two and two to a rope and driven to market. These are colliers going to London with coal.

About three hundred of these vessels now lay, all crowded together, in one dense mob, at Whitehaven. The tide was out. They lay completely helpless, clear of water, and grounded. They were sooty in hue. Their black yards were deeply canted,[9] like spears, to avoid collision. The three hundred grimy hulls lay wallowing in the mud, like a herd of hippopotami asleep in the alluvium of the Nile. Their sailless, raking masts, and canted yards, resembled a forest of fish-spears thrust into those same hippopotamus hides. Partly flanking one side of the grounded fleet was a fort, whose batteries were raised from the beach. On a little strip of this beach, at the base of the fort, lay a number of small rusty guns, dismounted, heaped together in disorder, as a litter of dogs. Above them projected the mounted cannon.

Paul landed in his own boat at the foot of this fort. He dispatched the other boat to the north side of the haven, with orders to fire the shipping there. Leaving two men at the beach, he then proceeded to get possession of the fort.

"Hold on to the bucket, and give me your shoulder," said he to Israel.

Using Israel for a ladder, in a trice he scaled the wall. The bucket and the men followed. He led the way softly to the guard-house, burst in, and bound the sentinels in their sleep. Then arranging his force, ordered four men to spike the cannon there.

"Now, Israel, your bucket, and follow me to the other fort." The two went alone about a quarter of a mile.

"Captain Paul," said Israel, on the way, "can we two manage the sentinels?"

"There are none in the fort we go to."

"You know all about the place, captain?"

"Pretty well informed on that subject, I believe. Come along. Yes, lad, I am tolerably well acquainted with Whitehaven. And this morning intend that Whitehaven shall have a slight inkling of *me*. Come on. Here we are."

Scaling the walls, the two involuntarily stood for an instant gazing upon the scene. The gray light of the dawn showed the crowded houses and thronged ships with a haggard distinctness.

"Spike and hammer, lad;—so,—now follow me along, as I go, and give me a spike for every cannon. I'll tongue-tie the thunderers. Speak no more!" and he spiked the first gun. "Be a mute," and he spiked the second. "Dumfounder thee," and he spiked the third. And so, on, and on, and on; Israel following him with the bucket, like a footman, or some charitable gentleman with a basket of alms.

"There, it is done. D'ye see the fire yet, lad, from the north? I don't."

"Not a spark, Captain. But day-sparks come on in the east."

"Forked flames into the hounds! What are they about? Quick, let us back to the first fort; perhaps something has happened, and they are there."

Sure enough, on their return from spiking the cannon Paul and Israel found the other boat back; the crew in confusion; their lantern having burnt out at the very instant they wanted it. By a singular fatality the other lantern, belonging to Paul's boat, was likewise extinguished. No tinder-box had been brought. They had no matches but sulphur matches. Loco-focos[10] were not then known.

The day came on apace.

"Captain Paul," said the lieutenant of the second boat, "it is madness to stay longer. See!" and he pointed to the town, now plainly discernible in the grey light.

"Traitor, or coward!" howled Paul, "how came the lanterns out? Israel, my lion, now prove your blood. Get me a light—but one spark!"

"Has any man here a bit of pipe and tobacco in his pocket?" said Israel.

A sailor quickly produced an old stump of a pipe, with tobacco.

"That will do;" and Israel hurried away towards the town.

"What will the loon do with the pipe?" said one. "And where goes he?" cried another.

"Let him alone," said Paul.

The invader now disposed his whole force so as to retreat at an instant's warning. Meantime, the hardy Israel, long experienced in all sorts of shifts and emergencies, boldly ventured to procure, from some inhabitant of Whitehaven, a spark to kindle all Whitehaven's habitations in flames.

There was a lonely house standing somewhat disjoined from the town; some poor laborer's abode. Rapping at the door, Israel, pipe in mouth, begged the inmates for a light for his tobacco.

"What the devil," roared a voice from within; "knock up a man this time of night, to light your pipe? Begone!"

"You are lazy this morning, my friend," replied Israel; "it is daylight. Quick, give me a light. Don't you know your old friend? Shame! open the door."

In a moment a sleepy fellow appeared, let down the bar, and Israel, stalking into the dim room, piloted himself straight to the fire-place, raked away the cinders, lighted his tobacco, and vanished.

All was done in a flash. The man, stupid with sleep, had looked on bewildered. He reeled to the door; but dodging behind a pile of bricks, Israel had already hurried himself out of sight.

"Well done, my lion," was the hail he received from Paul, who, during his absence, had mustered as many pipes as possible, in order to communicate and multiply the fire.

Both boats now pulled to a favorable point of the principal pier of the harbor, crowded close up to a part of which lay one wing of the colliers.

The men began to murmur at persisting in an attempt impossible to be concealed much longer. They were afraid to venture on board the grim colliers, and go groping down into their hulls to fire them. It seemed like a voluntary entrance into dungeons and death.

"Follow me, all of you but ten by the boats," said Paul, without noticing their murmurs. "And now, to put an end to all future burnings in America, by one mighty conflagration of shipping in England. Come on, lads! Pipes and matches in the van!"

He would have distributed the men so as simultaneously to fire different ships at different points, were it not that the lateness of the hour rendered such a course insanely hazardous. Stationing his party in front of one of the windward colliers, Paul and Israel sprang on board.

In a twinkling, they had broken open a boatswain's locker, and, with great bunches of oakum,[11] fine and dry as tinder, had leaped into the steerage. Here, while Paul made a blaze, Israel ran to collect the tar-pots, which being presently poured on the burning matches, oakum and wood, soon increased the flame.

"It is not a sure thing yet," said Paul, "we must have a barrel of tar."

They searched about until they found one: knocked out the head and bottom, and stood it like a martyr in the midst of the flames. They then retreated up the forward hatchway, while volumes of smoke were belched from the after one. Not till this moment did Paul hear the cries of his men, warning him that the inhabitants were not only actually astir, but crowds were on their way to the pier.

As he sprang out of the smoke towards the rail of the collier, he saw the sun risen, with thousands of the people. Individuals hurried close to the burning vessel. Leaping to the ground, Paul, bidding his men stand fast, ran to their front, and, advancing about thirty feet, presented his own pistol at now tumultuous Whitehaven.

Those who had rushed to extinguish what they had deemed but an accidental fire, were now paralyzed into idiotic inaction at the defiance of the incendiary; thinking him some sudden pirate or fiend dropped down from the moon.

While Paul thus stood guarding the incipient conflagration, Israel, without a weapon, dashed crazily towards the mob on the shore.

"Come back, come back," cried Paul.

"Not till I start these sheep, as their own wolves many a time started me!"

As he rushed bare-headed, like a madman, towards the crowd, the panic spread. They fled from unarmed Israel, further than they had from the pistol of Paul.

The flames now catching the rigging and spiralling around the masts, the whole ship burned at one end of the harbor, while the sun, an hour high, burned at the other. Alarm and amazement, not sleep, now ruled the world. It was time to retreat.

They re-embarked without opposition, first releasing a few prisoners, as the boats could not carry them.

Just as Israel was leaping into the boat, he saw the man at whose house he had procured the fire, staring like a simpleton at him.

"That was good seed you gave me," said Israel, "see what a yield;" pointing to the flames. He then dropped into the boat, leaving only Paul on the pier.

The men cried to their commander, conjuring him not to linger.

But Paul remained for several moments, confronting in silence the clamors of the mob beyond, and waving his solitary hand, like a disdainful tomahawk, towards the surrounding eminences, also covered with the affrighted inhabitants.

When the assailants had rowed pretty well off, the English rushed in great numbers to their forts, but only to find their cannon no better than so much iron in the ore. At length, however, they began to fire, having either brought down some ship's guns, or else mounted the rusty old dogs lying at the foot of the first fort.

In their eagerness they fired with no discretion. The shot fell short; they did not the slightest damage.

Paul's men laughed aloud, and fired their pistols in the air.

Not a splinter was made, not a drop of blood spilled throughout the affair. The intentional harmlessness of the result, as to human life, was only equalled by the desperate courage of the deed. It formed, doubtless, one feature of the compassionate contempt of Paul towards the town, that he took such paternal care of their lives and limbs.

Had it been possible to have landed a few hours earlier, not a ship nor a house could have escaped. But it was the lesson, not the loss, that told. As it was, enough damage had been done to demonstrate—as Paul had declared to the wise man in Paris—that the disasters caused by the wanton fires and assaults on the American coasts, could be easily brought home to the enemy's doors. Though, indeed, if the retaliators were headed by Paul Jones, the satisfaction would not be equal to the insult, being abated by the magnanimity of a chivalrous, however unprincipled a foe.

CHAPTER 17

They Call at the Earl of
Selkirk's; and Afterwards
Fight the Ship-of-war Drake

The Ranger now stood over the Solway Frith[1] for the Scottish shore, and at noon on the same day, Paul, with twelve men, including two officers and Israel, landed on St. Mary's Isle, one of the seats of the Earl of Selkirk.[2]

In three consecutive days this elemental warrior either entered the harbors, or landed on the shores of each of the Three Kingdoms.[3]

The morning was fair and clear. St. Mary's Isle lay shimmering in the sun. The light crust of snow had melted, revealing the tender grass and sweet buds of spring mantling the sides of the cliffs.

At once, upon advancing with his party towards the house, Paul augured ill for his project from the loneliness of the spot. No being was seen. But cocking his bonnet at a jaunty angle, he continued his way. Stationing the men silently round about the house, followed by Israel, he announced his presence at the porch.

A grey-headed domestic at length responded.

"Is the earl within?"

"He is in Edinburgh, sir."

"Ah—sure?—Is your lady within?"

"Yes, sir—who shall I say it is?"

"A gentleman who calls to pay his respects. Here, take my card."

And he handed the man his name, as a private gentleman, superbly engraved at Paris, on gilded paper.

Israel tarried in the hall while the old servant led Paul into a parlor.

Presently the lady appeared.

"Charming Madame, I wish you a very good morning."

"Who may it be, sir, that I have the happiness to see?" said the lady, censoriously drawing herself up at the too frank gallantry of the stranger.

"Madame, I sent you my card."

"Which leaves me equally ignorant, sir," said the lady coldly, twirling the gilded pasteboard.

"A courier dispatched to Whitehaven, charming Madame, might bring you more particular tidings as to who has the honor of being your visitor."

Not comprehending what this meant, and deeply displeased, if not vaguely alarmed at the characteristic manner of Paul, the lady, not entirely unembarrassed, replied, that if the gentleman came to view the isle, he was at liberty so to do. She would retire, and send him a guide.

"Countess of Selkirk," said Paul, advancing a step, "I call to see the earl. On business of urgent importance, I call."

"The earl is in Edinburgh," uneasily responded the lady, again about to retire.

"Do you give me your honor as a lady that it is as you say?"

The lady looked at him in dubious resentment.

"Pardon, Madame; I would not lightly impugn a lady's lightest word; but I surmised that, possibly, you might suspect the object of my call; in which case, it would be the most excusable thing in the world for you to seek to shelter from my knowledge the presence of the earl on the isle."

"I do not dream what you mean by all this," said the lady with decided alarm, yet even in her panic courageously maintaining her dignity, as she retired, rather than retreated, nearer the door.

"Madame," said Paul, hereupon waving his hand imploringly, and then tenderly playing with his bonnet with the golden band, while an expression poetically sad and sentimental stole over his tawny face; "it cannot be too poignantly lamented, that in the profession of arms, the officer of fine feelings and genuine sensibility should be sometimes necessitated to public actions which his own private heart cannot approve. This hard case is mine. The earl, Madame, you say is absent.—I believe those words. Far be it from my soul, enchantress, to ascribe a fault to syllables which have proceeded from so faultless a source."

This probably he said in reference to the lady's mouth, which was beautiful in the extreme.

He bowed very lowly, while the lady eyed him with conflicting and troubled emotions, but as yet all in darkness as to his ultimate meaning. But her more immediate alarm had subsided; seeing now, that the sailor-like extravagance of Paul's homage was entirely unaccompanied with any touch of intentional disrespect. Indeed, hyperbolical as were his phrases, his gestures and whole carriage were most heedfully deferential.

Paul continued: "The earl, Madame, being absent, and he being the sole object of my call, you can not labor under the least apprehension, when I now inform you, that I have the honor of being an officer in the American navy, who, having stopped at this isle to secure the person of the Earl of Selkirk as a hostage for the American cause, am, by your assurances, turned away from that intent; pleased, even in disappointment, since that disappointment has served to prolong my interview with the noble lady before me, as well as to leave her domestic tranquillity unimpaired."

"Can you really speak true?" said the lady in undismayed wonderment.

"Madame, through your window you will catch a little peep of the American colonial ship-of-war, Ranger, which I have the honor to command. With my best respects to your lord, and sincere regrets at not finding him at home, permit me to salute your ladyship's hand and withdraw."

But feigning not to notice this Parisian proposition, and artfully entrenching her hand, without seeming to do so, the lady, in a conciliatory tone, begged her visitor to partake of some refreshment ere he departed, at the same time thanking him for his great civility. But declining these hospitalities, Paul bowed thrice, and quitted the room.

In the hall he encountered Israel, standing all agape before a Highland target of steel, with a claymore and foil crossed on top.[4]

"Looks like a pewter platter and knife and fork, Captain Paul."

"So they do, my lion; but come, curse it, the old cock has flown; fine hen, though, left in the nest; no use; we must away empty-handed."

"Why, ain't Mr. Selkirk in?" demanded Israel in roguish concern.

"Mr. Selkirk? Alexander Selkirk,[5] you mean. No, lad, he's not on the Isle of St. Mary's; he's away off, a hermit, on the Isle of Juan Fernandes—the more's the pity; come."

In the porch they encountered the two officers. Paul briefly informed them of the circumstances; saying, nothing remained but to depart forthwith.

"With nothing at all for our pains?" murmured the two officers.

"What, pray, would you have?"

"Some pillage, to be sure—plate."[6]

"Shame. I thought we were three gentlemen."

"So are the English officers in America; but they help themselves to plate whenever they can get it from the private houses of the enemy."

"Come, now, don't be slanderous," said Paul; "these officers you speak of are but one or two out of twenty, mere burglars and light-fingered gentry, using the king's livery but as a disguise to their nefarious trade. The rest are men of honor."

"Captain Paul Jones," responded the two, "we have not come on this expedition in much expectation of regular pay; but we *did* rely upon honorable plunder."

"Honorable plunder! That's something new."

But the officers were not to be turned aside. They were the most efficient in the ship. Seeing them resolute, Paul, for fear of incensing them, was at last, as a matter of policy, obliged to comply. For himself, however, he resolved to have nothing to do with the affair. Charging the officers not to allow the men to enter the house on any pretence, and that no search must be made, and nothing must be taken away, except what the lady should offer them upon making known their demand, he beckoned to Israel and retired indignantly towards the beach. Upon second thoughts, he dispatched Israel back, to enter the house with the officers, as joint receiver of the plate, he being, of course, the most reliable of the seamen.

The lady was not a little disconcerted on receiving the officers. With cool determination they made known their purpose. There was no escape. The lady retired. The butler came; and soon, several silver salvers, and other articles of value, were silently deposited in the parlor in the presence of the officers and Israel.

"Mister Butler," said Israel, "let me go into the dairy and help to carry the milk-pans."

But, scowling upon this rusticity, or roguishness—he knew not which—the butler, in high dudgeon at Israel's republican familiarity, as well as black as a thunder-cloud with the general insult offered to an illustrious household by a party of armed thieves, as he viewed them, declined any assistance. In a quarter of an hour the officers left the house, carrying their booty.

At the porch they were met by a red-cheeked, spiteful-looking lass, who, with her brave lady's compliments, added two child's rattles of silver and coral to their load.

Now, one of the officers was a Frenchman, the other a Spaniard.

The Spaniard dashed his rattle indignantly to the ground. The Frenchman took his very pleasantly, and kissed it, saying to the girl that he would long preserve the coral, as a memento of her rosy cheeks.

When the party arrived on the beach, they found Captain Paul writing with pencil on paper held up against the smooth tabled side of the cliff. Next moment he seemed to be making his signature. With a reproachful glance towards the two officers, he handed the slip to Israel, bidding him hasten immediately with it to the house and place it in Lady Selkirk's own hands.

The note was as follows:—

"MADAME,—

"After so courteous a reception, I am disturbed to make you no better return than you have just experienced from the actions of certain persons under my command. Actions, lady, which my profession of arms obliges me not only to brook, but, in a measure, to countenance. From the bottom of my heart, my dear lady, I deplore this most melancholy necessity of my delicate position. However unhandsome the desire of these men, some complaisance seemed due them from me, for their general good conduct and bravery on former occasions. I had but an instant to consider. I trust, that in unavoidably gratifying them, I have inflicted less injury on your ladyship's property than I have on my own bleeding sensibilities. But my heart will not allow me to say more. Permit me to assure you, dear lady, that when the plate is sold, I shall, at all hazards, become the purchaser, and will be proud to restore it to you, by such conveyance as you may hereafter see fit to appoint.

"From hence I go, Madame, to engage, to-morrow morning, his majesty's ship Drake, of twenty guns, now lying at Carrickfergus. I should meet the enemy with more than wonted resolution, could I flatter myself that, through this unhandsome conduct on the part of my officers, I lie not under the disesteem of the sweet lady of the Isle of St. Mary's. But unconquerable as Mars[7] should I be, could I but dare to dream, that in some green retreat of her charming domain, the Countess of Selkirk offers up a charitable prayer for, my dear lady countess, one, who coming to take a captive, himself has been captivated.

"Your ladyship's adoring enemy,
"JOHN PAUL JONES."

How the lady received this super-ardent note, history does not relate. But history has not omitted to record, that after the return of the Ranger to France, through the assiduous efforts of Paul in buying up the booty, piece by piece, from the clutches of those among whom it had been divided, and not without a pecuniary private loss to himself, equal to the total value of the plunder, the plate was punctually restored, even to the silver heads of two pepper-boxes; and, not only this, but the earl, hearing all the particulars, magnanimously wrote Paul a letter, expressing thanks for his politeness. In the opinion of the noble earl, Paul was a man of honor. It were rash to differ in opinion with such high-born authority.

Upon returning to the ship, she was instantly pointed over towards the Irish coast. Next morning Carrickfergus was in sight. Paul would have gone straight in; but Israel, reconnoitering with his glass, informed him that a large ship, probably the Drake, was just coming out.

"What think you, Israel, do they know who we are? Let me have the glass."

"They are dropping a boat now sir," replied Israel, removing the glass from his eye, and handing it to Paul.

"So they are—so they are. They don't know us. I'll decoy that boat alongside. Quick—they are coming for us—take the helm now yourself, my lion, and keep the ship's stern steadily presented towards the advancing boat. Don't let them have the least peep at our broadside."

The boat came on; an officer in its bow all the time eyeing the Ranger through a glass. Presently the boat was within hail.

"Ship ahoy! Who are you?"

"Oh, come alongside," answered Paul through his trumpet, in a rapid off-hand tone, as though he were a gruff sort of friend, impatient at being suspected for a foe.

In a few moments the officer of the boat stepped into the Ranger's gangway. Cocking his bonnet gallantly, Paul advanced towards him, making a very polite bow, saying: "Good morning, sir, good morning; delighted to see you. That's a pretty sword you have; pray, let me look at it."

"I see," said the officer, glancing at the ship's armament, and turning pale. "I am your prisoner."

"No—my guest," responded Paul, winningly. "Pray, let me relieve you of your—your—cane."

Thus humorously he received the officer's delivered sword.

"Now tell me, sir, if you please," he continued; "what brings out his majesty's ship Drake, this fine morning? Going a little airing?"

"She comes out in search of you; but when I left her side half an hour since, she did not know that the ship off the harbor was the one she sought."

"You had news from Whitehaven, I suppose, last night, eh?"

"Aye: express; saying that certain incendiaries had landed there early that morning."

"What?—what sort of men were they, did you say?" said Paul, shaking his bonnet fiercely to one side of his head, and coming close to the officer. "Pardon me," he added derisively, "I had forgot; you are my *guest*. Israel, see the unfortunate gentleman below, and his men forward."

The Drake was now seen slowly coming out under a light air, attended by five small pleasure-vessels, decorated with flags and streamers, and full of gaily-dressed people, whom motives similar to those which draw visitors to the circus, had induced to embark on their adventurous trip. But they little dreamed how nigh the desperate enemy was.

"Drop the captured boat astern," said Paul; "see what effect that will have on those merry voyagers."

No sooner was the empty boat described by the pleasure-vessels, than forthwith surmising the truth, they with all diligence turned about and re-entered the harbor. Shortly after, alarm-smokes were seen extending along both sides of the channel.

"They smoke us at last, Captain Paul," said Israel.

"There will be more smoke yet before the day is done," replied Paul gravely.

The wind was right under the land; the tide unfavorable. The Drake worked out very slowly.

Meantime, like some fiery-heated duellist calling on urgent business at frosty daybreak, and long kept waiting at the door by the dilatoriness of his antagonist shrinking at the idea of getting up to be cut to pieces in the cold,—the Ranger, with a better breeze, impatiently tacked to and fro in the channel. At last, when the English vessel had fairly weathered the point, Paul, ranging ahead, courteously led her forth, as a beau might a belle in a ball-room—to mid-channel, and then suffered her to come within hail.

"She is hoisting her colors now, sir," said Israel.

"Give her the stars and stripes, then, my lad."

Joyfully running to the locker, Israel attached the flag to the halyards. The wind freshened. He stood elevated. The bright flag blew around him, a glorified shroud, enveloping him in its red ribbons and spangles, like up-springing tongues, and sparkles of flame.

As the colors rose to their final perch, and streamed in the air, Paul eyed them exultingly.

"I first hoisted that flag on an American ship, and was the first among men to get it saluted. If I perish this night, the name of Paul Jones shall live. Hark! they hail us."

"What ship are you?"

"Your enemy. Come on! What wants the fellow of more prefaces and introductions?"

The sun was now calmly setting over the green land of Ireland. The sky was serene; the sea smooth; the wind just sufficient to waft the two vessels steadily and gently. After the first firing, and a little manœuvering, the two ships glided on freely, side by side; in that mild air exchanging their deadly broadsides, like two friendly horsemen walking their steeds along a plain, chatting as they go. After an hour of this running fight, the conversation ended. The Drake struck. How changed from the big craft of sixty short minutes before! She seemed now, above deck, like a piece of wild western woodland into which choppers had been. Her masts and yards prostrate, and hanging in jack-straws; several of her sails ballooning out, as they dragged in the sea, like great lopped tops of foliage. The black hull and shattered stumps of masts, galled and riddled, looked as if gigantic woodpeckers had been tapping them.

The Drake was the larger ship; more cannon; more men. Her loss in killed and wounded was far the greater. Her brave captain and lieutenant were mortally wounded. The former died as the prize was boarded; the latter, two days after.

It was twilight; the weather still serence. No cannonade, nought that mad man can do, molests the stoical imperturbability of nature, when nature chooses to be still. This weather, holding on all through the following day, greatly facilitated the refitting of the ships. That done, the two vessels, sailing round the north of Ireland, steered towards Brest. They were repeatedly chased by English cruisers; but safely reached their anchorage in the French waters.

"A pretty fair four weeks' yachting, gentlemen," said Paul Jones, as the Ranger swung to her cable, while some French officers boarded her. "I bring two travellers with me, gentlemen," he continued. "Allow me to introduce you to my particular friend, Israel Potter, late of North America; and also to his Britannic Majesty's ship, Drake, late of Carrickfergus, Ireland."

This cruise made loud fame for Paul, especially at the court of France, whose king sent Paul a sword and a medal. But poor Israel, who also had conquered a craft, and all unaided too—what had he?

CHAPTER 18

The Expedition That Sailed
from Groix

Three months after anchoring at Brest, through Dr. Franklin's negotiations with the French king, backed by the bestirring ardor of Paul, a squadron of nine vessels of various force were ready in the road of Groix[1] for another descent on the British coasts. These craft were miscellaneously picked up; their crews a mongrel pack; the officers mostly French, unacquainted with each other, and secretly jealous of Paul. The expedition was full of the elements of insubordination and failure. Much bitterness and agony resulted to a spirit like Paul's. But he bore up; and though in many particulars the sequel more than warranted his misgivings, his soul still refused to surrender.

The career of this stubborn adventurer signally illustrates the idea, that since all human affairs are subject to organic disorder; since they are created in, and sustained by, a sort of half-disciplined chaos; hence, he who in great things seeks success, must never wait for smooth water; which never was, and never will be; but with what straggling method he can, dash with all his derangements at his object, leaving the rest to Fortune.

Though nominally commander of the squadron, Paul was not so in effect. Most of his captains conceitedly claimed independent commands. One of them in the end proved a traitor outright; few of the rest were reliable.

As for the ships, that commanded by Paul in person will be a good example of the fleet. She was an old Indiaman, clumsy and crank,[2] smelling strongly of the savor of tea, cloves, and arrack, the cargoes of former voyages. Even at that day, she was, from her venerable grotesqueness, what a cocked hat is, at the present age, among ordinary beavers.[3] Her elephantine bulk was houdahed with a castellated poop like the leaning tower of Pisa.[4] Poor Israel, standing on the top of this poop, spy-glass at his eye, looked more an astronomer than a mariner; having to do, not with the mountains of the billows, but the mountains in the moon. Galileo on Fiesole.[5] She was originally a single-decked ship; that is, carried her armament on one gun-deck. But cutting ports below, in her after part, Paul rammed out there six old eighteen pounders, whose rusty muzzles peered just above the water-line, like a parcel of dirty mulattoes from a cellar-way. Her name was the Duras; but, ere sailing, it was changed to that other appellation, whereby this sad old hulk became afterwards immortal. Though it is not unknown, that a compliment to Doctor Franklin was involved in this change of titles, yet the secret history of the affair will now for the first time be disclosed.

It was evening in the road of Groix. After a fagging day's work, trying to conciliate the hostile jealousy of his officers, and provide, in the face of endless obstacles (for he had to dance attendance on scores of intriguing factors and brokers ashore) the requisite stores for the fleet, Paul sat in his cabin in a half despondent reverie; while Israel, cross-legged at his commander's feet, was patching up some old signals.

"Captain Paul, I don't like our ship's name.—Duras? What's that mean?—Duras? Being cribbed up in a ship named Duras! a sort of makes one feel as if he were in durance[6] vile."

"Gad, I never thought of that before, my lion. Duras—Durance vile. I suppose it's superstition, but I'll change it. Come, Yellow-mane, what shall we call her?"

"Well, Captain Paul, don't you like Doctor Franklin? Hasn't he been the prime man to get this fleet together? Let's call her the Doctor Franklin."

"Oh no, that will too publicly declare him just at present; and Poor Richard wants to be a little shady in this business."

"Poor Richard!—call her Poor Richard,[7] then," cried Israel, suddenly struck by the idea.

"Gad, you have it," answered Paul, springing to his feet, as all trace of his former despondency left him;—"Poor Richard shall be the name, in honor to the saying, that 'God helps them that help themselves,' as Poor Richard says."

Now this was the way the craft came to be called the *Bon Homme Richard;* for it being deemed advisable to have a French rendering of the new title, it assumed the above form.

A few days after, the force sailed. Ere long, they captured several vessels; but the captains of the squadron proving refractory, events took so deplorable a turn, that Paul, for the present, was obliged to return to Groix. Luckily however, at this junction a cartel arrived from England with upwards of a hundred exchanged American seamen, who almost to a man enlisted under the flag of Paul.

Upon the resailing of the force, the old troubles broke out afresh. Most of her consorts insubordinately separated from the Bon Homme Richard. At length Paul found himself in violent storms beating off the rugged southeastern coast of Scotland, with only two accompanying ships. But neither the mutiny of his fleet, nor the chaos of the elements, made him falter in his purpose. Nay, at this crisis, he projected the most daring of all his descents.

The Cheviot Hills[8] were in sight. Sundry vessels had been described bound in for the Firth of Forth, on whose south shore, well up the Firth, stands Leith, the port of Edinburgh, distant but a mile or two from that capital. He resolved to dash at Leith, and lay it under contribution or in ashes. He called the captains of his two remaining consorts on board his own ship to arrange details. Those worthies had much of fastidious remark to make against the plan. After losing much time in trying to bring to a conclusion their sage deliberations, Paul by addressing their cupidity, achieved that which all appeals to their gallantry could not accomplish. He proclaimed the grand prize of the Leith lottery at no less a figure than £200,000; that being named as the ransom. Enough: the three ships entered the Firth, boldly and freely, as if carrying Quakers to a Peace-Congress.

Along both startled shores the panic of their approach spread like the cholera. The three suspicious crafts had so long lain off and on, that none doubted they were led by the audacious viking, Paul Jones. At five o'clock, on the following morning, they were distinctly seen from the capital of Scotland, quietly sailing up the bay. Batteries were hastily thrown up at Leith, arms were obtained from the castle at Edinburgh, alarm fires were kindled in all directions. Yet with such tranquillity of effrontery did Paul conduct his ships, concealing as much as possible their warlike character, that more than once his vessels were mistaken for merchantmen, and hailed by passing ships as such.

In the afternoon, Israel, at his station on the tower of Pisa, reported a boat with five men coming off to the Richard from the coast of Fife.[9]

"They have hot oat-cakes for us," said Paul, "let 'em come. To encourage them, show them the English ensign, Israel, my lad."

Soon the boat was alongside.

"Well, my good fellows, what can I do for you this afternoon?" said Paul, leaning over the side with a patronizing air.

"Why, captain, we come from the Laird of Crokarky, who wants some power and ball for his money."

"What would you with powder and ball, pray?"

"Oh! haven't you heard that that bloody pirate, Paul Jones, is somewhere hanging round the coasts?"

"Aye, indeed, but he won't hurt you. He's only going round among the nations, with his old hat, taking up contributions. So, away with ye; ye don't want any powder and ball to give him. He wants contributions of silver, not lead. Prepare yourselves with silver, I say."

"Nay, captain, the Laird ordered us not to return without powder and ball. See, here is the price. It may be the taking of the bloody pirate, if you let us have what we want."

"Well, pass 'em over a keg," said Paul laughing, but modifying his order by a sly whisper to Israel; "Oh, put up your price, it's a gift to ye."

"But ball, captain, what's the use of powder without ball?" roared one of the fellows from the boat's bow, as the keg was lowered in. "We want ball."

"Bless my soul, you bawl loud enough as it is. Away with ye, with what you have. Look to your keg, and hark ye, if ye catch that villain, Paul Jones, give him no quarter."

"But, captain, here," shouted one of the boatmen, "There's a mistake. This is a keg of pickles, not powder. Look," and poking into the bung-hole, he dragged out a green cucumber dripping with brine. "Take this back, and give us the powder."

"Pooh," said Paul, "the powder is at the bottom, pickled powder, best way to keep it. Away with ye, now, and after that bloody embezzler, Paul Jones."

This was Sunday. The ships held on. During the afternoon, a long tack of the Richard brought her close towards the shores of Fife, near the thriving little port of Kirkaldy.

"There's a great crowd on the beach, captain Paul," said Israel, looking through his glass. "There seems to be an old woman standing on a fish-barrel there, a sort of selling things at auction, to the people, but I can't be certain yet."

"Let me see," said Paul, taking the glass as they came nigher. "Sure enough, it's an old lady—an old quack-doctress, seems to me, in a black gown, too. I must hail her."

Ordering the ship to be kept on towards the port, he shortened sail within easy distance, so as to glide slowly by, and seizing the trumpet, thus spoke:—

"Old lady, ahoy! What are you talking about? What's your text?"

"The righteous shall rejoice when he seeth the vengeance. He shall wash his feet in the blood of the wicked."[10]

"Ah, what a lack of charity. Now hear mine;—God helpeth them that help themselves, as Poor Richard says."

"Reprobate pirate, a gale shall yet come, to drive thee in wrecks from our waters."

"The strong wind of your hate fills my sails well. Adieu," waving his bonnet—"tell us the rest at Leith."

Next morning the ships were almost within cannon-shot of the town. The men to be landed were in the boats. Israel had the tiller of the foremost one, waiting for his commander to enter, when just as Paul's foot was on the gangway, a sudden squall struck all three ships, dashing the boats against them, and creating indiscribable confusion. The squall ended in a violent gale. Getting his men on board with all dispatch, Paul essayed his best to withstand the fury of the wind; but it blew adversely, and with redoubled power. A ship at a distance went down beneath it. The disappointed invader was obliged to turn before the gale, and renounce his project.

To this hour, on the shores of the Firth of Forth, it is the popular persuasion, that the Rev. Mr. Shirra's, of Kirkaldy, powerful intercession,[11] was the direct cause of the elemental repulse experienced off the endangered harbor of Leith.

Through the ill qualities of Paul's associate captains: their timidity, incapable of keeping pace with his daring; their jealousy, blind to his superiority to rivalship—together with the general reduction of his force, now reduced, by desertion, from nine to three ships; and last of all, the enmity of seas and winds, the invader, driven, not by a fleet, but a gale, out of the Scottish waters, had the mortification in prospect of terminating a cruise, so formidable in appearance at the onset, without one added deed to sustain the reputation gained by former exploits. Nevertheless, he was not disheartened. He sought to conciliate fortune, not by despondency, but by resolution. And, as if won by his confident bearing, that fickle power suddenly went over to him from the ranks of the enemy, suddenly as plumed Marshal Ney to the stubborn standard of Napoleon from Elba, marching regenerated on Paris.[12] In a word, luck—that's the word—shortly threw in Paul's way the great action of his life: the most extraordinary of all naval engagements; the unparalleled death-lock with the Serapis.[13]

CHAPTER 19

They Fight the Serapis

The battle between the Bon Homme Richard and the Serapis stands in history as the first signal collision on the sea between the Englishman and the American.[1] For obstinacy, mutual hatred, and courage, it is without precedent or subsequent in the story of ocean. The strife long hung undetermined, but the English flag struck in the end.

There would seem to be something singularly indicatory in this engagement. It may involve at once a type, a parallel, and a prophecy. Sharing the same blood with England, and yet her proved foe in two wars;[2] not wholly inclined at bottom to forget an old grudge: intrepid, unprincipled, reckless, predatory, with boundless ambition, civilized in externals but a savage at heart, America is, or may yet be, the Paul Jones of nations.

Regarded in this indicatory light, the battle between the Bon Homme Richard and the Serapis—in itself so curious—may well enlist our interest.

Never was there a fight so snarled. The intricacy of those incidents which defy the narrator's extrication, is not ill figured in that bewildering intertanglement of all the yards and anchors of the two ships, which confounded them for the time in one chaos of devastation.

Elsewhere than here the reader must go who seeks an elaborate version of the fight, or, indeed, much of any regular account of it whatever. The writer is but brought to mention the battle, because he must needs follow, in all events, the fortunes of the humble adventurer whose life he records. Yet this necessarily involves some general view of each conspicuous incident in which he shares.

Several circumstances of the place and time served to invest the fight with a certain scenic atmosphere, casting a light almost poetic over the wild gloom of its tragic results. The battle was fought between the hours of seven and ten at night; the height of it was under a full harvest moon, in view of thousands of distant spectators crowding the high cliffs of Yorkshire.[3]

From the Tees to the Humber, the eastern coast of Britain, for the most part, wears a savage, melancholy, and Calabrian[4] aspect. It is in course of incessant decay. Every year the isle which repulses nearly all other foes, succumbs to the Attila[5] assaults of the deep. Here and there the base of the cliffs is strewn with masses of rock, undermined by the waves, and tumbled headlong below; where, sometimes, the water completely surrounds them, showing in shattered confusion detached rocks, pyramids, and obelisks, rising half-revealed from the surf,—the Tadmores[6] of the wasteful desert of the sea. Nowhere is this desolation more marked than for those fifty miles of coast between Flamborough Head and the Spurn.

Weathering out the gale which had driven them from Leith, Paul's ships, for a few days, were employed in giving chase to various merchantmen and colliers; capturing some, sinking others, and putting the rest to flight. Off the mouth of the Humber they ineffectually manœuvered with a view of drawing out a king's frigate, reported to be lying at anchor within. At another time a large fleet was encountered, under convoy of some ships of force. But their panic caused the fleet to hug the edge of perilous shoals very nigh the land, where, by reason of his having no competent pilot, Paul durst not approach to molest them. The same night he saw two strangers further out at sea, and chased them until three in the morning; when, getting pretty nigh, he surmised that they must needs be vessels of his own squadron, which, previous to his entering the Firth of Forth, had separated from his command. Daylight proved this supposition correct. Five vessels of the original squadron were now once more in company. About noon, a fleet of forty merchantmen appeared coming round Flamborough Head, protected by two English men-of-war, the Serapis and Countess of Scarborough.

Descrying the five cruisers sailing down, the forty sail, like forty chickens, fluttered in a panic under the wing of the shore. Their armed protectors bravely steered from the land, making the disposition for battle. Promptly accepting the challenge, Paul, giving the signal to his consorts, earnestly pressed forward. But, earnest as he was, it was seven in the evening ere the encounter began. Meantime his comrades, heedless of his signals, sailed independently along. Dismissing them from present consideration, we confine ourselves, for a while to the Richard and the Serapis, the grand duellists of the fight.

The Richard carried a motley crew, to keep whom in order one hundred and thirty-five soldiers—themselves a hybrid band—had been put on board, commanded by French officers of inferior rank. Her armament was similarly heterogeneous; guns of all sorts and calibres; but about equal on the whole to those of a thirty-two gun frigate. The spirit of baneful intermixture pervaded this craft throughout.

The Serapis was a frigate of fifty guns, more than half of which individually exceeded in calibre any one gun of the Richard. She had a crew of some three hundred and twenty trained man-of-war's men.

There is something in a naval engagement which radically distinguishes it from one on the land. The ocean, at times, has what is called its *sea* and its *trough of the sea;* but it has neither rivers, woods, banks, towns, nor mountains. In mild weather, it is one hammered plain. Stratagems,—like those of disciplined armies, ambuscades—like those of Indians, are impossible. All is clear, open, fluent. The very element which sustains the combatants, yields at the stroke of a feather. One wind and one tide at one time operate upon all who here engage. This simplicity renders a battle between two men-of-war, with their huge white wings, more akin to the Miltonic contests of archangels[7] than to *the comparatively squalid* tussels of earth.

As the ships neared, a hazy darkness overspread the water. The moon was not yet risen. Objects were perceived with difficulty. Borne by a soft moist breeze over gentle waves, they came within pistol-shot. Owing to the obscurity, and the known neighborhood of other vessels, the Serapis was uncertain who the

Richard was. Through the dim mist each ship loomed forth to the other vast, but indistinct, as the ghost of Morven.[8] Sounds of the trampling of resolute men echoed from either hull, whose tight decks dully resounded like drum-heads in a funeral march.

The Serapis hailed. She was answered by a broadside. For half an hour the combatants deliberately manœuvered, continually changing their position, but always within shot fire. The Serapis—the better sailer of the two—kept critically circling the Richard, making lounging advances now and then, and as suddenly steering off; hate causing her to act not unlike a wheeling cock about a hen, when stirred by the contrary passion. Meantime, though within easy speaking distance, no further syllable was exchanged; but an incessant cannonade was kept up.

At this point, a third party, the Scarborough, drew near, seemingly desirous of giving assistance to her consort. But thick smoke was now added to the night's natural obscurity. The Scarborough imperfectly discerned two ships, and plainly saw the common fire they made; but which was which, she could not tell. Eager to befriend the Serapis, she durst not fire a gun, lest she might unwittingly act the part of a foe. As when a hawk and a crow are clawing and beaking high in the air, a second crow flying near, will seek to join the battle, but finding no fair chance to engage, at last flies away to the woods; just so did the Scarborough now. Prudence dictated the step. Because several chance shot—from which of the combatants could not be known—had already struck the Scarborough. So, unwilling uselessly to expose herself, off went for the present this baffled and ineffectual friend.

Not long after, an invisible hand came and set down a great yellow lamp in the east. The hand reached up unseen from below the horizon, and set the lamp down right on the rim of the horizon, as on a threshold; as much as to say, Gentlemen warriors, permit me a little to light up this rather gloomy looking subject. The lamp was the round harvest moon; the one solitary foot-light of the scene. But scarcely did the rays from the lamp pierce that languid haze. Objects before perceived with difficulty, now glimmered ambiguously. Bedded in strange vapors, the great foot-light cast a dubious half demoniac glare across the waters, like the phantasmagoric stream sent athwart

a London flagging in a night-rain from an apothecary's blue
and green window. Through this sardonical mist, the face of
the Man-in-the-Moon—looking right towards the combatants,
as if he were standing in a trap-door of the sea, leaning forward
leisurely with his arms complacently folded over upon the edge
of the horizon,—this queer face wore a serious, apishly self-
satisfied leer, as if the Man-in-the-Moon had somehow secretly
put up the ships to their contest, and in the depths of his malignant old soul was not unpleased to see how well his charms
worked. There stood the grinning Man-in-the-Moon, his head
just dodging into view over the rim of the sea:—Mephistopheles[9]
prompter of the stage.

Aided now a little by the planet, one of the consorts of the
Richard, the Pallas, hovering far outside the fight, dimly discerned the suspicious form of a lonely vessel unknown to her.
She resolved to engage it, if it proved a foe. But ere they joined,
the unknown ship—which proved to be the Scarborough—
received a broadside at long gun's distance from another consort of the Richard, the Alliance. The shot whizzed across the
broad interval like shuttlecocks across a great hall. Presently
the battledores[10] of both batteries were at work, and rapid
compliments of shuttlecocks were very promptly exchanged.
The adverse consorts of the two main belligerents fought with
all the rage of those fiery seconds who in some desperate duels,
make their principal's quarrel their own. Diverted from the
Richard and the Serapis by this little by-play, the Man-in-
the-Moon, all eager to see what it was, somewhat raised himself from his trap-door with an added grin on his face. By this
time, off sneaked the Alliance, and down swept the Pallas,
at close quarters engaging the Scarborough; an encounter destined in less than an hour to end in the latter ship's striking her
flag.

Compared to the Serapis and the Richard, the Pallas and the
Scarborough were as two pages to two knights. In their immature way they showed the same traits as their fully developed
superiors.

The Man-in-the-Moon now raised himself still higher to obtain a better view of affairs.

But the Man-in-the-Moon was not the only spectator. From the high cliffs of the shore, and especially from the great promontory of Flamborough Head, the scene was witnessed by crowds of the islanders. Any rustic might be pardoned his curiosity in view of the spectacle presented. Far in the indistinct distance fleets of frightened merchantmen filled the lower air with their sails, as flakes of snow in a snow-storm by night. Hovering undeterminedly, in another direction, were several of the scattered consorts of Paul, taking no part in the fray. Nearer, was an isolated mist, investing the Pallas and Scarborough—a mist slowly adrift on the sea, like a floating isle, and at intervals irradiated with sparkles of fire and resonant with the boom of cannon. Further away, in the deeper water, was a lurid cloud, incessantly torn in shreds of lightning, then fusing together again, once more to be rent. As yet this lurid cloud was neither stationary nor slowly adrift, like the first mentioned one; but, instinct with chaotic vitality, shifted hither and thither, foaming with fire, like a valiant water-spout careering off the coast of Malabar.[11]

To get some idea of the events enacting in that cloud, it will be necessary to enter it; to go and possess it, as a ghost may rush into a body, or the devils into the swine, which running down the steep place perished in the sea; just as the Richard is yet to do.

Thus far the Serapis and the Richard had been manœuvering and chasseing[12] to each other like partners in a cotillon, all the time indulging in rapid repartee.

But finding at last that the superior managableness of the enemy's ship enabled him to get the better of the clumsy old Indiaman, the Richard, in taking position; Paul, with his wonted resolution, at once sought to neutralize this, by hugging him close. But the attempt to lay the Richard right across the head of the Serapis ended quite otherwise, in sending the enemy's jib-boom just over the Richard's great tower of Pisa, where Israel was stationed; who catching it eagerly, stood for an instant holding to the slack of the sail, like one grasping a horse by the mane prior to vaulting into the saddle.

"Aye, hold hard, lad," cried Paul, springing to his side with a coil of rigging. With a few rapid turns he knitted himself to his foe. The wind now acting on the sails of the Serapis forced her, heel and point, her entire length, cheek by jowl, alongside the Richard. The projecting cannon scraped; the yards interlocked; but the hulls did not touch. A long lane of darkling water lay wedged between, like that narrow canal in Venice which dozes between two shadowy piles, and high in air is secretly crossed by the Bridge of Sighs.[13] But where the six yard-arms reciprocally arched overhead, three bridges of sighs were both seen and heard, as the moon and wind kept rising.

Into that Lethean[14] canal,—pond-like in its smoothness as compared with the sea without—fell many a poor soul that night;—fell, for ever forgotten.

As some heaving rent coinciding with a disputed frontier on a volcanic plain, that boundary abyss was the jaws of death to both sides. So contracted was it, that in many cases the gun-rammers had to be thrust into the opposite ports, in order to enter to muzzles of their own cannon. It seemed more an intestine feud, than a fight between strangers. Or, rather, it was as if the Siamese Twins, oblivious of their fraternal bond, should rage in unnatural fight.

Ere long, a horrible explosion was heard, drowning for the instant the cannonade. Two of the old eighteen-pounders—before spoken of, as having been hurriedly set up below the main deck of the Richard—burst all to pieces, killing the sailors who worked them, and shattering all that part of the hull, as if two exploded steam-boilers had shot out of its opposite sides. The effect was like the fall of the walls of a house. Little now upheld the great tower of Pisa but a few naked crow stanchions. Thenceforth, not a few balls from the Serapis must have passed straight through the Richard without grazing her. It was like firing buck-shot through the ribs of a skeleton.

But, further forward, so deadly was the broadside from the heavy batteries of the Serapis,—levelled point-blank, and right down the throat and bowels, as it were, of the Richard—that it cleared everything before it. The men on the Richard's covered gun-deck ran above, like miners from the fire-damp.[15] Collecting on the forecastle, they continued to fight with grenades and muskets. The soldiers also were in the lofty tops, whence they kept up incessant volleys, cascading their fire down as pouring lava from cliffs.

The position of the men in the two ships was now exactly reversed. For while the Serapis was tearing the Richard all to pieces below deck, and had swept that covered part almost of the last man; the Richard's crowd of musketry had complete control of the upper deck of the Serapis, where it was almost impossible for a man to remain unless as a corpse. Though in the beginning, the tops of the Serapis had not been unsupplied with marksmen, yet they had long since been cleared by the overmastering musketry of the Richard. Several, with leg or arm broken by a ball, had been seen going dimly downward from their giddy perch, like falling pigeons shot on the wing.

As busy swallows about barn-eaves and ridge-poles, some of the Richard's marksmen quitting their tops, now went far out on their yardarms, where they overhung the Serapis. From thence they dropped handgrenades upon her decks, like apples, which growing in one field fall over the fence into another. Others of their band flung the same sour fruit into the open ports of the Serapis. A hail-storm of aerial combustion descended and slanted on the Serapis, while horizontal thunderbolts rolled crosswise through the subterranean vaults of the Richard. The belligerents were no longer, in the ordinary sense of things, an English ship, and an American ship. It was a co-partnership and joint-stock combustion-company of both ships; yet divided, even in participation. The two vessels were as two houses, through whose party-wall doors have been cut; one family (the Guelphs) occupying the whole lower story; another family (the Ghibelines) the whole upper story.[16]

Meanwhile determined Paul flew hither and thither like the meteoric corposant-ball, which shiftingly dances on the tips and verges of ships' rigging in storms. Wherever he went, he seemed to cast a pale light on all faces. Blacked and burnt, his Scotch bonnet was compressed to a gun-wad on his head. His Parisian coat, with its gold-laced sleeve laid aside, disclosed to the full the blue tatooing on his arm, which sometimes in fierce gestures streamed in the haze of the cannonade, cabalistically terrific as the charmed standard of Satan. Yet his frenzied manner was less a testimony of his internal commotion than intended to inspirit and madden his men, some of whom seeing him, in transports of intrepidity stripped themselves to their trowsers, exposing their naked bodies to the as naked shot. The same was done on the Serapis, where several guns were seen surrounded by their buff crews as by fauns and satyrs.

At the beginning of the fray, before the ships interlocked, in the intervals of smoke which swept over the ships as mist over mountain-tops, affording open rents here and there—the gun-deck of the Serapis, at certain points, showed, congealed for the instant in all attitudes of dauntlessness, a gallery of marble statues—fighting gladiators.

Stooping low and intent, with one braced leg thrust behind, and one arm thrust forward, curling round towards the muzzle of the gun:—there was seen the *loader*, performing his allotted part; on the other side of the carriage, in the same stooping posture, but with both hands holding his long black pole, pike-wise, ready for instant use—stood the eager *rammer and sponger*; while at the breech, crouched the wary *captain of the gun*, his keen eye, like the watching leopard's, burning along the range; and behind, all tall and erect, the Egyptian symbol of death, stood the *matchman*, immovable for the moment, his long-handled match reversed. Up to their two long death-dealing batteries, the trained men of the Serapis stood and toiled in mechanical magic of discipline. They tended those rows of guns, as Lowell girls the rows of looms in a cotton factory.[17] The Parcæ were not more methodical; Atropos not more fatal;[18] the automaton chess-player not more irresponsible.

"Look, lad; I want a grenade, now, thrown down their main hatch-way. I saw long piles of cartridges there. The powder monkeys have brought them up faster than they can be used. Take a bucket of combustibles, and let's hear from you presently."

These words were spoken by Paul to Israel. Israel did as ordered. In a few minutes, bucket in hand, begrimed with powder, sixty-feet in air, he hung like Apollyon[19] from the extreme tip of the yard over the fated abyss of the hatchway. As he looked down between the eddies of smoke into that slaughter-ous pit, it was like looking from the verge of a cataract down into the yeasty pool at its base. Watching his chance, he dropped one grenade with such faultless precision, that, striking its mark, an explosion rent the Serapis like a volcano. The long row of heaped cartridges was ignited. The fire ran horizontally, like an express on a railway. More than twenty men were instantly killed: nearly forty wounded. This blow restored the chances of battle, before in favor of the Serapis.

But the drooping spirits of the English were suddenly revived, by an event which crowned the scene by an act on the part of one of the consorts of the Richard, the incredible atrocity of which, has induced all humane minds to impute it rather to some incomprehensible mistake, than to the malignant madness of the perpetrator.

The cautious approach and retreat of a consort of the Serapis, the Scarborough, before the moon rose, has already been mentioned. It is now to be related how that, when the moon was more than an hour high, a consort of the Richard, the Alliance, likewise approached and retreated. This ship, commanded by a Frenchman, infamous in his own navy, and obnoxious in the service to which he at present belonged; this ship, foremost in insurgency to Paul hitherto, and which, for the most part had crept like a poltroon[20] from the fray; the Alliance now was at hand. Seeing her, Paul deemed the battle at an end. But to his horror, the Alliance threw a broadside full into the stern of the Richard, without touching the Serapis. Paul called to her, for God's sake to forbear destroying the Richard. The reply was, a second, a third, a fourth broadside; striking the Richard ahead, astern, and amidships. One of the volleys killed several men and one officer. Meantime, like carpenters' augurs, and the sea-worm called remora, the guns of the Serapis were drilling away at the same doomed hull. After performing her nameless exploit, the Alliance sailed away, and did no more. She was like the great fire of London, breaking out on the heel of the great Plague.[21] By this time, the Richard had received so many shot-holes low down in her hull, that like a sieve she began to settle.

"Do you strike?"[22] cried the English captain.

"I have not yet begun to fight,"[23] howled sinking Paul.

This summons and response were whirled on eddies of smoke and flame. Both vessels were now on fire. The men of either knew hardly which to do; strive to destroy the enemy, or save themselves. In the midst of this, one hundred human beings, hitherto invisible strangers, were suddenly added to the rest. Five score English prisoners, till now confined in the Richard's hold, liberated in his consternation, by the master at arms, burst up the hatchways. One of them, the captain of a letter of marque, captured by Paul, off the Scottish coast, crawled through a port, as a burglar through a window, from the one ship to the other, and reported affairs to the English captain.

While Paul and his lieutenants were confronting these prisoners, the gunner, running up from below, and not perceiving his official superiors, and deeming them dead; believing himself now left sole surviving officer, ran to the tower of Pisa to haul down the colors. But they were already shot down and trailing in the water astern, like a sailor's towing shirt. Seeing the gunner there, groping about in the smoke, Israel asked what he wanted.

At this moment, the gunner, rushing to the rail, shouted "quarter! quarter!" to the Serapis.

"I'll quarter ye," yelled Israel, smiting the gunner with the flat of his cutlass.

"Do you strike?" now came from the Serapis.

"Aye, aye, aye!" involuntarily cried Israel, fetching the gunner a shower of blows.

"Do you strike?" again was repeated from the Serapis; whose captain, judging from the augmented confusion on board the Richard, owing to the escape of the prisoners, and also influenced by the report made to him by his late guest of the port-hole, doubted not that the enemy must needs be about surrendering.

"Do you strike?"

"Aye!—I strike *back*," roared Paul, for the first time now hearing the summons.

But judging this frantic response to come, like the others, from some unauthorized source, the English captain directed his boarders to be called; some of whom presently leaped on the Richard's rail; but, throwing out his tatooed arm at them with a sabre at the end of it, Paul showed them how boarders repelled boarders. The English retreated; but not before they had been thinned out again, like spring radishes, by the unfaltering fire from the Richard's tops.

An officer of the Richard, seeing the mass of prisoners delirious with sudden liberty and fright, pricked them with his sword to the pumps; thus keeping the ship afloat by the very blunder which had promised to have been fatal. The vessels now blazed so in the rigging, that both parties desisted from hostilities to subdue the common foe.

When some faint order was again restored upon the Richard, her chances of victory increased, while those of the English, driven under cover, proportionably waned. Early in the contest, Paul, with his own hand, had brought one of his largest guns to bear against the enemy's main-mast. That shot had hit. The mast now plainly tottered. Nevertheless, it seemed as if, in this fight, neither party could be victor. Mutual obliteration from the face of the waters seemed the only natural sequel to hostilities like these. It is, therefore, honor to him as a man, and not reproach to him as an officer, that, to stay such carnage, Captain Pearson, of the Serapis, with his own hands hauled down his colors. But just as an officer from the Richard swung himself on board the Serapis, and accosted the English captain, the first lieutenant of the Serapis came up from below inquiring whether the Richard had struck, since her fire had ceased.

So equal was the conflict that, even after the surrender, it could be, and was, a question to one of the warriors engaged (who had not happened to see the English flag hauled down) whether the Serapis had struck to the Richard, or the Richard to the Serapis. Nay, while the Richard's officer was still amicably conversing with the English captain, a midshipman of the Richard, in act of following his superior on board the surrendered vessel, was run through the thigh by a pike in the hand of an ignorant boarder of the Serapis. While equally ignorant, the cannons below deck were still thundering away at the nominal conqueror from the batteries of the nominally conquered ship.

But though the Serapis had submitted, there were two misan-thropical foes on board the Richard which would not so easily succumb,—fire and water. All night the victors were engaged in suppressing the flames. Not until daylight were the flames got under; but though the pumps were kept continually going, the water in the hold still gained. A few hours after sunrise the Richard was deserted for the Serapis and the other vessels of the squadron of Paul. About ten o'clock, the Richard, gorged with slaughter, wallowed heavily, gave a long roll, and blasted by tornadoes of sulphur, slowly sunk, like Gomorrah,[24] out of sight.

The loss of life in the two ships was about equal; one-half of the total number of those engaged being either killed or wounded.

In view of this battle one may well ask—What separates the enlightened man from the savage? Is civilization a thing distinct, or is it an advanced stage of barbarism?

CHAPTER 20

The Shuttle

For a time back, across the otherwise blue-jean career of Israel, Paul Jones flits and re-flits like a crimson thread. One more brief intermingling of it, and to the plain old homespun we return.

The battle won, the squadron started for the Texel,[1] where they arrived in safety. Omitting all mention of intervening harassments, suffice it, that after some months of inaction as to anything of a warlike nature, Paul and Israel (both from different motives, eager to return to America), sailed for that country in the armed ship Ariel; Paul as commander, Israel as quarter-master.

Two weeks out, they encountered by night, a frigate-like craft, supposed to be an enemy. The vessels came within hail, both showing English colors, with purposes of mutual deception, affecting to belong to the English navy. For an hour, through their speaking trumpets, the captains equivocally conversed. A very reserved, adroit, hoodwinking, statesman-like conversation, indeed. At last, professing some little incredulity as to the truthfulness of the stranger's statement, Paul intimated a desire that he should put out a boat and come on board to show his commission, to which the stranger very affably replied, that unfortunately his boat was exceedingly leaky. With equal politeness, Paul begged him to consider the danger attending a refusal, which rejoinder nettled the other, who suddenly retorted that he would answer for twenty guns, and that both himself and men were knock-down Englishmen. Upon this, Paul said that he would allow him exactly five minutes for a sober, second thought. That brief period passed, Paul, hoisting the American colors, ran close under the other ship's stern, and engaged her. It was about eight o'clock at night; that this strange quarrel was picked in the middle of the ocean. Why cannot men be peaceable on that great common? Or does nature in those fierce night-brawlers, the billows, set mankind but a sorry example?

After ten minutes' cannonading, the stranger struck, shouting out, that half his men were killed. The Ariel's crew hurraed. Boarders were called to take possession. At this juncture, the prize shifting her position so that she headed away, and to leeward of the Ariel, thrust her long spanker boom diagonally over the latter's quarter; when Israel, who was standing close by, instinctively caught hold of it—just as he had grasped the jib-boom of the Serapis—and, at the same moment, hearing the call to take possession, in the valiant excitement of the occasion, he leaped upon the spar, and made a rush for the stranger's deck, thinking, of course, that he would be immediately followed by the regular boarders. But the sails of the strange ship suddenly filled; she began to glide through the sea; her spanker-boom, not having at all entangled itself, offering no hindrance. Israel clinging midway along the boom, soon found himself divided from the Ariel, by a space impossible to be leaped. Meantime, suspecting foul play, Paul set every sail; but the stranger, having already the advantage, contrived to make good her escape, though perseveringly chased by the cheated conqueror.

In the confusion, no eye had observed our hero's spring. But, as the vessels separated more, an officer of the strange ship spying a man on the boom, and taking him for one of his own men, demanded what he did there.

"Clearing the signal halyards, sir," replied Israel, fumbling with the cord which happened to be dangling near by.

"Well, bear a hand and come in, or you will have a bow-chaser at you soon," referring to the bow guns of the Ariel.

"Aye, aye, sir," said Israel, and in a moment he sprang to the deck, and soon found himself mixed in among some two hundred English sailors of a large letter of marque.[2] At once he perceived that the story of half the crew being killed was a mere hoax, played off for the sake of making an escape. Orders were continually being given to pull on this and that rope, as the ship crowded all sail in flight. To these orders Israel with the rest promptly responded, pulling at the rigging stoutly as the best of them; though heaven knows his heart sank deeper and deeper at every pull which thus helped once again to widen the gulf between him and home.

In intervals, he considered with himself what to do. Favored by the obscurity of the night and the number of the crew, and wearing much the same dress as theirs, it was very easy to pass himself off for one of them till morning. But daylight would be sure to expose him, unless some cunning plan could be hit upon. If discovered for what he was, nothing short of a prison awaited him upon the ship's arrival in port.

It was a desperate case; only as desperate a remedy could serve. One thing was sure, he could not hide. Some audacious parade of himself promised the only hope. Marking that the sailors, not being of the regular navy, wore no uniform; and perceiving that his jacket was the only garment on him which bore any distinguishing badge, our adventurer took it off, and privily dropped it overboard, remaining now in his dark blue woollen shirt, and blue cloth waistcoat.

What the more inspirited Israel to the added step now contemplated, was the circumstances, that the ship was not a Frenchman, or other foreigner, but her crew, though enemies, spoke the same language that he did.

So very quietly, at last, he goes aloft into the main-top, and sitting down on an old sail there, beside some eight or ten topmen, in an off-handed way asks one for tobacco.

"Give us a quid,[3] lad," as he settled himself in his seat.

"Halloo," said the strange sailor, "who be you? Get out of the top! The fore and mizzen-top men[4] won't let us go into their tops, and blame me if we'll let any of their gangs come here. So, away ye go."

"You're blind, or crazy, old boy," rejoined Israel. "I'm a top-mate; ain't I, lads?" appealing to the rest.

"There's only ten main-topmen belonging to our watch; if you are one, then there'll be eleven," said a second sailor. "Get out of the top!"

"This is too bad, maties," cried Israel, "to serve an old top-mate this way. Come, come, you are foolish. Give us a quid." And, once more, with the utmost sociability, he addressed the sailor next to him.

"Look ye," returned the other, "if you don't make away with yourself, you skulking spy from the mizzen, we'll drop you to deck like a jewel-block."[5]

Seeing the party thus resolute, Israel, with some affected banter, descended.

The reason why he had tried the scheme—and, spite of the foregoing failure, meant to repeat it—was this: As customary in armed ships, the men were in companies, allotted to particular places and functions. Therefore, to escape final detection, Israel must some way get himself recognized as belonging to some one of those bands; otherwise, as an isolated nondescript, discovery ere long would be certain; especially upon the next general muster.[6] To be sure, the hope in question was a forlorn sort of hope; but it was his sole one, and must therefore be tried.

Mixing in again for a while with the general watch, he at last goes on the forecastle among the sheet-anchor-men there, at present engaged in critically discussing the merits of the late valiant encounter, and expressing their opinion that by day-break the enemy in chase would be hull-down out of sight.

"To be sure she will," cried Israel, joining in with the group, "old ballyhoo that she is, to be sure. But didn't we pepper her, lads? Give us a chew of tobacco, one of ye? How many have we wounded, do ye know? None killed that I've heard of. Wasn't that a fine hoax we played on 'em? Ha! ha! But give us a chew."

In the prodigal fraternal patriotism of the moment, one of the old worthies freely handed his plug to our adventurer, who, helping himself, returned it, repeating the question as to the killed and wounded.

"Why," said he of the plug, "Jack Jewboy told me, just now, that there's only seven men been carried down to the surgeon, but not a soul killed."

"Good, boys, good!" cried Israel, moving up to one of the gun-carriages, where three or four men were sitting—"slip along, chaps, slip along, and give a watchmate a seat with ye."

"All full here, lad; try the next gun."

"Boys, clear a place here," said Israel, advancing, like one of the family, to that gun.

"Who the devil are *you*, making this row here?" demanded a stern-looking old fellow, captain of the forecastle, "seems to me you make considerable noise. Are you a forecastleman?"

"If the bowsprit belongs here, so do I," rejoined Israel, composedly.

"Let's look at ye, then?" and seizing a battle-lantern, before thrust under a gun, the old veteran came close to Israel before he had time to elude the scrutiny.

"Take that!" said his examiner, and fetching Israel a terrible thump, pushed him ignominiously off the forecastle as some unknown interloper from distant parts of the ship.

With similar perseverance of effrontery, Israel tried other quarters of the vessel. But with equal ill success. Jealous with the spirit of class, no social circle would receive him. As a last resort, he dived down among the *holders*.[7]

A group of them sat round a lantern, in the dark bowels of the ship, like a knot of charcoal burners in a pine forest at midnight.

"Well, boys, what's the good word?" said Israel, advancing very cordially, but keeping as much as possible in the shadow.

"The good word is," rejoined a censorious old *holder*, "that you had best go where you belong—on deck—and not be a skulking down here where you *don't* belong. I suppose this is the way you skulked during the fight."

"Oh, you're growly to-night, shipmate," said Israel, pleasantly—"supper sits hard on your conscience."

"Get out of the hold with ye," roared the other. "On deck, or I'll call the master-at-arms."

Once more Israel decamped.

Sorely against his grain, as a final effort to blend himself openly with the crew, he now went among the *waisters*;[8] the vilest caste of an armed ship's company; mere dregs and settlings— sea-Pariahs; comprising all the lazy, all the inefficient, all the unfortunate and fated, all the melancholy, all the infirm; all the rheumatical scamps, scape-graces, ruined prodigal sons, sooty faces, and swineherds of the crew, not excluding those with dismal wardrobes.

An unhappy, tattered, moping row of them sat along dolefully on the gun-deck, like a parcel of crest-fallen buzzards, exiled from civilized society.

"Cheer up, lads," said Israel, in a jovial tone, "homeward bound, you know. Give us a seat among ye, friends."

"Oh, sit on your head!" answered a sullen fellow in the corner.

"Come, come, no growling; we're homeward-bound. Whoop, my hearties!"

"Work-house bound, you mean," grumbled another sorry chap, in a darned shirt.

"Oh, boys, don't be down-hearted. Let's keep up our spirits. Sing us a song, one of ye, and I'll give the chorus."

"Sing if ye like, but I'll plug my ears for one," said still another sulky varlet, with the toes out of his sea-boots; while all the rest with one roar of misanthropy joined him.

But Israel, not to be daunted, began:

"'Cease, rude Boreas,[9] cease your growling!'"

"And you cease your squeaking, will ye," cried a fellow in a banged tarpaulin. "Did ye get a ball in the windpipe, that ye cough that way, worse nor a broken-nosed old bellows? Have done with your groaning; it's worse nor the death-rattle."

"Boys, is this the way you treat a watch-mate," demanded Israel reproachfully, "trying to cheer up his friends? Shame on ye, boys. Come, let's be sociable. Spin us a yarn, one of ye. Meantime, rub my back for me, another," and very confidently he leaned against his neighbor.

"Lean off me, will ye?" roared his friend, shoving him away.

"But who *is* this ere singing, leaning, yarn-spinning, chap? Who are ye? Be you a waister, or be you not?"

So saying, one of this peevish, sottish band staggered close up to Israel. But there was a deck above and a deck below, and the lantern swung in the distance. It was too dim to see with critical exactness.

"No such singing chap belongs to our gang, that's flat," he dogmatically exclaimed at last, after an ineffectual scrutiny. "Sail out of this!"

And with a shove, once more poor Israel was rejected.

Black-balled out of every club, he went disheartened on deck. So long, while night screened him at least, as he contented himself with promiscuously circulating, all was safe; it was the endeavor to fraternize with any one set which was sure to endanger him. At last, wearied out, he happened to find himself on the berth deck, where the watch below were slumbering. Some hundred and fifty hammocks were on that deck. Seeing one empty, he leaped in, thinking luck might yet some way befriend him. Here, at last, the sultry confinement put him fast asleep. He was wakened by a savage whiskerando of the other watch, who, seizing him by his waistband, dragged him most indecorously out, furiously denouncing him for a skulker.

Springing to his feet, Israel perceived from the crowd and tumult of the berth deck, now all alive with men leaping into their hammocks, instead of being full of sleepers quietly dosing therein, that the watches were changed. Going above, he renewed in various quarters his offers of intimacy with the fresh men there assembled; but was successively repulsed as before. At length, just as day was breaking, an irascible fellow, whose stubborn opposition our adventurer had long in vain sought to conciliate—this man suddenly perceiving, by the grey morning light, that Israel had somehow an alien sort of general look, very savagely pressed him for explicit information as to who he might be. The answers increased his suspicion. Others began to surround the two. Presently, quite a circle was formed. Sailors from distant parts of the ship drew near. One, and then another, and another, declared that they, in their quarters, too, had been molested by a vagabond claiming fraternity, and seeking to palm himself off upon decent society. In vain Israel protested. The truth, like the day, dawned clearer and clearer. More and more closely he was scanned. At length the hour for having all hands on deck arrived; when the other watch which Israel had first tried, reascending to the deck, and hearing the matter in discussion, they endorsed the charge of molestation and attempted imposture through the night, on the part of some person unknown, but who, likely enough, was the strange man now before them. In the end, the master-at-arms appeared with his bamboo, who, summarily collaring poor Israel, led him as a mysterious culprit to the officer of the deck; which gentleman having heard the charge, examined him in great perplexity, and, saying that he did not at all recognize that countenance, requested the junior officers to contribute their scrutiny. But those officers were equally at fault.

"Who the deuce *are* you?" at last said the officer of the deck, in added bewilderment. "Where did you come from? What's your business? Where are you stationed? What's your name? Who are you, any way? How did you get here? and where are you going?"

"Sir," replied Israel very humbly, "I am going to my regular duty, if you will but let me. I belong to the main top, and ought to be now engaged in preparing the top-gallant stu'n'-sail for hoisting."

"Belong to the main-top? Why, these men here say you have been trying to belong to the fore-top, and the mizen-top, and the forecastle, and the hold, and the waist, and every other part of the ship. This is extraordinary," he added, turning upon the junior officers.

"He must be out of his mind," replied one of them, the sailing-master.

"Out of his mind?" rejoined the officer of the deck. "He's out of all reason; out of all men's knowledge and memories! Why, no one knows him; no one has ever seen him before; no imagination, in the wildest flight of a morbid nightmare, has ever so much as dreamed of him. Who *are* you?" he again added, fierce with amazement. "What's your name? Are you down in the ship's books, or at all in the records of nature?"

"My name, sir, is Peter Perkins," said Israel, thinking it most prudent to conceal his real appellation.

"Certainly, I never heard that name before. Pray, see if Peter Perkins is down on the quarter-bills," he added to a midshipman. "Quick, bring the book here."

Having received it, he ran his fingers along the columns, and dashing down the book, declared that no such name was there.

"You are not down, sir. There is no Peter Perkins here. Tell me at once who are you?"

"It might be, sir," said Israel, gravely, "that seeing I shipped under the effects of liquor, I might, out of absent-mindedness like, have given in some other person's name instead of my own."

"Well, what name have you gone by among your shipmates since you've been aboard?"

"Peter Perkins, sir."

Upon this the officer turned to the men around, inquiring whether the name of Peter Perkins was familiar to them as that of a shipmate. One and all answered no.

"This won't do, sir," now said the officer. "You see it won't do. Who are you?"

"A poor persecuted fellow at your service, sir."

"*Who* persecutes you?"

"Every one, sir. All hands seem to be against me; none of them willing to remember me."

"Tell me," demanded the officer earnestly, "how long do you remember yourself? Do you remember yesterday morning? You must have come into existence by some sort of spontaneous combustion in the hold. Or were you fired aboard from the enemy, last night, in a cartridge? Do you remember yesterday?"

"Oh yes, sir."

"What was you doing yesterday?"

"Well, sir, for one thing, I believe I had the honor of a little talk with yourself."

"With *me?*"

"Yes sir; about nine o'clock in the morning—the sea being smooth and the ship running, as I should think, about seven knots—you came up into the main-top, where I belong, and was pleased to ask my opinion about the best way to set a top gallant stu'n'-sail."

"He's mad! He's mad!" said the officer, with delirious conclusiveness. "Take him away, take him away—put him somewhere, master-at-arms. Stay, one test more. What mess do you belong to?"

"Number 12, sir."

"Mr. Tidds," to a midshipman, "send mess No. 12 to the mast."

Ten sailors replied to the summons, and arranged themselves before Israel.

"Men, does this man belong to your mess?"

"No, sir; never saw him before this morning."

"What are those men's names?" he demanded of Israel.

"Well, sir, I am so intimate with all of them," looking upon them with a kindly glance, "I never call them by their real names, but by nick-names. So, never using their real names, I have forgotten them. The nick-names that I know them by, are Towser, Bowser, Rowser, Snowser."

"Enough. Mad as a March hare. Take him away. Hold," again added the officer, whom some strange fascination still bound to the bootless investigation. "What's *my* name, sir?"

"Why, sir, one of my messmates here called you Lieutenant Williamson, just now, and I never heard you called by any other name."

"There's method in his madness," thought the officer to himself. "What's the captain's name?"

"Why, sir, when we spoke the enemy, last night, I heard him say, through his trumpet, that he was Captain Parker; and very likely he knows his own name."

"I have you now. That ain't the captain's real name."

"He's the best judge himself, sir, of what his name is, I should think."

"Were it not," said the officer, now turning gravely upon his juniors, "were it not, that such a supposition were on other grounds absurd, I should certainly conclude that this man, in some unknown way, got on board here from the enemy last night."

"How could he, sir?" asked the sailing-master.

"Heaven knows. But our spanker-boom geared the other ship, you know, in manœuvering to get headway."

"But supposing he *could* have got here that fashion, which is quite impossible under all the circumstances—what motive could have induced him voluntarily to jump among enemies?"

"Let him answer for himself," said the officer, turning suddenly upon Israel, with the view of taking him off his guard, by the matter of course assumption of the very point at issue.

"Answer, sir. Why did you jump on board here, last night, from the enemy?"

"Jump on board, sir, from the enemy? Why, sir, my station at general quarters is at gun No. 3, of the lower deck, here."

"He's cracked—or else I am turned—or all the world is;—take him away!"

"But where am I to take him, sir?" said the master-at-arms. "He don't seem to belong anywhere, sir. Where—where am I to take him?"

"Take him out of sight," said the officer, now incensed with his own perplexity. "Take him out of sight, I say."

"Come along, then, my ghost," said the master-at-arms. And, collaring the phantom, he led it hither and thither, not knowing exactly what to do with it.

Some fifteen minutes passed, when the captain coming from his cabin, and observing the master-at-arms leading Israel about in this indefinite style, demanded the reason of that procedure, adding that it was against his express orders for any new and degrading punishments to be invented for his men.

"Come here, master-at-arms. To what end do you lead that man about?"

"To no end in the world, sir. I keep leading him about because he has no final destination."

"Mr. officer of the deck, what does this mean? Who is this strange man? I don't know that I remember him. Who is he? And what is signified by his being led about?"

Hereupon, the officer of the deck, throwing himself into a tragical posture, set forth the entire mystery; much to the captain's astonishment, who at once indignantly turned upon the phantom.

"You rascal—don't try to deceive me. Who are you? and where did you come from last?"

"Sir, my name is Peter Perkins, and I last came from the forecastle, where the master-at-arms last led me, before coming here."

"No joking, sir, no joking."

"Sir, I'm sure it's too serious a business to joke about."

"Do you have the assurance to say, that you, as a regularly

shipped man, have been on board this vessel ever since she sailed from Falmouth,[10] ten months ago?"

"Sir, anxious to secure a berth under so good a commander, I was among the first to enlist."

"What ports have we touched at, sir?" said the captain, now in a little softer tone.

"Ports, sir, ports?"

"Yes, sir, *ports*."

Israel began to scratch his yellow hair.

"What *ports*, sir?"

"Well, sir:—Boston, for one."

"Right there," whispered a midshipman.

"What was the next port, sir?"

"Why, sir, I was saying Boston was the *first* port, I believe; wasn't it?—and"—

"The *second* port, sir, is what I want."

"Well—New York."

"Right again," whispered the midshipman.

"And what port are we bound to, now?"

"Let me see—homeward-bound—Falmouth, sir."

"What sort of a place is Boston?"

"Pretty considerable of a place, sir."

"Very straight streets, ain't they?"

"Yes, sir; cow-paths, cut by sheep-walks, and intersected with hentracks."

"When did we fire the first gun?"

"Well, sir, just as we were leaving Falmouth, ten months ago—signal-gun, sir."

"Where did we fire the first *shotted* gun, sir?—and what was the name of the privateer we took upon that occasion?"

"'Pears to me, sir, at that time I was on the sick list. Yes, sir, that must have been the time; I had the brain fever, and lost my mind for a while."

"Master-at-arms, take this man away."

"Where shall I take him, sir?" touching his cap.

"Go, and air him on the forecastle."

So they resumed their devious wanderings. At last they descended to the berth-deck. It being now breakfast-time, the master-at-arms, a good-humored man, very kindly introduced our hero to his mess, and presented him with breakfast; during which he in vain endeavored, by all sorts of subtle blandishments, to worm out his secret.

At length Israel was set at liberty; and whenever there was any important duty to be done, volunteered to it with such cheerful alacrity, and approved himself so docile and excellent a seaman, that he conciliated the approbation of all the officers, as well as the captain; while his general sociability served in the end, to turn in his favor the suspicious hearts of the mariners. Perceiving his good qualities, both as a sailor and man, the captain of the main-top applied for his admission into that section of the ship; where, still improving upon his former reputation, our hero did duty for the residue of the voyage.

One pleasant afternoon, the last of the passage, when the ship was nearing the Lizard,[11] within a few hours' sail of her port, the officer of the deck, happening to glance upwards towards the main-top, descried Israel there, leaning very leisurely over the rail, looking mildly down where the officer stood.

"Well, Peter Perkins, you seem to belong to the main-top, after all."

"I always told you so, sir," smiled Israel, benevolently down upon him, "though, at first, you remember, sir, you would not believe it."

CHAPTER 21

Samson among the Philistines

At length, as the ship, gliding on past three or four vessels at anchor in the roadstead—one, a man-of-war just furling her sails—came nigh Falmouth town, Israel, from his perch, saw crowds in violent commotion on the shore, while the adjacent roofs were covered with sightseers. A large man-of-war cutter was just landing its occupants, among whom were a corporal's guard and three officers, besides the naval lieutenant and boat's crew. Some of this company having landed, and formed a sort of lane among the mob, two trim soldiers, armed to the teeth, rose in the stern-sheets; and between them, a martial man of Patagonian stature,[1] their ragged and handcuffed captive, whose defiant head overshadowed theirs, as St. Paul's dome[2] its inferior steeples. Immediately the mob raised a shout, pressing in curiosity towards the colossal stranger; so that, drawing their swords, four of the soldiers had to force a passage for their comrades, who followed on, conducting the giant.

As the letter-of-marque drew still nigher, Israel heard the officer in command of the party ashore shouting. "To the castle! to the castle!" and so, surrounded by shouting throngs, the company moved on, preceded by the four drawn swords, ever and anon flourished at the rioters, towards a large grim pile on a cliff about a mile from the landing. Long as they were in sight, the bulky form of the captive was seen at times swayingly towering over the flashing bayonets and cutlasses, like a great whale breaching amid a hostile retinue of sword-fish. Now and then, too, with barbaric scorn, he taunted them, with cramped gestures of his manacled hands.

When at last the vessel had gained her anchorage, opposite a distant detached warehouse, all was still; and the work of breaking out in the hold immediately commencing, and continuing till nightfall, absorbed all further attention for the present.

Next day was Sunday; and about noon Israel, with others, was allowed to go ashore for a stroll. The town was quiet. Seeing nothing very interesting there, he passed out, alone, into the fields along shore; and presently found himself climbing the cliff; whereon stood the grim pile before spoken of.

"What place is yon?" he asked of a rustic passing.

"Pendennis Castle."[3]

As he stepped upon the short crisp sward[4] under its walls, he started at a violent sound from within, as of the roar of some tormented lion. Soon the sound became articulate, and he heard the following words bayed out with an amazing vigor:—

"Brag no more, old England; consider you are but an island! Order back your broken battalions! home, and repent in ashes! Long enough have your hired tories across the sea forgotten the Lord their God, and bowed down to Howe and Knyphausen— the Hessian![5]——Hands off, red-skinned jackall! Wearing the king's plate,[6] as I do, I have treasures of wrath against you British."

Then came a clanking, as of a chain; many vengeful sounds, all confusedly together; with strugglings. Then again the voice:—

"Ye brought me out here, from my dungeon to this green— affronting yon Sabbath sun—to see how a rebel looks. But I show ye how a true gentleman and Christian can conduct in adversity. Back, dogs! Respect a gentleman and a Christian, though he *be* in rags and smell of bilge-water."

Filled with astonishment at these words, which came from over a massive wall, inclosing what seemed an open parade-space, Israel pressed forward; and soon came to a black archway, leading far within, underneath, to a grassy tract, through a tower. Like two boar's tusks, two sentries stood on guard at either side of the open jaws of the arch. Scrutinizing our adventurer a moment, they signed him permission to enter.

Arrived at the end of the arched-way, where the sun shone, Israel stood transfixed at the scene.

Like some baited bull in the ring, crouched the Patagonian-looking captive, hand-cuffed as before; the grass of the green trampled, and gored up all about him, both by his own movements and those of the people around. Except some soldiers and sailors, these seemed mostly town's-people, collected here out of curiosity. The stranger was outlandishly arrayed in the sorry remains of a half-Indian, half-Canadian sort of a dress, consisting of a fawn-skin jacket—the fur outside and hanging in ragged tufts—a half-rotten, bark-like belt of wampum; aged breeches of sagathy;[7] bedarned worsted stockings to the knee; old moccasins riddled with holes, their metal tags yellow with salt-water rust; a faded red woollen bonnet, not unlike a Russian night-cap, or a portentous, ensanguined full-moon; all soiled, and stuck about with bits of half-rotted straw. He seemed just broken from the dead leaves in David's outlawed Cave of Adullam.[8] Unshaven, beard and hair matted, and profuse as a corn-field beaten down by hail-storms, his whole marred aspect was that of some wild beast; but of a royal sort, and unsubdued by the cage.

"Aye, stare, stare! Though but last night dragged out of a ship's hold, like a smutty tierce;[9] and this morning out of your littered barracks here, like a murderer; for all that, you may well stare at Ethan Ticonderoga Allen,[10] the unconquered soldier, by——! You Turks never saw a Christian before. Stare on! I am he, who, when your Lord Howe wanted to bribe a patriot to fall down and worship him by an offer of a major-generalship and five thousand acres of choice land in old Vermont—(Hah! three-times-three for glorious old Vermont, and my Green-Mountain-boys![11] Hurrah! Hurrah! Hurrah!) I am he, I say, who answered your Lord Howe, 'You, *you* offer *our* land? You are like the devil in Scripture, offering all the kingdoms in the world, when the d——d soul had not a corner-lot on earth!' Stare on!"

"Look you, rebel, you had best heed how you talk against General Lord Howe," here said a thin, wasp-waisted, epauleted officer of the castle, coming near and flourishing his sword like a schoolmaster's ferule.

"General Lord Howe? Heed how I talk of that toad-hearted king's lickspittle of a scarlet poltroon; the vilest wriggler in God's worm-hole below? I tell you, that herds of red-haired devils are impatiently snorting to ladle Lord Howe with all his gang (you included) into the seethingest syrups of tophet's[12] flames!"

At this blast, the wasp-waisted officer was blown backwards as from before the suddenly burst head of a steam-boiler.

Staggering away, with a snapped spine, he muttered something about its being beneath his dignity to bandy further words with a low-lived rebel.

"Come, come, Colonel Allen," here said a mild-looking man in a sort of clerical undress; "respect the day better than to talk thus of what lies beyond. Were you to die this hour, or what is more probable, be hung next week at Tower-wharf, you know not what might become, in eternity, of yourself."

"Reverend Sir," with a mocking bow; "when not better employed braiding my beard, I have a little dabbled in your theologies. And let me tell you, Reverend Sir," lowering and intensifying his voice: "that as to the world of spirits, of which you hint, though I know nothing of the mode or manner of that world, no more than do you, yet I expect when I shall arrive there, to be treated as well as any other gentlemen of my merit. That is to say, far better than you British know how to treat an American officer and meek-hearted Christian captured in honorable war, by——! Every one tells me as you yourself just breathed, and as, crossing the sea, every billow dinned into my ear—that I, Ethan Allen, am to be hung like a thief. If I am, the great Jehovah and the Continental Congress shall avenge me; while I, for my part, shall show you, even on the tree, how a Christian gentleman can die. Meantime, sir, if you are the clergyman you look, act out your consolatory function, by getting an unfortunate Christian gentleman about to die, a bowl of punch."

The good-natured stranger, not to have his religious courtesy appealed to in vain, immediately dispatched his servant, who stood by, to procure the beverage.

At this juncture, a faint rustling sound, as of the advance of an army with banners, was heard. Silks, scarfs, and ribbons fluttered in the background. Presently, a bright squadron of fair ladies drew nigh, escorted by certain outriding gallants of Falmouth.

"Ah," sighed a soft voice; "what a strange sash, and furred vest, and what leopard-like teeth, and what flaxen hair, but all mildewed;—is that he?"

"Yea, is it, lovely charmer," said Allen, like an Ottoman,[13] bowing over his broad, bovine forehead, and breathing the words out like a lute; "it is he—Ethan Allen, the soldier; now, since ladies' eyes visit him, made trebly a captive."

"Why, he talks like a beau in a parlor; this wild, mossed American from the woods," sighed another fair lady to her mate; "but can this be he we came to see? I must have a lock of his hair."

"It is he, adorable Delilah;[14] and fear not, even though incited by the foe, by clipping my locks, to dwindle my strength. Give me your sword, man." turning to an officer;—"Ah! I'm fettered. Clip it yourself, lady."

"No, no—I am"——

"Afraid, would you say? Afraid of the vowed friend and champion of all ladies all round the world? Nay, nay: come hither."

The lady advanced; and soon, overcoming her timidity, her white hand shone like whipped foam amid the matted waves of flaxen hair.

"Ah, this is like clipping tangled tags of gold-lace," cried she; "but see, it is half straw."

"But the wearer is no man-of-straw, lady; were I free, and you had ten thousand foes—horse, foot, and dragoons—how like a friend I could fight for you! Come, you have robbed me of my hair; let me rob your dainty hand of its price. What, afraid again?"

"No, not that; but"——

"I see, lady; I may do it, by your leave, but not by your word; the wonted way of ladies. There, it is done. Sweeter that kiss, than the bitter heart of a cherry."

When at length this lady left, no small talk was had by her with her companions about someway relieving the hard lot of so knightly an unfortunate. Whereupon a worthy, judicious gentleman, of middle-age, in attendance, suggested a bottle of good wine every day, and clean linen once every week. And these, the gentle Englishwoman—too polite and too good to be fastidious—did indeed actually send to Ethan Allen, so long as he tarried a captive in her land.

The withdrawal of this company was followed by a different scene.

A perspiring man in top-boots, a riding whip in his hand, and having the air of a prosperous farmer, brushed in, like a stray bullock, among the rest, for a peep at the giant; having just entered through the arch, as the ladies passed out.

"Hearing that the man who took Ticonderoga was here in Pendennis Castle, I've ridden twenty-five miles to see him; and to-morrow my brother will ride forty for the same purpose. So let me have first look. Sir," he continued, addressing the captive; "will you let me ask you a few plain questions, and be free with you?"

"Be free with me? with all my heart. I love freedom of all things. I'm ready to die for freedom; I expect to. So be free as you please. What is it?"

"Then, sir, permit me to ask what is your occupation in life;—in time of peace, I mean."

"You talk like a tax-gatherer;" rejoined Allen, squinting diabolically at him; "what is my occupation in life? Why, in my younger days I studied divinity, but at present I am a conjuror by profession."

Hereupon everybody laughed, equally at the manner as the words, and the nettled farmer retorted:—

"Conjurer, eh? well, you conjured wrong that time you were taken."

"Not so wrong, though, as you British did, that time I took Ticonderoga, my friend."

At this juncture the servant came with the punch, when his master bade him present it to the captive.

"No!—give it me, sir, with your own hands; and pledge me as gentleman to gentleman."

"I cannot pledge a state-prisoner, Colonel Allen; but I will hand you the punch with my own hands, since you insist upon it."

"Spoken and done like a true gentleman, sir; I am bound to you."

Then receiving the bowl into his gyved[15] hands, the iron ringing against the china, he put it to his lips, and saying, "I hereby give the British nation credit for half a minute's good usage," at one draught emptied it to the bottom.

"The rebel gulps it down like a swilling hog at a trough;" here scoffed a lusty private of the guard, off duty.

"Shame to you!" cried the giver of the bowl.

"Nay, sir; his red coat is a standing blush to him, as it is to the whole scarlet-blushing British army." Then turning derisively upon the private: "you object to my way of taking things, do ye? I fear I shall never please ye. You objected to the way, too, in which I took Ticonderoga, and the way in which I meant to take Montreal. Selah![16] But, pray, now that I look at you, are not you the hero I caught dodging round, in his shirt, in the cattle-pen, inside the fort? It was the break of day, you remember."

"Come, Yankee," here swore the incensed private; "cease this, or I'll darn your old fawn-skins for ye, with the flat of this sword;" for a specimen, laying it lashwise, but not heavily, across the captive's back.

Turning like a tiger, the giant, catching the steel between his teeth, wrenched it from the private's grasp, and striking it with his manacles, sent it spinning like a juggler's dagger into the air; saying, "Lay your dirty coward's iron on a tied gentleman again, and these," lifting his handcuffed fists, "shall be the beetle of mortality to you!"

The now furious soldier would have struck him with all his force; but several men of the town interposed, reminding him that it were outrageous to attack a chained captive.

"Ah," said Allen, "I am accustomed to that, and therefore I am beforehand with them; and the extremity of what I say against Britain, is not meant for you, kind friends, but for my insulters, present and to come." Then recognizing among the interposers the giver of the bowl, he turned with a courteous bow, saying, "Thank you again and again, my good sir; you may not be the worse for this; ours is an unstable world; so that one gentleman never knows when it may be his turn to be helped of another."

But the soldier still making a riot, and the commotion growing general, a superior officer stepped up, who terminated the scene by remanding the prisoner to his cell, dismissing the towns-people, with all strangers, Israel among the rest, and closing the castle gates after them.

CHAPTER 22

*Something Further of Ethan Allen; with Israel's
Flight Towards the Wilderness*

Among the episodes of the Revolutionary War, none is stranger than that of Ethan Allen in England; the event and the man being equally uncommon.

Allen seems to have been a curious combination of a Hercules, a Joe Miller, a Bayard, and a Tom Hyer; had a person like the Belgian giants; mountain music in him like a Swiss; a heart plump as Cœur de Lion's.[1] Though born in New England, he exhibited no trace of her character. He was frank; bluff; companionable as a Pagan; convivial; a Roman; hearty as a harvest. His spirit was essentially western; and herein is his peculiar Americanism; for the western spirit is, or will yet be (for no other is, or can be) the true American one.

For the most part, Allen's manner while in England, was scornful and ferocious in the last degree; however qualified by that wild, heroic sort of levity, which in the hour of oppression or peril, seems inseparable from a nature like his; the mode whereby such a temper best evinces its barbaric disdain of adversity; and how cheaply and waggishly it holds the malice, even though triumphant, of its foes! Aside from that inevitable egotism relatively pertaining to pine trees, spires, and giants, there were, perhaps, two special incidental reasons for the Titanic Vermonter's singular demeanor abroad. Taken captive while heading a forlorn hope before Montreal, he was treated with inexcusable cruelty and indignity; something as if he had fallen into the hands of the Dyaks.[2] Immediately upon his capture he would have been deliberately suffered to have been butchered by the Indian allies, in cold blood on the spot, had he not, with desperate intrepidity, availed himself of his enormous physical strength, by twitching a British officer to him, and using him for a living target, whirling him round and round against the murderous tomahawks of the savages. Shortly afterwards, led into the town, fenced about by bayonets of the guard, the commander of the enemy, one General Prescott, flourished his cane over the captive's head, with brutal insults promising him a rebel's halter at Tyburn.[3] During his passage to England in the same ship wherein went passenger Colonel Guy Johnson,[4] the implacable tory, he was kept heavily ironed in the hold, and in all ways treated as a common mutineer; or, it may be, rather as a lion of Asia; which, though caged, was still too dreadful to behold without fear and trembling; and consequent cruelty. And no wonder, at least for the fear; for on one occasion, when chained hand and foot, he was insulted on shipboard by an officer; with his teeth he twisted off the nail that went through the mortise[5] of his handcuffs, and so, having his arms at liberty, challenged his insulter to combat. Often, as at Pendennis Castle, when no other avengement was at hand, he would hurl on his foes such howling tempests of anathema, as fairly to shock them into retreat. Prompted by somewhat similar motives, both on shipboard and in England, he would often make the most vociferous allusions to Ticonderoga, and the part he played in its capture, well knowing, that of all American names, Ticonderoga was, at that period, by far the most famous and galling to Englishmen.

Parlor-men, dancing-masters, the graduates of the Abbé Bellegarde[6] may shrug their laced shoulders at the boisterousness of Allen in England. True, he stood upon no punctilios with his jailers; for where modest gentleman-hood is all on one side, it is a losing affair; as if my Lord Chesterfield[7] should take off his hat, and smile, and bow, to a mad bull, in hopes of a reciprocation of politeness. When among wild beasts, if they menace you, be a wild beast. Neither is it unlikely that this was the view taken by Allen. For, besides the exasperating tendency to self-assertion which such treatment as his must have bred on a man like him, his experience must have taught him, that by assuming the part of a jocular, reckless, and even braggart barbarian, he would better sustain himself against bullying turnkeys than by submissive quietude. Nor should it be forgotten, that besides the petty details of personal malice, the enemy violated every international usage of right and decency, in treating a distinguished prisoner of war as if he had been a Botany-Bay[8] convict. If, at the present day, in any similar case between the same States, the repetition of such outrages would be more than unlikely, it is only because it is among nations as among individuals: imputed indigence provokes oppression and scorn; but that same indigence being risen to opulence, receives a politic consideration even from its former insulters.

As the event proved, in the course Allen pursued, he was right. Because, though at first nothing was talked of by his captors, and nothing anticipated by himself, but his ignominious execution, or, at the least, prolonged and squalid incarceration; nevertheless, these threats and prospects evaporated, and by his facetious scorn for scorn, under the extremest sufferings, he finally wrung repentant usage from his foes; and in the end, being liberated from his irons, and walking the quarter-deck where before he had been thrust into the hold, was carried back to America, and in due time at New York, honorably included in a regular exchange of prisoners.

It was not without strange interest that Israel had been an eye-witness of the scenes on the Castle Green. Neither was this interest abated by the painful necessity of concealing, for the present, from his brave countryman and fellow-mountaineer, the fact of a friend being nigh. When at last the throng was dismissed, walking towards the town with the rest, he heard that there were some forty or more other Americans, privates, confined on the cliff. Upon this, inventing a pretence, he turned back, loitering around the walls for any chance glimpse of the captives. Presently, while looking up at a grated embrasure in the tower, he started at a voice from it familiarly hailing him:—

"Potter, is that you? In God's name how came you here?"

At these words, a sentry below had his eye on our astonished adventurer. Bringing his piece to bear, he bade him stand. Next moment Israel was under arrest. Being brought into the presence of the forty prisoners, where they lay in litters of mouldy straw, strewn with gnawed bones, as in a kennel, he recognized among them one Singles, now Sergeant Singles, the man who, upon our hero's return home from his last Cape Horn voyage, he had found wedded to his mountain Jenny. Instantly a rush of emotions filled him. Not as when Damon found Pythias.[9] But far stranger, because very different. For not only had this Singles been an alien to Israel (so far as actual intercourse went), but impelled to it by instinct, Israel had all but detested him, as a successful, and perhaps insidious rival. Nor was it altogether unlikely that Singles had reciprocated the feeling. But now, as if the Atlantic rolled, not between two continents, but two worlds—this, and the next—these alien souls, oblivious to hate, melted down into one.

At such a juncture, it was hard to maintain a disguise; especially when it involved the seeming rejection of advances like the sergeant's. Still, converting his real amazement into affected surprise, Israel, in presence of the sentries, declared to Singles that he (Singles) must labor under some unaccountable delusion; for he (Potter) was no Yankee rebel, thank Heaven, but a true man to his king; in short, an honest Englishman, born in Kent, and now serving his country, and doing what damage he might to her foes, by being first captain of a carronade on board a letter-of-marque, that moment in the harbor.

For a moment, the captive stood astounded; but observing Israel more narrowly, detecting his latent look, and bethinking him of the useless peril he had thoughtlessly caused to a countryman, no doubt unfortunate as himself, Singles took his cue, and pretending sullenly to apologize for his error, put on a disappointed and crest-fallen air. Nevertheless, it was not without much difficulty, and after many supplemental scrutinies and inquisitions from a board of officers before whom he was subsequently brought, that our wanderer was finally permitted to quit the cliff.

This luckless adventure not only nipped in the bud a little scheme he had been revolving, for materially befriending Ethan Allen and his comrades, but resulted in making his further stay at Falmouth perilous in the extreme. And as if this were not enough, next day, while hanging over the side, painting the hull, in trepidation of a visit from the castle soldiers, rumor came to the ship that the man-of-war in the haven purposed impressing one-third of the letter of marque's crew; though, indeed, the latter vessel was preparing for a second cruise. Being on board a private armed ship, Israel had little dreamed of its liability to the same governmental hardships with the meanest merchantman. But the system of impressment is no respecter either of pity or person.

His mind was soon determined. Unlike his shipmates, braving immediate and lonely hazard, rather than wait for a collective and ultimate one, he cunningly dropped himself overboard the same night, and after the narrowest risk from the muskets of the man-of-war's sentries (whose gang-ways he had to pass), succeeded in swimming to shore, where he fell exhausted, but recovering, fled inland; doubly hunted by the thought, that whether as an Englishman, or whether as an American, he would, if caught, be now equally subject to enslavement.

Shortly after the break of day, having gained many miles, he succeeded in ridding himself of his seaman's clothing, having found some mouldy old rags on the banks of a stagnant pond, nigh a rickety building, which looked like a poorhouse,—clothing not improbably, as he surmised, left there, on the bank, by some pauper suicide. Marvel not that he should, with avidity, seize these rags; what the suicides abandon the living hug.

Once more in beggar's garb, the fugitive sped towards London, prompted by the same instinct which impels the hunted fox to the wilderness; for solitudes befriend the endangered wild beast, but crowds are the security, because the true desert of persecuted man. Among the throngs of the capital, Israel for more than forty years was yet to disappear, as one entering at dusk into a thick wood. Nor did ever the German forest, nor Tasso's enchanted one,[10] contain in its depths more things of horror than eventually were revealed in the secret clefts, gulfs, caves and dens of London.

But here we anticipate a page.

CHAPTER 23

Israel in Egypt

It was a grey, lowering afternoon that, worn-out, half-starved, and haggard, Israel arrived within some ten or fifteen miles of London, and saw scores and scores of forlorn men engaged in a great brickyard.[1]

For the most part, brick-making is all mud and mire. Where, abroad, the business is carried on largely, as to supply the London Market, hordes of the poorest wretches are employed; their grimy tatters naturally adapting them to an employ where cleanliness is as much out of the question as with a drowned man at the bottom of the lake in the Dismal Swamp.[2]

Desperate with want, Israel resolved to turn brick-maker; nor did he fear to present himself as a stranger; nothing doubting that to such a vocation, his rags would be accounted the best letters-of-introduction.

To be brief, he accosted one of the many surly overseers, or task-masters of the yard, who with no few pompous airs, finally engaged him at six shillings a week; almost equivalent to a dollar and a half. He was appointed to one of the mills for grinding up the ingredients. This mill stood in the open air. It was of a rude, primitive, Eastern aspect; consisting of a sort of hopper, emptying into a barrel-shaped receptacle. In the barrel was a clumsy machine turned round at its axis by a great bent beam, like a well-sweep, only it was horizontal; to this beam, at its outer end, a spavined[3] old horse was attached. The muddy mixture was shovelled into the hopper by spavined-looking old men; while trudging wearily round and round the spavined old horse ground it all up till it slowly squashed out at the bottom of the barrel, in a doughy compound, all ready for the moulds.

Where the dough squeezed out of the barrel, a pit was sunken, so as to bring the moulder here stationed down to a level with the trough, into which the dough fell. Israel was assigned to this pit. Men came to him continually, reaching down rude wooden trays, divided into compartments, each of the size and shape of a brick. With a flat sort of big ladle, Israel slapped the dough into the trays from the trough; then, with a bit of smooth board scraped the top even, and handed it up. Half buried there in the pit, all the time handing those desolate trays, poor Israel seemed some grave-digger, or church-yard man, tucking away dead little innocents in their coffins on one side, and cunningly disinterring them again to resurrectionists stationed on the other.

Twenty of these melancholy old mills were in operation. Twenty heart-broken old horses, rigged out deplorably in cast-off old cart harness, incessantly tugged at twenty great shaggy beams; while from twenty half-burst old barrels, twenty wads of mud, with a lava-like course, gouged out into twenty old troughs, to be slapped by twenty tattered men, into the twenty-times-twenty battered old trays.

Ere entering his pit for the first, Israel had been struck by the dismally devil-may-care gestures of the moulders. But hardly had he himself been a moulder three days, when his previous sedateness of concern at his unfortunate lot, began to conform to the reckless sort of half jolly despair expressed by the others. The truth indeed was, that this continual, violent, helterskelter slapping of the dough into the moulds, begat a corresponding disposition in the moulder; who, by heedlessly slapping that sad dough, as stuff of little worth, was thereby taught, in his meditations, to slap, with similar heedlessness, his own sadder fortunes, as of still less vital consideration. To these muddy philosophers, men and bricks were equally of clay. What signifies who we be—dukes or ditchers? thought the moulders; all is vanity and clay. So slap, slap, slap; care-free and negligent; with bitter unconcern, these dismal desperadoes flapped down the dough. If this recklessness were vicious of them, be it so; but their vice was like that weed which but grows on barren ground; enrich the soil, and it disappears.

For thirteen weary weeks, lorded over by the taskmasters, Israel toiled in his pit. Though this condemned him to a sort of earthy dungeon, or grave-digger's hole while he worked; yet even when liberated to his meals, naught of a cheery nature greeted him. The yard was encamped, with all its endless rows of tented sheds, and kilns, and mills, upon a wild waste moor, belted round by bogs and fens. The blank horizon, like a rope, coiled round the whole.

Sometimes the air was harsh and bleak; the ridged and mottled sky looked scourged; or cramping fogs set in from sea, for leagues around, ferreting out each rheumatic human bone, and racking it; the sciatic limpers shivered; their aguish rags sponged up the mists. No shelter, though it hailed. The sheds were for the bricks. Unless, indeed, according to the phrase, each man was a "brick," which, in sober scripture, was the case; brick is no bad name for any son of Adam; Eden was but a brick-yard; what is a mortal but a few luckless shovelfuls of clay, moulded in a mould, laid out on a sheet to dry, and ere long quickened into his queer caprices by the sun? Are not men built into communities just like bricks into a wall? Consider the great wall of China:[4] ponder the great populace of Pekin. As man serves bricks, so God him; building him up by billions into the edifices of his purposes. Man attains not to the nobility of a brick, unless taken in the aggregate. Yet is there a difference in brick, whether quick or dead; which, for the last, we now shall see.

All night long, men sat before the mouth of the kilns, feeding them with fuel. A dull smoke—a smoke of their torments—went up from their tops. It was curious to see the kilns under the action of the fire, gradually changing color, like boiling lobsters. When, at last, the fires would be extinguished, the bricks being duly baked, Israel often took a peep into the low vaulted ways at the base, where the flaming faggots had crackled. The bricks immediately lining the vaults would be all burnt to useless scrolls, black as charcoal, and twisted into shapes the most grotesque; the next tier would be a little less withered, but hardly fit for service; and gradually, as you went higher and higher along the successive layers of the kiln, you came to the midmost ones, sound, square, and perfect bricks, bringing the highest prices; from these the contents of the kiln gradually deteriorated in the opposite direction, upward. But the topmost layers, though inferior to the best, by no means presented the distorted look of the furnace-bricks. The furnace-bricks were haggard, with the immediate blistering of the fire—the midmost ones were ruddy with a genial and tempered glow—the summit ones were pale with the languor of too exclusive an exemption from the burden of the blaze.

These kilns were a sort of temporary temples constructed in the yard, each brick being set against its neighbor almost with the care taken by the mason. But as soon as the fire was extinguished, down came the kiln in a tumbled ruin, carted off to London, once more to be set up in ambitious edifices, to a true brick-yard philosopher, little less transient than the kilns.

Sometimes, lading out his dough, Israel could not but bethink him of what seemed enigmatic in his fate. He whom love of country made a hater of her foes—the foreigners among whom he now was thrown—he who, as soldier and sailor, had joined to kill, burn and destroy both them and theirs—here he was at last, serving that very people as a slave, better succeeding in making their bricks than firing their ships. To think that he should be thus helping, with all his strength, to extend the walls of the Thebes[5] of the oppressor, made him half mad. Poor Israel! well-named—bondsman in the English Egypt. But he drowned the thought by still more recklessly spattering with his ladle: "What signifies who we be, or where we are, or what we do?" Slap-dash! "Kings as clowns are codgers—who ain't a nobody?" Splash! "All is vanity and clay."[6]

CHAPTER 24

In the City of Dis

At the end of his brick-making, our adventurer found himself with a tolerable suit of clothes—somewhat darned—on his back, several blood-blisters in his palms, and some verdigris coppers in his pocket. Forthwith, to seek his fortune, he proceeded on foot to the capital, entering, like the king, from Windsor, from the Surrey side.[1]

It was late on a Monday morning, in November—a Blue Monday—a Fifth of November—Guy Fawkes' Day![2]—very blue, foggy, doleful and gunpowdery, indeed, as shortly will be seen,—that Israel found himself wedged in among the greatest every-day crowd which grimy London presents to the curious stranger. That hereditary crowd—gulf-stream of humanity—which, for continuous centuries, has never ceased pouring, like an endless shoal of herring, over London Bridge.

At the period here written of, the bridge, specifically known by that name, was a singular and sombre pile, built by a cowled monk—Peter of Colechurch[3]—some five hundred years before. Its arches had long been crowded at the sides with strange old rookeries of disproportioned and toppling height, converting the bridge at once into the most densely occupied ward, and most jammed thoroughfare of the town, while, as the skulls of bullocks are hung out for signs to the gateways of shambles,[4] so the withered heads and smoked quarters of traitors, stuck on pikes, long crowned the Southwark[5] entrance.

Though these rookeries, with their grisly heraldry, had been pulled down some twenty years prior to the present visit; still, enough of grotesque and antiquity clung to the structure at large, to render it the most striking of objects, especially to one like our hero, born in a virgin clime, where the only antiquities are the for ever youthful heavens and the earth.

On his route from Brentford to Paris, Israel had passed through the capital, but only as a courier. So that now, for the first, he had time to linger and loiter, and lounge—slowly absorb what he saw—meditate himself into boundless amazement. For forty years he never recovered from that surprise—never, till dead, had done with his wondering.

Hung in long, sepulchral arches of stone, the black, besmoked bridge seemed a huge scarf of crape, festooning the river across. Similar funereal festoons spanned it to the west, while eastward, towards the sea, tiers and tiers of jetty colliers lay moored, side by side, fleets of black swans.

The Thames, which far away, among the green fields of Berks,[6] ran clear as a brook, here, polluted by continual vicinity to man, curdled on between rotten wharves, one murky sheet of sewerage. Fretted by the ill-built piers, awhile it crested and hissed, then shot balefully through the Erebus[7] arches, desperate as the lost souls of the harlots, who, every night, took the same plunge. Meantime, here and there, like awaiting hearses, the coal-scows drifted along, poled broadside, pell-mell to the current.

And as that tide in the water swept all craft on, so a like tide seemed hurrying all men, all horses, all vehicles on the land. As ant-hills, the bridge arches crawled with processions of carts, coaches, drays, every sort of wheeled, rumbling thing, the noses of the horses behind touching the backs of the vehicles in advance, all bespattered with ebon mud, ebon mud that stuck like Jews' pitch. At times the mass, receiving some mysterious impulse far in the rear, away among the coiled thoroughfares out of sight, would start forward with a spasmodic surge. It seemed as if some squadron of centaurs, on the thither side of Phlegethon,[8] with charge on charge, was driving tormented humanity, with all its chattels, across.

Whichever way the eye turned, no tree, no speck of any green thing was seen; no more than in smithies. All laborers, of whatsoever sort, were hued like the men in foundries. The black vistas of streets were as the galleries in coal mines; the flagging, as flat tomb-stones minus the consecration of moss; and worn heavily down, by sorrowful tramping, as the vitreous rocks in the cursed Gallipagos,[9] over which the convict tortoises crawl.

As in eclipses, the sun was hidden; the air darkened; the whole dull, dismayed aspect of things, as if some neighboring volcano, belching its premonitory smoke, were about to whelm the great town, as Herculaneum and Pompeii, or the Cities of the Plain.[10] And as they had been upturned in terror towards the mountain, all faces were more or less snowed, or spotted with soot. Nor marble, nor flesh, nor the sad spirit of man, may in this cindery City of Dis[11] abide white.

On they passed; two-and-two, along the packed footpaths of the bridge; long-drawn, methodic, as funerals: some of the faces settled in dry apathy, content with their doom; others seemed mutely raving against it; while still others, like the spirits of Milton and Shelley in the prelatical Hinnom,[12] seemed undeserving their fate, and despising their torture.

As retired at length, midway, in a recess of the bridge, Israel surveyed them, various individual aspects all but frighted him. Knowing not who they were; never destined, it may be, to behold them again; one after the other, they drifted by, uninvoked ghosts in Hades. Some of the wayfarers wore a less serious look; some seemed hysterically merry; but the mournful faces had an earnestness not seen in the others; because man, "poor player,"[13] succeeds better in life's tragedy than comedy.

Arrived, in the end, on the Middlesex[14] side, Israel's heart was prophetically heavy; foreknowing, that being of this race, felicity could never be his lot.

For five days he wandered and wandered. Without leaving statelier haunts unvisited, he did not overlook those broader areas; hereditary parks and manors of vice and misery. Not by constitution disposed to gloom, there was a mysteriousness in those impulses which led him at this time to rovings like these. But hereby stoic influences were at work, to fit him at a soon-coming day, for enacting a part in the last extremities here seen; when by sickness, destitution, each busy ill of exile, he was destined to experience a fate, uncommon even to luck-less humanity; a fate whose crowning qualities were its remote-ness from relief and its depth of obscurity; London, adversity, and the sea, three Armageddons,[15] which, at one and the same time, slay, and secrete their victims.

CHAPTER 25

Forty-five Years

For the most part, what befell Israel during his forty years' wanderings in the London deserts, surpassed the forty years in the natural wilderness of the outcast Hebrews under Moses.[1]

In that London fog, went before him the ever-present cloud by day, but no pillar of fire by the night, except the cold column of the monument;[2] two hundred feet beneath the mocking gilt flames on whose top, at the stone base, the shiverer, of midnight, often laid down.

But these experiences, both from their intensity and his solitude, were necessarily squalid. Best not enlarge upon them. For just as extreme suffering, without hope, is intolerable to the victim, so, to others, is its depiction, without some corresponding delusive mitigation. The gloomiest and truthfulest dramatist seldom chooses for his theme the calamities, however extraordinary, of inferior and private persons; least of all, the pauper's; admonished by the fact, that to the craped palace of the king lying in state, thousands of starers shall throng; but few feel enticed to the shanty, where, like a pealed knucklebone, grins the unupholstered corpse of the beggar.

Why at one given stone in the flagging does man after man cross yonder street? What plebeian Lear or Œdipus;[3] what Israel Potter cowers there by the corner they shun? From this turning point then, we too cross over and skim events to the end; omitting the particulars of the starveling's wrangling with rats for prizes in the sewers; or his crawling into an abandoned doorless house in St. Giles',[4] where his hosts were three dead men, one pendant; into another of an alley nigh Houndsditch,[5] where the crazy hovel, in phosphoric rottenness, fell sparkling on him one

pitchy midnight, and he received that injury, which excluding activity for no small part of the future, was an added cause of his
prolongation of exile; besides not leaving his faculties unaffected
by the concussion of one of the rafters on his brain.

But these were some of the incidents not belonging to the beginning of his career. On the contrary, a sort of humble prosperity attended him for a time. Insomuch that once he was not
without hopes of being able to buy his homeward passage, so
soon as the war should end. But, as stubborn fate would have
it, being run over one day at Holborn Bars,[6] and taken into a
neighboring bakery, he was there treated with such kindliness
by a Kentish[7] lass, the shop-girl, that in the end he thought his
debt of gratitude could only be repaid by love. In a word, the
money saved up for his ocean voyage was lavished upon a rash
embarkation in wedlock.

Originally he had fled to the capital to avoid the dilemma of
impressment or imprisonment. In the absence of other motives,
the dread of those hardships would have fixed him there till the
peace. But now, when hostilities were no more; so was his
money. Some period elapsed ere the affairs of the two govern-
ments were put on such a footing as to support an American
consul at London. Yet, when this came to pass, he could only
embrace the facilities for a return here furnished, by deserting a
wife and child; wedded and born in the enemy's land.

The peace immediately filled England and more especially
London, with hordes of disbanded soldiers; thousands of
whom, rather than starve, or turn highwaymen (which no few
of their comrades did; stopping coaches at times in the most
public streets), would work for such a pittance, as to bring
down the wages of all the laboring classes. Neither was our adventurer the least among the sufferers. Driven out of his previous employ—a sort of porter in a river-side warehouse—by this
sudden influx of rivals, destitute, honest men like himself, with
the ingenuity of his race, he turned his hand to the village art of
chair-bottoming. An itinerant, he paraded the streets with the
cry of "old chairs to mend!" furnishing a curious illustration of
the contradictions of human life; that he who did little but
trudge, should be giving cosy seats to all the rest of the world.

Meantime, according to another well-known Malthusian enigma[8] in human affairs, his family increased. In all, eleven children were born to him in certain sixpenny garrets in Moorfields.[9] One after the other, ten were buried.

When chair-bottoming would fail, resort was had to matchmaking. That business being overdone in turn, next came the collecting of old rags, bits of paper, nails, and broken glass. Nor was this the last step. From the gutter, he slid to the sewer. The slope was smooth. In poverty,

      ——"Facilis descensus Averni."[10]

But many a poor soldier had sloped down there into the boggy canal of Avernus before him. Nay, he had three corporals and a sergeant for company.

But his lot was relieved by two strange things, presently to appear. In 1793 war again broke out; the great French war. This lighted London of some of its superfluous hordes, and lost Israel the subterranean society of his friends, the corporals and sergeant, with whom, wandering forlorn through the black kingdoms of mud, he used to spin yarns about sea prisoners in hulks, and listen to stories of the Black-hole of Calcutta;[11] and often would meet other pairs of poor soldiers, perfect strangers, at the more public corners and intersections of sewers—the Charing-Crosses[12] below; one soldier having the other by his remainder button, earnestly discussing the sad prospects of a rise in bread, or the tide; while through the grating of the gutters overhead, the rusty skylights of the realm, came the hoarse rumblings of bakers' carts, with splashes of the flood whereby these unsuspected gnomes of the city lived.

Encouraged by the exodus of the lost tribes of soldiers, Israel returned to chair-bottoming. And it was in frequenting Covent-Garden market,[13] at early morning, for the purchase of his flags,[14] that he experienced one of the strange alleviations hinted of above. That chatting with the ruddy, aproned, huckster-women, on whose moist cheeks yet trickled the dew of the dawn on the meadows; that being surrounded by bales of hay, as the raker by cocks and ricks in the field; those glimpses of garden

produce, the blood-beets, with the damp earth still tufting the
roots; that mere handling of his flags, and bethinking him of
whence they must have come; the green hedges through which
the wagon that brought them had passed; that trudging home
with them as a gleaner with his sheaf of wheat; all this was inex-
pressibly grateful. In want and bitterness, pent in, perforce, between dingy walls, he had rural returns of his boyhood's sweeter
days among them; and the hardest stones of his solitary heart
(made hard by bare endurance alone), would feel the stir of tender but quenchless memories, like the grass of deserted flagging,
upsprouting through its closest seams. Sometimes, when incited
by some little incident, however trivial in itself, thoughts of home
would—either by gradually working and working upon him, or
else by an impetuous rush of recollection—overpower him for a
time to a sort of hallucination.

Thus was it:—One fair half-day in the July of 1800, by good
luck, he was employed, partly out of charity, by one of the keepers, to trim the sward in an oval inclosure within St. James'
Park, a little green, but a three minutes' walk along the gravelled
way, from the brick-besmoked and grimy Old Brewery of the
palace,[15] which gives its ancient name to the public resort on
whose borders it stands. It was a little oval, fenced in with iron
palings, between whose bars the imprisoned verdure peered
forth, as some wild captive creature of the woods from its cage.
And alien Israel there—at times staring dreamily about him—
seemed like some amazed runaway steer, or trespassing Pequod
Indian, impounded on the shores of Narragansett Bay,[16] long
ago; and back to New England our exile was called in his soul.
For still working, and thinking of home; and thinking of home,
and working amid the verdant quietude of this little oasis, one
rapt thought begat another, till at last his mind settled intensely,
and yet half humorously, upon the image of Old Huckleberry,
his mother's favorite old pillion horse; and, ere long, hearing a
sudden scraping noise (some hob-shoe without, against the iron
paling), he insanely took it to be Old Huckleberry in his stall,
hailing him (Israel) with his shod fore-foot clattering against
the planks—his customary trick when hungry—and so, down
goes Israel's hook, and with a tuft of white clover, impulsively

snatched, he hurries away a few paces in obedience to the imaginary summons. But soon stopping midway, and forlornly gazing round at the inclosure, he bethought him that a far different oval, the great oval of the ocean, must be crossed ere his crazy errand could be done; and even then, Old Huckleberry would be found long surfeited with clover, since, doubtless, being dead many a summer, he must be buried beneath it. And many years after, in a far different part of the town, and in far less winsome weather too, passing with his bundle of flags through Red-Cross street, towards Barbican,[17] in a fog so dense that the dimmed and massed blocks of houses, exaggerated by the loom, seemed shadowy ranges on ranges of midnight hills; he heard a confused pastoral sort of sounds; tramplings, lowings, halloos, and was suddenly called to by a voice, to head off certain cattle, bound to Smithfield,[18] bewildered and unruly in the fog. Next instant he saw the white face—white as an orange blossom—of a black-bodied steer, in advance of the drove, gleaming ghost-like through the vapors; and presently, forgetting his limp, with rapid shout and gesture, he was more eager, even than the troubled farmers, their owners, in driving the riotous cattle back into Barbican. Monomaniac reminiscences were in him—"To the right, to the right!" he shouted, as, arrived at the street corner, the farmers beat the drove to the left, towards Smithfield: "To the right! you are driving them back to the pastures—to the right! that way lies the barn-yard!" "Barn-yard?" cried a voice; "you are dreaming, old man." And so, Israel, now an old man, was bewitched by the mirage of vapors; he had dreamed himself home into the mists of the Housatonic[19] mountains; ruddy boy on the upland pastures again. But how different the flat, apathetic, dead, London fog now seemed from those agile mists, which goat-like, climbed the purple peaks, or in routed armies of phantoms, broke down, pell-mell, dispersed in flight upon the plain; leaving the cattle-boy loftily alone, clear-cut as a balloon against the sky.

In 1817, he once more endured extremity; this second peace[20] again drifting its discharged soldiers on London, so that all kinds of labor were over-stocked. Beggars, too, lighted on the walks like locusts. Timber-toed cripples stilted along, numerous as French peasants in *sabots*.[21] And, as thirty years before, on all sides, the exile had heard the supplicatory cry, not addressed to him: "An honorable scar, your honor, received at Bunker-Hill, or Saratoga, or Trenton,[22] fighting for his most gracious Majesty, King George!" So now, in presence of the still-surviving Israel, our Wandering Jew,[23] the amended cry was anew taken up, by a succeeding generation of unfortunates: "An honorable scar, your honor, received at Corunna, or at Waterloo, or at Trafalgar!"[24] Yet not a few of these petitioners had never been outside of the London Smoke; a sort of crafty aristocracy in their way, who, without having endangered their own persons much if anything, reaped no insignificant share, both of the glory and profit of the bloody battles they claimed; while some of the genuine working heroes, too brave to beg, too cut-up to work, and too poor to live, laid down quietly in corners and died. And here it may be noted, as a fact nationally characteristic, that however desperately reduced at times, even to the sewers, Israel, the American, never-sunk below the mud, to actual beggary.

Though henceforth elbowed out of many a chance three-penny job by the added thousands who contended with him against starvation, nevertheless, somehow he continued to subsist, as those tough old oaks of the cliffs, which though hacked at by hail-stones of tempests, and even wantonly maimed by the passing woodman, still, however cramped by rival trees and fettered by rocks, succeed, against all odds, in keeping the vital nerve of the tap-root alive. And even towards the end, in his dismallest December, our veteran could still at intervals feel a momentary warmth in his topmost boughs. In his Moor-fields' garret, over a handful of re-ignited cinders (which the night before might have warmed some lord), cinders raked up from the streets, he would drive away dolor, by talking with his one only surviving, and now motherless child—the spared Benjamin of his old age—of the far Canaan beyond the sea; rehearsing to the lad those well-remembered adventures among New-England hills, and painting scenes of nestling happiness and plenty, in which the lowliest shared. And here, shadowy as it was, was the second alleviation hinted of above.

To these tales of the Fortunate Isles of the Free, recounted by one who had been there, the poor enslaved boy of Moorfields listened, night after night, as to the stories of Sinbad the Sailor.[25] When would his father take him there? "Some day to come, my boy;" would be the hopeful response of an unhoping heart. And "would God it were to-morrow!" would be the impassioned reply.

In these talks Israel unconsciously sowed the seeds of his eventual return. For with added years, the boy felt added longing to escape his entailed misery, by compassing for his father and himself, a voyage to the Promised Land. By his persevering efforts he succeeded at last, against every obstacle, in gaining credit in the right quarter to his extraordinary statements. In short, charitably stretching a technical point, the American Consul finally saw father and son embarked in the Thames for Boston.

It was the year 1826;[26] half a century since Israel, in early manhood, had sailed a prisoner in the Tartar frigate from the same port to which he now was bound. An octogenarian as he recrossed the brine, he showed locks besnowed as its foam. White-haired old ocean seemed as a brother.

CHAPTER 26

Requiescat in Pace

It happened that the ship, gaining her port, was moored to the dock on a Fourth-of-July; and half-an-hour after landing, hustled by the riotous crowd near Faneuil Hall,[1] the old man narrowly escaped being run over by a patriotic triumphal car in the procession, flying a broidered banner, inscribed with gilt letters:—

"BUNKER-HILL.
1775.
GLORY TO THE HEROES THAT FOUGHT!"

It was on Copp's Hill,[2] within the city bounds, one of the enemy's positions during the fight, that our wanderer found his best repose that day. Sitting down here on a mound in the grave-yard, he looked off across Charles River towards the battle-ground, whose incipient monument, at that period, was hard to see, as a struggling sprig of corn in a chilly spring. Upon those heights, fifty years before, his now feeble hands had wielded both ends of the musket. There too he had received that slit upon the chest, which afterwards, in the affair with the Serapis, being traversed by a cutlass wound, made him now the bescarred bearer of a cross.

For a long time he sat mute, gazing blankly about him. The sultry July day was waning. His son sought to cheer him a little ere rising to return to the lodging for the present assigned them by the ship-captain. "Nay," replied the old man, "I shall get no fitter rest than here by the mounds."

But from this true "Potters' Field,"[3] the boy at length drew him away; and encouraged next morning by a voluntary purse made up among the reassembled passengers, father and son started by stage for the country of the Housatonic. But the exile's presence in these old mountain townships proved less a return than a resurrection. At first, none knew him, nor could recall having heard of him. Ere long it was found, that more than thirty years previous, the last known survivor of his family in that region, a bachelor, following the example of three-fourths of his neighbors, had sold out and removed to a distant country in the west; where exactly, none could say.

He sought to get a glimpse of his father's homestead. But it had been burnt down long ago. Accompanied by his son, dim-eyed and dim-hearted, he next went to find the site. But the roads had years before been changed. The old road was now broused over by sheep; the new one ran straight through what had formerly been orchards. But new orchards, planted from other suckers, and in time grafted, throve on sunny slopes near by, where blackberries had once been picked by the bushel. At length he came to a field waving with buckwheat. It seemed one of those fields which himself had often reaped. But it turned out, upon inquiry, that but three summers since, a walnut grove had stood there. Then he vaguely remembered that his father had sometimes talked of planting such a grove, to defend the neighboring fields against the cold north wind; yet where precisely that grove was to have been, his shattered mind could not recall. But it seemed not unlikely that during his long exile, the walnut grove had been planted and harvested, as well as the annual crops preceding and succeeding it, on the very same soil.

Ere long, on the mountain side, he passed into an ancient natural wood, which seemed some way familiar, and midway in it, paused to contemplate a strange, mouldy pile, resting at one end against a sturdy beech. Though wherever touched by his staff, however lightly, this pile would crumble, yet here and there, even in powder, it preserved the exact look, each irregularly defined line, of what it had originally been—namely, a half-cord of stout hemlock (one of the woods least affected by exposure to the air), in a foregoing generation chopped and stacked up on the spot, against sledging-time; but, as sometimes happens in such cases, by subsequent oversight, abandoned to oblivious decay. Type now, as it stood there, of for ever arrested intentions, and a long life still rotting in early mishap.

"Do I dream?" mused the bewildered old man, "or what is this vision that comes to me, of a cold, cloudy morning, long, long ago, and I heaving yon elbowed log against the beech, then a sapling? Nay, nay; I can not be so old."

"Come away, father, from this dismal damp wood," said his son, and led him forth.

Blindly ranging to and fro, they next saw a man ploughing. Advancing slowly, the wanderer met him by a little heap of ruinous burnt masonry, like a tumbled chimney, what seemed the jams of the fire-place, now aridly stuck over here and there, with thin, clinging, round prohibitory mosses, like executors' wafers.[4] Just as the oxen were bid stand, the stranger's plough was hitched over sideways, by sudden contact with some sunken stone at the ruin's base.

"There; this is the twentieth year my plough has struck this old hearth-stone. Ah, old man,—sultry day, this."

"Whose house stood here, friend?" said the wanderer, touching the half-buried hearth with his staff, where a fresh furrow overlapped it.

"Don't know; forget the name; gone West, though, I believe. You know 'em?"

But the wanderer made no response; his eye was now fixed on a curious natural bend or wave in one of the bemossed stone jambs.

"What are you looking at so, father?"

"'Father!' here," raking with his staff, "my father would sit, and here, my mother, and here I, little infant, would totter between, even as now, once again, on the very same spot, but in the unroofed air, I do. The ends meet. Plough away, friend."

Best followed now is this life, by hurrying, like itself, to a close. Few things remain.

He was repulsed in efforts, after a pension,[5] by certain caprices of law. His scars proved his only medals. He dictated a little book, the record of his fortunes. But long ago it faded out of print— himself out of being—his name out of memory. He died the same day that the oldest oak on his native hills was blown down.

Appendix

SELECTIONS FROM *THE LIFE AND REMARKABLE ADVENTURES OF ISRAEL R. POTTER* (1824)

Melville's main source text for *Israel Potter* was the *Life and Remarkable Adventures of Israel R. Potter, (A Native of Cranston, Rhode-Island,) Who Was a Soldier in the American Revolution*, published by Henry Trumbull in Providence, Rhode Island, in 1824. The descriptive subtitle provided by Trumbull gives a good sense of the picaresque energy of Potter's autobiographical narrative: "And took a distinguished part in the Battle of Bunker Hill (in which he received three wounds) after which he was taken Prisoner by the British, conveyed to England, where for 30 years he obtained a livelihood for himself and family, by crying '*Old Chairs to Mend*' through the streets of London.—In May last, by the assistance of the American Consul, he succeeded (in the 79th year of his age) in obtaining a passage to his native country, after an absence of 48 years." The book came with a preface by Trumbull, in which he took credit for writing up Potter's first-person account, a closing deposition by one John Vial offering a "solemn oath" affirming the truth of aspects of Potter's account, and Potter's 106-page life history. That narrative is continuous (there are no chapter breaks) and ends with Potter's arrival in the United States in quest of a government pension for his service in the Revolutionary War. He would never receive that pension, and the evidence suggests that he died in 1826. As discussed in the Introduction to this Penguin Classics Edition, the known facts of Potter's life raise questions about many aspects of the story he and Trumbull tell in this narrative. Melville probably knew of Trumbull's reputation for publishing inaccurate histories and biographies. Still, something about Potter's narrative obviously appealed to Melville. The following selections from Potter's 1824 *Life and Adventures* constitute approximately half of the published book and the bulk of the material that Melville drew on for his novel.

The Life and Remarkable Adventures of Israel R. Potter

I was born of reputable parents in the town of Cranston, State of Rhode Island, August 1st, 1744.—I continued with my parents there in the full enjoyment of parental affection and indulgence, until I arrived at the age of 18, when, having formed an acquaintance with the daughter of a Mr. Richard Gardner, a near neighbour, for whom (in the opinion of my friends) entertaining too great a degree of partiality, I was reprimanded and threatened by them with more severe punishment, if my visits were not discontinued. Disappointed in my intentions of forming an union (when of suitable age) with one whom I really loved, I deemed the conduct of my parents in this respect unreasonable and oppressive, and formed the determination to leave them, for the purpose of seeking another home and other friends.

It was on Sunday, while the family were at meeting, that I packed up as many articles of my cloathing as could be contained in a pocket handkerchief, which, with a small quantity of provision, I conveyed to and secreted in a piece of woods in the rear of my father's house; I then returned and continued in the house until about 9 in the evening, when with the pretence of retiring to bed, I passed into a back room and from thence out of a back door and hastened to the spot where I had deposited my cloathes, &c.—it was a warm summer's night, and that I might be enabled to travel with the more facility the succeeding day, I lay down at the foot of a tree and reposed myself until about 4 in the morning when I arose and commenced my journey, travelling westward, with an intention of reaching if possible the new countries, which I had heard highly spoken of

as affording excellent prospects for industrious and enterpris-
ing young men—to evade the pursuit of my friends, by whom I
knew I should be early missed and diligently sought for, I confined my travel to the woods and shunned the public roads,
until I had reached the distance of about 12 miles from my
father's house.

At noon the succeeding day I reached Hartford, in Connecticut, and applied to a farmer in that town for work, and for
whom I agreed to labour for one month for the sum of six dollars. Having completed my month's work to the satisfaction of
my employer, I received my money and started from Hartford
for Otter Creek; but, when I reached Springfield, I met with a
man bound to the Cahos country, and who offered me four
dollars to accompany him, of which offer I accepted, and the
next morning we left Springfield and in a canoe ascended Connecticut river, and in about two weeks after much hard labour
in paddling and poling the boat against the current, we reached
Lebanon (N. H.), the place of our destination. It was with some
difficulty and not until I had procured a writ, by the assistance
of a respectable innkeeper in Lebanon, by the name of Hill,
that I obtained from my last employer the four dollars which
he had agreed to pay me for my services.

From Lebanon I crossed the river to New-Hartford (then
N. Y.) where I bargained with a Mr. Brink of that town for
200 acres of new land, lying in New Hampshire, and for which
I was to labour for him four months. As this may appear to
some a small consideration for so great a number of acres of
land, it may be well here to acquaint the reader with the situation of the country in that quarter, at that early period of its
settlement—which was an almost impenetrable wilderness,
containing but few civilized inhabitants, far distantly situated
from each other and from any considerable settlement; and
whose temporary habitations with a few exceptions were constructed of logs in their natural state—the woods abounded
with wild beasts of almost every description peculiar to this
country, nor were the few inhabitants at that time free from
serious apprehension of being at some unguarded moment suddenly attacked and destroyed, or conveyed into captivity by the

savages, who from the commencement of the French war, had improved every favourable opportunity to cut off the defence-less inhabitants of the frontier towns.

After the expiration of my four months labour the person who had promised me a deed of 200 acres of land therefor, having refused to fulfill his engagements, I was obliged to en-gage with a party of his Majesty's Surveyors at fifteen shillings per month, as an assistant chain bearer, to survey the wild un-settled lands bordering on the Connecticut river, to its source. It was in the winter season, and the snow so deep that it was impossible to travel without snow shoes—at the close of each day we enkindled a fire, cooked our victuals and erected with the branches of hemlock a temporary hut, which served us for a shelter for the night. The Surveyors having completed their business returned to Lebanon, after an absence of about two months. Receiving my wages I purchased a fowling-piece and ammunition therewith, and for the four succeeding months de-voted my time in hunting Deer, Beavers, &c. in which I was very successful, as in the four months I obtained as many skins of these animals as produced me forty dollars—with my money I purchased of a Mr. John Marsh, 100 acres of new land, lying on Water Quechy River (so called) about five miles from Hart-ford (N. Y.). On this land I went immediately to work, erected a small log hut thereon, and in two summers without any assis-tance, cleared up thirty acres fit for sowing—in the winter sea-sons I employed my time in hunting and entraping such animals whose hides and furs were esteemed of the most value. I remained in possession of my land two years, and then dis-posed of it to the same person of whom I purchased it, at the advanced price of 200 dollars, and then conveyed my skins and furs which I had collected the two preceding winters, to NO. 4 (now Charlestown), where I exchanged them for Indian blankets, wampeag and such other articles as I could conve-niently convey on a hand sled, and with which I started for Canada, to barter with the Indians for furs.—This proved a very profitable trip, as I very soon disposed of every article at an advance of more than two hundred per cent, and received payment in furs at a reduced price, and for which I received in

NO. 4, 200 dollars, cash. With this money, together with what I was before in possession of, I now set out for home, once more to visit my parents after an absence of two years and nine months, in which time my friends had not been enabled to receive any correct information of me. On my arrival, so greatly effected were my parents at the presence of a son whom they had considered dead, that it was sometime before either could become sufficiently composed to listen to or to request me to furnish them with an account of my travels.

Soon after my return, as some atonement for the anxiety which I had caused my parents, I presented them with most of the money that I had earned in my absence, and formed the determination that I would remain with them contented at home, in consequence of a conclusion from the welcome reception that I met with, that they had repented of their opposition, and had become reconciled to my intended union—but, in this, I soon found that I was mistaken; for, although overjoyed to see me alive, whom they had supposed really dead, no sooner did they find that my long absence had rather increased than diminished my attachment for their neighbor's daughter, than their resentment and opposition appeared to increase in proportion—in consequence of which I formed the determination again to quit them, and try my fortune at sea, as I had now arrived at an age in which I had an unquestionable right to think and act for myself.

After remaining at home one month, I applied for and procured a birth at Providence, on board the Sloop—, Capt. Fuller, bound to Grenada—having completed her loading (which consisted of stone lime, hoops, staves, &c.) we set sail with a favourable wind, and nothing worthy of note occurred until the 15th day from that on which we left Providence, when the sloop was discovered to be on fire, by a smoke issuing from her hold—the hatches were immediately raised, but as it was discovered that the fire was caused by water communicating with the lime, it was deemed useless to make any attempts to extinguish it—orders were immediately thereupon given by the captain to hoist out the long boat, which was found in such a leaky condition as to require constant bailing to keep her afloat; we had only time to put on board a small quantity of bread, a firkin of butter and a ten gallon keg of water, when we embarked, eight in number, to trust ourselves to the mercy of the waves, in a leaky boat and many leagues from land. As our provision was but small in quantity, and it being uncertain how long we might remain in our perilous situation, it was proposed by the captain soon after leaving the sloop, that we should put ourselves on an allowance of one biscuit and half a pint of water per day, for each man, which was readily agreed to by all on board—in ten minutes after leaving the sloop she was in a complete blaze, and presented an awful spectacle. With a piece of the flying-jib, which had been fortunately thrown into the boat, we made shift to erect a sail, and proceeded in a south-west direction in hopes to reach the spanish maine, if not so fortunate as to fall in with some vessel in our course—which, by the interposition of kind providence in our favour, actually took place the second day after leaving the sloop—we were discovered and picked up by a Dutch ship bound from Eustatia to Holland, and from the captain and crew met with a humane reception, and were supplied with every necessary that the ship afforded—we continued on board one week when we fell in with an American sloop bound from Piscataqua to Antigua, which received us all on board and conveyed us in safety to the port of her destination. At Antigua I got a birth on board an American brig bound to Porto Rico, and from thence to Eustatia. At Eustatia I received my discharge and entered on board a Ship belonging to Nantucket, and bound on a whaling voyage, which proved an uncommonly short and successful one—we returned to Nantucket full of oil after an absence of the ship from that port of only 16 months. After my discharge I continued about one month on the island, and then took passage for Providence, and from thence went to Cranston, once more to visit my friends, with whom I continued three weeks, and then returned to Nantucket. From Nantucket I made another whaling voyage to the South Seas and after an absence of three years, (in which time I experienced almost all the hardships and deprivations peculiar to Whalemen in long voyages) I succeeded by the blessings of providence in reaching once more my native home, perfectly sick of the sea, and willing to return to the bush and exchange a mariner's life for one less hazardous and fatiguing.

I remained with my friends at Cranston a few weeks, and then hired myself to a Mr. James Waterman, of Coventry, for 12 months, to work at farming. This was in the year 1774, and I continued with him about six months, when the difficulties which had for some time prevailed between the Americans and Britons, had now arrived at that crisis, as to render it certain that hostilities would soon commence in good earnest between the two nations; in consequence of which, the Americans at this period began to prepare themselves for the event—companies were formed in several of the towns in New England, who received the appellation of "minute men," and who were to hold themselves in readiness to obey the first summons of their officers, to march at a moment's notice;—a company of this kind was formed in Coventry, into which I enlisted, and to the command of which Edmund Johnson, of said Coventry, was appointed.

It was on a Sabbath morning that news was received of the destruction of the provincial stores at Concord, and of the massacre of our countrymen at Lexington, by a detached party of the British troops from Boston: and I immediately thereupon received a summons from the captain, to be prepared to march with the company early the morning ensuing—and, although I felt not less willing to obey the call of my country at a minute's notice, and to face her foes, than did the gallant Putnam, yet, the nature of the summons did not render it necessary for me, like him, to quit my plough in the field; as having the day previous commenced the ploughing of a field of ten or twelve acres, that I might not leave my work half done, I improved the sabbath to complete it.

By the break of day Monday morning I swung my knapsack, shouldered my musket, and with the company commenced my march with a quick step for Charlestown, where we arrived about sunset and remained encamped in the vicinity until about noon of the 16th June; when, having been previously joined by the remainder of the regiment from Rhode Island, to

which our company was attached, we received orders to proceed and join a detachment of about 1000 American troops,
which had that morning taken possession of Bunker Hill, and
which we had orders immediately to fortify, in the best manner
that circumstances would admit of. We laboured all night without cessation and with very little refreshment, and by the dawn
of day succeeded in throwing up a redoubt of eight or nine rods
square. As soon as our works were discovered by the British in
the morning, they commenced a heavy fire upon us, which was
supported by a fort on Copp's hill; we however (under the command of the intrepid Putnam) continued to labour like beavers
until our breast-work was completed.

About noon, a number of the enemy's boats and barges,
filled with troops, landed at Charlestown, and commenced a
deliberate march to attack us—we were now harangued by
Gen. Putnam, who reminded us, that exhausted as we were, by
our incessant labour through the preceding night, the most im- .
portant part of our duty was yet to be performed, and that
much would be expected from so great a number of excellent
marksmen—he charged us to be cool, and to reserve our fire
until the enemy approached so near as to enable us to see the
white of their eyes—when within about ten rods of our works
we gave them the contents of our muskets, and which were
aimed with so good effect, as soon to cause them to turn their
backs and to retreat with a much quicker step than with what
they approached us. We were now again harangued by "old
General Put," as he was termed, and requested by him to aim
at the officers, should the enemy renew the attack—which they
did in a few moments, with a reinforcement—their approach
was with a slow step, which gave us an excellent opportunity
to obey the commands of our General in bringing down their
officers. I feel but little disposed to boast of my own performances on this occasion, and will only say, that after devoting
so many months in hunting the wild animals of the wilderness,
while an inhabitant of New Hampshire, the reader will not
suppose me a bad or unexperienced marksman, and that such
were the fare shots which the epauletted red coats presented in
the two attacks, that every shot which they received from me, I

am confident on another occasion would have produced me a deer skin.

So warm was the reception that the enemy met with in their second attack, that they again found it necessary to retreat, but soon after receiving a fresh reinforcement, a third assault was made, in which, in consequence of our ammunition failing, they too well succeeded—a close and bloody engagement now ensued—to fight our way through a very considerable body of the enemy, with clubbed muskets (for there were not one in twenty of us provided with bayonets) were now the only means left us to escape;—the conflict, which was a sharp and severe one, is still fresh in my memory, and cannot be forgotten by me while the scars of the wounds which I then received, remain to remind me of it!—fortunately for me, at this critical moment, I was armed with a cutlass, which although without an edge, and much rust-eaten, I found of infinite more service to me than my musket—in one instance I am certain it was the means of saving my life—a blow with a cutlass was aimed at my head by a British officer, which I parried and received only a slight cut with the point on my right arm near the elbow, which I was then unconscious of, but this slight wound cost my antagonist at the moment a much more serious one, which effectually dis-armed him, for with one well directed stroke I deprived him of the power of very soon again measuring swords with a "yankee rebel!" We finally however should have been mostly cut off, and compelled to yield to a superiour and better equipped force, had not a body of three or four hundred Connecticut men formed a temporary breast work, with rails &c. and by which means held the enemy at bay until our main body had time to ascend the heights, and retreat across the neck;—in this retreat I was less fortunate than many of my comrades—I received two musket ball wounds, one in my hip and the other near the ankle of my left leg—I succeeded however without any assistance in reaching Prospect Hill, where the main body of the Americans had made a stand and commenced fortifying—from thence I was soon after conveyed to the Hospital in Cambridge, where my wounds were dressed and the bullet extracted from my hip by one of the Surgeons; the house was nearly filled with the poor fellows who like myself had received wounds in the late engagement, and presented a melancholly spectacle.

Bunker Hill fight proved a sore thing for the British, and will I doubt not be long remembered by them; while in London I heard it frequently spoken of by many who had taken an active part therein, some of whom were pensioners, and bore indelible proofs of American bravery—by them the Yankees, by whom they were opposed, were not unfrequently represented as a set of infuriated beings, whom nothing could daunt or intimidate: and who, after their ammunition failed, disputed the ground, inch by inch, for a full hour with clubbed muskets, rusty swords, pitchforks and billets of wood, against the British bayonets.

I suffered much pain from the wound which I received in my ankle, the bone was badly fractured and several pieces were extracted by the surgeon, and it was six weeks before I was sufficiently recovered to be able to join my Regiment quartered on Prospect Hill, where they had thrown up entrenchments within the distance of little more than a mile of the enemy's camp, which was full in view, they having entrenched themselves on Bunker Hill after the engagement.

On the 3d July, to the great satisfaction of the Americans, General WASHINGTON arrived from the south to take command—I was then confined in the Hospital, but as far as my observations could extend, he met with a joyful reception, and his arrival was welcomed by every one throughout the camp—the troops had been long waiting with impatience for his arrival as being nearly destitute of ammunition and the British receiving reinforcements daily, their prospects began to wear a gloomy aspect.

The British quartered in Boston began soon to suffer much from the scarcity of provisions, and General Washington took every precaution to prevent their gaining a supply—from the country all supplies could be easily cut off, and to prevent their receiving any from Tories, and other disaffected persons by water, the General found it necessary to equip two or three armed vessels to intercept them—among these was the brigantine

Washington of 10 guns, commanded by Capt. Martindale,—as seamen at this time could not easily be obtained, as most of them had enlisted in the land service, permission was given to any of the soldiers who should be pleased to accept of the offer, to man these vessels—consequently myself with several others of the same regiment went on board of the Washington, then lying at Plymouth, and in complete order for a cruise.

We set sail about the 8th December, but had been out but three days when we were captured by the enemy's ship Foy, of 20 guns, who took us all out and put a prize crew on board the Washington—the Foy proceeded with us immediately to Boston bay where we were put on board the British frigate Tartar and orders given to convey us to England.—When two or three days out I projected a scheme (with the assistance of my fellow prisoners, 72 in number) to take the ship, in which we should undoubtedly have succeeded, as we had a number of resolute fellows on board, had it not been for the treachery of a renegade Englishman, who betrayed us—as I was pointed out by this fellow as the principal in the plot, I was ordered in irons by the Officers of the Tartar, and in which situation I remained until the arrival of the ship at Portsmouth (Eng.) when I was brought on deck and closely examined, but protesting my innocence, and what was very fortunate for me in the course of the examination, the person by whom I had been betrayed, having been proved a British deserter, his story was discredited and I was relieved of my irons.

The prisoners were now all thoroughly cleansed and conveyed to the marine hospital on shore, where many of us took the small-pox the natural way, by some whom we found in the hospital effected with that disease, and which proved fatal to nearly one half our number. From the hospital those of us who survived were conveyed to Spithead, and put on board a Guard Ship, and where I had been confined with my fellow prisoners about one month, when I was ordered into the boat, to assist the bargemen (in consequence of the absence of one of their gang) in rowing the lieutenant on shore. As soon as we reached the shore and the officer landed, it was proposed by some of the boat's crew to resort for a few moments to an ale-house, in

the vicinity, to treat themselves to a few pots of beer; which being agreed to by all, I thought this a favourable opportunity
and the only one that might present to escape from my Floating Prison, and felt determined not to let it pass unimproved;
accordingly, as the boat's crew were about to enter the house,
I expressed a necessity of my separating from them a few
moments, to which they (not suspecting any design), readily
assented. As soon as I saw them all snugly in and the door
closed, I gave speed to my legs, and ran, as I then concluded,
about four miles without once halting—I steered my course
toward London as when there by mingling with the crowd, I
thought it probable that I should be least suspected.

When I had reached the distance of about ten miles from
where I quit the bargemen and beginning to think myself in little danger of apprehension, should any of them be sent by the
lieutenant in pursuit of me, as I was leisurely passing a public
house, I was noticed and hailed by a naval officer at the door
with "ahoi, what ship?"—"no ship," was my reply, on which
he ordered me to stop, but of which I took no other notice
than to observe to him that if he would attend to his own business I would proceed quietly about mine—this rather increas-
ing than diminishing his suspicions that I was a deserter,
garbed as I was, he gave chase—finding myself closely pursued
and unwilling again to be made a prisoner of, if it was possible to escape, I had once more to trust to my legs, and should
have again succeeded had not the officer, on finding himself
likely to be distanced, set up a cry of "stop thief!" this brought
numbers out of their houses and work shops, who, joining in
the pursuit, succeeded after a chase of nearly a mile in over-
hauling me.

Finding myself once more in their power and a perfect
stranger to the country, I deemed it vain to attempt to deceive
them with a lie, and therefore made a voluntary confession to
the officer that I was a prisoner of war, and related to him in
what manner I had that morning made my escape. By the officer I was conveyed back to the Inn, and left in custody of two
soldiers—the former (previous to retiring) observing to the landlord that believing me to be a true blooded yankee, requested

him to supply me at his expense with as much liquor as I should call for.

The house was thronged early in the evening by many of the "good and faithful subjects of King George," who had assembled to take a peep at the "yankee rebel," (as they termed me) who had so recently taken an active part in the rebellious war, then ranging in his Majesty's American provinces—while others came apparently to gratify a curiosity in viewing, for the first time, an "American Yankee!" whom they had been taught to believe a kind of non descripts—beings of much less refinement than the ancient Britains, and possessing little more humanity than the Buccaneers.

As for myself I thought it best not to be reserved, but to reply readily to all their inquiries; for while my mind was wholly employed in devising a plan to escape from the custody of my keepers, so far from manifesting a disposition to resent any of the insults offered me, or my country, to prevent any suspicions of my designs, I feigned myself not a little pleased with their observations, and in no way dissatisfied with my situation. As the officer had left orders with the landlord to supply me with as much liquor as I should be pleased to call for, I felt determined to make my keepers merry at his expense, if possible, as the best means that I could adopt to effect my escape.

The loyal group having attempted in vain to irritate me, by their mean and ungenerous reflections, by one (who observed that he had frequently heard it mentioned that the yankees were extraordinary dancers), it was proposed that I should entertain the company with a jig! to which I expressed a willingness to assent with much feigned satisfaction, if a fiddler could be procured—fortunately for them, there was one residing in the neighbourhood, who was soon introduced, when I was obliged (although much against my own inclination) to take the floor—with the full determination, however that if John Bull was to be thus diverted at the expense of an unfortunate prisoner of war, uncle Jonathan should come in for his part of the sport before morning, by showing them a few *Yankee steps* which they then little dreamed of.

By my performances they were soon satisfied that in this kind of exercise, I should suffer but little in competition with the most nimble footed Britain among them nor would they release me until I had danced myself into a state of perfect perspiration; which, however, so far from being any disadvantage to me, I considered all in favour of my projected plan to escape—for while I was pleased to see the flowing bowl passing merrily about, and not unfrequently brought in contact with the lips of my two keepers, the state of perspiration that I was in, prevented its producing on me any intoxicating effects.

The evening having become now far spent and the company mostly retiring, my keepers (who, to use a sailor's phrase I was happy to discover "half seas over") having much to my dissatisfaction furnished me with a pair of handcuffs spread a blanket by the side of their bed on which I was to repose for the night. I feigned myself very grateful to them for having humanely furnished me with so comfortable a bed, and on which I stretched myself with much apparent unconcern, and remained quiet about one hour, when I was sure that the family had all retired to bed. The important moment had now arrived in which I was resolved to carry my premeditated plan into execution, or die in the attempt—for certain I was that if I let this opportunity pass unimproved, I might have cause to regret it when it was too late—that I should most assuredly be conveyed early in the morning back to the floating prison from which I had so recently escaped, and where I might possibly remain confined until America should obtain her independence, or the differences between Great-Britain and her American provinces were adjusted. Yet should I in my attempt to escape meet with more opposition from my keepers, than what I had calculated from their apparent state of inebriety, the contest I well knew would be very unequal—they were two full grown stout men, with whom (if they were assisted by no others) I should have to contend, handcuffed! but, after mature deliberation, I resolved that however hazardous the attempt, it should be made, and that immediately.

After remaining quiet, as I before observed, until I thought it probable that all had retired to bed in the house, I intimated to my keepers that I was under the necessity of requesting permission to retire for a few moments to the back yard; when both instantly arose and reeling toward me seized each an arm, and proceeded to conduct me through a long and narrow entry to the back door, which was no sooner unbolted and opened by one of them, than I tripped up the heels of both and laid them sprawling, and in a moment was at the garden wall seeking a passage whereby I might gain the public road—a new and unexpected obstacle now presented, for I found the whole garden enclosed with a smooth bricken wall, of the heighth of twelve feet at least, and was prevented by the darkness of the night from discovering an avenue leading therefrom—in this predicament, my only alternative was either to scale this wall handcuffed as I was, and without a moment's hesitation, or to suffer myself to be made a captive of again by my keepers, who had already recovered their feet and were bellowing like bullocks for assistance—had it not been a very dark night, I must certainly have been discovered and re-taken by them;—fortunately before they had succeeded in rallying the family, in groping about I met with a fruit tree situated within ten or twelve feet of the wall, which I ascended as expeditiously as possible, and by an extraordinary leap from the branches reached the top of the wall, and was in an instant on the opposite side. The coast being now clear, I ran to the distance of two or three miles, with as much speed as my situation would admit of;—my next object now was to rid myself of my handcuffs, which fortunately proving none of the stoutest, I succeeded in doing after much painful labour.

It was now as I judged about 12 o'clock, and I had succeeded in reaching a considerable distance from the Inn from which I had made my escape, without hearing or seeing any thing of my keepers, whom I had left staggering about in the garden in search of their "Yankee captive!"—it was indeed to their intoxicated state, and the extreme darkness of the night, that I imputed my success in evading their pursuit.—I saw no one until about the break of day, when I met an old man, tottering beneath the weight of his pick-ax, hoe and shovel, clad in tattered garments, and otherwise the picture of poverty and distress; he had just left his humble dwelling, and was proceeding thus early to his daily labour;—and as I was now satisfied that it would be very difficult for me to travel in the day time garbed as I was, in a sailor's habit, without exciting the suspicions of his Royal Majesty's pimps, who (I had been informed) were constantly on the look-out for deserters, I applied to the old man, miserable as he appeared, for a change of cloathing, offering those which I then wore for a suit of inferior quality and less value—this I was induced to do at that moment, as I thought that the proposal could be made with perfect safety, for whatever might have been his suspicions as to my motives in wishing to exchange my dress, I doubted not, that with an object of so much apparent distress, self-interest would prevent his communicating them.—The old man however appeared a little surprised at my offer, and after a short examination of my pea-jacket, trousers, &c. expressed a doubt whether I would be willing to exchange them for his "Church suit," which he represented as something worse for wear, and not worth half so much as those I then wore—taking courage however from my assurances that a change of dress was my only object, he deposited his tools by the side of a hedge, and invited me to accompany him to his house, which we soon reached and entered, when a scene of poverty and wretchedness presented, which exceeded every thing of the kind that I had ever before witnessed— the internal appearance of the miserable hovel, I am confident would suffer in a comparison with any of the meanest stables of our American farmers—there was but one room, in one corner of which was a bed of straw covered with a coarse sheet, and on which reposed his wife and five small children. I had heard much of the impoverished and distressed situation of the poor in England, but the present presented an instance of which I had formed no conception—little indeed did I then think that it would be my lot, before I should meet with an opportunity to return to my native country, to be placed in an infinitely worse situation! but, alas, such was my hard fortune!

*   *   *

Being continually harassed by night and day by the soldiers, and driven from place to place, without an opportunity to perform a day's work, I was advised by one whose sincerity I could not doubt, to apply for a berth as a labourer in a garden of his Royal Majesty, situated in the village of Quew, a few miles from Brintford; where, under the protection of his Majesty, it was represented to me that I should be perfectly safe, as the soldiers dare not approach the royal premises, to molest any one therein employed—he was indeed so friendly as to introduce me personally to the overseer, as an acquaintance who possessed a perfect knowledge of gardening, but from whom he carefully concealed the fact of my being an American born, and of the suspicion entertained by some of my being a prisoner of war, who had escaped the vigilance of my keepers.

The overseer concluded to receive me on trial;—it was here that I had not only frequent opportunities to see his Royal Majesty in person, in his frequent resorts to this, one of his country retreats, but once had the honour of being addressed by him. The fact was, that I had not been one week employed in the garden, before the suspicion of my being either a pris-oner of war, or a Spy, in the employ of the American Rebels, was communicated, not only to the overseer and other persons employed in the garden, but even to the King himself! As I was one day busily engaged with three others in gravelling a walk, I was unexpectedly accosted by his Majesty: who, with much apparent good nature, enquired of me of what country I was— "an American born, may it please your Majesty," was my reply (taking off my hat, which he requested me instantly to replace on my head),—"ah! (continued he with a smile) an American, a stubborn, a very stubborn people indeed!—and what brought you to this country, and how long have you been here?" "the fate of war, your Majesty—I was brought to this country a prisoner about eleven months since,"—and thinking this a favourable opportunity to acquaint him with a few of my grievances, I briefly stated to him how much I had been harassed by the soldiers—"while here employed they will not trouble you," was the only reply he made, and passed on. The familiar manner in which I had been interrogated by his Majesty, had I must confess a tendency in some degree to pre-posses me in his favour—I at least suspected him to possess a disposition less tyrannical, and capable of better view than what had been imputed to him; and as I had frequently heard it represented in America, that uninfluenced by such of his ministers, as unwisely disregarded the reiterated complaints of the American people, he would have been foremost to have redressed their grievances, of which they so justly complained.

*   *   *

After partaking of a little refreshment I set out at 12 o'clock at night, and reached White Waltam at half past 11 the succeeding day, and immediately waited on and presented the letter to the gentleman to whom it was directed, and who gave me a very cordial reception, and whom I soon found was as real a friend to America's cause as the three gentlemen in whose company I had last been. It was from him that I received the first information of the evacuation of Boston by the British troops, and of the declaration of INDEPENDENCE, by the American Congress—he indeed appeared to possess a knowledge of almost every important transaction in America, since the memorable battle of Bunker-Hill, and it was to him that I was indebted for many particulars, not a little interesting to myself, and which I might otherwise have remained ignorant of, as I have always found it a principle of the Britains, to conceal every thing calculated to diminish or tarnish their fame, as a "great and powerful nation!"

I remained in the family of this gentleman about a fortnight, when I received a letter from 'Squire Woodcock, requesting me to be at his house without fail precisely at 2 o'clock the morning ensuing—in compliance of which I packed up and started immediately for Brintford, and reached the house of 'Squire Woodcock at the appointed hour—I found there in company with the latter, the two gentlemen whose names I have before mentioned, and by whom the object of my mission to Paris was now made known to me—which was to convey in the most secret manner possible a letter to Dr. FRANKLIN; every thing was in readiness, and a chaise ready harnessed which was to convey me to Charing Cross, waiting at the door—I was presented with a pair of boots, made expressly for me, and for the safe conveyance of the letter of which I was to be the bearer, one of them contained a false heel, in which the letter was deposited, and was to be thus conveyed to the Doctor. After again repeating my former declarations, that whatever might be my fate, they should never be exposed, I departed, and was conveyed in quick time to Charing Cross, where I took the post coach for Dover, and from thence was immediately conveyed in a packet to Calais, and in fifteen minutes after landing, started for Paris; which I reached in safety, and delivered to Dr. Franklin the letter of which I was the bearer.

What were the contents of this letter I was never informed and never knew, but had but little doubt but that it contained important information relative to the views of the British cabinet, as regarded the affairs of America; and although I well knew that a discovery (while within the British dominions) would have proved equally fatal to me as to the gentlemen by whom I was employed, yet, I most solemnly declare, that to be serviceable to my country at that important period, was much more of an object with me, than the reward which I had been promised, however considerable it might be. My interview with Dr. Franklin was a pleasing one—for nearly an hour he conversed with me in the most agreeable and instructive manner, and listened to the tale of my sufferings with much apparent interest, and seemed disposed to encourage me with the assurance that if the Americans should succeed in their grand object, and firmly establish their Independence, they would not fail to remunerate their soldiers for their services—but, alas! as regards myself, these assurances have not as yet been verified!—I am confident, however, that had it been a possible thing for that great and good man (whose humanity and generosity have been the theme of infinitely abler pens than mine) to have lived to this day, I should not have petitioned my country in vain for a momentary enjoyment of that provision, which has been extended to so great a portion of my fellow soldiers; and whose hardships and deprivations, in the cause of their country, could not I am sure have been half so great as mine!

After remaining two days in Paris, letters were delivered to me by the Doctor, to convey to the gentlemen by whom I had been employed, and which for their better security as well as my own, I deposited as the other, in the heel of my boot, and with which to the great satisfaction of my friends I reached Brintford, in safety, and without exciting the suspicion of any one as to the important (although somewhat dangerous) mission that I had been engaged in. I remained secreted in the house of 'Squire Woodcock a few days, and then by his and the two other gentlemen's request, made a second trip to Paris, and in reaching which and in delivering my letters, was equally as fortunate as in my first. If I should succeed in returning in safety to Brintford this trip, I was (agreeable to the generous proposal of Doctor Franklin) to return immediately to France, from whence he was to procure me a passage to America; —but, although in my return I met with no difficulty, yet, as if fate had selected me as a victim to endure the miseries and privations which afterward attended me, but three hours before I reached Dover to engage a passage for the third and last time to Calais, all intercourse between the two countries was prohibited!

My flattering expectations of being enabled soon to return to my native country, and once more to meet and enjoy the society of my friends, (after an absence of more than twelve months) being thus by an unforeseen circumstance completely destroyed, I returned immediately to the gentlemen by whom I had been last employed to advise with them what it would be best for me to do, in my then unpleasant situation—for indeed, as all prospects were now at an end, of meeting with an opportunity very soon to return to America, I could not bear the idea of remaining any longer in a neighbourhood where I was so strongly suspected of being a fugitive from justice and under continual apprehension of being retaken, and immured like a felon in a dungeon.

By these gentlemen I was advised to repair immediately to London, where employed as a labourer, if I did not imprudently betray myself, they thought there was little probability of my being suspected of being an American. . . .

* * *

In the winter of 1781, news was received in London of the surrender of the army of Lord Cornwallis, to the French and American forces!—the receipt of news of an event so unexpected operated on the British ministers and members of Parliament, like a tremendous clap of thunder—deep sorrow was evidently depicted in the countenances of those who had been the most strenuous advocates for the war—never was there a time in which I longed more to exult, and to declare myself a true blooded yankee—and what was still more pleasing to me, was to find myself even surpassed in expresssions of joy and satisfaction, by my wife, in consequence of the receipt of news, which, while it went to establish the military fame of my countrymen, was so calculated to humble the pride of her own! greater proofs of her regard for me and my country I could not require.

*　*　*

There was no one engaged in the cause of America, that did more to establish her fame in England, and to satisfy the high boasting Britains of the bravery and unconquerable resolutions of the Yankees, than that bold adventurer capt. Paul Jones; who, for ten or eleven months kept all the western coast of the island in alarm—he boldly landed at Whitehaven, where he burnt a ship in the harbour, and even attempted to burn the town . . .

*　*　*

When I first entered the city of London, I was almost stunned, while my curiosity was not a little excited by what is termed the "cries of London"—the streets were thronged by persons of both sexes and of every age, crying each the various articles which they were exposing for sale, or for jobs of work at their various occupations;—I little then thought that this was a mode which I should be obliged myself to adopt to obtain a scanty pittance for my needy family—but, such indeed proved to be the case. The great increase of labourers produced by the cessation of hostilities, had so great an effect in the reduction of wages, that the trifling consideration now allowed me by my employers for my services, in the line of business in which I had been several years engaged, was no longer an object, being insufficient to enable me to procure a humble sustenance. Having in vain sought for more profitable business, I was induced to apply to an acquaintance for instruction in the art of chair bottoming, and which I partially obtained from him for a trifling consideration.

It was now (which was in the year 1789) that I assumed a line of business very different from that in which I had ever before been engaged—fortunately for me, I possessed strong lungs, which I found very necessary in an employment the success of which depended, in a great measure, in being enabled to drown the voices of others (engaged in the same occupation) by my own—"Old Chairs to Mend," became now my constant cry through the streets of London, from morning to night; and although I found my business not so profitable as I could have wished, yet it yielded a tolerable support for my family some time, and probably would have continued so to have done, had not the almost constant illness of my children, rendered the expenses of my family much greater than they otherwise would have been—thus afflicted by additional cares and expense, (although I did every thing in my power to avoid it) I was obliged, to alleviate the sufferings of my family, to contract some trifling debts which it was not in my power to discharge.

I now became the victim of additional miseries—I was visited by a bailiff employed by a creditor, who seizing me with the claws of a tiger, dragged me from my poor afflicted family and inhumanly thrust me into prison! indeed no misery that I ever before endured equalled this—separated from those dependent on me for the necessaries of life, and placed in a situation in which it was impossible for me to afford them any relief!— fortunately for me at this melancholly moment, my wife enjoyed good health, and it was to her praise-worthy exertions that her poor helpless children, as well as myself, owed our preservation from a state of starvation!—this good woman had become acquainted with many who had been my customers, whom she made acquainted with my situation, and the sufferings of my family, and who had the humanity to furnish me with work during my confinement—the chairs were conveyed to and from the prison by my wife—in this way I was enabled to support myself and to contribute something to the relief of my afflicted family. I had in vain represented to my unfeeling creditor my inability to satisfy his demands, and in vain represented to him the suffering condition of those wholly dependent on me; unfortunately for me, he proved to be one of those human beasts, who, having no soul, take pleasure in tormenting that of others, who never feel but in their own misfortunes, and never rejoice but in the afflictions of others—of such beings, so disgraceful to human nature, I assure the reader London contains not an inconsiderable number.

After having for four months languished in a horrid prison, I was liberated therefrom a mere skeleton; the mind afflicted had tortured the body; so much is the one in subjection to the other—I returned sorrowful and dejected to my afflicted family whom I found in very little better condition. We now from necessity took up our abode in an obscure situation near Moorfields; where, by my constant application to business, I succeeded in earning daily a humble pittance for my family, bearly sufficient however to satisfy the cravings of nature; and to add to my afflictions, some one of my family were almost constantly indisposed.

*   *   *

In February 1793, War was declared by Great Britain against the republic of France—and although war is a calamity that ought always to be regretted by friends of humanity, as thousands are undoubtedly thereby involved in misery; yet, no event could have happened at that time productive of so much benefit to me, as this—it was the means of draining the country of those who had been once soldiers, and who, thrown out of employ by the peace, demanded a sum so trifling for their services, as to cause a reduction in the wages of the poor labouring class of people, to a sum insufficient to procure the necessaries of life for their families;—this evil was now removed—the old soldiers preferred an employment more in character of themselves, to doing the drudgery of the city—great inducements were held out to them to enlist, and the army was not long retarded in its operations for the want of recruits. My prospects in being enabled to earn something to satisfy the calls of nature, became now more flattering;—the great number that had been employed during the Peace in a business similar to my own, were now reduced to one half, which enabled me to obtain such an extra number of jobs at chair mending that I no longer found it necessary to collect the scrapings of the streets as I had been obliged to do for the many months past. I was now enabled to purchase for my family two or three pounds of fresh meat each week, an article to which (with one or two exceptions) we had

been strangers for more than a year—having subsisted princi-
pally on potatoes, oat meal bread, and salt fish, and sometimes,
but rarely however, were enabled to treat ourselves to a little
skim milk.

Had not other afflictions attended me, I should not have had
much cause to complain of very extraordinary hardships or privations from this period, until the conclusion of the war in
1817;—my family had increased, and to increase my cares there
was scarcely a week passed but that some one of them was seriously indisposed—of ten children of which I was the father, I
had the misfortune to bury seven under five years of age, and
two more after they had arrived to the age of twenty—my last
and only child now living, it pleased the Almighty to spare to
me, to administer help and comfort to his poor afflicted parent,
and without whose assistance I should (so far from having been
enabled once more to visit the land of my nativity) 'ere this have
paid the debt of nature in a foreign land, and that too by a death
no less horrible than that of starvation!

*   *   *

In long and gloomy winter evenings, when unable to furnish
myself with any other light than that emitted by a little fire of
sea coal, I would attempt to drive away melancholy by amusing
my son with an account of my native country, and of the many
blessings there enjoyed by even the poorest class of people—
of their fair fields producing a regular supply of bread—their
convenient houses, to which they could repair after the toils of
the day, to partake of the fruits of their labour, safe from the
storms and the cold, and where they could lay down their heads
to rest without any to molest them or to make them afraid.
Nothing could have been better calculated to excite animation
in the mind of the poor child, than an account so flattering of a
country which had given birth to his father, and to which he had
received my repeated assurances he should accompany me as
soon as an opportunity should present—after expressing his
fears that the happy day was yet far distant, with a deep sigh he
would exclaim "would to God it was to morrow!"

About a year after the decease of my wife, I was taken extremely ill, insomuch that at one time my life was despaired of,

and had it not been for the friendless and lonely situation in which such an event would have placed my son, I should have welcomed the hour of my dissolution and viewed it as a consummation rather to be wished than dreaded; for so great had been my sufferings of mind and body, and the miseries to which I was still exposed, that life had really become a burden to me—indeed I think it would have been difficult to have found on the face of the earth a being more wretched than I had been for the three years past.

During my illness my only friend on earth was my son Thomas, who did every thing to alleviate my wants within the power of his age to do—sometimes by crying for old chairs to mend (for he had become as expert a workman at this business as his father) and sometimes by sweeping the cause-ways, and by making and selling matches, he succeeded in earning each day a trifle sufficient to procure for me and himself a humble sustenance. When I had so far recovered as to be able to creep abroad, and the youth had been so fortunate as to obtain a good job, I would accompany him, although very feeble, and assist him in conveying the chairs home—it was on such occasions that my dear child would manifest his tenderness and affection for me, by insisting (if there were four chairs) that I should carry but one, and he would carry the remaining three, or in that proportion if a greater or less number.

From the moment that I had informed him of the many blessings enjoyed by my countrymen of every class, I was almost constantly urged by my son to apply to the American Consul for a passage—it was in vain that I represented to him, that if such an application was attended with success and the opportunity should be improved by me, it must cause our separation, perhaps forever; as he would not be permitted to accompany me at the expense of government—"never mind me (he would reply) do not father suffer any more on my account; if you can only succeed in obtaining a passage to a country where you can enjoy the blessings that you have described to me, I may hereafter be so fortunate as to meet with an opportunity to join you—and if not, it will be a consolation to me, whatever my afflictions may be, to think that yours have ceased!" My ardent wish to return to America, was not less than that of my son, but could not bear the thoughts of a separation; of leaving him behind exposed to all the miseries peculiar to the friendless poor of that country;—he was a child of my old age, and from whom I had received too many proofs of his love and regard for me, not to feel that parental affection for him to which his amiable disposition entitled him.

* * *

When I parted with the Consul he presented me with half a crown, and directions where to apply for board—it was at a public Inn where I found many American seamen, who, like myself, were boarded there at the Consul's expence, until passages could be obtained for them to America—I was treated by them with much civility, and by hearing them daily recount their various and remarkable adventures, as well as by relating my own, I passed my time more agreeably than what I probably should have done in other society.

In eight weeks I was so far recruited by good living, as in the opinion of the Consul, to be able to endure the fatigues of a passage to my native country, and which was procured for me on board the ship Carterian, bound to New-York. We set sail on the 5th April, 1823, and after a passage of 42 days, arrived safe at our port of destination. After having experienced in a foreign land so much ill-treatment from those from whom I could expect no mercy, and for no other fault than that of being an American, I could not but flatter myself that when I bid adieu to that country, I should no longer be the subject of unjust persecution, or have occasion to complain of ill treatment from those whose duty it was to afford me protection. But the sad reverse which I experienced while on board the Carterian, convinced me of the incorrectness of my conclusions. For my country's sake, I am happy that I have it in my power to say that the crew of this ship, was not composed altogether of Americans—there was a mixture of all nations; and among them some so vile, and destitute of every humane principle, as to delight in nothing so much as to sport with the infirmities of one, whose grey locks ought at least to have protected him. By these unfeeling wretches (who deserve not the name of sailors)

I was not only most shamefully ill-used on the passage, but was robbed of some necessary articles of cloathing, which had been charitably bestowed on me by the American Consul.

We arrived in the harbour of New-York about midnight, and such were the pleasing sensations produced by the reflection that on the morrow I should be indulged with the priviledge of walking once more on American ground after an absence of almost 50 years, and that but a short distance now separated me from my dear son, that it was in vain that I attempted to close my eyes to sleep. Never was the morning's dawn so cheerfully welcomed by me. I solicited and obtained the permission of the captain to be early set on shore, and on reaching which, I did not forget to offer up my unfeigned thanks to that Almighty Being, who had not only sustained me during my heavy afflictions abroad, but had finally restored me to my native country. The pleasure that I enjoyed in viewing the streets thronged by those, who, although I could not claim as acquaintances, I could greet as my countrymen, was unbounded, I felt a regard for almost every object that met my eyes, because it was American.

Great as was my joy on finding myself once more among my countrymen, I felt not a little impatient for the arrival of the happy moment when I should be able to meet my son. Agreeable to the orders which I received from the American Consul, I applied to the Custom House in New-York for a passage from thence to Boston, and with which I was provided on board a regular packet which sailed the morning ensuing—in justice to the captain, I must say that I was treated by him as well as by all on board, with much civility. We arrived at the Long Wharf in Boston after a short and pleasant passage. I had been informed by the Consul, previous to leaving London, of the name of the gentleman with whom my son probably lived, and a fellow passenger on board the packet was so good as to call on and inform him of my arrival—in less than fifteen minutes after receiving the information my son met me on the wharf! Reader, you will not believe it possible for me to describe my feelings correctly at this joyful moment! if you are a parent, you may have some conception of them; but a faint one however unless you and an only and beloved child have been placed in a similar situation.

After acquainting myself with the state of my boy's health, &c. my next enquiry was whether he found the country as it had been described by me, and how he esteemed it—"well, extremely well (was his reply) since my arrival I have fared like a Prince, I have meat every day, and have feasted on American puddings and pies (such as you used to tell me about) until I have become almost sick of them!" I was immediately conducted by him to the house of the gentleman with whom he lived, and by whom I was treated with much hospitality—in the afternoon of the day succeeding (by the earnest request of my son) I visited Bunker Hill, which he had a curiosity to view, having heard it so frequently spoken of by me while in London, as the place where the memorable battle was fought and in which I received my wounds.

I continued in Boston about a fortnight, and then set out on foot to visit once more my native State. My son accompanied me as far as Roxbury, when I was obliged reluctantly to part with him, and proceeded myself no farther on my journey that day than Jamaica plains, where at a public house I tarried all night—from thence I started early the next morning and reached Providence about 5 o'clock in the afternoon, and obtained lodgings at a public Inn in High-Street.

It may not be improper here to acquaint my readers that as I had left my father possessed of very considerable property, and of which at his decease I thought myself entitled to a portion equal to that of other children, which (as my father was very economical in the management of his affairs) I knew could not amount to a very inconsiderable sum, it was to obtain this if possible, that I became extremely anxious to visit immediately the place of my nativity—accordingly the day after I arrived in Providence, I hastened to Cranston, to seek my connexions if any were to be found; and if not to seek among the most aged of the inhabitants, some one who had not forgotten me, and who might be able to furnish me with the sought for information. But, alas, too soon were blasted my hopeful expectations of finding something in reserve for me, that might have afforded me a humble support, the few remaining years of my life. It was by a distant connection that I was informed that my brothers had many years since removed to a distant part of the country— that having credited a rumour in circulation of my death, at the decease of my father had disposed of the real estate of which he died possessed, and had divided the proceeds equally among themselves! This was another instance of adverse fortune that I had not anticipated!—it was indeed a circumstance so foreign from my mind that I felt myself for the first time, unhappy, since my return to my native country, and even believed myself now doomed to endure, among my own countrymen (for whose liberties I had fought and bled) miseries similar to those that had attended me for many years in Europe. With these gloomy forebodings I returned to Providence, and contracted for board with the gentleman at whose house I had lodged the first night of my arrival in town, and to whom for the kind treatment that I have received from him and his family, I shall feel till death under the deepest obligations that gratitude can dictate; for I can truly say of him, that I was a stranger and he took me in, I was hungry and naked, and he fed and cloathed me.

As I had never received any remuneration for services rendered, and hardships endured in the cause of my country, I was now obliged, as my last resort, to petition Congress to be included in that number of the few surviving soldiers of the Revolution, for whose services they had been pleased to grant pensions—and I would to God that I could add, for the honour of my country, that the application met with its deserving success—but, although accompanied by the deposition of a respectable gentleman (which deposition I have thought proper to annex to my narrative) satisfactorily confirming every fact as therein stated—yet, on no other principle, than that *I was absent from the country when the pension law passed*—my Petition was REJECTED!!! Reader, I have been for 30 years (as you will perceive by what I have stated in the foregoing pages) subject, in a *foreign* country, to almost all the miseries with which poor human nature is capable of being inflicted—yet, in no one instance did I ever feel so great degree of a depression of spirits, as when the fate of my Petition was announced to me! I love too well the country which gave me birth, and entertain too high a respect for those employed in its government, to reproach them with ingratitude; yet, it is my sincere prayer that this strange and unprecedented circumstance, of withholding from me that reward which they have so generally bestowed on others, may never be told in Europe, or published in the streets of London, least it reach the ears of some who had the effrontery to declare to me personally, that for the active part that I had taken in the "rebellious war" misery and starvation would ultimately be my reward!

To conclude—although I may be again unfortunate in a renewal of my application to government, for that reward to which my services so justly entitle me—yet I feel thankful that I am priviledged (after enduring so much) to spend the remainder of my days, among those who I am confident are possessed of too much humanity, to see me suffer; and which I am sensible I owe to the divine goodness, which graciously condescended to support me under my numerous afflictions, and finally enabled me to return to my native country in the 79th year of my age—for this I return unfeigned thanks to the Almighty; and hope to give during the remainder of my life, convincing testimonies of the strong impression which those afflictions made on my mind, by devoting myself sincerely to the duties of religion.

Explanatory Notes

TO HIS HIGHNESS
THE BUNKER-HILL MONUMENT

1. *Bunker Hill*: The first significant military conflict between the colonial army and British forces, the Battle of Bunker Hill took place on June 17, 1775, in Charlestown, Massachusetts. Although the British troops emerged victorious, they suffered significant casualties (nearly half of the approximately 2,200 men engaged in the battle). The out-armed and inexperienced colonists therefore claimed a moral victory in a battle that came to take on mythic proportions in the patriots' imagination. In 1823 a civic group formed the Bunker Hill Monument Association with the goal of constructing a commemorative monument. The 221-foot granite obelisk was completed in 1842 and dedicated on June 17, 1843.

2. *your Highness*: The Bunker Hill Monument, which is located at Breed's Hill, in Charlestown, Massachusetts, where the battle of Bunker Hill actually took place.

3. *Israel Potter's autobiographical story*: Melville's principal source text, *Life and Remarkable Adventures of Israel R. Potter, (A Native of Cranston, Rhode-Island,) Who Was a Soldier in the American Revolution* (Providence, Rhode Island: 1824). For more on this text, see the Appendix.

4. *cripple by the Beautiful Gate*: See Acts 3:1–11, which describes Peter's healing of a lame man.

5. *Sparks*: The prolific historian Jared Sparks (1789–1866) published more than 100 biographies and editions, including an edition of Benjamin Franklin's *Works* (10 vol., 1836–1840).

CHAPTER 1: THE BIRTHPLACE OF ISRAEL

1. *Berkshire, Mass.*: In western Massachusetts. Melville lived in Pittsfield, Massachusetts, in the Berkshires, from 1850 to 1862.
2. *Windsor*: A town in the Berkshires north of Pittsfield.
3. *Housatonic*: The Housatonic River flows through this valley in the Berkshires.
4. *Boótes*: In Greek myth, the inventor of the plow, and visible in the constellation known as Boötes.
5. *Titans*: In Greek myth, the preternaturally strong sons and daughters of Uranus and Gaea, who were unsuccessful in their attempt to rebel against the gods of Olympus.
6. *Sisyphus . . . Samson*: The mythic Greek king Sisyphus was condemned by Zeus to an eternity of attempting to push a heavy rock to the summit of a hill; the biblical Samson pulled down the stone columns of the Philistines' temple, killing himself and his enemies (Judges 13–16).
7. *Taconic . . . Saddleback*: The Taconic Mountains and Saddleback (also known as Mount Greylock) are in the Berkshires. Rome's St. Peter's Basilica is the world's largest Roman Catholic church.
8. *Rhenish*: Of the river Rhine, which flows through Switzerland, Germany, and the Netherlands.
9. *Potter wandered . . . hardships and ills*: Throughout the novel, Melville emphasizes the biblical dimensions of the title character's experiences. Like the children of Israel, Israel Potter is depicted as "wander[ing] in the wilderness forty years" (Numbers 14:33).
10. *Thames*: River flowing through London.

CHAPTER 2: THE YOUTHFUL
ADVENTURES OF ISRAEL

1. *French war*: The North American conflict between Great Britain and France known as the French and Indian War (1754–1763) ended with a British victory in which France relinquished its control over Canada.
2. *chain-bearer*: Person who carried and placed the land surveyor's chain, a measuring device.
3. *Putnam*: According to Revolutionary legend, at the battle at Bunker Hill, General Israel Putnam (1718–1790) ordered his

troops not to fire upon the British until they saw the whites of the enemies' eyes.

4. *No. 4*: A reference to Fort No. 4, which was a military post near the southern New Hampshire town of Charlestown.

5. *barrows*: Wheelbarrows.

6. *Eustatia*: Saint Eustatius, an important trading center in the Dutch West Indies.

7. *Piscataqua to Antiqua*: Maine's Piscatagua River flows into the Atlantic; Antiqua was at the time a British colony in the West Indies.

CHAPTER 3: ISRAEL GOES TO THE WARS

1. *General Patterson*: In April 1775, John Patterson (1744–1808) of Lenox, Massachusetts, upon hearing the news of the Battle of Lexington, quickly raised a military regiment and led his men to Cambridge, Massachusetts, to confront the British.

2. *battle of Lexington*: Military confrontation between the British and the colonists, which flared when the British attempted to seize munitions from the Minute Men of Concord, Massachusetts, whom they encountered in Lexington. Several colonists were killed in what came to be regarded as a key opening engagement of the Revolutionary War.

3. *gad*: Pointed stick (colloquial).

4. *broadcloth . . . linsey-woolsey*: Fine wool cloth (broadcloth), worn by the well-to-do, contrasted against the homespun cloth made of flax or cotton (linsey-woolsey), worn by workers and soldiers.

5. *furred grenadiers*: British soldiers often wore a furry headdress.

6. *Shetland seal*: Seal found at Antarctica's South Shetland Islands.

7. *Sicinius Dentatus*: Roman tribunal and warrior renowned for his military prowess. He was murdered by an assassination team dispatched by a political rival around B.C. 405.

8. *brigantine Washington*: Commanded by Sion Martindale of Rhode Island, this was the first ship in the U.S. navy named after George Washington. It was captured by the British in December of 1775, shortly after it sailed from Plymouth, Massachusetts.

9. *Portsmouth*: A principal British naval base at Portsmouth, Hampshire.

10. *Jaffa*: A seaport city on the Mediterranean in what was once part of the Ottoman Empire. In 1799 Napoleon's troops cap-

tured the city and massacred many of its Turkish inhabitants.
Melville also alludes to Jonah, who fled to Jaffa instead of proceeding to Nineveh as the Lord commanded (Jonah 1:1–4).

11. *Spithead*: Harbor area at Portsmouth, and the site of a famous
British mutiny of 1797, which Melville presents as important
background in his posthumous novella, *Billy Budd, Sailor*.

12. *belly of the whale*: See Jonah 1:17.

13. *gentleness of the dove . . . wisdom of the serpent*: In Matthew
10:16, Jesus states to the disciples: "Behold, I send you forth as
sheep to the midst of wolves: be ye therefore as serpents, and
harmless as doves."

14. *Fontenoy*: Site of a major battle of 1745, in what is now Belgium, in which British and Austrian forces engaged the French.

15. *stush*: Stop (colloquial).

16. *White swelling*: A tubercular arthritis.

CHAPTER 4: FURTHER WANDERINGS
OF THE REFUGEE

1. *Staines*: Town approximately twenty miles southwest of London.

2. *Round House*: Guardhouse.

3. *Brentford*: Market town west of London.

4. *Sir John Millet*: Mentioned in the 1824 *Life and Remarkable Adventures of Israel R. Potter*, the relatively obscure Millet was a
farmer who appears to have supported the colonists' revolutionary cause.

5. *this garden was the Princess Amelia's*: The daughter of George
II, Princess Amelia (1710–1786) resided at the southwestern
end of Kew Gardens, the royal gardens west of London, which
was also the site of Kew Palace, the home of George III (1738–
1820) and Queen Charlotte.

6. *phaeton*: A light, four-wheeled carriage.

7. *hostler*: Person in charge of taking care of horses.

8. *Abrahamic*: Coinage suggesting Millet's biblical patriarchal kindness.

9. *skuttle*: A small lidded opening on a roof.

CHAPTER 5: ISRAEL IN THE LION'S DEN

1. *Kew*: See chapter 4, note 5.
2. *den of the British lion*: An allusion to the story of Daniel in the lion's den (Daniel 6:1–23); the lion is also the heraldic symbol of the British Crown.
3. *Ravaillac*: The religious fanatic François Ravaillac (1578–1610) fatally stabbed Henry IV of Navarre (1553–1610), king of France.

CHAPTER 6: ISRAEL MAKES THE ACQUAINTANCE OF CERTAIN SECRET FRIENDS OF AMERICA

1. *Squire Woodcock*: In *Life and Remarkable Adventures of Israel R. Potter*, the gentleman of Brentford is called "J. Woodcock." Melville names him John Woodcock.
2. *Horne Tooke and James Bridges*: The politician John Horne Tooke (1736–1812) supported a number of liberal causes, including the colonists' efforts to gain their independence. His *Diversions of Purley* (1786), a philological examination of Old English, made important contributions to the scientific study of language. James Bridges is obscure and possibly invented.
3. *Perry*: A fermented beverage made from pear juice.
4. *Doctor Franklin, then in that capital*: In 1776, Benjamin Franklin (1706–1790) was elected by the Second Continental Congress to serve on a commission charged with negotiating a treaty with France. He arrived in Paris in December of that year, and he quickly secured aid for the revolutionaries' cause. Franklin would remain in Paris until 1785.
5. *White Waltham*: Small town approximately twenty miles west of Brentford.
6. *Charing Cross . . . for Dover . . . to Calais*: Potter travels from a district in central London, to a seaport in southeast England, to a seaport in northern France.

CHAPTER 7: AFTER A CURIOUS
ADVENTURE UPON THE PONT NEUF

1. *Pont Neuf*: The most famous bridge in Paris, it was completed in 1606 under the direction of Henry IV of Navarre. (See also chapter 5, note 3.)
2. *statue of Henry IV*: A statue was erected in 1614 and destroyed in 1792; a second was erected in 1818.
3. *Bon jour*: Good day; hello (French).
4. *Seine*: River flowing through Paris to the English Channel.
5. *Poor Richard's Almanac*: Almanac published by Franklin from 1733 to 1758. The purported author, Franklin's fictional persona Richard Saunders, became famous for his proverbial sayings about economy, temperance, and industry.
6. *Plato*: Greek philosopher (B.C.E. 427–347) known for his philosophical idealism.

CHAPTER 8: WHICH HAS SOMETHING
TO SAY ABOUT DR. FRANKLIN AND
THE LATIN QUARTER

1. *Jacob*: Patriarchal biblical ancestor of the Hebrew people. The son of Isaac and Rebecca, Jacob as a young man exhibited a shrewd worldliness in obtaining his twin brother Esau's birthright for a meal of pottage (a thick soup); see Genesis 25–50. After wrestling with an angel, he received the name of Israel. His sons were the ancestors of the twelve tribes of Israel.
2. *Arcadian*: Simple, rustic—as in Arcadia, the region of ancient Greece traditionally known for its pastoral innocence.
3. *the apostolic serpent and dove*: Allusion to the apostle Matthew; see chapter 3, note 13.
4. *Machiavelli in tents*: The Italian political philosopher Niccolò Machiavelli (1446–1527), author of *The Prince* (1532), is best known for his writings on how to acquire and maintain power. In Genesis 25:27, Jacob is called "a plain man, dwelling in tents."
5. *Hobbes of Malmsbury*: Convinced that sovereign power was necessary to control the selfishness of individuals, the En-

glish philosopher Thomas Hobbes (1588–1679) argued in *Leviathan* (1651) for the virtues of absolute monarchy. His birthplace is also spelled Malmesbury.

6. *Broadbrims*: Quakers, or Society of Friends; the term was derived from the broad-brimmed hats favored by some in this religious group.

7. *magians*: Allusion to the three wise men who paid homage to the infant Jesus (Matthew 2:1–12).

8. *faubourgs*: Districts.

9. *Latin Quarter*: Neighborhood in Paris by the university district, and thus known for its intellectuals and indigent scholars. During the medieval period, Latin was the main language spoken by those at the theological college.

10. *Sorbonne*: The name of the theological college founded in 1257 and suppressed in 1792; the University of Paris took control of the grounds and facilities in 1808.

11. *grizzets*: Young working-class women.

12. *Garden of the Luxembourg*: The renowned gardens of the Luxembourg Palace, which was built near the Sorbonne during the Renaissance.

13. *theurgic*: Magically connected to divine spirits.

14. *Paracelsus or Friar Bacon*: The Swiss physician Philippus Aureolus Paracelsus (1493–1541), and the English Franciscan monk Roger Bacon (c. 1214–1294?). Both were interested in magic and the occult.

15. *Augustus Cæsar*: First Roman emperor (B.C.E. 63–C.E. 14), he was hailed as a beneficent leader who helped to foster Rome's commitment to the arts.

16. *Palais des Beaux Arts*: Probably a reference to the École des Beaux-Arts (School of Fine-Arts), founded in 1648 and located near Paris's Latin Quarter.

17. *Passy*: At the time a separate country village on the Right Bank of the Seine, Passy was annexed to Paris in 1860.

18. *savan*: Savant; man of learning.

19. *pocket congress of all humanity*: An allusion to the revolutionary Prussian baron Anacharsis Clootz (1755–1794), who in June 1790 led an international delegation to the French National Assembly, declaring that they were ambassadors of the human race.

CHAPTER 9: ISRAEL IS INITIATED INTO THE MYSTERIES OF LODGING-HOUSES IN THE LATIN QUARTER

1. *Otard*: Cognac made by Otard, DuPuy, and Company.
2. *Ammonite*: As described in the Hebrew Bible, the Ammonites were lewd and morally corrupt, in the genealogical line of a daughter of Lot who seduced her drunken father (Genesis 19:30–38).
3. *'Way to Wealth'*: Widely reprinted pamphlet with Poor Richard's sayings, first appearing as part of Franklin's 1758 *Poor Richard's Almanack*.
4. *Dunker*: A denomination of German Baptists, some of whom settled in Pennsylvania in the eighteenth century. The name derived from the group's ritual practice of baptismal dipping.

CHAPTER 10: ANOTHER ADVENTURER APPEARS UPON THE SCENE

1. *à-la-mode*: In fashion (French).
2. *Paul Jones*: The great naval hero John Paul Jones (1747–1792) was born in Scotland but fought with the American Revolutionaries. He had already led several ships in battle, and was expecting captaincy of the *Indien*, but for political reasons that particular ship was given to a French captain. In the 1824 *Life and Remarkable Adventures of Israel R. Potter*, Jones is mentioned only briefly. In Melville's novel, he has a central role.
3. *Sodom*: Ancient city destroyed by the Lord for its descent into evil (Genesis 18–19).
4. *Jersey privateers*: Privately owned, armed ships off Jersey, an island in the English Channel, which were commissioned by the British government.
5. *Brest*: Seaport in western France.
6. *cat's paws*: Light breeze.
7. *outwitted the Solebay frigate, fought the Milford, and captured the Mellish . . . off Louisbergh*: References to three British ves-

sels that Jones either outwitted or captured during 1776 while he was captain of the *Providence*. Louisbergh, now spelled Louisberg, is a seaport on Cape Breton Island, Nova Scotia.

8. *keel*: The lowest and principal timber of a vessel. "Leeward": The direction opposite to which the wind blows.

9. *The Duke de Chartres, and Count D'Estaing*: Historical figures and naval men who supported the American Revolutionary cause: Louis Philippe Joseph, Duc d'Orléans (1747–93), also known as Duc de Chartres; and Charles Hector Théodat, Comte D'Estaing (1729–1794).

CHAPTER 11: PAUL JONES IN A REVERIE

1. *Whitehaven*: Seaport in northwest England.

2. *Andes*: Extensive mountain range along the west of South America.

3. *Borneo*: Large island in the Malay Archipelago known for its dense jungles.

CHAPTER 12: RECROSSING THE CHANNEL

1. *diligence*: Public stagecoach. The Place-du-Carrousel is an area in Paris near the Louvre.

2. *Dutchess D'Abrantes*: Probably Melville's fictional creation.

3. *Templars*: Order of Catholic soldier-monks established in the twelfth century to protect pilgrims journeying to the Holy Land. Henry I introduced the order to England; it was dissolved in 1312 after it developed a reputation for corruption. In his short fiction "The Paradise of Bachelors and the Tartarus of Maids" (1855), Melville ironically links present-day London lawyers to the Templars.

4. *the reign of Queen Elizabeth*: Elizabeth I (1533–1603) was queen of England from 1558 to 1603.

5. *prophetic days and years of Daniel*: See chapter 5, note 2; and Daniel 7–12.

CHAPTER 13: HIS ESCAPE
FROM THE HOUSE

1. *cocks*: Piles.
2. *tatterdemalion*: Person in tattered clothing.
3. *razeed to a spencer*: Cut down to a short jacket.
4. *Highlands*: Mountainous region in Scotland.
5. *English clergyman translated Lucian; another . . . wrote Tristram Shandy; and a third, an ill-natured appreciator of good-natured Rabelais, died a dean*: The historical Took himself translated the Greek satirist Lucian (C.E. 120–180); Laurence Stern (1713–68) wrote the multivolume comic novel *Tristram Shandy* (1759–1767); and Jonathan Swift (1667–1745), dean of Dublin's St. Patrick's Cathedral, drew on the French comic writer François Rabelais (c. 1490–1533) for *Gulliver's Travels* (1726).
6. *kidnapped into the naval service*: During this time, and especially later during the Napoleonic Wars, the practice of impressment—forcibly putting young men to service in the king's navy—was rampant. In his posthumous novella, *Billy Budd*, Melville's title character is similarly impressed and made into a fore-topman (the person responsible for manning a front mast from an elevated platform).
7. *cribbing*: Imprisoning.
8. *crimp*: Person who forcibly recruits sailors.
9. *gaolers*: Jailors.
10. *Sir Edward Hughes*: English admiral (1720?–1794) who served as commander-in-chief of British operations in the East Indies, where England was battling France for control of India. Melville invents the names of the three ships.
11. *the famous engagement off the coast of Coromandel, between Admiral Suffren's fleet and the English squadron*: In 1778, the forces of Hughes and the French admiral Pierre André de Suffren (1726–1788) fought a series of indecisive battles near Coromandel, which is on India's eastern coast.

CHAPTER 14: IN WHICH ISRAEL IS
SAILOR UNDER TWO FLAGS

1. *the seventy-four*: Warship with seventy-four guns, typically manned by a crew of around six hundred.
2. *between Scilly and Cape Clear*: The Scilly Isles are off the western coast of England; Cape Clear is on an island off southern Ireland.
3. *cutter*: Single-masted ship.
4. *Gibraltar*: British fortress and seaport near the southern tip of Spain. The mountainous Rock of Gibraltar is approximately fourteen hundred feet high.
5. *jibing of a boom*: Quick shifting from one side to the other of the heavy pole extending from one of the ship's masts.
6. *stern-sheets*: The space to the rear of rowing seats in a small boat.
7. *dobbin*: Contemptuous term for an old horse.
8. *hap*: Situation or circumstances (archaic).
9. *scuppers*: Drain holes in the deck's gutters.
10. *stays*: Ropes supporting segments of the mast.
11. *taffrail*: Deck railing at the rear of the ship.
12. *halyards*: The main ropes supporting the sails.
13. *the Ranger*: A one-masted sailing vessel commanded by John Paul Jones in the spring of 1778. The historical Israel Potter did not accompany Jones on the missions and battles described in subsequent chapters.
14. *broadside*: All the guns that can be fired from one side of a ship.
15. *battle-lanthorns*: battle lanterns (archaic).
16. *Penzance*: Cornwall seaport in southwest England.
17. *Fejee*: Fiji; South Pacific island group. Throughout the novel, Melville associates Jones with "savage" wildness.
18. *flogged a sailor, one Mungo Maxwell, to death*: In 1770, Jones was tried by an Admiralty Court for flogging the allegedly disobedient Maxwell, and was acquitted. Months later he was imprisoned and sued by the Maxwell family for wrongful death, because Maxwell had died on the return voyage. Jones posted bond and the suit was eventually dismissed.
19. *like Caesar, at Sandwich*: The Roman statesman and general Julius Caesar (c. B.C.E. 102—B.C.E. 44) invaded England in B.C.E. 55.

20. *farthingales*: Hoop skirts.
21. *smack*: Ship.
22. *Earl of Selkirk*: Dunbar Hamilton, later Douglas, Fourth Earl of Selkirk (1722–1799). The historical evidence suggests he was not a friend or counselor of George III.

CHAPTER 15: THEY SAIL AS FAR AS THE CRAG OF AILSA

1. *Wales*: In southwest England.
2. *Gath*: Goliath, killed by David (I Samuel, 17).
3. *Coriolanus*: The Roman patrician Gnaeus Marcius Coriolanus sought to end democratic rule in Rome; when thwarted, he joined with Rome's enemies in attacking the city in B.C.E. 491.
4. *mizzen-shrouds*: Fixed rigging supporting the rearmost mast.
5. *Colonial Commissioner*: Benjamin Franklin.
6. *Isle of Man . . . Cumberland shore*: Island in the Irish Sea north of Wales and south of Cumberland (in northwest England).
7. *wherry*: Long, light boat.
8. *Mull of Galloway*: Promontory off region in southwest Scotland.
9. *Lochryan*: Calm waters (loch) off Galloway.
10. *Levanter*: Trader or warrior in the Levant (Middle East), with suggestion of Jones's take-no-prisoners mode of craftiness.
11. *Clyde*: The Firth of Clyde, off southwest Scotland, forms a large area of coastal water, sheltered from the Atlantic by a peninsula.
12. *Juan Fernandez-like Crag of Ailsa*: Located in the Firth of Clyde, Ailsa Craig (as it is currently spelled) is a volcanic island, approximately two miles in circumference. The Juan Fernández islands are located five hundred miles west of the Chilean coast.
13. *submarine Grampians*: Mountains in Scotland extending from the Firth of Clyde.
14. *Cheops*: Egyptian king c. B.C.E. 2680 who built the Great Pyramid of Cheops near Cairo.
15. *cock of the walk*: One who crows of getting the better of rivals or competitors (colloquial).

CHAPTER 16: THEY LOOK IN
AT CARRICKFERGUS

1. *Drake*: Jones captured the British warship *Drake* on April 24, 1778.
2. *grapnels*: Anchor-like devices.
3. *City Hall, St. Paul's, and the Astor House, from the triangular Park in New York*: In lower Manhattan, from City Hall Park, one could see City Hall, St. Paul's Church on Broadway, and the resplendent hotel the Astor House.
4. *Whitehaven*: See chapter 11, note 1.
5. *harrows*: Agricultural tool for weeding and loosening soil.
6. *Peter the Great*: Peter I (1672–1725), tsar of Russia (1682–1725), who shrewdly encouraged the country's imperial expansion.
7. *collieries*: Coal mines, including all buildings and equipment.
8. *Lisbon, in 1755*: The year of the cataclysmic earthquake in Lisbon, Portugal.
9. *yards were deeply canted*: The poles used to hold up the masts were tilted and secured.
10. *Loco-focos*: Friction matches, which came into use in the 1830s. The term was also used to describe a reform faction of New York's Democratic party, which split from the regular party in 1835, and was said to have done key organizational work at an evening meeting by lighting up the room with locofoco matches.
11. *oakum*: Fibers from unraveled rope.

CHAPTER 17: THEY CALL AT
THE EARL OF SELKIRK'S

1. *Solway Frith*: Near Whitehaven; usually spelled Solway Firth (an estuary).
2. *Earl of Selkirk*: See chapter 14, note 22. St. Mary's Isle is also near Whitehaven.
3. *Three Kingdoms*: Ireland, Scotland, England.
4. *Highland target of steel, with a claymore and foil crossed on top*: Sword with double-edged blade used by Scottish Highlanders in the sixteenth century.

5. *Alexander Selkirk*: Scottish seaman (1617–1721), whose adventures inspired Daniel Defoe's *Robinson Crusoe* (1719). Selkirk had been marooned on the Juan Fernández Islands.

6. *plate*: In 1778, during the unsuccessful effort to kidnap the Earl of Selkirk, who was not at home, Jones's men stole the family's silver plate and other valuable items. Jones later apologized and offered to return the plate, which he did in 1785. Melville's account of the raid on the Earl of Selkirk's estate follows the broad historical outline, though much is invented.

7. *Mars*: Roman god of war.

CHAPTER 18: THE EXPEDITION
THAT SAILED FROM GROIX

1. *Groix*: An island off the northwest coast of France.

2. *crank*: Ship that could easily capsize.

3. *beavers*: Hats.

4. *houdahed with a castellated poop like the leaning tower of Pisa*: The ship's high covered deck (poop) is compared to the seat (houdah) on the back of an elephant and to the famous Pisan tower.

5. *Galileo on Fiesole*: The Italian astronomer Galileo Galilei (1564–1642), a professor at the University of Pisa, also lived in Florence, the site of the hill Fiesole.

6. *durance*: Duration (archaic) or imprisonment.

7. *call her Poor Richard*: In historical fact, Jones named the ship *Bonhomme Richard* (Good Man Richard).

8. *Cheviot Hills*: A highland range of more than thirty miles that marks the boundary between England and Scotland.

9. *Fife*: Forty miles north of Edinburgh.

10. *The righteous shall rejoice . . . in the blood of the wicked*: Psalms 58:10.

11. *the Rev. Mr. Shirra's, of Kirkaldy, powerful intercession*: According to local history, the prayers of the Reverend Robert Shirra of Kirkcaldy (the usual spelling of the town around thirteen miles from Edinburgh) were instrumental in saving the community from Jones's attack in 1778. Melville's probable source is Robert C. Sands, *Life and Correspondence of John Paul Jones* (1830).

12. *Marshal Ney to the stubborn standard of Napoleon from Elba, marching regenerated on Paris*: In 1815, Napoleon escaped

from the Tuscan island of Elba, where he had been exiled by the allies, and returned to Paris with supporters, including the French soldier Michel Ney, who had been instructed to arrest him.

13. *Serapis*: Famed British warship named after the Greco-Egyptian god of the dead.

CHAPTER 19: THEY FIGHT THE SERAPIS

1. *the first signal collision on the sea between the Englishman and the American*: The famous battle took place on September 23, 1779, off Flamborough Head, a promontory in northeast England.

2. *two wars*: The American Revolution and the War of 1812.

3. *Yorkshire*: County in northeast English. The various locales Melville describes in this chapter, such as Flamborough Head, the Tees River, the Humber River, and the Spurn (land projecting across the Humber), are located near or off the Yorkshire coast.

4. *Calabrian*: Resembling Calabria, the mountainous peninsula in southwest Italy.

5. *Attila*: King of the Huns (c. 406–453), a nomadic European people, Attila was known for his skills as a warrior.

6. *Tadmores*: Tadmore was a biblical oasis city in the Syrian desert, founded by Solomon (II Chronicles 8:4).

7. *Miltonic contests of archangels*: See *Paradise Lost*, Book VI, which tells of how Michael and Gabriel set forth to battle Satan and his angels.

8. *ghost of Morven*: An allusion to the ghost of Morven in the Scottish poet Jamees Macpherson's mystical *The Works of Ossian* (1765).

9. *Mephistopheles*: The devil.

10. *battledores*: Rackets used to strike shuttlecocks.

11. *Malabar*: In southwest India.

12. *chasseing*: A gliding step in a dance.

13. *Bridge of Sighs*: The bridge in Venice connecting the palace and the prison.

14. *Lethean canal*: In Greek mythology, the river in Hades from which the dead drink to forget the past.

15. *fire-damp*: Dangerously combustible gas formed in coal mines.

16. *one family (the Guelphs) . . . another family (the Ghibelines)*: Opposing political factions in Germany and Italy during the late me-

dieval period. The Guelphs supported the papacy while the Ghibelines supported worldly empire.

17. *Lowell girls . . . in a cotton factory*: During the 1840s and 1850s, the textile mills of Lowell, Massachusetts, which hired only single young women, were celebrated as models of their kind. Charles Dickens made an admiring visit in 1842; but Melville expressed his skepticism in "The Paradise of Bachelors and the Tartarus of Maids" (1855).

18. *The Parcae were not more methodical; Atropos not more fatal*: In Roman mythology, the Parcæ were the three goddesses who wove the thread of life, and Atropos was the Fate who cut it.

19. *Apollyon*: The angel of destruction (Revelation 9:11).

20. *poltroon*: coward.

21. *great fire of London . . . great Plague*: The destructive London fire occurred in 1666 and was preceded by the plague of 1664–65.

22. *strike*: To lower the sail or flag as a sign of surrender.

23. *"I have not yet begun to fight"*: Most historians doubt that Jones actually spoke these now-mythic words, which were reported in John Henry Sherburne's *Life and Character of John Paul Jones* (1825).

24. *Gomorrah*: City destroyed by the Lord for its wickedness (Genesis 19:24–25).

CHAPTER 20: THE SHUTTLE

1. *Texel*: Netherlands island in the North Sea.

2. *letter of marque*: Privately owned ship licensed by a state to attack ships of other nations.

3. *quid*: Chewing tobacco.

4. *fore and mizzen-top men*: Those manning the platforms of the front and rear sails.

5. *jewel-block*: Pulley at the end of the ropes extending from sails.

6. *muster*: Assembling of the crew.

7. *holders*: Those who man the large storage area beneath the decks.

8. *waisters*: Seamen stationed in the central section of the deck.

9. *Boreas*: Ancient Greek personification of the north wind. Here Potter echoes a line from the popular naval song "The Storm," attributed to the British writer George A. Stevens (1710–784): "Cease, rude Boreas, blustering railer!"

10. *Falmouth*: Seaport in Cornwall, southwest England.
11. *Lizard*: Peninsula near Falmouth.

CHAPTER 21: SAMSON AMONG
THE PHILISTINES

1. *martial man of Patagonian stature*: Ethan Allen; see note 10 below. Natives of Patagonia, in the southernmost region of South America, were reputed to be tall.
2. *St. Paul's dome*: St. Paul's Cathedral in London, constructed during the sixteenth century, has one of the largest Cathedral domes in the world.
3. *Pendennis Castle*: Built by Henry VIII in 1540–45 in Falmouth, Cornwall, the castle was intended to protect this strategic area from the threat of invasion from Catholic France and Spain.
4. *sward*: Grassy surface.
5. *Howe and Knyphausen—the Hessian!*: William Howe (1729–1814) commanded the British army in America; and Wilhelm von Knyphausen (1716–1810) commanded German mercenaries in America during the Revolutionary War (hence the deprecatory "Hessian!"—Hessen is a state in West Germany).
6. *Wearing the king's plate*: Meaning, probably, certain manacles. [This footnote appeared in both the *Putnam's* serialization and the book publication, and was probably supplied by Melville.]
7. *sagathy*: A woolen fabric.
8. *David's outlawed Cave of Adullam*: David's refuge when he was outlawed by Saul (1 Samuel 22:1–2).
9. *tierce*: Cask.
10. *Ethan Ticonderoga Allen*: The celebrated Revoutionary hero Ethan Allen (1738–1789) was best known for leading the attack on the British headquarters at Fort Ticonderoga, New York, on May 10, 1775. In September of that year, after leading a failed attack on the British in Montreal, he was captured and taken to Pendennis Castle, where he was held for two years. Melville draws on Allen's own *A Narrative of Colonel Ethan Allen's Captivity* (1779), which went through more than fifteen printings by 1854. Allen is not mentioned in *Life and Remarkable Aventures of Israel R. Potter*. Melville skews chronology here, for Allen was freed as part of a prisoner exchange in May 1778, several months before the battle between the *Serapis* and the *Bonhomme Richard*.

11. *Green-Mountain-boys*: Name given to the Allen-commanded regiments in a part of New Hampshire, now Vermont, that sought to defend lands that were being claimed by British-aligned New Yorkers; these regiments eventually joined the Revolutionary cause.

12. *tophet's*: Hell's.

13. *Ottoman*: Native of Turkey.

14. *Delilah*: In the Hebrew Bible, Delilah cuts Samson's hair (a sign of his vows to God), robbing him of his strength. Eventually Samson regains his strength and destroys his enemies, the Philistines. An analogy between Ethan Allen and Samson (and the English and the Philistines) had already been established by the title of this chapter. See Judges 13–16.

15. *gyved*: Shackled.

16. *Selah*: Recurring word in Psalms, suggestive of emphasis or praise.

CHAPTER 22: SOMETHING FURTHER
OF ETHAN ALLEN

1. *a Joe Miller, a Bayard, and a Tom Hyer . . . a person like the Belgian giants . . . a heart plump as Cœr de Lion's*: Though these various associations, Melville emphasizes Allen's strength and performative abilities: Joseph Miller (1684–1736) was an English actor; Seigneur de Bayard (c. 1473–1524) was a French soldier known for his valor; Tom Hyer (1819–1864) was the first nationally recognized U.S. champion prizefighter (1841–1848); the Belgian giant Mon E. Bihin, said to be over over seven feet tall, appeared in Boston, New York, and Philadelphia during the 1830s and 1840s; and King of England Richard I (1145–1199) was known as "the Lion-hearted" (Coeur de Lion) for his martial skills and conduct.

2. *Dyaks*: Indigenous people of Borneo; see chapter 11, note 3.

3. *General Prescott . . . Tyburn*: The British officer Richard Prescott (1725–1788) was himself twice captured by the American enemy (in 1775 and 1777) and was released as part of prisoner exchanges. Tyburn was then a village just outside London best known as a place of public execution.

4. *Colonel Guy Johnson*: Irish-born New York loyalist (c.1740–1788), who, according to Allen's *Narrative*, encouraged the British to treat Allen harshly.

5. *mortise*: Slot or groove.

6. *Abbé Bellegarde*: Morvan de Bellegarde (1648–1734), the author of popular etiquette books.
7. *Lord Chesterfield*: Philip Dormer Stanhope, Fourth Earl of Chesterfield (1694–1773), best known for his letters to his illegitimate son, Philip Stanhope, on fashion, education, and etiquette. First published in 1774, the letters were widely reprinted.
8. *Botany-Bay*: English penal colony in Australia in operation from 1787 to 1840.
9. *Damon found Pythias*: Legendary Greek friends from the fourth century B.C.E. When Pythias was condemned to death for plotting against Dionysius I, Damon offered to die in his friend's place. Moved by their friendship, Dionysius freed both men.
10. *German forest, nor Tasso's enchanted one*: The Harz Mountains of Central Germany was by legend a meeting place of witches; the Italian poet Torquato Tasso (1544–1595) wrote of an enchanted forest in his epic of the First Crusade, *Jerusalem Delivered* (1575).

CHAPTER 23: ISRAEL IN EGYPT

1. *brickyard*: As the title of the chapter suggests, Melville depicts Israel Potter in Egypt as analogous to the Israelites in Egypt. In Exodus 1:13–14, the Israelites are depicted as working in brickyards: "And the Egyptians made the children of Israel to serve with rigour: And they made their lives bitter with hard bondage, in mortar, and in brick."
2. *Dismal Swamp*: Massive swamp across parts of Virginia and North Carolina.
3. *spavined*: Suffering from a disease of the joints.
4. *great wall of China*: Approximately 1,500 miles long, dating from 1388–1644. "Pekin": Peking.
5. *Thebes*: Ancient Greek city; during the Persian Wars, Thebes sided with the Persians against the Athenians (B.C.E. 480–479).
6. *All is vanity and clay*: See Ecclesiastes 1:2.

CHAPTER 24: IN THE CITY OF DIS

1. *entering, like the king, from Windsor, from the Surrey side*: Windsor Castle, the chief residence of England's sovereignity, and the county of Surrey are both west of London.

SOUTH OF RIVER THAMES

2. *Guy Fawkes' Day*: Holiday celebrating the thwarting of the "Gunpowder Plot" by the Roman Catholic Guy Fawkes (1570–1606), who sought to kill James I and blow up Parliament on November 5, 1605.

3. *Peter of Colechurch*: Peter de Colechurch (?–1205), the chaplain of St. Mary Colechurch, did architectural work on London Bridge for more than thirty years.

4. *shambles*: Meat markets.

5. *Southwark*: Borough of central London. ⌐SOUTH OF R.·THAMES

COUNTY! 6. *Berks*: ~~Town~~ in a valley west of London.

7. *Erebus*: In Greek mythology, the dark, cavernous passage through which the dead must travel on their way to Hades.

8. *Phlegethon*: In Greek mythology, the fiery river that the dead cross on their way to Hades.

9. *Gallipagos*: Galapagos. For similar language, see Melville's sketch of the volcanic rock and tortoises of the Galapagos Islands in "The Encantadas" (1854). The islands are located in the Pacific Ocean, approximately four hundred miles west of Ecuador.

10. *Herculaneum and Pompeii, or the Cities of the Plain*: The eruption of Mount Vesuvius in C.E. 79 buried Herculaneum and Pompeii; Sodom and Gomorrah (the Cities of the Plain) were destroyed by God's "brimstone and fire" (see Genesis 19:23–25).

11. *City of Dis*: In Roman mythology, Dis ruled the Underworld. In Dante's *Inferno* (c. 1305), Dis is the capital city of Hell (see Canto 9).

12. *Hinnom*: In Milton's *Paradise Lost*, Hinnom is "the type of Hell" (I, 404–5). The suggestion here is that the poets Milton and Shelley do not deserve to be condemned to hell, as they were by some ecclesiastical authorities.

13. *"poor player"*: See Shakespeare's *Macbeth* act 5, scene 5.

14. *Middlesex*: County bordering northwest London.

15. *Armageddons*: In Revelation 16:14–16, Armageddon is the place of the last battle at the Day of Judgment; the word has come to be loosely associated with apocalyptic conflict.

CHAPTER 25: FORTY-FIVE YEARS

1. *forty years . . . under Moses*: In Deuteronomy 4, the Lord condemns Moses and the Hebrew people to forty years of wandering

in the desert; before his death Moses has a vision of the Promised Land from Mount Pisgah but he does not enter it.

2. *no pillar of fire by night, except the cold column of the monument*: The column or monument is the commemorative column built by Christopher Wren during the 1670s in memory of the tragedy of the Great Fire of 1666. In Exodus 13:21, the Lord guides the Hebrew people with the help of "a pillar of fire."

3. *Lear or Œdipus*: The tragic heroes of Shakespeare's *King Lear* (1608) and Sophocles's *Oedipus Rex* (c. B.C.E. 430).

4. *St. Giles*: At the time, a run-down area of central London.

5. *Houndsditch*: Area in east London, which at the time was made noxious by a huge ditch used for rubbish, including dead hounds.

6. *Holborn Bars*: In west London.

7. *Kentish*: From a county in southeast England.

8. *Malthusian enigma*: In his *Essay on the Principle of Population* (1798) and other writings, the British political economist Thomas Robert Malthus (1766–834) conveyed his concerns about the failure of the means of subsistence to keep pace with the rise in population. For Malthus, the "enigma" was why humans allowed for such population growth.

9. *Moorfields*: At the time, a poor district in London near Houndsditch.

10. *"Facilis descensus Averni"*: From Virgil, *Aeneid*, VI, 126: "The descent to Avernus is easy." A crater lake west of Naples, Avernus was known for its noxious fumes and in classical literature was analogized to the passageway to Hell.

11. *Black-hole of Calcutta*: A small dungeon where troops of the ruler of Bengal confined British prisoners on June 20, 1756. According to disputed accounts by a survivor, 123 of 146 prisoners died of heat exhaustion in the confined conditions. Historians now believe the number to be approximately fifty.

12. *Charing-Crosses*: Charing Cross is a lively district and transportation center in central London.

13. *Covent-Garden market*: At the time, England's largest open market, located in central London.

14. *flags*: Reeds or stems used to repair bottoms of chairs.

15. *St. James Park . . . Old Brewery of the Palace*: Buckingham Palace is located within St. James Park; the Truman Brewery was built in the seventeenth century.

16. *Narragansett Bay*: Atlantic inlet in east Rhode Island.

17. *Barbican*: District named after a medieval tower north of London.

18. *Smithfield*: The site of a large cattle market in northwest London, near Barbican.

19. *Housatonic*: See chapter 1, note 3.

20. *this second peace*: Following the Napoleonic Wars (1803–1815) and the War of 1812.

21. *sabots*: Clogs (French).

22. *Saratoga, or Trenton*: The Battle of Saratoga (New York) in September of 1777 was a major victory for the American forces and a turning point of the war; the Battle of Trenton (New Jersey) in December of 1776 resulted in a crucial early victory for the colonists.

23. *Wandering Jew*: Israel is compared to the figure from medieval folklore who supposedly taunted Jesus and was cursed to wander the globe until the Second Coming.

24. *Corunna . . . Waterloo . . . Trafalgar*: Sites of key battles in the Napoleonic Wars: In January 1809, the British suffered major casualties and were defeated in the Battle of Corunna (in Spain); in the June 1815 Battle of Waterloo (in present-day Belgium), which was the last major battle in the Napoleonic Wars, Napoleon was defeated by the British; and in the Battle of Trafalgar, in October 1805, the British defeated the French and Spanish fleet at Cape Trafalgar in southwest Spain.

25. *Sinbad the Sailor*: Story-cycle of Persian origin popularized in *The Book of One Thousand and One Nights*.

26. *It was the year 1826*: The historical Israel Potter returned to the United States in 1823.

CHAPTER 26: REQUIESCAT IN PACE

1. *Faneuil Hall*: A meeting hall and market in Boston, built in 1742. Samuel Adams and other patriots gave speeches there calling for American independence.

2. *Copp's Hill*: Burial ground in Boston, founded in 1659.

3. *"Potter's Field"*: A place of burial of unknown or indigent people, derived from Matthew 27:7, when priests took the thirty pieces of silver returned by the repentant Judas to purchase a potter's field as a burial place for foreigners and strangers. The field was called "potter's" because the land was unfit to grow crops, and therefore was used by potters as a source for clay.

4. *executors' wafers*: The wax seal used to affix a ribbon to a legal document, such as a will.

5. *after a pension*: In his old age, the historical Israel Potter returned to the United States in quest of a government pension to honor his military service during the Revolutionary War. The avowed purpose of the 1824 *Life and Remarkable Adventures of Israel R. Potter* was to make a case for the pension, but because of legal technicalities, the pension never was approved. Potter is said to have died in 1826, like Melville's character. Melville's title of the closing chapter of the novel, "Requiescat in Pace" is Latin for "May he rest in peace," and thus speaks to both the historical and fictional Potter.